SEVENTEEN BOOK TWO

WARRIOR

A.D. STARRLING

COPYRIGHT

Warrior (A Seventeen Series Novel) Book Two

First published as King's Crusade: Seventeen Book Two in 2013.
Third hardback edition: 2024
ISBN-13: 978-0-9955013-6-2

www.ADStarrling.com
shop.adstarrling.com

Edited by Invisible Ink Editing & Right Ink On The Wall

DEDICATION

As always, to my family and friends

THE IMMORTALS

The Crovirs and the Bastians: two races of immortals that have lived side by side with humans since the beginning of civilization and once ruled an empire that stretched across Europe, Asia, and North Africa. Each possessing the capacity to survive up to sixteen deaths, they have been engaged in a bloody and savage war from the very dawn of their existence. This unholy battle has, for the most part, remained a well-guarded secret from the eyes of ordinary humans, despite the fact that they have been used as pawns in some of the most epic chapters of the immortal conflict. It was not until the late fourteenth century that the two races were forced to forge an uneasy truce following a deadly plague that wiped out more than half of their numbers and made the majority of survivors infertile.

Each immortal society is ruled by a hierarchy of councils made up of nobles. The First Council consists of the heads of seven Immortal Sections: the Order of the Hunters, the Counter-Terrorism group, Human Relations, Commerce,

Immortal Legislations and Conventions, Research and Development, and Immortal Culture and History. The Head of the Order of the Hunters is the most powerful member of the First Council. The Second Council, or the Assembly, comprises the regional division directors under each Head of Section, while the Congress of the Council is made up of local authority chiefs.

Though they have been instrumental to the most significant events in world history, religion, and culture, the Immortals' existence is known to only a select few humans, among them the political leaders of the most powerful states on Earth and the Secretary General of the United Nations.

PART I
TOMBS

PROLOGUE

NOVEMBER 1700. BATTLE OF NARVA. SWEDISH TERRITORY.

THE LITTLE GIRL STARED INTO THE DEAD MAN'S EYES, HER expression steady and unflinching. All around her rose the cries of soldiers and the clash of swords, while cannons boomed on a distant hill, and the sharp reports of musket shots echoed across the banks of the nearby river.

The morning's blizzard had turned the battlefield into a gray and bloody mire. The snow and rain that had been falling steadily during the night had grown heavy at dawn, and visibility was worsened by vicious gusts blowing in from the west. When the wind shifted to the south at midday, it provided an unprecedented advantage for the eight-thousand-strong army of Sweden's King Karl the Twelfth. They had been able to advance virtually unseen on the significantly larger Russian contingent, which laid siege to the city of Narva in early November of that year.

Although tired and hungry after traveling across miles of treacherous back roads and countryside laid to waste by the invaders, the better-equipped and more experienced Swedes managed to get within fifty yards of the enemy's front lines without being detected and led a swift attack on two fronts.

After overcoming Russian General Veyde's and Prince Trubetskoy's men, they now marched for the troops on the adversary's left flank, which were under the charge of Duke de Cröy, the field marshal whom Tsar Peter I of Russia had left in charge of his army.

As he carefully made his way across the treacherous ground, Dimitri Reznak glanced at the bruised skies overhead. Though the worst of the storm had passed, heavy flakes still fell from the low clouds that covered the land in eerie twilight. Interspersed with rain and sleet, the snow melted rapidly in crimson puddles that dotted the plain, forming brief teardrops on the cooling skin of the hundreds of Russian and Swedish soldiers who had fallen since the start of the battle. Reznak frowned at the gruesome sight.

Given that he was an immortal who had witnessed countless wars and conflicts over the five centuries of his existence thus far, he knew he should have been immune to the spectacle of blood and gore that surrounded him. Yet, despite the fact that he and the two hundred Crovir immortals under his command were assisting the young Swedish King in his endeavor to keep the new territories his predecessors had acquired during Europe's bloody Thirty Years' War, Reznak could not help but feel overwhelmed by sadness at the needless loss of human life. Which was why he headed straight for the little girl when he saw her standing on the knoll in the middle of the battleground.

Although he hadn't expected to see a child in the midst of the war zone, Reznak was not surprised. Some civilians had still been trying to reach the safety of the fortified city when they were caught between the advancing armies, and those who had not succumbed to the fierce blizzard perished in the subsequent crossfire. He could only presume that the child had become separated from her parents during the ensuing chaos. The chances of finding them alive, he knew, would be slim at best.

When he got within twenty feet of her, the little girl finally looked up. It was not the panicked, wild movement he had been anticipating. Instead, it was a slow and measured gesture. Reznak froze.

Her eyes were a clear gray, the irises wide and almost silvery in their sheen. Her skin, where it was visible beneath the dirty yet elegant ivory dress she wore, was an alabaster white. Thick, dark curls crowned her head and fell in waves to her shoulders, framing a surprisingly slim face and neck. She looked to be about eight years old and was without a doubt the most shockingly beautiful being he had ever seen.

Yet it was not her startling appearance that stopped him in his tracks; it was the look on her face that sent a sharp chill through his bones and a shiver down his spine, immobilizing his legs.

There was only one word to describe the expression in her eyes: fearlessness.

Pure and unadulterated, the feeling seemed to seep through her pores and emanate from the very core of her being, an almost palpable energy focused in a lance-like beam projected from her dark pupils.

That was when Reznak knew she was not human.

The little girl blinked. Reznak suddenly found that he could move again. His gaze drifted down to her right hand, where the handle of an ugly knife was clasped firmly between her slender fingers. Red droplets still gleamed wetly on the edge of the blade and dropped into an expanding pool by her bare feet. His eyes followed the crimson trail to the dead man lying inches from where she stood. There was a deep, linear wound on the left side of the soldier's chest; by the looks of it, she had stabbed him in the heart.

It would have taken the man less than a minute to die.

Reznak's gaze shifted to the girl. 'Hello,' he said gently in German, conscious of the weight of the sword at his waist. 'My name is Dimitri. What's your name?'

The little girl remained silent. He hesitated. Certain he would not get a reply, he repeated the question in the local Estonian dialect. He was shocked when, in a clear and low voice that was oddly devoid of emotion, she said, 'Alexandria.'

Reznak took a cautious step forward, his eyes never leaving hers. Her chin tilted as she stared up at him. 'Where's your mother, Alexandria?' he continued quietly in the same vernacular.

A faint frown dawned on her face at his words. 'I don't know,' she said.

Less than two hundred feet from where they stood, scores of soldiers fought to the death, their swords and daggers carving through the flesh and bones of their enemies. The harsh breaths of their nervous horses misted the cold air, while musket rounds peppered the ground around them.

Reznak took another step forward. 'Can you tell me where you came from?'

The little girl's frown deepened while she considered the question. 'I don't know,' she repeated.

It was then that he noticed the fresh blood matted in her hair. She had suffered a blow to the side of her head. His gaze dropped to the red finger marks on her arm. His eyes narrowed.

'Did that man hurt you?' Reznak asked stiffly, indicating the dead soldier at her feet.

Her chin dipped in a brief nod.

He stared at her for a moment before slowly squatting down. With his face level with hers, he carefully extended a hand. 'Would you like to come with me, Alexandria? It's not safe here.'

The little girl gazed at him silently. Undaunted, Reznak stood up and waited. She turned on her heels and stared through the thin veil of snow at the river and the city beyond it. The wind picked up and ruffled her hair.

He peered at the back of her neck curiously. Imprinted a scant inch beneath her hairline, in the very middle of her delicate spine, was a triangular mark—a trishula. Although generically shaped like a trident, the more intricate details of the design reminded him strongly of the weapons he had seen wielded by fearsome Asian warriors in battles past. It was not a tattoo. It looked more like a birthmark.

The knife thudded softly in the deepening snowdrift when the little girl opened her fingers. Still gazing at the battlefield before them, she raised her bloodied hand toward him. Reznak clasped it in his own and was surprised at how warm her skin felt.

'Are you my father now?' she asked calmly.

'No,' he said with a weak smile. He glanced at the top of her head. The dark curls shivered slightly in the wind. Beneath them, the child's body was as still as stone. 'Can I call you Alexa? Alexandria is a bit of a mouthful.'

She gave this some thought. 'Yes,' she said finally with a curt nod.

CHAPTER ONE

November 2010. Eastern Desert. Egypt.

Dimitri Reznak mopped his forehead with a handkerchief and muttered a few expletives in Czech. The midday sun beat down relentlessly from an azure sky devoid of clouds. According to the temperature sensor in the Jeep that had brought him to the desert from the city of Aswan, it was thirty-seven degrees Celsius in the shade. It was technically winter in North Africa.

He sighed, took a sip from the glass of tepid water in his hand, and concentrated on what his chief research scientist, Professor Simon Goodwin, was saying as he led him inside a tent.

'– and then the GPR units went mad! I mean, we started to get readings like nobody's business. Here, take a look!' The normally mild-mannered and immaculate archaeologist ran a hand through his disheveled red hair, grabbed several feet of data sheets from a pile next to a laptop, and reverently laid them out on a camping table.

Reznak stared at the reams of gray, monochromatic images for several long seconds. As an avid and obsessive collector, and more importantly as the Head of the Immortal Culture and History Section of the Crovir First Council, he had a good idea of the technology behind ground-penetrating radars, or GPRs. Using the reflected signals from high-frequency, polarized radio waves transmitted into the ground, GPR receivers produced radar grams showing profiles of subsurface sections. By analyzing these, Reznak's team could identify the presence of discrete objects, changes in rock strata, voids, and even cracks a considerable distance beneath the earth. 'What am I looking at, exactly?' he said finally.

Fingers trembling slightly, Goodwin pointed at a stretch of darker gray below a series of hyperbolic reflections on the radar gram. 'We found two caves. The first one is fifty feet below the surface of our current elevation and measures approximately sixty by forty feet. The second cave is deeper.' He tapped the paper. 'We have yet to determine its size, although we suspect it's smaller than the first. Were it not for a subtle line that seemed to indicate some sort of narrow channel leading from the first cave, we would have missed it entirely. Of course, the fact that these mountains are mostly made of granite and limestone rendered ground penetration by the radio waves more effective, which explains—'

Reznak stopped listening. The scientist's words washed over him in a buzz while he stared at the shadow on the picture. He felt his heartbeat rise. Could this be it? Could they finally have found the very thing he had been searching for throughout the last six hundred years? A small flicker of hope, that treacherous and yet more often than not disappointing feeling, blossomed in his chest. He took a deep breath and chastised himself silently; he had experienced too much disillusionment in the past to allow himself to get easily carried away, unlike the scientist across the table from him. The only way he would believe it was if he saw it for himself.

'Simon?' he interrupted quietly. The professor continued talking, seemingly oblivious to his employer's voice. 'Simon,' Reznak said more forcefully. Undaunted, Goodwin's eyes had glazed with emotion, and he pressed on with his impromptu lecture on rock strata. 'Simon!' Reznak finally barked.

Goodwin jumped. 'What?' he said, sounding mildly hurt.

'How far are you into the excavation?' asked the Crovir immortal as patiently as he could.

The scientist blinked. A grin broke across his face. 'We're about five feet from the tunnel leading to the first cave,' he gushed with barely concealed enthusiasm. 'I have to say, it was damn good of the Egyptians to lend us one of their air core drills. That thing blasted through the granite like it was marshmallow. What could have taken weeks using conventional digging methods has taken us a mere couple of days to accomplish!'

Reznak smiled faintly. 'Lend' was far too altruistic a word for how he had gotten his hands on the expensive drilling equipment from one of the local gold mines. 'Coerce' and 'threaten' were much closer to the real deal. Of course, he saw no need to tell this to the professor; the Cambridge and Harvard graduate did not possess an unkind bone in his body, and there was nothing to be gained by burdening him with details of his employer's shadowy transactions. 'Would you be so kind as to take me to the site?' he requested instead.

'Of course,' Goodwin replied, nodding energetically. A

hesitant expression dawned on his face. 'I hope you don't mind us starting the dig without you. I tried to contact you when we made the discovery a week ago.'

'I know. Things have been kind of…busy lately,' said Reznak, grimacing slightly. That was the understatement of the century. He had just returned from a trip to Europe, where he had attended a most disturbing meeting of the Crovir First Council. After more than six hundred years of relative peace, another war was brewing between the Crovirs and their immortal enemy, the Bastians. This time, Agatha Vellacrus, the current Head of the Order of Crovir Hunters and the de facto leader of the Crovir Councils, was intent on wiping out the Bastian race for good.

As one of the authors of the original peace treaty between the two immortal races, Reznak was damned if he was going to sit back and let the woman destroy centuries of his hard work. Besides, some of the people he respected most in this world and counted among his closest friends were Bastians.

'Here, catch,' said Goodwin.

Reznak looked up in time to grab the yellow hardhat the scientist lobbed across the table. He stared at the plastic helmet.

'Health and safety first,' said the professor with a friendly grin, putting on his own hardhat.

Reznak followed him out of the tent. Of course, there was also no point telling the scientist that if a rock were to fall on Reznak's head and kill him, he would wake up a short while later as fresh as a daisy. That would, however, bring him one death closer to the final one, and with only seven more to go, he had mixed feelings about the idea.

As they headed past the Jeep that had brought him to the site, two men clad in dark clothing fell into step behind them.

Goodwin glanced at the bodyguards curiously but never said a word; he was used to them by now. A sigh left Reznak's lips.

All that the professor had been told about his employer was that he was the CEO of a large, private organization interested in funding difficult archaeological projects around the world for the benefit of furthering international academic and cultural knowledge. The fact that this organization appeared to have almost limitless resources and access to the latest state-of-the-art equipment to work with were enough to keep him content. The bodyguards had been assigned to Reznak the day he became a member of the Crovir First Council; it was unfortunately a condition of the job, one that the immortal found faintly insulting considering he knew he could take on both Hunters in a fight.

Goodwin led them through a camp perched on a narrow shelf on the side of the mountain. The land fell away sharply to the west, giving way to endless miles of rolling sand dunes. They walked past the trailers that served as homes and mobile labs for the scientists before heading up a trail freshly carved into the earth by a digger. The yellow dust that covered the plains and peaks of the Eastern Desert whirled around their feet as the wind picked up. Reznak wiped his brow again, grateful for the breeze. Moments later, they reached the summit of the rise and stopped on the edge of a ridge some thirty feet away. The Crovir immortal shielded his eyes against the glare of the sun and stared into the narrow valley at their feet.

The track they stood on followed the natural curves of the underlying rock face as it wound along a steep incline all the way to the floor of the canyon. A group of figures stood around a large excavator at the bottom. An improvised workstation and a machine that looked like a portable oil rig on caterpillar tracks sat close by; a loud, percussive hum emanated from the metal structure as it hammered into the ground.

Even from a distance, Reznak could feel the palpable excitement in the air. He tried not to let it get to him moments later, when he reached the bottom of the valley with Goodwin. On closer inspection, the canyon resembled one of the hundreds of ancient, dry riverbeds that criss-crossed this part of the Eastern Desert. As he approached the helmeted scientists, he noticed the thick layer of dust that coated their skin and clothes. Although a low, restrained mumble ran through the group, he could see the expectant gleam in everyone's eyes.

'How long until we breach the roof of the tunnel?' said Goodwin briskly. He had addressed a short, bearded man Reznak knew to be an immortal.

'About a half hour,' replied Russell Brennan, glancing at a radar gram attached to a GPR unit. The scientist gave a curt nod of acknowledgement to Reznak. Graham Walcott, a second immortal, stood next to Brennan; his gaze never left the complex control panel of the million-dollar mining drill several feet from him.

More than half of the research team Reznak had assembled over the centuries for this quest were Crovir immortals. To keep their secret safe, the human colleagues who had joined them over the last two hundred years were only ever given fixed, five-year, non-renewable contracts on the project, with ironclad confidentiality agreements attached. So far, the safeguards appeared to have worked.

A frown crossed Reznak's face at that thought. There was one man who had gotten uncomfortably close to the truth about a decade ago. Had it not been for that particular individual's constant prying and all-out insubordination, they would have progressed much further and faster in their venture, for he had been without a doubt one of the most intellectually gifted humans Reznak had ever encountered.

'It's strange, really,' said Goodwin pensively as they listened to the sound of rock being pulverized into pieces.

Reznak glanced at him questioningly.

'We came across what seemed to be the primary tunnel leading to the first cave before we found the chamber itself,' the scientist continued. 'The passage appears to end abruptly after some thirty feet. The hyperbolic reflections on the radar gram suggest a collapse. We have yet to determine the exact location of the original entrance.'

'Can't you hazard a guess as to where it might have been by extrapolating on the direction and angle?' asked Reznak.

Goodwin smiled. 'We're scientists—we try not to guess. But you're right. We did just that. Unfortunately, either our calculations are incorrect or the truth is seriously baffling.'

'Why?' said Reznak.

'Because it would appear that whoever dug the tunnel started it a thousand feet up the vertical side of a mountain,' Goodwin replied laconically. 'I suspect they started excavating much lower down, with an ascending passage like the one in the pyramid of Giza.'

Reznak was still frowning when a shout of jubilation erupted from the team of scientists. The mining drill had finally penetrated through the roof of the tunnel. It took several minutes to move the heavy, track-mounted machine out of the way. Everyone gathered around the edges of the rapidly darkening abyss.

'Would you like to do the honors?' asked Goodwin excitedly, glancing at Reznak.

The immortal nodded and felt the first flutter of anticipation thrum through his veins. Of all the remote and inaccessible places he had excavated in Europe, Asia, and Africa in this seemingly endless quest, their current location held the most promise to date. Though the search had spanned centuries, the advent of space technology and satellite imagery over the previous two decades had finally helped narrow their target area to this part of the old continent; for the first time in a long time, Reznak felt confident they were on the right track.

He waited patiently while a technician fitted a harness with a climbing rope to his waist. His two bodyguards shifted restlessly at the edge of the crowd, their expressions troubled; he had banned them from following him into the tunnel.

He was finally lowered into the opening via a winch attached to the excavator. About ten feet down, the harsh desert light started to fade. After another ten feet, he was cast into pitch-blackness. He removed a glow stick from his belt and cracked it against the wall of the vertical shaft. The fluorescent green light washed across the tight confines of the hole and showed the roof of the tunnel some thirty feet below him.

Moments later, he stepped carefully onto a mound of rubble and released the climbing rope from his harness.

'Are you there?' Goodwin's tense voice came over the walkie-talkie strapped to his shoulder.

'Yes,' said Reznak. He cracked another pair of glow sticks and threw one down either side of the rock pile before unhooking a torch from his belt.

'What do you see?' said the scientist animatedly.

'A lot of darkness,' Reznak replied calmly. The air was cool and dry, yet not as stale as he had expected it to be. The walls of the passage he stood in were roughly six feet apart and so smooth they might have been carved out by a machine. His voice bounced hollowly against the bare rock and the low ceiling. The stillness was otherwise deafening.

By the time Goodwin followed him down the shaft, Reznak had already started to move south along the tunnel. The powerful light beam from his torch swept across the ground before him, exposing a layer of yellow dust covering the hard rock surface. If there had ever been footprints in the dirt, they had long since been erased by the passage of time. Some fifty feet later, the tunnel ended abruptly. He stepped through an arched doorway into a large chamber and froze.

Reznak's heart slammed against his ribs as he played the torchlight across the domed ceiling of a cave. Footsteps sounded behind him. Seconds later, Goodwin appeared at his side and rocked to a standstill, a gasp escaping his lips. Brennan and Walcott stopped next to the professor and gazed silently at the dark cavern. Walcott lit a powerful gas lantern and placed it carefully on the ground.

Elation turned to disappointment when the interior of the cave was revealed in the harsh, white light. 'It's empty,' Goodwin murmured in a dejected tone.

Reznak studied the chamber and felt coldness spread through him. He glanced at the two immortal scientists and saw his own apprehension reflected in their faces. 'No,' he said somberly, a sudden sweat drenching his back. 'It's been ransacked.'

The cave was approximately sixty by forty feet, with smooth, arched walls that joined to form a ceiling nearly twenty feet high at its peak. A perfect symmetrical oval in design, it was bare but for two large, rectangular, shallow depressions in the middle of the granite floor. They each measured eight by four feet and stood side by side. Reznak was willing to bet his entire fortune that they would be perfectly aligned in an east-west direction.

A three-foot gap separated the two impressions. A small, rectangular imprint was visible in the center of the narrow space.

'How do you know that?' asked Goodwin, his eyes widening.

'There are fresh footprints in the dust,' replied Reznak.

Goodwin looked down for the first time, his mouth agape as he finally saw what Reznak and the two immortals had spotted within seconds of entering the cave. A flurry of faint shoe prints covered the ground. Most of them were clustered around the hollow impressions in the middle of the floor.

Reznak walked to the center of the chamber. 'I suspect there were two tombs here,' he said stiffly, stopping in front of the first depression. Anger was replacing the dread in his gut. Who on this Earth had the resources and ability to discover these caves before he did? In all his centuries of searching, he had never crossed paths with—or even heard of—another individual or organization on a similar quest as his.

The professor looked up from the floor. 'You mean, like a pair of sarcophagi?'

'No,' said Reznak. 'Not "like". I believe they would have been the precursor to the ancient Egyptians' coffin.' He looked around the cave. 'The question is, how did our looters get in here, and how did they remove the tombs?'

They started to walk around the chamber, torchlight running across the smooth rock face while they searched for signs of the long-departed intruders.

'I can feel a faint draft,' said Brennan moments later from the east wall of the chamber.

'So can I,' said Walcott from the opposite side.

Reznak watched the two men meet in the center of the

south wall. Walcott stopped and studied the rock face with a frown. The faintest ripple suddenly disturbed the solid surface. The immortal's eyes widened. He raised his hand and touched the wall gingerly. It gave slightly beneath his fingertips. He took a knife from his belt and stabbed the blade into the rock.

They all stared in amazement when the surface ripped open smoothly.

Walcott tugged the knife down a few inches. Then, together with Brennan, he grabbed the edges of the vertical slit and pulled. Both men staggered backwards as a large sheet of beige-colored canvas came apart in their hands.

'What the —' Goodwin stammered.

Reznak swore and crossed the floor swiftly to the mouth of the tunnel concealed behind the stone-colored covering. The passage had been carved only recently; there was fresh rubble on the ground. Whoever had gone to the trouble of hiding the tunnel had obviously not wanted its presence to be discovered for a while.

He raised his torch and shined it into the dark opening. 'So that's how they got in,' he muttered. There were faded shoe marks in the dirt. He stepped inside the passage and headed into the gloom. Goodwin and the two Crovir scientists followed.

Reznak came to a halt a minute later. The tunnel ended abruptly in a blind wall. He frowned. The draft was stronger here. He squinted at the edges of the passage and switched the torch off. They were plunged into darkness.

'Why did you—' Goodwin started.

'Look ahead,' said Reznak sharply.

Goodwin's gaze switched to the wall in front of them. 'What is that?' he murmured after a few seconds.

A faint glow surrounded the edges of the wall. Reznak slid

his fingers carefully along the top right-hand corner of the rock face until he felt the faintest gap. He removed a knife from his belt, stabbed it into the narrow space, and pulled down. Canvas ripped under the blade and fluttered outward in a strong breeze. Sunlight flooded the passage, dazzling them with its brilliance. Goodwin stepped eagerly past him.

'Stop!' shouted Reznak. He grabbed the back of the professor's shirt just before the man walked out into the nothingness before him. Goodwin uttered a strangled cry and jerked backward from the ledge.

Reznak moved carefully to the edge of the opening that had been carved into the side of the mountain. Another peak loomed in the blue sky ahead of him. Four hundred feet below, a riverbed snaked along the floor of a valley. He studied the steep, almost vertical wall beneath him and spotted the steel struts embedded in the rock.

'They used a crane,' he said in a voice stiff with rising anger. 'That's the only way they could have gotten this high. A goddamned bloody crane!' His words echoed down the walls of the canyon.

He closed his eyes briefly, took a deep shuddering breath, turned, and stormed past the scientists. He entered the cave and stopped in the middle of the floor.

'It doesn't look like they found the second chamber; otherwise, we'd be looking at another hole in the ground,' he said, struggling to mask his fury while he looked around. 'They may not have known of its existence.' He turned to Goodwin. 'Where was the entrance?'

It didn't take long for one of the GPR units to be lowered from the worksite above them into the borehole where they had entered the tunnel. Twenty minutes later, Brennan muttered, 'Bingo,' under his breath. They crowded around him and studied the images on the radar gram.

Ironically, the tomb raiders had dug their tunnel exactly five feet from the opening to the second cave. It was impossible to tell with the naked eye that a heavy stone slab lay next to the southwest wall; the edges were so well concealed they resembled the underlying rock.

Another ten minutes with pickaxes finally revealed the entrance to the cave. Below it, a staircase chiseled out of the rock spiraled down into darkness. This time, Reznak descended the steps without ceremony. Fifteen feet beneath the main cave, he reached the bottom of the stairway and paused. As his torchlight washed across the space before him, his eyes slowly widened.

Over the centuries of his existence thus far, Reznak had borne witness to some of the most incomparable wonders of this world. Yet, he had never beheld such a sight as the one that now lay in front of him. It took another pair of gas lanterns brought down by Goodwin and the two Crovir scientists for him to truly appreciate what they had discovered.

Like the cave above it, the second chamber was a perfectly designed, symmetrical oval, measuring about thirty by twenty feet. Except here, the walls did not curve up to meet the ceiling, which in this instance was flat. Instead, they ran vertically around the space to form an almost continuous facade but for the opening to the staircase. From the appearance and color of the granite, the second cave looked to be in an entirely different rock formation.

In the center of the floor stood two large, plain, circular pillars that rose to meet the ceiling. Judging by their orientation, Reznak suspected they were positioned exactly beneath the impressions of the missing tombs in the cave above. Carved within each granite column, at about waist level, was an alcove that held a large clay pot. Although his heart was slamming against his ribs and his fingers itched to discover what the earthenware contained, Reznak could not stop his gaze from straying to the most impressive aspect of the room.

Engraved into the walls of the chamber, untouched by time and man, complex pictographs covered the rock face from floor to ceiling, forming a huge, circular, ornamental scroll that looked as fresh as the day it was inscribed.

'My god…these are cuneiform scripts,' Goodwin whispered as he stepped to the nearest wall, his fingers shaking around the torch in his hand. 'They must be—goodness—thousands of years old!'

Though he was not an expert on ancient Sumerian-derived languages, Reznak was nonetheless familiar with the characteristic wedge-shaped writings on the walls; the oldest known Crovir and Bastian texts had been etched in the descendants of the original Sumerian script, namely Assyrian and Aramaic. The fact that the inscriptions looked to be from that period of history only confirmed that these caves were more than likely of immortal origin and design.

'These may be older than the clay tablets found at Jemdet Nasr,' said Goodwin in a dazed voice. 'I think they're in the original proto-writings that came before the Sumerian language.' The scientist turned and stared at Reznak. 'You do realize that this is the archaeological find of the century? We're going to need an Assyriologist to translate this!'

Impatience replaced awe in Reznak's mind. He nodded briskly. 'I know several. Now, let's look at the pots.'

He had to wait while more scientists brought containers of equipment from the campsite. Everyone who entered the second chamber had to don sterile suits so as to preserve the original environment of the site, a measure Reznak himself had insisted on since the technology had become available.

An hour after they had started to photograph and record the provenance and association of the various elements within the cave, a voice suddenly interrupted the reverent hush that had fallen across the group.

'What's that on the floor?' asked one of the scientists.

They stopped what they were doing and stared at where the woman was pointing. Her boots had disturbed the dirt between the two pillars in the center of the room. A faint impression was apparent between the grains of dust.

'That looks like another inscription,' said Goodwin, alarm raising the pitch of his voice. 'Everybody stand still!'

They froze.

'Can you see any other markings on the floor around you?' said Goodwin anxiously.

Several minutes passed while the team inspected the ground. Slowly, one 'No,' after another began to echo around the cave.

Goodwin sagged. 'Good. Step back carefully, Patricia. Let me take a closer look.'

Reznak stood over the professor while the latter lay on the floor and carefully cleared the indentation with a fine brush. It soon became apparent that the floor engraving was not Sumerian, nor was it derived from any of the other cuneiform languages. Instead, it seemed to be a unique, triangular-shaped design that had been chiseled into the epicenter of the space between the pillars. The immortal wondered briefly what had stood in that exact spot in the cave above, where he had observed the small rectangular imprint between the larger tombs. As the details of the motif were slowly revealed, his eyes widened, and a shiver raced down his spine.

When the entire etching finally lay exposed under the glare of the projection lights, Reznak could no longer deny the evidence before his own eyes. Carved into the floor of the cave was a large trishula.

It looked identical to the marking he had discovered on a little girl's neck exactly three hundred and ten years previously.

For several seconds, the immortal felt too stunned to breathe. When air finally left his lungs in a harsh exhale, Reznak knew his life would never be the same again. In this one day, not only had he finally uncovered one of the greatest secrets in the history of the immortal races, he had also come a step closer to solving the second biggest enigma of his existence to date: the mysterious origin of the little girl who had come to mean so much to him.

Moments later, the contents of the clay pots were finally revealed. Several of the scientists paled and rushed out of the cave, heaving as they did so. The chill coursing through Reznak's veins turned to ice as he stared inside the ancient containers.

The sun was low in the sky when the Crovir immortal finally emerged from the tunnel and climbed the wall of the canyon. He stopped at the summit of the rise and watched blindly while the orange orb sank toward the purple horizon. A dozen questions swarmed his mind, the most pressing of which concerned the identity of the unknown tomb raiders. However unpleasant the thought, he had to consider the possibility that someone on his team had betrayed him.

Reznak reached for his cell phone and started to dial a number. He hesitated before canceling the call. He needed more information before he could talk to her.

The sooner he got the cuneiform scriptures analyzed, the better. The only way he trusted this to be done in complete secrecy was if he transported the entire second cave and its contents to his main research facility in Europe. It would be a difficult but not impossible task. He was on the phone making the arrangements before he even reached the Jeep.

On the ride back to Aswan, Reznak got a call that would put half of his best-laid plans on hold. Agatha Vellacrus, the leader of the Crovirs, had finally made her move.

The battle to avert a second immortal war had begun.

THOUGH THE CAVE WAS EVENTUALLY EXCAVATED AND MOVED TO Europe, Reznak did not get to the clay pot artifacts and the scriptures on the walls for another fortnight, during which time the entire face of the immortal societies had changed. Following the death of Agatha Vellacrus and her only surviving son and successor at the hands of an army of Bastian and Crovir allies, he found himself in the unenviable position of being promoted to temporary Head of the Order of Crovir Hunters and became, for all intents and purposes, the leader of the Crovirs.

A week after he started his analysis of the data from the cave, Reznak called Victor Dvorsky, one of his closest friends and the new Head of the Order of Bastian Hunters. In between reorganizing their respective immortal societies, the two friends met up in the Crovir's research lab to discuss the astonishing findings from the Eastern Desert cave. Reznak then asked his Bastian friend for the biggest favor of their relationship to date. After much deliberation, Dvorsky eventually accepted and provided him with the biological sample he had requested: a drop of blood from an extraordinary immortal whose very existence had determined the course and outcome of the recent immortal battle. A few days later, Reznak had the answers he had been looking for.

He called Dvorsky again, this time to arrange a meeting with that very special immortal. Finally, before he left Europe for the States, he spoke to the woman whose existence he sensed was undeniably linked to the oldest secret in immortal history.

'Hi, Alexa? We need to talk.'

CHAPTER TWO

December 2010. California. USA.

The wintry sun beat relentlessly upon the barren wasteland of the Mojave Desert as a cold wind coursed through the valleys and canyons of the National Preserve. It shook the Yucca palms and Juniper trees that covered the arid terrain and whistled through clusters of mesquite and creosote bushes, disturbing the lizards and snakes that lazed within the shelter of the scrub brush. As it danced over the vast sand dunes that dominated the landscape, the wind caused a low booming noise to echo against the foothills of the mountains.

Two thousand feet above the desert floor, Alexa King stood motionless on a ledge on the side of a cliff. A short distance to her left, a red-tailed hawk watched her curiously from its rocky perch. The bird of prey seemed strangely unaffected by her presencc; it had yet to let out a fierce, rasping cry to indicate its displeasure at her intrusion of its territory.

Feet planted firmly apart and hands hanging loosely at her sides, she stared unblinkingly through her skydiving goggles at the bright landscape before her. Strapped to the back of the white, bespoke, nylon cordura and spandex wing-suit she wore was a small parachute. Beneath it, her custom-made body holster held her two stainless steel Sig Sauer P229 pistols and her twin sai daggers.

The red-tailed hawk cocked its head to the north. A second later, Alexa picked up the low-pitched hum of an approaching aircraft. She glanced at the Timex on her left wrist. The target was on time; from her covert surveillance over the last two weeks, she knew he would have left the Las Vegas airport exactly forty minutes ago on his way to Palm Springs to make the drop. She started the chronograph on the watch, reached behind her back, and slid the sais out of their sheaths.

Half a minute passed. The aircraft's engine grew louder. Her watch beeped.

Alexa took off toward the edge of the ledge and jumped just as a white Cessna 172 Skyhawk with a red fuselage and tail shot past the curve of the mountain to her right. The aircraft was around five years old and registered to one Abraham McIntyre.

As she dropped toward the desert floor, she spread her arms and legs to open the wings of the suit, then turned and dived after the plane. She had practiced the jump a dozen times in the past few days; there was little margin for error. If the Cessna was traveling at a slower speed than it had the previous four times she had timed it, she would overshoot in front of the propeller and be torn to shreds.

As it turned out, McIntyre was a creature of habit. He kept the aircraft at a cruising speed of a hundred and twenty-two knots and maintained a steady altitude.

Less than fifteen seconds after she cleared the edge of the

cliff, she glided to the rear deck of the Cessna and stabbed the sai daggers into the metal of the fuselage.

The impact jarred her wrists and the wind drag nearly tore her off the aircraft. The plane pitched backward and rolled, offering her a dizzying view of the desert far below when her body tilted with it. The engine roared as the pilot struggled to level the Cessna.

She unclipped the wings of the suit and renewed her grip on the daggers. Moving the blades one at a time, she pulled herself toward the front of the aircraft and dropped down the trailing edge of the left wing. Steadying her feet against the strut and the wheel fairing of the landing gear, she sheathed her left sai and yanked the cabin door open.

The pilot stared at her, goggle-eyed.

'Abraham McIntyre, in the name of the Crovir First Council, I hereby arrest you on charges of—' she started to say.

McIntyre blinked and reached for the gun on the seat next to him.

Alexa twisted to the left and narrowly avoided the bullet that whizzed past her chest. Frowning, she gripped the support strut, slipped the right sai in her holster, and pulled a knife from a scabbard on her thigh. McIntyre blanched when she leaned inside the aircraft and cut his seatbelt. She grabbed him by the neck of his shirt. He wriggled desperately in her grip and aimed the gun at her head.

Alexa raised her right knee and hook-kicked the weapon from his hand. A cry of pain left his lips when the gun fell from his fingers. She ignored it and heaved backwards. McIntyre screamed, knuckles whitening on the edge of his seat.

A grim smile crossed her lips. She let go of the wing strut and fell away from the plane.

His shriek of terror was lost in the wind as they dropped

like lead weights toward the distant ground. Alexa tightened her arm around the man's neck and wrapped her legs around his waist before reaching behind her back and pulling the activation handle on her chute. It deployed swiftly behind her.

McIntyre choked at the sudden deceleration.

She reached for the steering toggles and guided them smoothly toward the desert floor. Halfway down, the red-tailed hawk dove past them with a shrill cry, likely on the trail of an unseen prey. She followed the bird with her eyes until it disappeared from view.

Ten feet from the ground, Alexa let go of McIntyre. He hit the dirt with a dull thud and lay there, groaning. She landed a few steps ahead of him, steadied herself, and shrugged the chute harness off her back. She strode back toward the prostrate figure and stopped a couple of inches from his head. She unclipped her GPS device from her hip and studied it.

They had touched down exactly a mile and a half from her rental Jeep.

A minute passed. Alexa stared at the man lying still at her feet. 'Get up,' she ordered coldly.

McIntyre's hand suddenly snaked out and gripped her booted ankle. He yanked on her leg and tried to pull her to the ground. Her weight barely shifted. A sigh left her lips. She removed one of her Sigs from its holster and shot him in the hand.

His howl of agony reverberated against the nearby sand dunes. McIntyre scrambled wildly to his knees and gripped his bleeding appendage. 'You bitch!' he growled, glaring at her from under the layer of grime that covered his face.

The gun shifted in her hand. 'Unless you want to lose your right eye, I suggest you get up and start to walk,' she said in a dull monotone. He stared into the barrel of the Sig and gritted his teeth before rising unsteadily to his feet.

Ten minutes before they reached the Jeep, Alexa heard the distant boom of an explosion and saw a flare of smoke rise on the horizon. The Cessna had crashed into the desert.

She had parked the vehicle in the shadow of a giant boulder and camouflaged it with netting to reduce its visibility from the sky. She handcuffed a disgruntled McIntyre to the passenger door, changed out of the wing-suit, and climbed behind the wheel.

Less than an hour after she had jumped off the side of the cliff, Alexa guided the Jeep onto Interstate Fifteen and drove toward Las Vegas. As the vehicle quickly ate the distance that separated them from the city, she glanced at the man next to her.

McIntyre slouched in his seat and alternated between scowling at her and staring worriedly at the landscape outside the window. An occasional wince crossed his face when he moved his injured hand.

She had wrapped a bandage around it; she did not want him bleeding all over the rental.

'Who the hell are you anyway?' he finally asked when they were thirty miles out from the city.

Alexa stared at the road ahead. 'That's on a need-to-know basis.'

'Look, if this is about money, I can—' McIntyre started. He stopped abruptly at her expression.

'Don't insult my intelligence,' she said.

He lapsed into silence and gnawed at his lips.

She studied him for several seconds before turning her attention to the highway.

Abraham McIntyre was a thief and a fool. A clever thief,

granted, but still a fool. He had to be if he thought he could pull a fast one on the Crovir First Council.

McIntyre was an engineer for one of the most lucrative oil companies in the world. It was owned by a Crovir noble who also happened to be a member of the First Council. Not content with his generous salary, McIntyre started embezzling money from the company. When an accountant finally picked up an irregularity in the balance sheets a year ago, it became apparent that someone had been siphoning cash from one of the corporation's subsidiary funds. The trail eventually led to McIntyre through a series of anonymous postal box companies.

It turned out the immortal was even greedier than originally thought. In an attempt to make his ill-earned fortune grow, he set up business with a drug cartel in South America, where he was based for his job. Twice a week, he would fly from Vegas to Palm Springs to make a drop to one of the cartel's principal cocaine distributors in California. The money he earned was then wired to one of his many foreign bank accounts.

At that stage, the oil company should have notified the FBI's Financial Crimes Section and the DEA.

But that was not the way immortals carried out their affairs. Although they adhered to most of the rules and regulations of human society in order to preserve the secrets of their race, they had a whole set of their own laws to abide by, most of which stemmed from the very inception of the immortal societies. In cases like these, immortal decrees overrode those made by humans. And immortals firmly believed in obtaining their pound of flesh. Or, in this case, a life for a sin.

In the two weeks that she had been watching him, Alexa had come up with six ways to capture and dispose of McIntyre. Five of them would have involved injuring or killing the bodyguards from the security firm he had hired to protect him; although he was an immortal, McIntyre was no fool when it came to investing in his personal protection. However discreet she was, the death of humans would have brought attention from the Federal police, something she was keen to avoid. After all, it was the reason she had been assigned this task.

Dealing with an immortal embezzler was a job that would ordinarily have been handled by the Order of Crovir Hunters. But the Hunters, while excellent at what they did, sometimes left traces. McIntyre needed to disappear off the face of the Earth, as if he had never existed.

That was her area of expertise.

The sixth method was the one she had finally chosen. The only time the immortal was truly alone was when he made the flight to Palm Springs; he never took a bodyguard with him on his trips.

By the time the authorities and McIntyre's business partners realized his body was not in the remains of the burnt-out Cessna, he would be long gone.

She exited the freeway at Junction 27 and took the St. Rose Parkway. Two miles later, she turned right and headed for the Henderson Executive airport. She drove past the main terminal and administrative buildings and parked the Jeep by one of the private corporate hangars.

McIntyre tensed when he saw the Learjet next to it. The color drained from his face as four Crovir Hunters stepped out of the shadow of the plane. Alexa pulled the cursing immortal from the vehicle and dragged him toward the group of silent men.

Frank Schmidt, the Crovir team leader, was tall and broad-shouldered, with a chiseled face lifted straight from a Roman bust. Alexa knew him from the brief time she had spent in the

Order. He was one of a handful of Hunters who did not fear her.

A breeze ruffled Schmidt's suit and revealed the faint outline of the holster under his arm as he walked toward them. 'You're dead on time,' he said with a faint grin. He glanced at McIntyre's hand. 'What happened?'

'He got frisky,' said Alexa. McIntyre glowered at her.

Schmidt raised his eyebrows. His expression indicated that a man would have to be mad to attempt any such thing around her. His gaze ran over her figure briefly. 'You look good,' he said quietly.

'Thanks,' said Alexa.

The Hunters behind Schmidt shifted slightly. She glanced impassively at their troubled expressions.

She had long been aware of the rumors that circulated about her in the upper echelons of the Crovir Councils and the Order. She was a cold and calculating bitch without feelings. She would just as soon kill you as look at you. She wasn't a team player. She ate raw meat and drank the blood of her lovers. The gossip was wild and fanciful. Some of it was true.

Alexa knew she had bruised many egos over the centuries. She was faster, stronger, and deadlier than any Hunter working for the Order today, and was without a doubt the best covert agent the First Council had had access to in the last three hundred years. She thought this without pride or pleasure. It was a simple fact. She was also the only Crovir operative who had yet to suffer a death.

Fifteen minutes later, she watched the Learjet taxi along the runway. She turned and walked back to the Jeep. McIntyre would be taken to Europe to face the charges against him in a Crovir court. The evidence was damning. She knew what the outcome would be; she had carried out enough executions for the Crovir First Council to know they did not forgive easily.

She had just made it onto Interstate Fifteen when her cell phone rang.

Alexa looked at the display with narrowed eyes. She knew the number well. She took the call.

'Hi, Alexa? We need to talk,' said Dimitri Reznak without preamble.

She was silent for several seconds. 'Where are you?' she finally said.

'I'm in Europe,' said Reznak. 'I'll be in LA tonight.'

She frowned at the underlying tension in his voice. 'Where do you want to meet?'

FOUR HOURS LATER, SHE DROVE INTO A PARKING LOT AT LOS Angeles International Airport. After returning the Jeep to the rental company's local office, she made her way to one of the terminal's executive lounges. She settled down with a cup of coffee and a paper while she waited for Reznak.

A shadow soon fell across her. Alexa looked up.

'Hello,' said the tall, trim man before her. Her gaze flickered over the stranger's expensive suit, manicured hands, and Rolex watch. A second man, undoubtedly his business associate, stood next to him.

'Would you like some company?' asked the first man with an easy, confident smile.

'No,' she replied.

He inhaled sharply at her blunt tone.

His friend stiffened. 'Hey, I'm sure we can —' started the stranger with an amicable expression.

Alexa placed her cup down carefully on the table and glanced around the lounge. Shy of taking a Sig out and shooting the two men, she was going to have to make it inherently clear why it would be a bad idea to associate with her.

'The tan line on the fourth finger of your left hand indicates that you were on a holiday with your wife in the last month,' she said, staring steadily at the first man. 'Your wedding ring is in the right breast pocket of your suit.'

She ignored his startled gasp and turned to his business partner. 'As for you, I'm sure your friend here would like to know why you're sleeping with his wife.'

The second man's jaw sagged open. 'How the hell did you—'

'Barry?' said the first man in a stunned voice, turning to look at his associate.

Alexa picked up her cup and leaned back in her seat. 'You have the same scratch marks on your overnight cases from her diamond ring,' she said, her gaze scanning the paper once more. 'And you both smell like her.'

She tuned out the heated voices of the two men as they walked off in the midst of an argument. Not for the first time, she cursed her face and physique. Despite the nondescript way she dressed, her dark hair, silver eyes, sculpted cheekbones, and pale skin made her stand out in a crowd.

Reznak landed in LA nine hours later. Alexa watched him cross the lounge toward her and experienced the same mixture of irritating emotions his presence always engendered. Officially, Reznak was one of her employers. Unofficially, he was her godfather, her mentor, and the closest thing to a family she had in this world.

She bore only hazy recollections of the time when he had found her on the battlefield outside Narva. Once the Crovir noble realized that she would not regain her memory, and after his attempts to trace her family came to a dead end, he took her under his wing and brought her to his home. Over the following decade, Alexa was educated by the finest human and immortal tutors in Europe, not only in conventional subjects such as the sciences, languages, and literature, but also in the art of war; as Reznak quickly discovered, she excelled in all forms of combat.

It was not until she entered immortal adulthood at the age of eighteen and her aging slowed that she sensed her mentor had developed an attraction for her. Yet Reznak never once acted on his desires. Alexa had always wondered whether this was because of some outdated feeling of chivalry and morality or just that the prospect had literally scared him. As time passed, he seemed to come to terms with his feelings for her.

Though she would never admit it to him, Reznak was not an unattractive man. Nearly seven hundred years old in immortal terms, he looked like a human in his fifties, and had kept himself in shape over the years. He had a strong and compelling presence most women found alluring.

'Alexa,' Reznak said with a formal nod as he took the seat opposite hers.

'Dimitri,' she murmured in response. She glanced to where his bodyguards hovered by the door and the bar, their hooded eyes scanning the room before acknowledging her with a stare. 'What's this about?' she said, her gaze switching to her mentor's face.

Reznak did not reply immediately. 'I hear your mission went well,' he said with a faintly indulgent smile.

Alexa clenched her teeth. All she wanted to do right now was catch the next flight to New York and return to the peaceful solitude of her apartment in Manhattan. 'It did,' she said briskly.

'Good,' said Reznak. His expression sobered. He leaned forward and rested his elbows on his thighs. 'I have another assignment for you.'

'I haven't heard anything from the First Council,' she said after a short silence.

Reznak shook his head. 'You won't be working for the First Council on this occasion.' His eyes were steady on her face. 'You'll be answering directly to me.'

Alexa raised her eyebrows. 'Is the Council aware of this?'

A grimace crossed Reznak's lips. 'Not yet,' he replied grudgingly. 'I'll be informing them shortly that I've appropriated you for a…special quest for the Immortal Culture and History Section. That's if you accept the mission, of course.'

She studied his troubled countenance. 'It's not really my territory,' she said.

Reznak sighed.

Alexa observed the shadows under his eyes with a trace of concern. She knew of the pressures that had befallen him in the weeks following the death of the last leader of the Crovirs. Because of the latter's actions, they had been on the verge of another immortal war with the Bastians, their enemy of old. Reznak had been part of a group of Crovir and Bastian nobles who had helped avert the disaster. She had been on a mission in South America at the time and had not been directly involved in the action.

'I know it isn't,' her godfather murmured. Something shifted in his eyes. 'But I need you for this. You're the only one who can take on this assignment.'

The look on his face was unsettling. Alexa had never seen it before. 'You have access to dozens of specialists in your section,' she said calmly. 'If you need somebody to do the grunt work, ask the Hunters.'

Reznak gazed at her unwaveringly. It was then that she realized what his expression reminded her of. It was the look of someone about to impart unwanted news. 'None of them have the birthmark on the back of your neck,' he said quietly.

She stiffened. 'What do you mean?' she demanded in a voice laced with an edge of steel.

For the next half hour, her godfather recounted his extraordinary findings in Egypt over a month ago. Having lived with him for several decades, Alexa was long aware of his obsessive quest to discover the truth about the origins of the immortal races. She found the whole thing faintly amusing, as the only time he showed any real passion was when he discussed the subject.

She grew still when he described the carving in the floor of the second cave he had discovered. She listened intently as he told her of his suspicions about what had gone missing from the first cave.

A strained hush fell between them after he finished talking. Alexa sensed he had not told her everything. 'You want me to find out who looted the first cave and bring back the missing artifacts?' she asked, her tone not betraying her displeasure.

'Yes, essentially,' Reznak replied. 'I have hope that this mission will also shed some light on your past.' His gaze shifted to his hands. 'You'll have to keep this a secret from the Crovir First Council. The fewer people who know about it, the better.'

She stared at him. Her origins were not something she worried about excessively; despite her missing years, she knew who and what she was. But she was aware that the subject had long frustrated Reznak. For some reason, he felt he owed her the truth. It was the only other thing he was truly passionate about.

'You're hiding something,' Alexa finally said bluntly.

Her godfather's expression grew shuttered. He leaned back in the chair. 'I won't deny that,' he said carefully. 'I have never lied to you. Just call it a deliberate…omission.'

She scowled. 'Why?'

'Let's just say that there are other people involved in this, and it's not up to me to reveal their secrets,' he said with a sigh. 'If and when it becomes appropriate to tell you the rest of their story, I shall do so.'

She mulled this over for a silent moment. 'Okay,' she said finally.

A smile dawned on Reznak's face. It lost some of its shine when he appeared to recall something unpleasant. 'There's one more thing.'

CHAPTER THREE

TEN HOURS LATER, ALEXA STOOD IN THE MIDDLE OF AN apartment near the Back Bay area of Boston and wondered briefly whether her godfather had lost his mind. She studied the mess around her.

It had been childishly easy to break into the building. No doorman guarded the entrance to the tower block, and she had yet to see a single security camera in the entire place. Getting past the front door of the apartment had taken less than five seconds; there were no alarm systems for her to override, and a monkey could have picked the lock.

It was glaringly obvious from the narrow vestibule that the place belonged to a man. It had the generic air of chaos that only the male half of the human species could generate.

A pile of unopened mail sat on a side table in the hallway. Half of it was bills. The rest was a mixture of junk post and letters from distinguished universities and museums from around the world. There were several invites to conferences and lectures on obscure subjects in anthropology.

A door on the right opened onto a kitchen. It would have been warm and inviting but for the stack of dirty dishes spilling over the sink, the cluttered countertops, and the mildly offensive smell drifting from the direction of the garbage container. Alexa walked to the fridge and examined its contents with a critical eye. It contained a surprising quantity of healthy food, a positive find that was nullified by the open carton of milk next to the microwave.

Opposite the kitchen was a study that looked like ground zero of some catastrophic doomsday event. The polished floorboards were barely visible under a scattering of journals and books, while the MacBook Pro on the mahogany desk looked perilously close to being crushed under the avalanche of tomes piled atop it. The walls were solid floor-to-ceiling bookcases.

The bathroom was unexpectedly bright and clean. A pair of worn running shoes was neatly arranged under the sink.

Alexa stopped briefly in the open doorway to the bedroom and frowned at what she saw. She decided it could wait. At the bottom of the hall was a large sitting room with panoramic bay windows. She stopped in the middle of the hardwood floor and stared at the dark blue waters of the Charles River Basin visible through the gap between the buildings at the end of the road. She turned and looked around.

One wall of the room was taken up with dozens of picture frames depicting shots of archaeological digs from around the world. A bright-eyed man with an infectious smile was featured in most of them. A set of used boxing gloves hung from a hook above a narrow mantel, which held several university boxing trophies. An eclectic collection of furniture, sculptures, and artifacts made up the rest of the decor.

There were more books and a half-eaten pizza wilting on the coffee table.

The place was as far removed from her own apartment in New York as the sun was from the moon. Her frown deepened. She had seen enough.

She strolled back to the bedroom, stopped at the foot of the bed, and stared at the two figures sleeping under the sheets.

'Zachary Jackson?' she said coldly.

There was no response from the inert forms on the mattress. She kicked the oak frame sharply.

A startled 'Whaza–huh?!' erupted from the figure on the right. The man jerked upright and looked at her blearily. The cotton sheet slid down and came to rest just above his groin.

Zachary Jackson looked to be a good six-foot-two. The muscles of his chest, stomach, and arms were hard and well defined, and he had a surprisingly athletic frame for an academic. Alexa recalled the boxing gloves and the running shoes in the apartment.

Fine stubble dusted his strong jaw and upper lip. Above it, ice-blue eyes gazed at her sleepily under a mop of dark blond hair.

According to Reznak, she was currently looking at one of the most intelligent humans on the planet.

Alexa was not impressed. She sensed the other things Reznak had told her about the man would turn out to be unerringly true.

The languid expression in his blue eyes slowly cleared. The man stared at her with a puzzled air. Male appreciation dawned on his features as his gaze skimmed her figure.

The woman next to him stirred and pushed herself up on one elbow. She clutched the sheet to her naked breasts and blinked at Alexa. Her eyes widened. 'You didn't tell me you had a girlfriend,' she said, turning an accusing glare on Jackson.

'I don't,' the latter replied with a casual shrug, still staring at Alexa. 'Besides, if I had a lady friend, she would be…bustier.' His gaze dropped briefly to her chest.

Alexa let the insult slide and looked at the woman in the bed. 'Get dressed and get out.' She picked up the scattered lingerie, high heels, and cocktail dress on the floor, and threw them toward her.

An outraged gasp left the woman's lips when the bundle landed on her chest. 'Hey! Are you going to let her talk to me like that?' she demanded shrilly of Jackson.

An amused smile tugged at the man's lips. He glanced at the woman beside him. 'Not that last night wasn't fun babe,' he drawled, 'but I'd do as the scary lady said if I were you. She looks like she's in a filthy mood.'

The woman scowled at Alexa. 'Well, I won't tolerate this bitch—' The bullet hit the headboard next to her right shoulder with a muffled thud. A sharp cry escaped her lips.

'What the—' Jackson's smile slipped from his face and he stared at the gash in the oak wood frame. He turned and watched Alexa as if she were a rabid dog.

She lowered the Sig. For the sake of discretion, she had put a suppressor on the end of the gun.

The woman in the bed opened and closed her mouth soundlessly. She stumbled out from under the covers, wrapped one of the sheets hastily around her, grabbed her clothes and shoes, and ran from the room. The sound of the front door slamming shut came seconds later.

Alexa's eyes never left the man in the bed.

'Who the hell are you and what do you want?' said Jackson. He folded his arms and leaned back against the headboard, his face stony.

'My name is Alexa King. Dimitri Reznak wants to hire you for a job.'

'Reznak? I thought that guy never wanted to have anything to do with me again.' His face darkened. 'In fact, the last time I spoke to him, he threatened to sue me.'

Alexa watched him steadily. She wished he would put some clothes on; his nakedness was starting to irritate her. 'He believes you're the only one who possesses the necessary knowledge and skills to assist with this particular assignment,' she said in a flat tone.

Jackson looked singularly unconvinced. He kicked off the sheet, grabbed a pair of jeans from the floor, and stepped into them. She did not avert her gaze from his naked body. 'Look,' said the man in a disgruntled tone, 'tell Reznak I'm busy. I have a hundred other things to do, and I really don't have time for one of his games—'

'The fee is five million dollars,' said Alexa bluntly.

Jackson froze in the act of zipping up his jeans. He turned slowly and stared at her. 'What?'

'Reznak is willing to pay you five million dollars if you take the job,' said Alexa.

'That's more than...' he looked at his fingers dazedly, 'a hundred times what he paid me for that dig ten years ago!' He sat down heavily on the bed. The mattress springs creaked beneath him. He gazed blindly at the wall.

Alexa shifted impatiently. 'So, what's it to be?'

Jackson looked at her with a glazed expression. 'What exactly is this "assignment"?'

'I can only tell you that after you've accepted and signed a confidentiality agreement,' she replied.

His blue eyes grew more focused and the frown returned to

his face. 'He wants me to put my name to one of those convoluted legal documents again?' he said darkly.

She shrugged. 'That's the deal.'

He rose and walked past her. Alexa caught his scent as she turned to follow him out of the bedroom. It made her think of campfires and expensive bourbon.

She stood in the doorway to the kitchen and watched him turn the coffee machine on. He leaned against the sink, his expression thoughtful, seemingly oblivious to her presence. Sunbeams slipped through the blinds of the window behind him and shone on his skin. He had a golden tan. She wondered whether he worked outdoors—or maybe he liked running without a shirt on.

'Can you at least tell me where it is?' said Jackson.

Distracted by the scattering of freckles above his collarbone, Alexa looked at him blankly. 'Egypt,' she said, successfully masking the irritation darting through her. She must be more tired than she thought.

Jackson's eyebrows rose. 'Egypt?' he said skeptically. 'That's kind of a broad statement.'

She stared at him impassively.

He sighed. 'How long is this likely to take? I've got work commitments that I'll need to reschedule if I accept Reznak's offer.'

'Two weeks at the most.' Alexa would be surprised if it took them longer than that to find the missing artifacts.

Jackson watched her silently. 'Okay, I'll bite,' he finally said gruffly. 'But tell Reznak the deal's off if I see something I don't like. He's been involved in some strange business in the past.' He grabbed a cup from the draining board, poured hot coffee into it, and splashed in some milk from the open carton on the counter.

Alexa hid a grimace.

'You want some?' he asked with a raised eyebrow, mistaking her expression.

'No, thank you.'

'I'll need a few days to organize things,' he said, sipping the drink.

Alexa noted the hardened skin over the knuckles of the hand holding the cup. He obviously still boxed.

His brow furrowed as he stared at the floor. 'I have to cancel appointments with my post-grad students at Harvard and—'

Alexa glanced at her Timex. 'You have an hour.'

Jackson choked and spluttered. 'What?' he exclaimed distractedly when he got his breath back. A drop of coffee slid down his chest. The liquid was the same color as his freckles. He reached for a dish cloth and wiped his chin before dabbing at the stray droplet rolling toward the open zip of his low riding jeans.

Alexa blinked and tore her gaze away from his fingers. 'Our flight leaves at two.'

He looked up and scowled. 'You were so damn sure I was gonna say yes?' he said accusingly.

'No,' she said with a shrug.

He mumbled something unsavory under his breath and stalked out of the room.

Sixty minutes later, they walked out into the cold morning air. Jackson carried a large duffel bag on his shoulder. Alexa had watched with faint interest as he strode around his apartment, unconsciously muttering to himself while he examined and discarded various textbooks. He finally packed a small selection in the bag, along with some clothes and toiletries. Before they left, he made a series of terse phone calls to his colleagues at

Harvard. He frowned at her almost continuously while he spoke.

Alexa negotiated the snowdrifts in front of the tower block with practiced ease and headed swiftly down a public alley. Jackson followed more cautiously in her footsteps. She reached a parking bay, opened the door of her car, and climbed in the driver's seat.

Jackson stopped and stared from the sidewalk.

She leaned across the console and opened the passenger door. 'Get in.'

He pointed at the low, black sports car. 'What the hell is that?'

'It's a Maserati,' she replied curtly. The vehicle was the most expensive thing she owned in the world, besides her apartment. It had been especially designed for her by the Italian carmaker.

'Do you drive it or does it fly?' said Jackson, boots still firmly planted in the snow.

She looked pointedly at her watch. 'We're going to miss our flight.'

He sighed, climbed in the passenger seat, and threw the duffel bag in the back. 'This thing looks fast.' He gazed warily at the sleek dashboard.

A sly smile crossed Alexa's lips. 'It is.'

She engaged the transmission and sent the Maserati squealing out of the parking bay a second after he clipped in his safety belt. There was a muffled gasp at her side. She hid a grin and changed gears as the car shot down the road. The engine roared under the hood.

A set of traffic lights appeared ahead of them. She took the corner sharply onto the next avenue and caught a glimpse of a small, saffron-robed figure standing on the pavement to the right. It was a young Asian man with a bald head and a cryptic smile.

It was not the way that he was dressed that drew her attention. Instead, it was his absolute stillness among the sea of jostling bodies that immediately captured her gaze.

Alexa blinked and looked over her shoulder. The figure had disappeared. She glanced at the rearview and side mirrors as she sped away.

'What is it?' said Jackson. He looked back the way they had come, his puzzled stare shifting from the road behind them to her.

'Nothing,' she murmured. She was certain she had not imagined the stranger.

She took the Callahan Tunnel beneath Boston Harbor and reached the outskirts of Logan International Airport ten minutes later. Jackson glanced at her when she ignored the motorway exit to the main terminal buildings and headed for a small complex to the north of the grounds. She guided the Maserati inside a hangar and parked next to a sleek Gulfstream jet.

'I presumed when you said we were gonna be late that we were flying economy,' Jackson muttered dully at her side after several seconds.

Alexa glanced at him. 'Reznak's lending us his plane.' She stepped out of the car, grabbed her backpack, and handed him the duffel bag. He took it from her grasp reluctantly, his gaze still fixed on the aircraft.

The cabin door opened and a tall, thin, middle-aged man dressed in a pilot's uniform stepped out. 'Miss King,' he said warmly. 'It's a pleasure to see you.' His gaze moved to the man at her side. 'Mr. Jackson? Come this way please.' He indicated the interior of the aircraft with a welcoming hand.

Alexa's lips curved in a small smile as she studied the older man. Tom Garibaldi Fawkes had worked for Dimitri Reznak under a variety of guises for as long as she could remember. A retired member of the Order of the Crovir Hunters, he was a constant, serene presence in the background whenever she visited Reznak's estate in central Europe. He had taught her how to use a gun.

A second man appeared behind the pilot. Although shorter and younger looking than Fawkes, Sidney Carrington was another Crovir immortal who had been in Reznak's service for centuries. His eyes brightened when he saw the Maserati, and he caught the keys she threw at him without looking away from the sports car.

'You want me to park it in the usual spot?' said Carrington, his face wrinkling with a grin. A pale line ran from the angle of his mouth to his right ear, the remnant of an old battle scar.

'Yes,' said Alexa. Her eyes narrowed at his expression. 'If there's scratch on it when I get back, I'll shoot you,' she added.

Carrington's grin widened. 'Yeah, yeah.' He nodded at Jackson briefly and crossed the tarmac toward the Maserati, whistling a happy tune under his breath. He would drive the car back to New York for her.

Alexa watched him climb behind the wheel. 'Why does he always think I'm joking when I say that?'

The pilot smiled. 'He probably thinks Reznak will save him if you do try to carry out your threat.'

While Fawkes filed a flight plan with the control tower, Alexa showed Jackson where to stow his luggage. They settled at a table as the aircraft started to roll down a runway. He took the seat opposite hers and looked around the plush interior of the cabin with guarded interest. 'Reznak's organization must be loaded if their executives can afford to travel in this style,' he said.

She took a memory stick from her pocket and plugged it in the onboard computer. 'This is his personal jet.'

Jackson's eyes glazed over. 'Holy cow,' he whispered. His gaze switched to the files on the display. His expression cleared. 'So, you finally gonna tell me why we're going to Egypt?'

Alexa spent the next twenty minutes giving him a condensed account of Reznak's discovery in North Africa. Images from the excavation site flickered across the screen while she spoke; she had already viewed the pictures once and deleted the shots that showed the engraved trishula in the floor of the second cave.

A strange feeling had stolen over her when she first saw the photographs. For a moment, she had a brief insight into Reznak's compulsion to uncover her past. It was odd to see her birthmark in a place she had never visited. It felt like a violation of her person.

'What was in the clay pots?' asked Jackson, his gaze riveted to the image on the monitor.

Alexa studied him curiously. The expression in his eyes was one she would never have imagined seeing on the face of an academic. It reflected absolute focus and single-minded ferocity, as if the enigma before him was an enemy he had to defeat. It reminded her oddly of her own mindset in battle.

She was beginning to get an inkling of why her godfather had chosen Jackson for this task, despite the fact that he had personally sacked the man for breaching the terms of his contract during a dig a decade previously.

'They were empty,' she said finally in reply to his question.

It was a barefaced but necessary lie. She herself found it hard to believe that the clay pots had held the hearts of two immortals who had perished more than four millennia ago. Apart from mentioning it briefly, Reznak had refused to expand on the topic any further, much to her annoyance.

A distracted frown appeared on Jackson's face. 'Has he had the cuneiform scripts translated?' His fingers moved on the keyboard, and he scrolled down the images of the engravings on the walls of the second cave.

'Some of them, yes,' said Alexa.

'Oh.' His eyes gleamed with intellectual fervor. 'Do you have the transcriptions?'

'No,' she replied. 'They have nothing to do with our mission.'

Jackson scowled. 'What do you mean?'

'Our task is find out who looted the first cave and retrieve the missing artifacts,' said Alexa.

'Why does he need me for that? I'm not a detective.'

'He believes your eyes and brain will be helpful to me,' she said steadily.

'I was gonna mention that next,' said Jackson, features locked in a grim expression. 'What do you mean "we"? And "our" mission?'

'It's exactly as it sounds,' said Alexa. 'I've been assigned the job as well.'

Jackson's eyebrows rose. He studied her from head to toe, his gaze somewhat derogatory. 'I'm sorry if I sound rude, but if I'm the brain, what are you?'

'I'm the muscle,' she replied with a mirthless smile.

CHAPTER FOUR

TWELVE HOURS LATER, THEY LANDED IN THE CITY OF ASWAN, IN south Egypt. While Fawkes arranged for the jet to be refueled for his return trip to the States, Alexa and Jackson made their way to the tan Jeep Wrangler that awaited them. She took the keys from the rental company rep, while Jackson placed their bags in the rear of the vehicle and hopped in the passenger seat.

Alexa climbed behind the steering wheel, started the engine, and rolled onto the highway, heading east. As they passed the Aswan Dam and the dark blue waters of Lake Nasser, she became aware of Jackson's watchful gaze.

'What?' she asked tersely. She was irritable after their flight. Normally a sound sleeper, her slumber on the plane had been fitful, and she had awoken feeling less than fresh. Jackson, on the other hand, had lain back in his seat and zoned out for a solid eight hours. Only the occasional faint snore had indicated that he was still alive. Alexa had never met anyone so relaxed. It annoyed her for some unfathomable reason.

Jackson stirred in the passenger seat and shook his head

slightly. 'I still don't see it. You're like, what? Five-foot-eight and a hundred and thirty pounds? Hardly the beefed up image I have in mind for a bodyguard.'

She turned a steely stare on him. 'I could break your arm to demonstrate.'

Jackson grinned. 'Yeah, right.'

Alexa gritted her teeth. Shooting the man would achieve nothing, she told herself.

An hour passed. The Eastern Desert mountains appeared on the horizon. As the Jeep ate away the miles that separated them from the far off peaks, the landscape grew more barren. Acacias and wormwood scrubs dotted the wide-open space; except for the occasional Barbary sheep and desert hare, they did not see a living thing for miles.

Almost two hours after they left Aswan, she guided the vehicle off a gravel road and headed into the desert.

It was early afternoon when they spotted the narrow mountain shelf where Reznak's team had set up camp during the excavation. Instead of driving up to the site, Alexa went around the south end of the foothill until she located the entrance to the canyon the tomb raiders had used to gain access to the caves. She braked half a mile later.

They stepped out of the vehicle and stared up the sheer wall of the mountain.

'That's how they got in?' said Jackson skeptically.

Alexa nodded.

They could just about see the opening carved in the granite rock face a good four hundred feet above them. Reznak had had the passage enlarged to facilitate the removal of the sections of the second cave he had transported to his research lab in Europe. A tall pile of rubble littered the ground at the base of the mountain.

Alexa turned and studied the valley for a silent moment. She started to walk north, her gaze focused on the dry riverbed. Twenty feet later, she paused and stared at the desert floor. She crouched down, curled her palm around a handful of yellow sand, and let the particles sift through her fingers. A shadow fell across her.

'What are you looking for?' asked Jackson.

'Track marks,' she said, scanning the canyon floor ahead. 'Reznak saw some the last time he was here.' She sensed his surprise.

'Didn't you say that he discovered the caves more than a month ago?' said Jackson.

'Yes.' Alexa rose to her feet and headed due north again.

He followed in her footsteps. 'You'd be damn lucky to find any traces of a vehicle after all this time. This place doesn't look like it's seen any rain for months.'

She stopped abruptly, her gaze riveted to the ground. 'You're wrong.'

'I am?' said Jackson.

Alexa dropped on her haunches and touched a dark smudge in the dust. She brought her hand to her nose, rubbed the thin smear between her fingertips, and sniffed. 'Engine oil,' she said after a few seconds.

He stared at her before looking at the ground. 'You're kidding,' he said dully.

With Jackson guiding while she drove, Alexa followed the oil trail out of the canyon and headed north across the desert. Ten miles later, she saw something glimmering in the distance to her right. She stopped the Jeep, removed a pair of binoculars from her bag, and stared through them at the far-off object.

'What is it?' said Jackson curiously.

She passed him the glasses.

'It's a communications tower,' he said after a while. 'There's a chain-link fence below it.'

'They have cameras,' said Alexa.

While Jackson shifted the binoculars to have a better look, she took a slim, hardback case out of her backpack. She booted up the computer inside and removed a satellite smartphone from a side compartment. The Harvard professor turned and stared at her while she dialed a number.

'This is Alexa King,' she said once the connection was made. The Crovir tech at the other end acknowledged her. 'I need level-one access to the network. Team leader is Dimitri Reznak.' She waited a minute, ignoring Jackson's puzzled frown. 'Can you confirm my GPS location?' she finally asked. 'Good. There's a mine about half a mile east of my position. I want access to their camera feeds.'

'You mean you're *hacking* into that mine's computer system?' said Jackson. Alexa shrugged. His shocked gaze switched to the laptop. 'Not that I'm condoning your action,' he said uneasily, 'but I could probably do that from here.'

She shook her head. 'The guys I've called won't be traceable. This device is.'

'Good point,' said Jackson with a grave nod. 'We don't want the mine owners to know we're doing something illegal now, do we?'

Alexa ignored his sarcastic remark. 'You've got them?' she said into the phone moments later. 'Send the pictures from eight to six weeks ago to this address.'

The laptop beeped after several seconds. She opened the new file.

They spent the next fifteen minutes studying the hijacked security feeds. The images spanned a period of fourteen days starting before Reznak's scientists arrived at the site where they would eventually discover the caves. Alexa could sense Jackson's quiet disapproval at her side. Despite it, he stared intently at the computer as she skimmed through hours of film.

'Gotcha,' she finally murmured. She froze an image on the screen.

They stared at the picture. 'Those are trucks,' said Jackson.

The cameras had captured four vehicles driving past the mine three days before Reznak's team had set up camp. One of them was a large crawler crane.

'The third truck is riding low,' he added thoughtfully.

'You're right,' Alexa concurred, surprised that he had picked up on such a minor detail. 'It was carrying something heavy.'

'The tombs Reznak suspected were in the cave?' wondered Jackson, glancing at her.

'Maybe.' She zoomed in on the crawler. 'Balcher Cranes,' she said slowly as the lettering on the side of the gantry became clear. She got back on the satellite phone and brought up a map of Egypt on the screen while she waited for the connection to go through. 'I need information on a crane company by the name of Balcher,' she said to the Crovir tech. 'I want to know where they operate in this area.' She waited quietly while he searched the databases. 'Saudi Arabia? You're sure?' she queried with a frown.

'Check the shipping manifests from eight weeks ago,' said Jackson. Alexa glanced at him. He pointed at the map. 'There's a port in Duba, in the Tabuk province, on the north west coast of Saudi Arabia. There's also a port in Safaga, two hundred miles from here and across the Red Sea from Duba.'

Alexa looked at the screen. He was right. She told the Crovir tech where to look. Ten minutes later, they had the cargo manifest for a ship that arrived at Safaga from Duba seven days before the cameras at the mine had captured images of the trucks. A Balcher crawler crane was listed among the transported goods.

'Why Saudi Arabia? They could have gotten a crawler crane from any city in Egypt,' she pondered with a thoughtful frown after ending the call.

'Visibility.' Jackson indicated the map again. 'They would have had to travel on the main roads to get here. You don't exactly want to be noticed if you're looting treasure.'

Alexa had to agree with him. She started the Jeep and continued driving north. Less than an hour later, they rolled onto an asphalt road and headed for a motorway that ran along the Egyptian coastline.

Night was falling by the time they saw the cluster of lights that was Safaga. Alexa guided the vehicle through the old city and eventually turned in the direction of the port. She negotiated a couple of narrow side roads before finally parking the Jeep next to a derelict warehouse.

One hundred feet away, lights were still on in the two-storey edifice that housed the offices of the company that owned the Ras Abu, the ship that had transported the crane from Duba. Several people left over the next hour. The parking lot in front of the building gradually emptied until a single car remained.

Alexa opened the door of the Jeep and stepped out onto the warm asphalt. Jackson joined her.

'I'm not sure this is a good idea,' he said, following her across the road.

'What isn't a good idea?' She scanned their surroundings briefly.

'Breaking and entering,' said Jackson.

She glanced at him. 'It's more discreet than walking in and asking them for the information.'

The front door of the building was locked. Alexa removed a lock pick from her jacket and inserted it in the keyhole. It clicked open a couple of seconds later.

'You're a woman of many worrying talents,' said Jackson drily, as they entered a small lobby.

Alexa shone a pen torch on a signboard on the wall to their right. El Bashir Shipping Ltd. was on the second floor of the building. She headed up the stairs and turned down a narrow corridor, Jackson on her heels.

Light was coming from under a closed door at the end of the passage. Alexa ignored it and entered a large room on the right. It was the main office of the shipping firm. She switched a desk lamp on and looked around. A series of filing cabinets occupied the west wall. The drawers were labeled by month and year. Jackson opened the one for October, and they went through the files together.

There was no mention of the Balcher crane in any of the paperwork.

While Jackson continued to search the other cabinets, Alexa turned her attention to the old computer sitting on one of the desks. Ten minutes later, they still had not found any trace of the Ras Abu's October shipping orders.

'Now what?' said Jackson.

Alexa turned off the desk lamp and headed back into the corridor. She stared at the door at the end. A shadow moved across the light that shone through the gap at the bottom.

Jackson raised his eyebrows. 'Tell me you're not thinking of going in there?'

A grim smile crossed her lips. She strode down the passageway, turned the handle of the door, and pushed it open.

A short, portly, dark-skinned man with a beard stared at them blankly from the other side of the room beyond. His stubby, multi-ringed fingers froze in the process of placing a document in the wall safe in front of him.

'Perfect,' murmured Alexa. She crossed the floor toward him.

The stranger unfroze, reached inside the safe, and brought out a gun. Jackson shouted a warning behind her.

She raised her right knee, pivoted on her left foot, and kicked the Beretta pistol out of the man's grasp. There was a loud snap as his thumb broke.

A strangled gurgle escaped the man's lips when she closed her hand around his throat in a chokehold, lifted him bodily from the floor, and slammed him down on the desk next to the window. Her gaze shifted briefly to the papers beneath his head.

'Mr. El Bashir?' she said. The man struggled frantically beneath her, his heels banging against the side of the table while his fists tugged ineffectively at her arm. His eyes were like golf balls in his reddening face. Alexa increased her grip on his Adam's apple. 'A nod would suffice.'

'You're killing him,' said Jackson darkly. He had picked up the Beretta and stood holding it as if it were a bag full of snakes.

Alexa ignored him. The stranger was nodding frantically. She let go, took a step back, and waited.

El Bashir sucked in air and tried to stand up. His knees buckled and he sagged against the desk with a groan. 'Who—who the devil are you?' he croaked after several seconds, rubbing the skin of his neck gingerly. His right thumb was red and swelling up visibly.

'That's irrelevant,' said Alexa. 'We're looking for the October shipping orders for the Ras Abu. Where are they?'

The man's eyes betrayed him. For a fraction of a second, his gaze shifted to the wall safe.

'Search it,' she told Jackson brusquely.

The Harvard professor frowned as he walked to the opening in the wall. He ignored the piles of foreign currency stacked neatly at the back of the metal box and inspected a pile of document holders. 'Found it,' he said after a minute. He pulled out a pair of sheets from a file and scanned the pages quickly. 'It doesn't say who ordered the Balcher crane.'

Alexa turned her attention to the fat man. Sweat stained the collar of his shirt, and beads of perspiration dotted his forehead and upper lip. She glanced at her watch. Almost fifteen minutes had elapsed since they had entered the building. They were wasting precious time.

She reached behind her back and brought one of her Sigs out of her body holster. El Bashir blanched when she placed the tip of the suppressor against his forehead.

'You have ten seconds to tell me who hired you to bring the crawler crane from Duba,' said Alexa.

The fat man's lips opened and closed soundlessly. 'These people—these people are dangerous!' he finally stammered. 'They said they would kill me if I mentioned a—'

She moved her hand and fired a shot into the desk. The fat man jumped, emitting a short cry. Across the room, Jackson audibly sucked in a breath.

'Five seconds,' Alexa said in a conversational tone. 'Three, two, one. Goodbye, Mr. El Bash—'

'All right, all right!' the fat man shouted shrilly as she started to squeeze the trigger. She stopped. 'The order was placed over the phone, with strict instructions not to record any of the details. The man who collected the crane called himself Dragov. Boyko Dragov. That's the only thing I know, I swear!'

'He didn't give you a contact number or address?'

'No! He always called me,' said El Bashir shakily.

'What does he look like?' asked Alexa.

El Bashir's eyes grew large with panic. 'I really don't want to—'

She fired another shot into the desk. Jackson took a step toward her.

'He was—he was tall!' The words rushed out of El Bashir's mouth in a breathless stutter. 'And big! Like that—that green monster from that American TV series!'

Jackson's eyebrows rose. 'You mean, "The Hulk"?'

'Yes, that's the one!' said El Bashir, nodding wildly.

Alexa frowned. The man was holding something back. 'What are you not telling us?'

El Bashir gulped and looked pleadingly at Jackson.

'It'd be better if you talked,' said Jackson, glancing at her.

El Bashir hesitated. 'This Dragov—he—he wanted me to tell him if I knew of any fishing vessels that would travel to Port Said.'

'You mean up through the Suez Canal?' said Jackson sharply.

El Bashir nodded.

'What did you tell him?' said Alexa. El Bashir's panicked gaze shifted to the desk. She lowered the gun. Wincing at his swollen thumb, the fat man grabbed a piece of paper and hastily wrote down three lines. He handed her the sheet.

She studied the names on the list. 'Do you know whether he hired any of these ships?'

El Bashir shook his head vigorously. 'No. Look, all I did was bring the crane across! I'm not involved in anything else that might be going on here!'

Alexa gazed at him for several seconds. 'We're leaving,' she said finally.

El Bashir's shoulders sagged, relief evident in his eyes.

'But,' she continued, 'if you tell anyone about this, I'll kill you. You'll be under surveillance from now on.' She turned and walked out of the room, leaving the fat man sweating profusely by the desk.

'You were kidding about killing him, weren't you?' asked Jackson as he followed her out of the building. 'And that surveillance thing was just to scare him, right? Hey, I asked you a couple questions!'

Alexa halted in the parking lot and looked at him over her shoulder. 'If he were to pose a threat to our mission, I would not hesitate to dispose of him.'

'I don't believe that!' exclaimed Jackson.

'You don't know me,' she retorted, striding to the Jeep and climbing in the vehicle.

'No, I don't, do I?' He got in and slammed the door forcefully behind him.

Alexa took the satellite phone out of the hardback case and called up the Crovir techs. 'I need intel on three fishing boats,' she said and quickly ran through the names on the piece of paper El Bashir had handed her. 'I want to know if any of them docked in Port Said in the last six weeks.' She stared blindly at the road ahead while she waited, aware of Jackson brooding at her side. 'The Juzur Tawilah?' she said finally, frowning at the windscreen. 'Any chance of finding out where it unloaded?'

The Crovir immortal on the other end of the line went silent for a moment. 'That information is not held in the Port Authority database,' he replied. 'They're probably still using paper records. The only way to find out is to go there.'

It was Alexa's turn to be quiet. 'Can you find me a boat? A fast one?' she said eventually. 'No, further up the coast would be better. I want to be in Port Said by lunchtime tomorrow. Also, see what you've got on a Boyko Dragov. He's probably of Bulgarian origin. I'll wait for your call back.'

'We could drive to Port Said,' Jackson suggested in a distinctly reluctant tone as she disconnected.

She shook her head. 'A boat will be quicker.'

The phone rang a while later. Alexa listened closely while the Crovir tech spoke. 'The Abu Tig marina? Good. And Dragov?' She scowled at the tech's response. 'Nothing? All right. I'll be in touch if I need anything else.' She ended the call.

'The Abu Tig marina is fifty miles north of here,' said Jackson.

She raised her eyebrows. 'Have you been there before?'

'No.' He shrugged. 'I read about it once.'

Alexa recalled Reznak's words as she started the engine. It seemed her godfather had also been correct about Jackson's eidetic memory.

Seconds after she pulled away from the curb, El Bashir exited the building that housed his shipping company. The fat man froze in his tracks when he saw the Jeep go by.

'That guy is gonna have a heart attack before the week's out,' Jackson muttered pityingly.

IT WAS AFTER TEN WHEN THEY REACHED THE RESORT TOWN OF EL Gouna and the Abu Tig marina. Lights were still on in the restaurants and bars that lined the harbor, and tourists and locals strolled along the busy promenades.

Alexa drove to a hotel close to the waterfront and checked them into a room. Jackson's eyes widened when he saw the pair of fake passports she showed to the receptionist.

'Mr. and Mrs. Thompson? I hope you enjoy your stay with us,' the man behind the main desk said with a bright smile.

'We'll need an early checkout in the morning,' said Alexa.

'Not a problem,' the receptionist replied with a gracious nod. His smile grew stilted when his gaze fell on their bare ring fingers.

'She's allergic to jewelry,' said Jackson, flashing a grin at the man.

The receptionist's eyebrows rose slightly. He glanced at their bags. 'Do you have any other luggage?'

'No,' said Alexa. She took the passkey and headed in the direction of the room.

'And men. She's allergic to men,' Jackson added under his breath as he strode after her. 'Hey, can I have a look at that passport?'

She handed him the document.

'When did you do this? And isn't this picture from my Harvard ID badge?' he said as he scanned the passport.

'I had it made while you were packing yesterday. Fawkes had it ready at the airport.' She stopped in front of the door to their room and swiped the passkey across the lock. The lights came on automatically when they crossed the threshold.

Jackson stared at the layout of the twin room with a deadpan expression. 'For a second there, I thought we were gonna share a bed.'

Alexa gave him a flinty look.

'A man can but hope,' he added with an unapologetic shrug.

'Get some rest.' She dropped her bag on the bed closest to the door. 'We have a long day ahead of us tomorrow.'

CHAPTER FIVE

THEY CHECKED OUT OF THE HOTEL SHORTLY AFTER SEVEN THE next morning and made the short journey to the marina on foot. Alexa headed past several luxury yachts until she reached a berth where a sleek, black and chocolate-brown Hunton powerboat was docked.

A man stood on the polished teak deck; a good six feet tall, with wavy dark hair and gray eyes, he looked like a model who had just stepped off a runway in Milan. 'Miss Adams?' he said in a faint Florentine accent, his gaze running appreciatively over her form.

'Yes,' she replied impassively.

'You're dead on time,' said the Italian. His lips curved in a dazzling smile.

'Adams? What'd you do, get a divorce overnight?' Jackson murmured darkly behind her. She ignored him and stepped onto the boat. He hesitated before following her cautiously.

The Italian man's gaze shifted curiously between them. 'And this would be?'

'An associate,' said Alexa. She caught Jackson's scowl out of the corner of her eye and felt an odd sense of satisfaction.

She was irascible again after last night. While the Harvard professor had fallen asleep seconds after she turned off the lights, she had lain awake for a good few hours, conscious of his every breath and the movements of his body on the bed next to hers. She had never been so aware of another being's presence, be they immortal or human, in her entire life. It maddened her.

The Italian man nodded lazily, unfazed by her demeanor. 'The money has been wired to my account?'

'It's being done as we speak,' said Alexa.

'Great. I'll pick up the boat in two days.' He handed her a set of keys, stepped onto the pier, and untied the vessel.

She caught the dock lines he threw at her and stored them on the deck.

Jackson stuck his head through the open hatch to the cabin. 'Hey, there's a galley kitchen and all sorts of stuff down here.'

Alexa turned on the engines and guided the powerboat out of the marina. The Italian waved from the pier before walking off. Jackson eventually returned from his explorations and took the bolster seat next to her.

'By the way, did I happen to mention that I get sea sick?' he said with a grimace.

She glanced at him. 'You were fine on the plane.'

'Yeah, well, planes and trains are okay. Boats are a problem.'

She waited until they were out at sea before pushing the twin throttles. The boat leapt forward and gathered speed.

'How fast does this thing go, anyway?' Jackson watched the choppy waters at the side with a queasy expression as the powerboat bounced over the wash of a fishing vessel.

'It can do seventy knots.'

'That's almost eighty miles an hour,' he said after a second. She looked at him impassively. 'Oh boy,' he murmured.

They passed several islands on their way up the Red Sea and entered the mouth of the Gulf of Suez at the Strait of Jubal less than an hour later. The mountains of the Eastern Desert appeared on their left and tapered off toward the Nile Delta to the north. In the west, bridging the African and Asian continents, rose the Sinai Peninsula; its highest peak, Mount Sinai, was soon visible through a haze of yellow desert dust.

The wind picked up and the waves doubled in size. Jackson grew pale and threw up over the side twice. Alexa ignored him and held the wheel firmly in her grip. Fishing vessels, oil platforms, and reefs dotted the waters around them as they headed toward the southern end of the Suez Canal and Port Tawfik.

The Hunton's owner had already filed the paperwork for his transit through the waterway. A hefty, undeclared fee to personal contacts on either side of the canal also ensured that the powerboat would make the normal twelve-hour trip in less than half a day.

After notifying port control of their approach on the Hunton's radio, Alexa slowed the vessel and joined the northbound shipping convoy.

The transit up the waterway was smoother than their passage through the Gulf of Suez, even with the powerboat doing three times the canal's recommended top speed, a fact that was blatantly overlooked by the Egyptian soldiers posted at regular intervals along the banks. The fields lining the west of the canal were a vivid green under the harsh winter sun. On the eastern side, the yellow dunes of the Sinai Peninsula occasionally disappeared behind episodic sandstorms.

They went through the Great Bitter Lake before Ismailia,

passed under the Suez Canal Bridge at El Qantara, and reached Port Said shortly after midday. Alexa guided the boat into the marina on the eastern bank of the canal and docked it in the empty berth assigned to the Hunton's owner.

A sigh left Jackson's lips when he stepped onto the jetty. 'Man, I'm glad that's over,' he muttered under his breath.

She finished securing the powerboat and took her bag off him wordlessly. They turned and headed down the road to the ferry terminal, where they caught the next service to Port Said.

As she leaned against the port bulwark of the ship and examined the looming western bank of the canal, Alexa was conscious of Jackson hovering close to her, his stance strangely protective. She was only vaguely aware of the local men's stares. Although form-fitting, the dark cargo pants, combat boots, army T-shirt, and leather jacket she wore were comfortable, utilitarian in their design, and helped mask her custom-made body holster. She saw no need for false modesty unless it was crucial to the mission at hand. Besides, she could count the number of dresses she owned on one hand. All of them had been ridiculously expensive gifts from her godfather.

They landed at the port terminal shortly and were making their way through the crush of bodies when the back of her neck suddenly prickled.

Alexa froze. Her head snapped around. She caught a glimpse of a short, bald, saffron-robed figure before it melted in the crowd.

She stood perfectly still as she scanned the sea of unfamiliar faces. She was certain it was the same man she had spied close to Jackson's apartment in Boston.

The Harvard professor stopped a few steps ahead and looked at her curiously over his shoulder. 'What is it?'

Alexa hesitated. 'It's—nothing.' She filed the event under 'things to investigate further' and joined him.

A trip to the administrative offices of the port authority revealed that the Juzur Tawilah had stopped briefly at a cargo handling yard less than a mile south of their current location, before proceeding up the canal to the fishing harbor. They left the building and made their way along the busy streets of the city to the address they had been given. It turned out to be a large depot in the middle of a row of similar constructions, all of which looked out over the water. The place was bustling with activity.

'Now what?' said Jackson. They stood in the shadow of a shipping container and studied the warehouse two hundred feet down and across the road from their position.

Alexa observed the layout of the yard with a thoughtful frown. 'We wait until nightfall.'

Jackson stiffened. 'You mean, we're breaking and entering again?' he countered, staring at her.

'Yes,' she replied without compunction.

A sigh left his lips. 'I worry about how easily you said that,' he murmured.

They headed into town and found a quiet cafe a short distance from the harbor. Alexa called Reznak and updated him with the recent developments. She omitted her sightings of the mysterious, saffron-robed figure.

'Boyko Dragov?' said Reznak.

She could picture the frown on her godfather's face. 'Yes. The techs didn't have anything on him,' she said quietly.

'I'll see what I can dig up,' he said before disconnecting.

She sat back and closed her eyes while Jackson got on the phone to his contacts in the universities and museums in North Africa and the Middle East. No one had heard of any tombs being dug up in the Eastern Desert in the last two months.

'The people who did this will not be using normal channels to move the stolen goods.' Alexa opened her eyes and looked calmly at the Harvard professor's troubled face.

'I don't get it. If they're not intending to display the artifacts, then what're they planning to do with them?' said Jackson testily. 'Dispose of them on the black market?'

'Reznak would have heard of it by now if that were the case,' she said dismissively.

They returned to the warehouse at eight that evening. The shipping yard was quieter than it had been that afternoon, and they easily avoided detection in the darkness. Alexa completed her second perimeter check of the day before joining Jackson in the shadows of the adjoining depot.

'There's a light on at the back. The place looks dead otherwise.' She pulled on a pair of black leather cross training gloves, removed the Sigs from their holsters, and screwed a pair of suppressors on the ends.

Jackson watched her warily while she clipped magazines to her waist. 'What are you intending to do with those?'

'Shoot anyone who gets in our way,' said Alexa. She removed El Bashir's Beretta from her jacket and handed it to him. He took the weapon gingerly. 'Do you know how to handle a gun?'

'Of course!' he exclaimed with an affronted air. 'I grew up in Montana.'

Her frown deepened. 'When was the last time you fired one?'

'1992,' Jackson replied promptly.

Alexa stared at him stonily. 'That's eighteen years ago.'

He shrugged. 'So?'

Her fingers flexed unconsciously on her Sigs. She gritted her teeth and spent the next minute showing him how to use the Beretta. 'If the bullets start to fly, stick behind me,' she warned him over her shoulder as they made their way across the alley to the warehouse. Jackson grunted something unintelligible in response.

The side exit to the building was closed. Alexa picked the padlock, drew the external bolt, and carefully pulled the door open. There was a faint creak of metal on metal as it moved on its hinges. She crossed the narrow threshold into the dark space beyond and closed the door behind Jackson.

They stood still while their eyes adjusted to the gloom. Shapes slowly materialized in front of them. Rows of shipping crates and containers appeared, soaring on pallets along a series of wide, intersecting aisles that ran the length and width of the warehouse. Suspended high above was a bridge crane on rails.

The building was as silent as a tomb.

Alexa turned and headed quietly toward the back of the warehouse. Jackson fell into step behind her. A dim light soon filtered around the hulking towers of boxes. Faint voices followed. Though she could not make out the words, the general tone indicated that an argument was in progress.

They had barely covered another dozen yards when the sound of a single gunshot boomed across the cavernous interior of the warehouse.

Jackson flinched. His right foot collided with a pile of metal pipes and sent them crashing to the concrete floor. The resulting clatter was almost as deafening as the gun blast.

Alexa stared at him.

'Oops,' he whispered with a contrite grimace.

Heavy footsteps rose on the other side of a wall of crates.

'Who's there?' a thick male voice demanded.

The man's accent was distinctly eastern European. As Alexa

pondered whether the voice belonged to the elusive Boyko Dragov, another sound reached her ears above the noise of the approaching footfall.

She whipped around, shoved Jackson against the crates, and shot the figure creeping up behind them. The dead man hit the ground with a dull noise, gun falling from limp fingers.

Jackson gaped at the body on the floor. Before he could utter a single word, Alexa caught another flash of movement above them. She leapt into a back flip and narrowly avoided the spray of bullets that peppered the ground where she had been standing. She landed solidly on her feet, fired a defensive volley at the men atop the crates, grabbed a stunned Jackson by his arm, and dragged him into the closest aisle.

Loud thuds rose from the roof of the shipping containers that lined the right wall of the passage. Excitement fluttered through her. She smiled grimly. Their invisible assailants were keeping track.

A junction appeared in the gloom ahead. Several figures stepped into view.

Alexa pushed Jackson to the floor, jumped, and high-kicked the closest man in the chest. He stumbled back into a wall of boxes with a grunt, the gun in his hand clattering to the ground. She swept the weapon out of the way with one foot, shot the second man raising his gun to her left, and delivered a hooking knee strike to the thigh of the third man to her right. There was a loud snap as his femur shattered. He screamed and fell. A savage grin flashed across her lips. She stepped up to him and dropped her leg in an axe kick that broke his right wrist. A strangled gurgle escaped his throat, and he curled up in a ball on the floor.

Bullets thudded into the crates next to her head.

Alexa dropped on her back, raised both Sigs, and fired

rapidly at the shadows on the top of the containers. Two men landed on the ground with loud, fleshy thumps and lay still. There was a faint noise behind her. She rolled to one knee and leveled a gun at the figure standing above her.

It was Jackson. He inhaled sharply when the tip of the Sig froze an inch from his left eye.

She stood. 'Don't do that,' she said steadily. 'I could have shot you.'

Jackson opened his mouth to speak. Before he could utter a single word, someone gripped him around the neck in a chokehold. He gasped.

Alexa looked at the figure behind the Harvard professor. It was the man she had kicked in the chest.

Jackson grabbed his assailant's arm with one hand and elbowed him in the stomach. His aggressor grunted and maintained his hold. The Harvard professor stepped back and stamped down on the man's foot. The latter groaned and sagged, his arm slipping a fraction from his victim's neck. Jackson turned and punched him squarely in the jaw.

The man's eyes rolled back in his head and he dropped to the floor.

Jackson coughed and rubbed his neck while he gazed at his unconscious assailant. 'Were you having fun watching?' he said, glancing at her accusingly.

Alexa shrugged. 'I wanted to see what you could do,' she said. 'Your uppercut could do with some tighten—'

A shadow blocked out the light coming from the rear of the warehouse. Jackson stared at something behind her. His eyes widened. Acting on instinct, she dropped to the floor and rolled toward him.

❄

CHAPTER SIX

A FIST THE SIZE OF A LEAD SEWER PIPE ARCED THROUGH THE AIR where her head had been a second before and smashed into the boxes at the side of the aisle. Wood splintered and shattered. The tower of crates trembled. Alexa rose to her feet and looked at the giant figure filling the width of the alley.

'Is it me, or does this guy look like the Hulk?' said Jackson dully at her side.

She silently assessed the man facing them. About six-foot-seven and built like a tank, the stranger moved with deceptive silence for his size. His neck was almost as wide as her thigh, and thick, corded muscles bulged under his tight-fitting sweater and linen trousers. Small, dark eyes were set in a coarse, pockmarked face. He watched them dispassionately from under a pair of thinning eyebrows.

'Boyko Dragov?' said Alexa.

The man's expression did not change. 'Who wants to know?'

She had spent enough decades in fighting rings to know that the giant was pumped up on steroids. Her gaze dropped to his torso. She raised a Sig and fired four shots in rapid succession. The bullets struck Dragov's chest with a series of dull thumps. The force of the impacts did not even rock him on his heels. The giant man blinked and looked down curiously at the holes in his sweater.

Alexa holstered the guns and shrugged her jacket off her shoulders. 'Stay back,' she told Jackson, her eyes never leaving Dragov. Anticipation of the fight buzzed along her limbs. 'I want him alive.'

The Harvard professor gazed at her, slack jawed. 'You just shot him!'

'He's wearing body armor,' she retorted.

Jackson stared at the gray material visible through the tears in the giant's top. 'Would it have hurt to ask?' he said, glancing at her. 'I mean, look at him. The guy is seriously pissed!'

Dragov's thick lips parted in a feral smile. Alexa flexed her gloved fingers, bent her arms slightly at the elbows, turned her body sideways, and moved her legs into a fighting stance.

The giant took a step forward and swung his right hand around in a hook punch. She didn't even attempt to block the attack. Instead, she slipped deftly to the side, twisted, and delivered a powerful back kick with her left foot. Her heel struck the inner side of Dragov's left knee at the same time that his fist passed a good foot from her head and pulverized a wooden crate.

Dragov looked at her over his shoulder. His smile broadened.

The kick would have incapacitated an ordinary man. Alexa darted back half a dozen steps and scrutinized her opponent. Although Dragov was strong, his size would undoubtedly limit his speed. A shadow above his head caught her eyes.

The giant turned and lumbered steadily in her direction.

Alexa ran toward him, kicked up against a container on her right, pushed off the crate on the opposite side of the aisle to gain more altitude, spun in the air, and aimed a spinning reverse kick at Dragov's head.

Her right foot connected with his jaw with a loud snap. The impact jarred her ankle and momentarily stopped him in his tracks. As she dropped toward the ground, his hand snaked out with unearthly speed and grabbed her left thigh in an iron grip. He swung her body up and across the alley as if he was swatting a fly.

Alexa saw the approaching pallet of crates, raised her arms to cover up her head, and rotated her body slightly.

Despite her defensive posture, she struck the boxes with enough force to cause her teeth to vibrate in her jaws. A gush of blood slid across her tongue as she inadvertently bit the inside of her cheek.

A savage thrill flooded her senses at the same time that a surge of adrenaline spiked through her body. It had been some time since she had experienced an emotion in battle. She grabbed the edge of the crate above her head, twisted, and grinned fiercely over her shoulder at Dragov.

A glimmer of confusion dawned on the giant's face.

Alexa knew what he saw in her eyes. It was utter fearlessness overlaid with a brutal determination to win.

There was a sharp cry below them as someone rushed Dragov and hit him on the leg. She looked down. Jackson had found a metal pipe from somewhere. He swung it back to attack the giant again.

Dragov reached down, closed his fingers around Jackson's throat, and lifted him effortlessly off the ground. The Harvard professor choked. The pipe dropped from his grasp. A look of alarm clouded his face as he pulled and punched in vain at the giant's arm.

Alexa jabbed her right leg into a straight foot thrust at Dragov's face and felt his nose give beneath the heel of her boot. His grip momentarily loosened on her thigh.

It was enough for her to pull free. She kicked against the wall of boxes, back-flipped across the alley, and landed against the side of a crate. She climbed nimbly to the top of the tower of containers.

Dragov turned slowly, a trickle of blood oozing out of his left nostril.

Jackson's face had gone an unhealthy shade of purple in the giant man's grip. He managed to turn his head and stared at her with a desperate, wide-eyed expression. His mouth formed the word 'Run'.

An unfamiliar emotion stabbed through Alexa at the look in Jackson's ice-blue eyes. She took a few steps back, ran to the edge of the container, and jumped. Her body arced through the air and her hands closed around the loop of the iron chain she had seen hanging from the bridge crane. Gravity brought her down on Dragov's head. She landed on his shoulders, dropped to wrap her thighs around his neck, and twisted the chain under his jaw.

Dragov's hand opened and he released Jackson. The Harvard professor fell to the ground with a thud. A series of hoarse, rasping coughs left his lips and he audibly sucked in air.

The giant's fingers closed on Alexa's thighs. He dug deep into her flesh and tried to throw her off. She ignored the bone crushing pain, smiled viciously, and tightened her hold on the chain. He let out a grunt and stumbled back a step.

Alexa leaned down and brought her lips to his ear. 'Where are the tombs?' she demanded coldly.

Dragov's grip switched to the chain. He pulled at it with all his might. Alexa felt a couple of links slide through her fingers. She increased her grasp on the thick metal.

She was stronger than a human and stronger still than most immortals. It was the first time she had met someone who could prove to be more powerful than her.

There was a bang and a loud thunk next to her head. A splinter from a bullet-damaged crate slashed across her cheek. She looked irritably over her shoulder.

Jackson was already up and moving toward the man he had knocked out earlier, and who now stood with a firearm aimed at her head. The gunman's finger moved on the trigger a split second after Jackson tackled him to the ground. The bullet whistled through the air, entered the soft flesh of her inner arm, exited through the other side, and slammed into a metal container. Blood dripped onto her hand.

Fleshy thuds and grunts rose from behind as Jackson fought her attacker. Below her, Dragov heaved on the chain once more.

The links slipped an inch through her grasp. She heard air travel down Dragov's throat.

He groaned, reached up with his right hand, and curled his fingers into the wound on her arm. Alexa gritted her teeth against the stinging pain. The flow of blood from her injury doubled and the links slid through her increasingly wet hands. A hiss of disgust left her lips.

She let go of the chain and dropped off the giant's back. As she landed lightly on her feet, Alexa caught a glimpse of a tattoo on the back of his neck.

It was a cross with a red rose entwined around it.

Jackson was pushing himself off Dragov's unconscious accomplice; the man's face was a bloodied pulp. He retrieved the gun from the floor and threw it toward the top of a container.

Barely eight minutes had elapsed since they entered the warehouse.

Dragov slowly turned to face them. A feral smile flashed on Alexa's lips as she observed the fresh, red marks around his neck.

The giant swung the chain in his hands. She leaned out of the way and felt the iron links whistle past her face before they struck a crate with enough force to split it. He yanked on the chain. The crate groaned; the metal links were firmly wedged inside the thick wood. Dragov scowled, dropped the chain, and came at her with his fists.

She bobbed and weaved, effortlessly avoiding his punches. Rage darkened the giant man's eyes. His lips curled back to expose his teeth.

A faint noise suddenly reached her ears. She looked over her shoulder.

A figure stood in the shadows at the end of the aisle behind them. It was holding a long, tubular object to its shoulder. A flash of light and a whoosh of noise erupted from the gaping mouth of the rocket launcher.

Alexa twisted on her heels, grabbed Jackson's arm, and pulled him into a passage to the right a second before the grenade detonated against the tower of crates next to where they had been standing. A wave of compressed hot air and flames washed over them as debris pelted their backs. Jackson stumbled.

An ominous rumble rose behind them, underpinning the fading roar of the blast. Alexa glanced back and saw the wall of boxes come tumbling down. She pushed Jackson to the ground, dropped on top of him, and braced herself as she wrapped her arms around their heads.

A crushing weight landed on her back, pinning both of them to the floor. Darkness engulfed them. She felt Jackson's heart race frantically against her chest and his breath wash shallowly over her face. She ground her teeth as more boxes dropped on them.

It was almost ten seconds before the avalanche came to a thunderous close and the final thuds sounded dimly around them. Alexa blinked in the stifling gloom.

'Are you okay?' said Jackson in her ear.

She nodded and realized he could not see her. 'Yes,' she said steadily.

'Not that I mind the close intimacy, but how the hell do we get out of here?' he drawled after a while.

Alexa placed her hands on the floor on either side of his head and heaved up with her body. The crates above them barely shifted. She felt Jackson's arms rise around her and push at the deadweight. She heaved again.

A moment later, something slipped above them.

Now that her eyes had adjusted to the darkness, she could make out Jackson's features. He was grinning.

'What?' she snapped.

'This is kinda nice,' he murmured. His gaze switched to her lips.

She wondered whether the fall had given him a concussion. 'Two days ago, I was kicking a woman out of your bed,' she said.

Jackson shrugged. 'Hey, she knew what she was getting herself into,' he responded. 'I don't do relationships.'

She ignored the disturbing feel of his heated breath on her cheek and murmured, 'On the count of three.'

It was another half-minute before dim light stabbed through the shadows of the tomb-like space where they lay trapped. Alexa used her elbows and heels in a succession of rapid strikes and kicks to shatter the remaining boxes that held them captive. Once clear, she snatched the Sigs from her body holster, rose, and quickly scanned their surroundings, the guns tracking her line of sight.

They were alone. From the warehouse's empty feel, Dragov and his accomplices had long left the building.

Jackson climbed to his feet and brushed fragments of the wreckage off his clothes. 'We should get that checked out,' he said, his gaze falling on her wounded arm.

Alexa glanced at the bullet hole. She had forgotten about it. 'It'll heal,' she said and turned on her heels.

'Hey, where're you going?' Jackson called out.

She climbed over the debris from the explosion, retrieved her jacket, and headed toward the back of the warehouse. The source of the light became visible when she rounded a wall of containers. It was spilling onto the concrete floor through an open doorway ahead. She stopped on the threshold and studied the room beyond.

Filing cabinets lined the confines of a narrow office. A desk stood next to the far wall. Seated in the metal chair behind it was a dark-skinned man. Dull brown eyes stared unseeingly at the ceiling. There was a single bullet hole in the middle of his forehead. Blood and brain matter had splattered across the back of the chair and the wall behind him.

Jackson came up behind her and froze in his tracks.

Alexa crossed the floor and started to examine the papers on the desk.

'Shouldn't we be calling the cops?' asked the Harvard professor quietly, still staring at the dead man from the doorway.

'No,' she replied, glancing at his troubled expression. 'I want to find out who this guy is and why Dragov killed him.'

'And then we'll call the cops?' said Jackson in a hopeful voice. Silence ensued. 'We're not calling anyone, are we?'

'This warehouse is in use,' said Alexa. 'He'll be discovered in the morning.'

They found the identity of the man from his wallet. Jawaed Hassan was forty-six years old and the father to two children; there was a picture of his family tucked behind his Egyptian ID card. A search of the desk revealed that he was the general manager of three warehouses in Port Said and oversaw the shipping and delivery of goods for a number of companies in mainland Europe and the Middle East.

'What kind of martial arts was that?' asked Jackson as they started to look through the filing cabinets lining the walls. He glanced at the dead man uneasily before meeting Alexa's blank stare. 'You know, when you were fighting the Hulk? I thought I recognized some kickboxing moves.'

'You're correct.' She turned her attention to the folder in her hand.

'And?' prompted Jackson.

'And what?'

His eyebrows rose. 'There must be more to it than that. I mean, that guy was as strong as an ox and you were seriously kicking his butt! Also, I don't know about you, but people trying to kill me with guns and rocket launchers don't usually feature on my daily compass.'

Alexa's eyes narrowed. She was starting to entertain thoughts of shooting him again. 'I know all of them,' she said brusquely. She started to examine another document.

'All of what?' said Jackson.

'The martial arts.' She saw no point in revealing that, in

addition to sparring with the best fighters in every branch of unarmed and armed combat in the last three centuries, she had also beaten several of the current world champions in private fighting rings.

'Really?' he said skeptically.

She stared at him. 'Would you like me to demonstrate?'

'No, thanks. I'll pass,' said Jackson with a grunt.

Ten minutes later, Alexa came across several bank statements and bills tucked inside a document folder at the bottom of one of the cabinets. 'Hassan owed a lot of money,' she said thoughtfully, studying the numbers on the papers. 'His account's been in the red for more than a year.'

Jackson looked at the figures and whistled softly. 'He had a lot of credit cards in his wallet.'

She stared blindly at the wall. 'The artifacts were probably stored in this warehouse before being shipped elsewhere. Hassan must have been in on the job.'

'The cave was raided more than a month ago,' said Jackson with a puzzled frown. 'Why kill the poor bastard now?'

'I think Hassan got greedy.' Alexa tapped the bills with a finger. 'He must have contacted Dragov for more money.'

'You mean our dead guy was blackmailing the Hulk?' said Jackson dubiously, glancing at the body in the chair.

'Yes,' she said. 'We need to figure out what it was that he knew.'

It was another half hour before they discovered a possible link between the dead man and the tombs. The shipping orders for a cargo vessel that left with containers from Hassan's warehouses four weeks previously were missing from the records. A search through the dock receipts for the month of November showed that the freight ship returned from Mersin several days later.

'That's a major port in southeast Turkey,' said Jackson close to her ear. He was studying the paperwork over her shoulder. 'It's about four hundred and fifty miles from here.'

Alexa frowned faintly, her gaze fixed on the dock receipt; she was starting to find Jackson's proximity strangely unsettling. She turned to hide her unease and walked to a cabinet that held the contracts for the warehouse. 'There are three depots that Hassan normally dealt with in Mersin,' she said, looking up from the documents. 'I guess we won't find out which one may have held the tombs until we get there.'

Jackson stared at her. 'We're going to Turkey?'

'Yes.'

A queasy grimace washed across his face. 'We're not taking a boat, are we?'

'No,' Alexa replied and was startled to find her lips twitching. She forcibly suppressed the smile threatening to emerge.

It was midnight when they finally left the warehouse. Jackson breathed in the night air deeply and blinked at the star-lit sky. 'I'm not sure I like where this assignment is going,' he said quietly.

Alexa looked at him steadily. 'I'll tell Reznak you want out,' she said, startled at the odd sense of disappointment that flitted through her.

Jackson's eyes bore into her. 'What will you do if I quit?' There was an edge to his voice that she had not heard before.

She shrugged. 'I'll finish the mission.'

'On your own?' he said harshly. 'I can't let you do that. These men are killers! Hell, does Reznak even know what kind of dangers you're exposing yourself to?'

Alexa scowled. 'Dimitri Reznak is not my keeper. And I'm not some weakling who needs protecting.' She was bewildered by the anger that modulated her voice. Few people in the world had the ability to rattle her. She turned to mask her confusion and took a step away from him.

'Wait!' said Jackson. He grabbed her shoulder.

She froze and glared at him. 'Let go,' she said.

The blue eyes darkened with annoyance. 'Look, I just want to talk. This is far too—'

Alexa turned, gripped him above the elbow, hooked her arm under his shoulder, lifted him in the air, and threw him to the ground in front of her.

Jackson's breath left his lungs in an audible whoosh. He stared up at her with a stunned expression, his face mere inches from hers.

'You were saying?' she said.

'Wow,' he whispered. All trace of anger had vanished from his voice. 'Was that some kind of judo move?'

'It was,' Alexa admitted reluctantly. She felt her own irritation drain away and stood back.

Jackson winced as he rose to his feet. 'What's it called? "Woman kicking man's ass"?' he said, rubbing his lower back.

'No.' She hesitated. 'It's the Ippon Seoi Nage.'

His eyebrows rose. 'The "one-arm shoulder throw"?'

Alexa concealed her surprise and nodded impassively. 'You know Japanese?'

Jackson shrugged. 'Yes.'

They headed for the place where she had hidden their bags. 'How many languages are you proficient in?' she asked, curious despite herself.

'Spoken or written?' said Jackson.

She raised her eyebrows. 'Both.'

'Too many,' he replied. A smile crossed his lips at her expression. 'Hey, two can play this game, lady.'

Alexa lifted his duffel bag from under a forklift and kept a hold of the strap as she passed it across. 'Does this mean you don't want me to call Reznak?'

Jackson went still and stared at her. Clouds drifted past in the sky and muted the light from the stars. She could barely make out the expression in his eyes.

'Hell, I'd never be able to live with myself if I walked away now,' he said in disgust.

CHAPTER SEVEN

It was morning by the time they located a helicopter to take them across the Mediterranean Sea to Turkey.

Jackson watched with a faint frown while Alexa paid the representative of the private charter company they had hired. The number of zeroes he glimpsed on the bill made his eyes smart.

'Did you just put that on an AMEX black card?' he asked as they headed across the tarmac to a black Sikorsky helicopter. Alexa nodded briefly. 'Man, I've only ever heard of those,' he murmured. 'Aren't they like, the Holy Grail of credit cards?'

She shrugged.

Jackson sighed. In the sixty-nine hours since he'd met her, he had come to realize that Alexa King was a riddle wrapped in a mystery inside an enigma. He still found it hard to believe that she worked as a henchman for Dimitri Reznak. Although he continued to have doubts on the subject, what he had seen of her skills in the last two days was quickly changing his opinion.

He also could not dismiss the strange pull he felt toward her.

Although she dressed pragmatically and was not his usual, full-figured type, there was no denying the fact that she was stunningly beautiful. With her silver-gray eyes, pale skin, high cheekbones, and dark hair, she could have graced the cover of any fashion magazine or runway in the world. Jackson strongly suspected his life would be in mortal danger if he ever came on to her. The woman was one scary package.

The aircraft had just lifted off the tarmac at Port Said Airport and turned to make its way to the city of Adana when she mentioned the tattoo she had seen on Dragov's neck.

'A cross and a red rose?' said Jackson thoughtfully.

Alexa nodded.

'Sounds like a Rose Cross,' he said.

She stared at him blankly. 'Isn't that what I just said?'

'No,' he replied with a rueful smile, 'what I meant was that the symbol of a cross entwined with a rose is called the Rose Cross. It's also known as the Rosy Cross or the *Rose Croix*. It's generally associated with Rosicrucianism and Rosicrucian Orders, but has existed under various guises in other esoteric societies like the Freemasons, the Hermetic Order of the Golden Dawn, and the Ordo Templi Orientis.'

A puzzled expression appeared on her face. 'What's an esoteric society?'

'Without wanting to sound crass, I could talk about Esotericism for an entire day,' Jackson said with a grimace.

Alexa glanced at the Timex on her wrist. 'You have just over two hours,' she said in the dispassionate tone of voice he had gotten accustomed to.

As the helicopter flew over the cargo ships, fishing boats, and leisure crafts dotting the dark waters of the Mediterranean, she listened attentively while he explained the concept of Esotericism. Derived from the Greek word *esōterikos*, which literally translated to "belonging to an inner circle", the term described a set of arcane religious belief systems, wisdoms, and philosophies understood by and taught to a select group of specially initiated, enlightened individuals throughout the history of mankind.

'The core principle of Esotericism centers around the possession of secret mystic *gnosis*,' said Jackson.

'*Gnosis*?' repeated Alexa. 'Isn't that the Greek word for knowledge?'

'Yes, it is,' he replied with a nod. 'In the current context, gnosis signifies spiritual knowledge or mystical enlightenment.'

She gazed silently out the window. '"We are not human beings having a spiritual experience, but spiritual beings having a human experience",' she murmured slowly.

He pulled back slightly, startled. 'Yes. Do you know who said those words?'

'No,' replied Alexa. 'I came across it in a newspaper a while ago.'

Jackson was somewhat bemused. He had not heard of such a feature article in the last half decade. 'It's from *Le Phénomène Humain*, a book written in 1955 by Pierre Teilhard de Chardin, a French priest, scientist, and philosopher,' he said. 'Although he was not thought to be a member of an esoteric society, his words underpin the most original idea of Esotericism—that our outer physical body is but a shell that hides our inner, higher spiritual self. It's one of the binding concepts of the divine truths.'

Another frown appeared on her face. 'Where exactly does the *Rose Croix* come into this?'

'I'll get to that,' said Jackson. His reply did nothing to impress her. 'Now, Esotericism has spawned a range of alternative spiritual movements and philosophies over the millennia, among them Alchemy, Astrology, Herbalism, Christian Mysticism, Magic, Mesmerism, and Rosicrucianism. Egypt itself is thought to have been one of the places where Esotericism originated, with secret centers for learning established during the reign of Thutmose the Third and his stepmother Hatshepsut. These centers were used to explore the mysteries of life. From there, the mystic knowledge eventually spread to Greece and Rome. It's a strongly held belief that Plato and Aristotle belonged to one of these esoteric orders. In more recent times, Dante, da Vinci, Bonaparte, and even Benjamin Franklin were thought to have been Rosicrucians.'

Her eyebrows rose slightly. 'And the Cross?'

He grinned at her obvious impatience. 'Depending on who you talk to, Rosicrucianism either originated from the Egyptian secret schools or takes its name from Christian Rosenkreuz, a mythical German doctor, philosopher, and alchemist from the fourteenth century. The *Rose Croix* symbolizes the Rosicrucianism Order or secret society. Some surmised it represented Rosenkreuz himself, whereas others adhere to the belief that the cross epitomizes the human body, with the rose representing the unfolding human consciousness.'

Alexa digested this wealth of information with a guarded expression. 'Does this mean that Dragov belongs to some sort of secret sect?'

Jackson shrugged. 'Possibly. The caves that Reznak discovered were in Egypt after all, although they weren't close enough to Thutmose's tomb in the Valley of the Kings to be directly linked to the Egyptian secret societies.'

The helicopter flew over Cyprus and Cape Andreas, the promontory at the tip of the Karpass Peninsula. From his calculations, they were about a hundred miles from Adana Airport.

'You mentioned the Freemasons,' said Alexa after a while.

'I did,' Jackson replied. 'Strictly speaking, the Freemasons are not a Rosicrucian Order, but they *are* an esoteric society. It's thought that Rosicrucianism impacted on Freemasonry as it evolved in Scotland in the late eighteenth century.'

'So if the Freemasons don't use the *Rose Croix* as a symbol of their order, who does?' she said with a scowl.

'Strangely enough, the largest Rosicrucian Order in existence today who uses a golden cross with a red rose in the center is not as secret as you might think,' said Jackson. 'The Ancient and Mystical Order Rosae Crucis, or AMORC as it's abbreviated, is an international organization dedicated to studying the elusive mysteries of life and the universe. They're based in New York.'

'So Dragov could be a member of AMORC?' asked Alexa doggedly.

Jackson smiled. 'It's possible, but I doubt it. There would be a lot more people walking around with *Rose Croix* tattoos on the back of their necks if that were the case.' His expression grew sober. 'He could be a member of another Rosicrucian order or any other esoteric society that uses the symbol of the Rose Cross as part of their systems of beliefs and rituals. There's a wealth of conspiracy theories out there about a New World Order that refer to Rosicrucian- and Masonic-influenced societies such as the Illuminati, as well as other spiritual and religious organizations like the Round Table and the New Age movements.'

Alexa remained silent for the remainder of the trip, apparently brooding over what he had told her. From their discussions the night before, he sensed she was certain Dragov was the key to tracing the tomb raiders. The potential link between the giant and secret societies holding alternative religious and spiritual beliefs was not one that she seemed to welcome.

THE AIRPORT AT ADANA WAS CONVENIENTLY SMALL AND THE charter company's representative swiftly whisked them through the international terminal. Alexa left Jackson on the curb outside the building and headed toward the offices of a local car rental company. She drove out ten minutes later with a black Range Rover Defender pickup and braked to a screeching halt a couple of feet from where he stood.

Jackson stared at the vehicle. 'Where the hell does she get these cars?' he muttered. He threw their bags into the back of the pickup and got in. She performed an illegal U-turn right in front of a dumbfounded policeman and guided the vehicle toward the motorway that would take them to the Port of Mersin, sixty-nine miles to the west.

'How's your arm?' he asked after a while. He glanced at the sleeve of her leather jacket. The night before, he had watched her clean and dress her injured arm with a proficiency that suggested she had performed similar tasks many times before. Yet, from what he had seen of her pale skin, she bore no visible scars.

'It's fine,' she replied curtly, her gaze fixed on the road ahead.

Jackson remained silent for the rest of the drive and gazed blindly at the dusty, dry landscape rolling past the window. Though he could not quite put his finger on the crux of the matter, something about this whole affair did not ring true with him. He had felt the same way the last time he worked on a project with Dimitri Reznak. He had been fully aware then that he had been actively breaching the terms of his contract when he started to investigate the mysterious organization funding their dig in ancient Mesopotamia; when Reznak questioned him about his motives before sacking him, Jackson had been unable to come up with an answer to justify his actions.

To put it simply, he could not help himself; mysteries, old and new, had always fascinated him. It explained a lot about his nature.

Five years after that first dig with Reznak, Jackson came across an old photograph that baffled him even more. All his attempts to investigate the matter further reached a dead end. He had always felt that formidable powers had been at work behind the scenes to prevent him from getting to the truth.

There was no denying from what he had seen in the last few days that the people behind Reznak and King were extremely wealthy and influential. That fact alone made him uncomfortable. In his experience, institutions wielding that much authority were usually without scruples and would protect their secrets at any cost.

On the other hand, he was not exactly beyond reproach. He had not accepted this assignment out of charity. Five million dollars was five million dollars. It would be enough to fund dozens of his research projects.

'We're here,' said Alexa, interrupting his thoughts.

Jackson shifted in the seat and looked around. The D400 state road had brought them straight past the city of Tarsus and through the southeast fringe of Mersin, close to the tracks of the Adana-Mersin railway line. Mertim Tower, the second tallest skyscraper in Turkey, was visible in the distance ahead and to the right. To the left, the waters of the Mediterranean shimmered under the midday sun. The weather was cooler than it had been in Egypt.

Alexa took the next exit and headed toward the Mersin Free

Zone. Established in the 1980s, the zone was a free economic trade area intended for foreign investors. The companies within it operated outside customs and were exempt from corporate and income taxes. Home to a variety of import-export firms, offices, production facilities, and warehouses, the Mersin Free Zone was the first of about two dozen such areas that now operated in Turkey.

She turned down a side street and parked the pickup opposite the offices of the trading company that owned the three warehouses Jawaed Hassan had done business with in Mersin. Jackson exited the vehicle and followed her inside.

A young woman sat behind the reception desk, next to a noisy fan. She smiled politely when she saw them.

'We had a container delivered to one of your warehouses about a month ago,' said Alexa after they exchanged greetings. Jackson was faintly surprised at her flawless Turkish. 'We've been away to South America on business and have only just returned to the country. Unfortunately, there was a fire at our offices in our absence and we've lost our shipping receipt.'

'Oh. I hope nobody was injured,' said the receptionist with a sympathetic expression. Her eyes darted to Jackson while she spoke. A hint of a blush tinted her cheeks.

Alexa glanced at him with a frown. Jackson shrugged his shoulders in a 'It's-not-my-fault-I'm-sexy' gesture that he knew would infuriate her. The gleam in her pale eyes told him he had succeeded.

'If you'd like to give me your company details, I'll see what I can do for you,' said the young woman, glancing curiously between the two of them. She indicated the computer in front of her.

Alexa told her the name and address of a fictitious firm in Adana.

The woman typed the information in. A moment later, she pursed her lips. 'I'm afraid I don't have your shipment on our database,' she said hesitantly. 'Where did you say it originated from again?'

'Jawaed Hassan's warehouse in Port Said,' said Alexa smoothly.

The receptionist checked her records again. 'Oh. We did receive shipments from Mr. Hassan's warehouses around that time, but none of the docking receipts list your company as a customer.'

'Can you tell us which of your depots took delivery of that order?' asked Alexa. 'We'd like to talk to the manager of the warehouse if possible.'

The woman's expression grew wary. 'I'm afraid I can't release that information without the relevant paperwork,' she said apologetically.

Jackson leaned across the desk. 'Please, could you do it as a favor?' he requested with an engaging smile. 'Like you said, we won't be able to take delivery of the container, anyway.' He cocked a thumb toward Alexa. 'Honestly, she's already cranky as it is. You'll save me a whole afternoon of nagging if you just tell us where the shipment was delivered.'

The woman opened her mouth, hesitated, and bit her lower lip. She glanced over her shoulder at the busy office space behind her.

'We won't tell. Honest,' said Jackson.

The receptionist looked down at the computer with a flustered expression and brought up another screen. 'It's depot number four,' she said breathlessly. 'Follow the road to the water. It's the warehouse at the end on the left.'

'Thank you,' said Jackson warmly. He winked at the young woman as they turned to leave. She giggled.

Alexa gave him a stern look once they were outside the building. 'What was that?'

'I've always found that a bit of harmless flirting often gets you what you want,' said Jackson. His grin seemed to irritate her further.

They climbed in the pickup and drove to the end of the free zone. Alexa pulled up in the shadow of a tree next to the last warehouse on their left. The sea glittered beyond a rocky beach less than five hundred feet ahead of them.

'Though I'm certain I'm not going to like the answer,' said Jackson, 'but now what?'

She studied the depot. 'We've wasted enough time as it is. I don't care if we do this in broad daylight.'

'Do what in broad daylight?' said Jackson.

She pulled El Bashir's Beretta out of her bag.

'You're kidding, right?' he said dully.

She handed the gun to him. The metal was disturbingly cool against the skin of his palm as he clasped it.

'I never kid.' She opened the door of the pickup and stepped onto the asphalt.

'Great,' muttered Jackson. He scowled at the dashboard while he debated his options. There were very few of them left. The only legal one involved him walking away from this entire mess and going straight to the cops.

The passenger door opened. 'Well, what's it gonna be?' said Alexa. She stared at him impassively. 'I'll understand if you'd rather stay,' she added in a faintly condescending tone. 'Things might get heated.'

Jackson sighed. He was going to live to regret this. 'I'm coming.'

❄

CHAPTER EIGHT

No amount of careful planning can beat pure luck.

The words of one of her mentors resonated in Alexa's mind when they entered the depot through a fire exit at the rear seconds later. The place appeared strangely deserted for the time of day, and she had just realized why: the workers were on their lunch break.

The building was practically empty.

Several feet inside, she revised her previous thoughts about their good fortune. The office was not where she thought it would have been. Instead of a simple boarded room at the back, it was a loft-style, portable cabin on a mezzanine floor at the top of a flight of stairs halfway along the east wall of the warehouse. A pair of windows looked out over the depot below. There was no movement behind the glass.

They headed swiftly along the deserted aisles, past empty forklifts, and soon reached the end of the storage area.

An empty concrete floor separated them from the staircase

twenty feet away. Alexa peered around the edge of a pallet of crates and looked toward the front of the warehouse. Jackson moved up behind her.

A couple of men in overalls stood conversing near a roller shutter door some hundred feet to the right. They were both smoking cigarettes and their general demeanor suggested they were still on their break. The direction the pair faced would make it impossible for Jackson and her to reach the cabin office without being detected. She shifted back and bumped into the Harvard professor.

'Sorry,' he murmured in her ear.

She ignored the disconcerting feel of his breath across her skin. 'We need a distraction.'

'Oh.' His pupils dilated in the shadows cast by the boxes on either side of the aisle. 'What do you propose?'

'I want you to go out the back, walk around, and engage those men in conversation,' said Alexa bluntly.

Jackson's jaw dropped. 'You're joking, right?'

She looked at him steadily. 'Or I could start a fire. The choice is yours.'

He closed his eyes briefly. 'Fine, I'll go talk to them,' he said with a resigned expression. 'Just don't go near anything flammable.' He turned on his heels and disappeared around the corner.

Moments later, his voice rose from the front of the warehouse. 'Hello,' she heard him say in Turkish. She looked around the edge of the tower of crates.

Jackson had crossed the loading bay in front of the depot. The sea shone brightly behind him, outlining his silhouette. He walked out of the sunlight and into the shadow of the overhang above the shutter door. 'I appear to have lost my way,' he continued, addressing the men with the cigarettes. 'I'm looking for someone.' The pair turned to look at him curiously.

Alexa moved. She was at the top of the flight of stairs in less than five seconds and opened the door to the cabin.

The office was empty. She entered the room and closed the door behind her. Her eyes landed on the filing cabinets against the walls. They were labeled alphabetically. It would take too long to go through them.

She turned her attention to the computer on the desk.

Voices reached her through the steel walls of the cabin a minute later. Her gaze shifted from the display in front of her. She rose from the chair, took a few steps toward the door, and stole a glance through the window that overlooked the front of the warehouse.

The two men in overalls were heading across the concrete floor toward the office.

Jackson followed reluctantly a few steps behind them. 'Look, honestly, I don't want to trouble you,' he said loudly with a strained smile. 'I'll walk around and find him myself.'

'It's no trouble,' said the man in the lead. 'I'll give them a ring and find out if he's there.'

Alexa glanced at the phone on the desk. She moved to the wall behind the door just as footsteps clattered on the landing outside.

The first man who crossed the threshold never even saw her. The edge of her hand connected sharply with a vital pressure point on the side of his neck, and he was unconscious before he hit the floor.

The second man cried out when he saw his companion fall. His shout became a strangled gurgle after Jackson struck him on the back of the head with the butt of the Beretta. He slumped across the landing.

Alexa dragged the two inert figures inside the room.

'Please tell me I didn't kill him,' said Jackson anxiously. He entered the office and closed the door.

'He'll live,' she said shortly. She cocked her head toward the desk. 'Remember that time in the desert, when you said you could hack into the mine's computer frame?'

'Uh-huh,' said Jackson. He glanced at the desktop computer. 'Where're you going with this?'

'My techs won't be able to get into that hard drive,' said Alexa. 'It's not connected to a network. And whoever owns the thing has decent encryption software in place. I've barely scratched the surface.'

Jackson took the seat behind the desk. He started to type.

Alexa moved to the window. 'How much time do you need?' she asked, looking out at the empty warehouse.

The keyboard clattered under his fingers. 'Five minutes. Maybe ten,' he said distractedly. His eyebrows rose. 'You were right. This guy has some pretty good programs in place.'

She stared at him. 'Does this mean you can't access the data?'

He looked up with a mildly affronted air. 'I said it was good —I didn't say I couldn't override it.'

She turned her attention back to the window. A couple of men appeared in the sunlit yard at the front of the building. Three more followed. 'You haven't got ten minutes,' she said crisply. 'These guys' friends are coming off their break.' She indicated the unconscious men by the door.

'Great,' muttered Jackson. 'Nothing like a bit of pressure to get the job done.'

Alexa watched the warehouse fill up with men in blue overalls. Forklifts were activated. The building grew noisy. She heard babbles of conversation and the occasional bark of laughter.

She spotted a figure in casual clothes at the loading bay. The workers nodded respectfully at the man striding across the concrete floor.

'Hmm,' she murmured thoughtfully.

'What?' said Jackson.

'Are you done yet?' said Alexa, her eyes never moving from the figure approaching the cabin.

He frowned at the display. 'I need another minute.'

'The warehouse manager is coming this way,' she said. 'He'll be at the door in thirty seconds.'

Jackson paled. 'Shit.' He hunkered over the computer and started to type faster.

Alexa looked around the room. The metal mezzanine juddered under the feet of the man climbing the stairs.

She strode to the back wall of the cabin, smashed the front plate of the fire alarm unit with her elbow, and pulled the handle down.

A loud, piercing ringing erupted around the warehouse. Footsteps stopped on the other side of the cabin door. Agitated shouts rose from the main floor and punctuated the shrill noise of the fire alarm. The mezzanine shook again as the man outside rapidly descended the stairs.

'Got it!' Jackson exclaimed. The printer attached to the computer hummed into life and spat out a sheet of paper. He grabbed it and came around the desk.

Alexa opened the door and stepped outside the cabin.

Chaos reigned inside the building. The fire alarm had activated the sprinkler system in the ceiling, and water rained down over the crated goods that crowded the aisles. Men in overalls rushed across the floor toward the open shutter doors at the front of the warehouse.

Jackson shoved the paper inside his jacket and followed her

down the stairs. They were nearly at the bottom when the warehouse manager turned around and spotted them. A puzzled expression dawned on his face.

'Hey, you there! What are you doing?' he called out and headed toward them.

'Go!' shouted Alexa. She broke into a dead run toward the back of the warehouse, Jackson close behind. Shouts erupted from around the building as the manager and several of his men gave chase. The Harvard professor slipped on the wet floor and almost fell. He grabbed the edge of a container and pulled himself up moments before one of the men reached him.

They hit the fire door running and burst out into bright sunlight. It took mere seconds to cover the distance to the black pickup.

Alexa yanked the driver's door open, jumped inside, and started the engine a heartbeat before Jackson reached the vehicle. She threw it into reverse while he was still climbing in.

The men chasing them stumbled to a halt on the verge of the grass and watched with open mouths as the Range Rover spun around in a screeching U-turn and shot down the road.

Jackson stared over his shoulder as they sped away, his breath coming in short, fast pants. 'Well, that was kinda close.' He ran a hand down his wet face and glanced at her. 'I'm surprised you didn't shoot your way out of there.'

'Violence is a last resort.' The water had plastered strands of her hair to her face, and she was aware of the wet shirt clinging to her chest beneath her jacket. 'Those men are not involved in this.' She looked at him. 'Where to?'

'Huh?' said Jackson blankly.

'The data you printed. What does it say?'

'Oh.' He took the paper from his jacket, unfolded it, and scanned the writing. 'Of the containers that were brought across by Hassan's shipping company from Port Said a month ago, all have been accounted for by the receiving clerk except for one,' he said after a moment.

She did not like the sound of that. 'There's no mention of a forwarding address?'

He was silent as he continued to study the paper. 'Well, there is something here, but it's not so much an address as a series of numbers.' He showed her the printout. 'Do these look familiar?'

Alexa browsed the sheet quickly, then turned back to watch the road. 'Those are geographical coordinates.'

'That's what I thought,' said Jackson.

She reached for the GPS device in her bag and threw it on his lap. 'Type them in.'

Moments later, the machine guided them to their destination. It was just over a mile from their point of origin.

Alexa braked to a stop and turned the engine off. She stepped out of the vehicle and looked around. 'You sure this is the place?' she asked Jackson when he joined her.

'Yes.' His mystified expression reflected her own puzzlement.

'This doesn't make sense,' she said. 'Why would they go through all that subterfuge to bring the container here?'

They were standing next to one of the general cargo berths on a pier in the Port of Mersin, just to the west of the Free Zone. Mobile cranes, trucks, and cargo forklifts rumbled busily around them as men moved crated goods and containers on and off the ships anchored at the dock.

'It might be because of the Free Zone,' said Jackson thoughtfully. 'They wouldn't have had to go through customs to get the artifacts into the country if they landed on the other side of the harbor.'

Alexa ignored the curious glances being cast their way and

scanned their surroundings slowly. 'But why bring it *here,* exactly? Those coordinates were precise.' She glanced at Jackson. 'Was it to load the tombs onto another vessel? If so, it seems a complicated way to go about transporting them to their final destination, wherever that may have been.'

'You're right,' he said absentmindedly. He was staring at something over her shoulder.

'We're missing something' she muttered.

'Yeah,' said Jackson woodenly, his gaze still focused beyond her. 'And I think it's a big something.'

Alexa turned to see what had captured his attention.

A diesel locomotive was coming down the dock on a set of rail tracks. It slowed to a stop just before it reached the end of the pier. A couple of men oversaw the locomotive's linkup with the row of goods wagons that stood at the ready.

She scowled. 'A freight train?'

Jackson slapped his forehead with the palm of his hand. 'Of course!' he exclaimed. 'The Istanbul-Baghdad railway!'

She turned and looked at him carefully. 'What are you talking about?'

He went to the pickup, grabbed his duffel bag, and took out a thick, worn tome. 'In 1903, work began to extend the Anatolian Railway, which was originally built by the Germans in the late 1800s to connect Istanbul to Ankara and Konya,' he said, riffling through the book and stopping at a page. She joined him and looked at the section he indicated. 'Previous to that, the German Empire constructed the Oriental Railway to link Berlin and Istanbul,' Jackson continued with an animated expression. 'The Germans wanted to access Baghdad and the Ottoman Empire directly from Berlin and ultimately build a port in the Persian Gulf. From there, they would be able to bypass the Suez Canal and reach their easternmost colonies.

This would have given them economic and political dominance in the area, never mind the direct oil supply for their flourishing industry.' He gave Alexa a wry grimace. 'Of course, the British, French, and Russians were not exactly ecstatic about this. The Germans' plans greatly threatened their interests in the region. A series of technical and financial setbacks, not to mention the advent of the First World War, slowed down the construction of the new railway. It wasn't completed until 1940.'

Alexa digested this information thoughtfully. 'Is it still in use today?' She stared at the map depicting the projected Istanbul-Baghdad route.

'Quite a lot of it is in fair working order and most of the original stations still stand,' Jackson replied. He perused the busy port. 'And there are at least half a dozen dockside rail connections from here to the main lines that link Mersin to Adana.'

She twisted on her heels and stared at the freight train. 'Are you saying the artifacts may have been loaded on a train here?'

Jackson sighed and closed the book. 'I'm not saying anything. But it would seem a strange coincidence that the geographic coordinates for the forwarding address of the missing container from Hassan's shipment led us directly to a set of rail tracks, don't you think?'

Alexa drummed the fingers of her right hand against her thigh. The tomb raiders had gone to a lot of trouble to cover their tracks. That fact, combined with what had transpired in Port Said, spoke volumes about their adversaries. 'They could have gone anywhere from here,' she muttered.

'I think I have a good idea where they went,' said Jackson. An amused smile lit up his face. 'In fact, I'd bet big money on it.'

She stared at him. 'Well?'

His blue eyes gleamed in the bright sunlight. 'Istanbul.'

'And what makes you so sure they've gone there?' asked Alexa.

Jackson grinned. 'Because the last time I visited the place, I heard rumors of a secret society expanding its influence in the city's underworld.'

PART II
HUNT

CHAPTER NINE

THEY ARRIVED IN ISTANBUL AROUND SUNSET THAT DAY. ALEXA had hired the private charter Sikorsky helicopter again, this time to take them from Adana Airport to Ataturk International, fifteen miles from the center of the city. Jackson asked whether her AMEX card had ever maxed out.

She didn't reply. There was no need for him to know that the credit limit on it could buy her a small island in the Caribbean.

She had booked another rental car before leaving Adana. The silver Ford Taurus sat waiting outside the terminal building. They put their bags in the boot and got in.

'This doesn't feel right,' said Jackson as she pulled away from the curb.

'What doesn't?' asked Alexa with a faint frown. A light snow had started to fall over the city.

'This car. It just isn't you.' He shook his head, a smile teasing the corners of his mouth. 'I was expecting some sort of kick-ass black SUV.'

She felt her lips quiver in an involuntary smile and turned her head to hide the unexpected reaction. She glared at the traffic outside while she tried to clamp down on her emotions; she was starting to get annoyed at her response to the man sitting a few inches from her.

The satellite phone rang minutes later. She glanced at the number and handed the receiver to Jackson. 'It's your friend.'

He took the call. 'Ismael? Hi. Thanks for ringing back. Can we meet up?' He glanced outside the window. 'We're just passing Topkapi Park.' He listened for several seconds, then grabbed a pen and paper from his bag. 'Okay, tell me where.'

Earlier that day, Alexa had contacted the Crovir techs to see if they could uncover information on possible Rosicrucian-linked orders making waves in Istanbul's criminal underworld. Despite access to one of the largest databases in the world, the Crovirs had failed to come up with any useful intel on the subject.

It was Jackson who suggested they talk to his friend, a retired university professor who had lived in Istanbul his entire life. The man was apparently well-versed in the religious and political undercurrents of his hometown. They arranged to meet in the Kumkapi neighborhood of the Fatih district, on the historic peninsula south of the Golden Horn.

Alexa parked the Taurus outside the pedestrian-only area and they walked to a small square with a quaint water fountain. Despite the cold and the snow flurry, the place was packed with locals and tourists. Jackson led her down a crowded passage to a seafood restaurant. They ordered some beer while they waited.

Ismael Sadik arrived fifteen minutes later. He greeted Jackson with a bear hug and a hearty slap on the back. Alexa studied him silently while he removed his winter coat.

It was difficult to believe that the plump, elderly gentleman with the well-worn clothes and faded, scuffed shoes was an internationally renowned emeritus professor of philosophy and religious studies at Istanbul University.

Sadik smiled pleasantly when Jackson introduced her.

It did not take long for Alexa to realize that the professor's intellect had not faded with age. His perceptive eyes were bright and sparkled with humor while he and Jackson traded tales across the table. The older man reminded her of the tutors Reznak had hired to teach her three centuries ago, when she went to live with him.

'How did you two meet?' she asked curiously after a waiter had taken their orders.

Sadik grinned at Jackson. 'Why, this young man here came to deliver a lecture at our university some twenty years ago.' He patted Jackson heavily on the shoulder, making him wince. 'He was passionate, arrogant, ridiculously naïve, and the youngest professor of philosophy and religious studies the world had seen. Actually, he was *the* youngest professor the world had seen. How old were you at the time?'

Alexa could tell Sadik knew the answer well. It was nonetheless amusing to see Jackson squirm in his seat.

'Seventeen,' he muttered into his beer. The tips of his ears had turned bright red.

Sadik laughed out loud and leaned across the table. 'Do you know what the funniest thing was?' he said. 'He couldn't even drink alcohol at the reception held in his honor afterward—because he was still underage.'

She clenched her jaw to stop herself from smiling. 'I thought your area of expertise was socio-cultural anthropology and archaeology,' she said, turning to stare at Jackson with a deadpan expression.

Sadik shook his head. 'I can tell you don't know our Jackson very well!' he said with a chortle. 'That's only one of his pet subjects. He has postdoctoral degrees in several of the social and natural sciences.'

Alexa was impressed despite herself. She knew that Jackson was smart, and she was coming to accept Reznak's opinion that he was quite likely the most gifted human he had ever crossed paths with; she was certain they would not have gotten this far this fast without his insight. Yet, she found herself vaguely troubled about all that she did *not* know about the man who had been her constant companion for the last four days.

It was not until their empty dishes had been taken away that Jackson finally broached the subject of secret societies. Although she appreciated the subtle way he introduced the topic into the conversation, she could tell from Sadik's sharp expression that the retired professor was not falling for the trick.

'What's this really about, Jackson?' he asked finally. He shook his head at the waiter who came to ask whether they wanted any coffee and leaned back in his chair. 'The only time you ever play your cards this close to your chest is when you're working on something big.'

Jackson smiled. 'I guess there's no pulling the wool over your eyes.' He glanced at Alexa hesitantly.

She placed her elbows on the table, folded her arms, and gazed steadily at the retired professor. 'Just over a month ago, my employer discovered a pair of interlinked caves in the Eastern Desert mountains in Egypt. The first and largest of these caves had unfortunately been raided by an unknown party, and my employer believes valuable artifacts were stolen from it. Jackson and I have been charged with finding the missing relics.'

Sadik went still. 'Even though I'm not working at the university anymore, I think I would have heard about such a substantial discovery,' said the professor.

'My employer works for a very…private organization,' said Alexa quietly.

Sadik studied her for a while, then looked at Jackson. 'I never thought I'd see the day when you'd become a treasure hunter.' Despite the professor's light tone, she detected mild disapproval in his voice.

Jackson grimaced. 'Trust me, old friend, this is more than a simple treasure hunt,' he said. 'I'll tell you about it someday—if I live through the next week.'

'It sounds like you've gotten yourself involved in something dangerous,' said Sadik.

'That's why I'm asking for your help,' said Jackson.

The retired professor mulled over these words for a moment. 'You've always been an excellent friend,' he said finally. 'I'd be remiss were I not to honor the bonds of our long-lived relationship. What is it that you wish to know?'

'Thank you,' said Jackson with a soft sigh. He leaned across the table. 'When I was here five years ago, I heard stories of a secret sect that had infiltrated the city's underworld and was expanding its influence in Istanbul's corridors of power.'

A guarded look appeared in Sadik's eyes. 'You are correct,' he said. 'There were indeed such rumors circulating, not just in Istanbul but in other cities and countries in the region.'

'Was there any truth to them?' asked Jackson, sitting back in the chair. 'I mean, have you personally ever come across any concrete evidence that would support these speculations?'

'In what way is this linked to your quest?' said Sadik.

Jackson looked questioningly at Alexa. She dipped her chin slightly.

'We came across a symbol during our search for the missing artifacts,' said Jackson. 'It's a cross with a rose entwined around it.'

The older man went still. 'The *Rose Croix*?' he said. 'You're certain?'

Jackson nodded and glanced at her. She knew from the look in his eyes that they were thinking the same thing.

Sadik knew something—and the retired professor did not appear thrilled about that fact.

The older man stared at his hands for almost a full minute before speaking again. 'The rumors you mentioned are not just in the past, Jackson,' he said slowly. 'They still exist to this very day. In fact, I have recently seen and heard of things happening in the upper echelons of our society that make me fear for the very future of our country.'

Sadik looked up then. Alexa was surprised by the trepidation in his eyes. Jackson straightened at her side.

'You and I both know the history and legends about secret societies from the time of the Egyptian dynasties through the antiquities and beyond, so I won't bore you with a lecture on the subject,' Sadik continued solemnly. 'As you're well aware, there have been many conspiracy theories involving ancient secret orders thought to have influenced world events over the last century. Some of these cabals or secret societies, such as the Illuminati, have been accused of wanting to establish a New World Order, where the entire planet would come under the rule of a single, authoritarian government consisting of the members of a powerful elite.' He stopped at this point, as if to gather his thoughts. 'What has become evident from my observation of general events since I entered academia is that one such secret order has been coming to the fore in ways that the others have not been able to achieve.'

'Surely the press would have been all over this if that were the case,' said Jackson. 'We all know they like nothing better than a good conspiracy theory.'

Sadik nodded briefly. 'You're right. And there have been articles in newspapers—not just in this country but in many others, including Europe and the States—over the last forty to fifty years. But, and this is an important "but", they have never made the headlines. And it's frankly astonishing how many of the journalists who authored those features have been discredited, faded into anonymity, been made redundant, or suffered "accidents" that have put a stop to their careers, if not their very lives.'

'Are you suggesting those reporters were deliberately targeted?' said Jackson.

Sadik shrugged. 'There has never been any conclusive evidence to support ardent advocates of conspiracy theories. There have, however, been too many such…incidents…for it to be mere coincidence or fate.'

Alexa scrutinized the professor. 'What are these "ways" in which this so-called secret order has been outdoing others before it?' she asked.

'There is no single definable event that I can point to,' said Sadik, lowering his voice. 'Instead, it's the general undertone of the decisions and ideas being cast in the political, social, and religious arenas of this country and other powerful states in this region that arouses my suspicions—and the suspicions of others like me. This goes far beyond the "Deep State" in Turkey. Already we're seeing governments intruding into our personal lives, above and beyond the rights of a legitimate democracy; and this they profess to do in the name of the greater good.' His tone grew sharper and a flush darkened his skin. 'There are laws and bills being passed that would see our freedoms and our right to voice our opinions severely restricted. More worrying still are the whisperings about covert police and armed forces being set up to control and subdue potential public uprisings in the future.' He took a deep breath. The color in his cheeks subsided slightly. 'Of course, these are, as you said, just rumors and speculations. But I believe there is a common strategy, a higher purpose shall we say, underpinning all these actions. It's as if whoever is behind this is preparing for something. Something big.'

Alexa did not like the sound of that. 'Something big?' she repeated tersely.

'Yes,' said Sadik with a firm nod. 'Something that will bring radical change to the world as we know it. Call it...an event, of sorts.'

She felt the skin on the back of her neck prickle at the professor's words.

'Radical change doesn't happen without bloodshed and the loss of countless innocent lives,' said Jackson quietly.

Sadik nodded. 'Which is exactly why I'm so afraid,' he said in a weary voice. 'People who embark on what they feel is a righteous path to bring about a revolution are often the very ones who commit the most unforgivable of atrocities. We have to only look at our recent history to see that.' A mirthless smile crossed his lips. 'I'm old enough to remember the aftermath of the Second World War.'

Alexa felt her blood grow cold. If what Sadik proclaimed was true, then whatever was transpiring would have significant implications for the immortal societies.

Although the Crovirs and the Bastians could survive without humans, they would rather not have to do so. Immortals once ruled over whole human dominions and even enslaved the more fragile race into their service. Over the millennia of their common existence, a symbiotic relationship had evolved between the races, especially after the plague that wiped out more than half of the immortal population. Humans now provided many of the resources vital for the normal function of the immortal societies, while the immortals stayed in the shadows and tried to keep out of human affairs.

But immortals as a whole had invested too many centuries in molding the history and culture of the weaker species to relinquish their long-held influence without a fight. The clash, Alexa knew, would not be your average bar brawl.

It would be an all-out battle that would paint the land red, color the rivers crimson, and darken the skies with ash.

It had crossed her mind to wonder whether immortals had had anything to do with these secret societies over the centuries. It would not shock her if some had; there were many megalomaniacs among her kind.

It would, however, surprise her if either race had suddenly elected to achieve unilateral dominion over the humans. Though there had been numerous attempts by certain factions in the past to attain world supremacy—more often than not using humans as pawns in their strategies—the lessons of the ages had taught the immortals that down that path lay only bloodshed and misery.

The events that had rocked the immortal world in the last few months had only served to emphasize this belief. No one in full possession of their faculties wanted another war.

Sadik interrupted her dark thoughts.

'Which brings us back to the *Rose Croix*,' the professor continued. 'Over the centuries, there have been other societies apart from the Rosicrucian orders that have used the symbol of a cross with a rose. Though nothing definitive is known about the members of this secret sect we're alluding to, a number of people have professed to have seen the *Rose Croix* with alarming frequency in all spheres of life in Istanbul in the last few years.' He hesitated. 'I have no idea whether the symbol you've come across during your search has anything do with what I've told you this evening. But I know of a place where you might find information that could point you in the right direction.'

Alexa straightened in her seat. 'Where?'

THEY LEFT THE RESTAURANT MINUTES LATER AND MADE THEIR way out of Kumkapi, Jackson and Alexa walking the professor to where he had parked his old Volkswagen Bora. 'Please be careful,' Sadik said through the open window of his car. 'The forces you're meddling with are very dangerous.' He turned the key in the ignition. 'One last thing. Although I have no way of proving this or anything else we've talked about tonight, I do believe this secret sect is old. Very old indeed.'

'What makes you say that?' asked Alexa.

'A cult with this much power and influence is not born overnight. It wouldn't surprise me if they've been lurking in the shadows for centuries,' replied Sadik.

They stood on the side of the road and watched the lights of the Bora fade into the distance. Waves lapped against a rocky shore a short distance from where they stood. Jackson shivered in the icy wind blowing off the Sea of Marmara.

'Let's go,' said Alexa. She turned on her heels.

'You're the boss,' Jackson said mostly to himself before following her.

She guessed from his brooding silence on their walk to the

car that Sadik's words lay heavy on Jackson's mind. She had to admit she was not too pleased with this latest development either. If there was indeed a link between the tomb raiders and this secret society that the retired professor feared so much, then the task that Reznak had assigned them was far more complex than a simple treasure hunt.

CHAPTER TEN

THEY DROVE THROUGH A FINE VEIL OF SLEET TOWARD THE GALATA Bridge and headed across the Golden Horn. The domes and minarets crowning the mosques that straddled the summits of the hills upon which the old city had been built shone with a radiance that outdid the lights on the south shore of the bay. Brightly lit ferryboats dotted the Bosphorus below them. A short distance from the water, crowds thronged the market and restaurants that lined the lower level of the bridge. The pale, medieval stone tower of Galata loomed against the dark sky to the north of the estuary.

The address Sadik had given them was in Beyoglu, a historic district and cosmopolitan area on the European side of Istanbul. Home to Istiklal Avenue, one of the most famous streets in Istanbul, the area also hosted scores of memorable landmarks, churches, and foreign consulates housed in Neoclassical and Art Nouveau buildings that had come to epitomize the grandiose elegance and sophistication of its past.

Alexa maneuvered the Taurus through the narrow, steep

streets that populated the neighborhood and parked the vehicle less than a quarter of a mile west of Taksim Square. From there they walked to Istiklal. The first thing they saw on entering the avenue was an old, red and white tram gliding past slowly on electrified tracks. Billboards, shop signs, and neon lights illuminated the noisy pedestrian walkway around them.

They merged with the crowd and turned left, their breath misting in the frosty air. Sadik's directions led them past the richly decorated, towering gates of Galatasaray High School and the beautiful red brick buildings of the St. Anthony of Padua Catholic Church. Moments later, they headed down a side passage.

Unlike the bright and busy thoroughfare behind them, this alley was dark and deserted. Blocks of flats and commercial buildings rose three to five storeys on either side of the narrow lane, the upper levels overhanging the cramped space and lending to its claustrophobic feel. Halfway down the passageway, they came to a dimly lit staircase leading down to a basement-level entrance. Faint yellow light surrounded the edges of the large door at the bottom. The dull clamor of voices rose from behind the thick, bleached wood.

'I'm starting to get a bad feeling about this,' said Jackson uneasily.

Alexa ignored him and strolled down the steps. Heat washed over her when she crossed the narrow landing and opened the door.

The room beyond was a traditional Turkish beer hall. The décor was stark and functional: bare stone walls and a few naked bulbs hanging from a low, irregular ceiling. Smoke wreathed the air and the weak light showed groups of men drinking at low wooden tables crowding the dirty, stained floor.

The noise level inside the tavern dropped when she stepped across the threshold. It picked up slightly after Jackson joined her.

'You do know that women are not welcome in these kind of places, right?' he whispered in her ear as they headed toward the bar.

Alexa glanced at him with a raised eyebrow. His sigh was audible above the low mutters around them. Ignoring the stares from the other men in the room, she stopped at the counter and ordered a couple of beers.

The man on the other side smiled at them nervously and reached for a pair of glasses. 'You tourists?' he asked in a heavy accent, glancing furtively from her to Jackson.

'No,' she retorted curtly.

'Oh.' The smile slipped from the bartender's face. 'You, er, sound American,' he added hesitantly. 'You live in Istanbul?'

Alexa frowned. The man gulped and brought their drinks swiftly before busying himself at the opposite end of the bar. She took a sip of the lukewarm beer and turned to study the tavern.

'It wouldn't hurt to be a bit friendly,' said Jackson in a low voice. 'We could have asked him about the *Rose Croix*.'

She glanced at the bartender's reflection in the mirror on the opposite wall. Her eyes narrowed fractionally before shifting to the rest of the room.

The men in the beer hall were mostly locals enjoying a quiet drink after a hard day's work. The majority were middle-aged, blue-collar workers who nervously looked away from her penetrating stare. Several of the younger men ogled her more openly, emboldened by the alcohol in their bloodstream and the muted jeers of their companions.

Her attention was drawn to a table near the far left wall.

Three men sat around it, silently nursing drinks. Two of them were olive-skinned with dark hair and eyes. The third man was fair and had pale blue eyes set high in a long, equine face. Their glasses were nearly full and their expressions detached.

There was movement in the mirror. Alexa watched the bartender put down a dishtowel and head for a thick, beaded curtain at the rear of the tavern. A door stood behind it. A second before he disappeared through the opening, the man glanced over his shoulder.

She put her drink down on the counter and started after him.

'Where are you going?' asked Jackson, trailing in her footsteps.

'The bartender knows something,' she said in a low voice.

'And you deduced this how?' responded Jackson incredulously.

'He flinched when you mentioned the *Rose Croix*.' She indicated the mirror with a brief tilt of her head.

They reached the back of the beer hall. Alexa pulled the beaded curtain aside to find the door ajar. She pushed the bottom edge gently with the tip of her boot; the door opened with a faint creak to reveal a dingy corridor.

She entered the narrow passageway silently, Jackson close behind. They passed a fetid restroom and a storage area. The corridor twisted to the right. A fire exit appeared at the far end. There was another door about a dozen feet from it.

Alexa put her hand against Jackson's chest and stopped him in his tracks.

'What?' he whispered.

She studied the weak light seeping through the bottom of the doorframe on the left. A shadow moved across it. A low mumble of voices rose from the other side. 'Stay close,' she said quietly. She flexed her gloved fingers, walked to the side of the doorjamb, and turned the handle.

The room beyond was small and dreary. A row of beer barrels stood next to the wall on the left. A single, naked light bulb hung from the low ceiling. It cast a dull glow on the five men seated around the table in the middle of a concrete floor. Papers lay scattered across the old, pitted wood. A map of Europe was pinned to a corkboard on the wall behind them.

The facial features of four of the strangers suggested an Eastern and Southern European origin. The pair with their chairs angled toward the door bore faintly visible *Rose Croix* tattoos just below their hairline.

It was the man at the head of the table, however, who immediately caught and held her gaze. Older than his companions by a good couple of decades, his red hair and beard were richly peppered with streaks of white. Deep-set, pale gray eyes watched her inscrutably from beneath thick eyebrows. His thin, white lips were fixed in a rigid, uncompromising line below his high, straight nose.

The bartender hovered next to the table, his posture apprehensive and his voice hushed while he spoke. He looked around distractedly at the sound of their footsteps. His face went ashen. 'You—you cannot be here! Please go! Go now!'

Alexa saw the bartender's eyes flicker, shoved Jackson against the wall next to her, reached up, and grabbed the arm closing around her neck in a stranglehold. She twisted on her heels, hit the man behind her in the face with the back of her fist, locked her fingers on his armpit, and threw him up and over her shoulder. She jabbed a straight punch at his solar plexus as he crumpled to the floor in front of her.

A harsh grunt left her attacker's lips, and his pale blue eyes reflected his shock. It was the man from the tavern.

She dropped below the hook strike from one of his dark-skinned accomplices, pivoted on one foot, and hit the man in the stomach with a spinning heel kick. He stumbled backward and crashed into the wall across the corridor before sliding silently to the ground.

Jackson deflected a blow from the third henchman, head butted him in the nose, yanked him down by the shoulders, and struck him in the face with his knee. He winced and rubbed his forehead gingerly as his stunned assailant fell at his feet.

A thrill of satisfaction coursed through Alexa. The Harvard professor was learning fast.

A horrified whimper erupted from the other side of the room. His dark eyes glazed with terror, the bartender gaped briefly at the unconscious men on the floor before fleeing from the room. His sandaled footsteps echoed down the passage as he disappeared in the direction of the beer hall.

Alexa straightened and scrutinized the men at the table. They had not moved. Her gaze shifted to the figure with the red hair and deep-set eyes. 'Where's Boyko Dragov?' she demanded curtly.

'Who the hell are you?' retorted the man closest to her.

She glanced at him. 'Answer the question.'

One of his companions leveled a calculating stare at her. 'What makes you think we know someone by that name?'

Faint groans rose from the injured henchmen on the floor. Alexa's eyes never moved from the still figure at the head of the table.

'Well, the *Rose Croix* tattoo on your neck is a bit of a giveaway,' said Jackson darkly.

The second man grinned and glanced at his companions. Alexa smiled thinly. She had the Sig out and was squeezing the trigger before he had fully straightened the arm holding the semi-automatic Makarov pistol he had been hiding under the table.

The bullet struck his shoulder with a dull thump. He jerked back in his chair, a startled cry leaving his lips. The gray eyes of the man at the head of the table never flickered.

'We just want to talk,' said Alexa. Though she sighted down the barrel of the Sig at the man with the pistol, she kept her stare on the silent, red-haired figure.

The injured man swore, features contorted in a grimace. He gripped his bleeding limb and brought the gun up again. Her eyes shifted briefly to his companions as they reached for their own weapons.

A bullet suddenly whistled past her right arm from behind and took a stone chip out of the ceiling. She glanced over her shoulder.

The blue-eyed man on the floor steadied the handgun in his grip and aimed the pistol at her head once more.

Alexa brought out the second Sig, twisted sideways, and fired both guns.

The blue-eyed man jerked as two 9mm Parabellum bullets entered his chest.

One of the figures at the table grunted and crumpled to the ground, his face frozen beneath the gunshot wound in the middle of his forehead.

She backed into Jackson and bore him to the ground behind the beer barrels a second before a hail of bullets peppered the space where they had stood. The men at the table crowded protectively around the older, red-haired figure and ran from the room, guns jerking in their hands as they discharged their weapons.

Their shots punched harmlessly through the wooden casks and riddled the wall above Alexa and Jackson, showering them in a fine layer of plaster dust. She straightened, looked briefly at the documents on the table, and headed after the fleeing figures.

'Hey, wait a—' Jackson called out after her.

The dark-skinned henchmen scrambled out of her way when she reached the corridor. The exit door at the end banged against the outer wall of the building. She moved toward the opening.

A bullet whined through the night and struck the ground an inch from her right foot when she entered the narrow courtyard at the back of the tavern. She dropped to the cobblestones, rolled to one knee, and fired at a figure on the high concrete wall to her right. The man dropped from view.

Alexa rose, holstered the Sigs, took a step back, and ran at the wall. She stepped up against the vertical surface, jumped, and caught the top edge of the rampart with the tips of her fingers. She pulled herself up with a silent grunt.

A narrow alley ran behind the tavern. It was empty. Running footsteps faded in the direction of the main street to the right.

Jackson shouted her name at her back. She ignored him, swung her legs over the wall, and landed lightly in the passage on the other side. She headed briskly toward Istiklal.

Though barely half an hour had passed since they arrived in Beyoglu, the avenue was less crowded than it had been earlier. Alexa scanned the thin press of people and made out four running figures. She started after them, the excitement of the chase making her blood sing in her veins.

The man at the rear of the group turned when he heard her footfall. There was a flash and a bang in the night. A bullet hissed past her head. She raised a Sig and fired a volley in their direction. The men bolted down the street.

A woman screamed somewhere to her right. Shouts of alarm echoed further along the avenue.

A uniformed guard stepped out of a cabin outside the Dutch Consulate as Alexa drew close to the building. He backed hurriedly inside the hut when he saw the gun in her hand and was reaching for the phone on his desk when she darted past.

Seconds later, the running men ducked inside an opening on the left. Alexa skidded to a stop in front of a wide portal flanked by commercial buildings. A flight of stairs descended into deepening gloom beyond it, with a darkened church at the bottom.

She glanced at the gray statue of the Virgin Mary guarding the lintel of the ancient stone frontage above and headed down the steps. Her gaze skimmed the shadowy recesses of the steep forecourt before focusing on the double doors guarding the entrance to the church. The one on the right swung slightly on its hinges. She pushed it and stepped inside the building.

A large chandelier hung from the middle of a beautiful vaulted ceiling. At the other end of the chancel, stained-glass windows framed a wide, marble altar. Alexa barely had time to assimilate these details before a bullet thudded into the wall next to her. Shadows shifted to the left of the nave.

Gunfire shattered the peaceful tranquility of the church as she sprinted down the aisle toward the fleeing figures. Flanked by the guard with the injured shoulder, the red-haired man stared at her briefly with cold, gray eyes before disappearing through an open archway beyond the nave.

The remaining two men rounded on her.

Alexa holstered the Sig and slid the sais out of their sheaths just as the first man raised his gun toward her. She blocked the barrel of the weapon between the shaft and prong of one of the daggers, twisted it to the right as he fired, and brought the handle of the second blade down on his wrist. Bone shattered under the metal. A strangled cry left the man's lips. It was choked off when she elbowed him in the throat. He collapsed to the ground.

She shifted and felt heat flash past her face as the bullet from the second man's gun missed her skin by an inch before striking a marble pillar. A second later, footsteps sounded from the direction of the church entrance.

'Alexa!' shouted Jackson.

Her attacker leveled his gun at the doors and squeezed the trigger once. Jackson gasped and jerked backward.

Alexa scowled, twisted on one foot, and back-kicked the pistol out of the gunman's hand. He stumbled a couple of steps before lunging forward. A snarl left his lips as he aimed a straight jab at her head. She bobbed and countered with a cross punch to his jaw. He blocked it with one arm and came at her with a wide swing. She leaned back, pivoted, and jumped, her heel striking his chest with a back kick.

His feet left the ground and he hit the metal rail behind him. There was a snap of breaking ribs. She straightened and lowered her foot to the ground, her breathing slow and even.

'What did Dragov do with the tombs?' she demanded sharply.

A thin trail of blood trickled past the man's lips as he panted with exertion and pain. He wiped the corner of his mouth with the back of his hand and grinned at her wildly. 'You'll never find out, bitch!'

His left fist sailed toward her head. Baring her teeth, she parried his strike with her right forearm, hooked the prong of the left sai behind his neck, pulled him down sharply, and kneed him in the face. His nose broke with an audible crunch. He groaned and slumped unconscious to the floor.

She looked over her shoulder. Jackson was cursing liberally while he staunched the flow of blood from the wound on his arm. He turned an accusing glare on her. 'Will you wait a goddamned minute?' he growled.

The mild unease that tempered her fierce excitement faded; he did not look like he was going to die anytime soon. She turned and headed for the opening through which the other two men had vanished.

The figures of several monks appeared in the dim light that illuminated the inner recesses of the church. Alexa disregarded their anxious queries and focused on the fresh crimson spatters that dotted the corridors of their living quarters. Moments later, she reached a rooftop terrace adjoining the church bell tower.

She halted in front of a concrete archway and studied the pattern of blood several feet ahead of her. The floor was wet from the sleet and snow that had been falling steadily over the last hour; ice patches had started to form on the cold stone. Lights glimmered brightly along the Bosphorus Strait to the far right. The noise of the city below was a dull clamor that would effectively mask the sounds of any ambush.

Her lips thinned in a grim smile. She walked through the opening to the terrace.

There was movement on her right. She blocked the gun aimed at her head with her sai and deflected it toward the ground. The metal barrel of the Makarov pistol clanged against the prong of her dagger and a bullet whispered close to her face before striking the stone floor.

She turned and thrust her left knee up into her assailant's stomach. The man with the wounded shoulder leapt back with a grunt and barely avoided the full impact of the blow. His face contorted in an expression of unadulterated fury. He raised the pistol once more.

Alexa threw her right sai in the air, drew her Sig, and shot him twice in the chest.

The man gasped. Blood burst past his lips and he started to fall. She holstered the Sig and caught the falling dagger by the handle just as his body thudded dully to the ground.

A silver blur erupted at the corner of her eye. She leaned backwards sharply at the waist. A blade sang past her cheek with a low hum and sheared a sliver off the end of a stray lock of hair at her temple.

She dropped to the ground, rolled toward the archway, and jumped to her feet, her heart thudding against her ribs.

The older man with the red hair and gray eyes stood facing her across the empty terrace, a beautifully polished, double-edged Schiavona broadsword clasped in his right hand. From the look of the hand guard, the weapon was well used. Although his face remained impassive, Alexa detected a brief flash of emotion in the slate colored gaze. He was seething with fury.

'You will not get in my way, immortal,' he stated irrevocably in a low, hard voice.

A chill darted down her spine at his words. This man was dangerous.

The gray eyes watching her darkened. The old man moved, the heavy sword twisting in his grip as if it weighed nothing.

Alexa spun the sais and countered with a flurry of strikes and blocks, the daggers blurring with the speed of her movements. Metal clashed against metal as their blades met repeatedly under the icy rainfall.

It did not take long for her to appreciate her opponent's

expert skills. Her brow furrowed as the weapon whispered close to her skin once more.

He handled the broadsword better than some of the tutors who had taught her fencing.

Seconds later, she captured the tip of his blade inside the prongs of one sai, brought the other dagger down sharply higher up the double-edged sword, and tried to yank it out of the old man's grasp. A muffled grunt left his lips. His fingers whitened on the hilt of the sword.

The back of her neck prickled.

Alexa dropped to the ground a second before gunshots erupted from the neighboring rooftops and was reaching for the Sigs even as she rolled toward the shelter of the bell tower. She rose to her feet, backed up against the wall, and looked to her right. The old man had disappeared.

Bullets struck the other side of the tower. One pinged against a bell and produced a dull, musical clang.

A thrill rushed through her at the sound of the gunfire. She smiled savagely, shifted, and fired at the shadows on the roof of the adjoining buildings. Her first shots took out two of the seven men targeting her.

Her feeling of elation was short-lived. Jackson had appeared in the archway to the terrace. He raised the Beretta and started to fire at her assailants.

CHAPTER ELEVEN

ALARM TORE THROUGH ALEXA, THE FEELING UNEXPECTED AND all the more shocking in its intensity. She scowled and darted from behind the wall, the Sigs rigid in her grip as she repeatedly pulled the triggers. Two more men fell under her charge. Bullets pelted the floor and the wall of the terrace behind her.

She slammed into Jackson and knocked him to the ground beyond the arch. A harsh gasp left his lips when she landed on top of him. She rolled, grabbed his shirt, and pulled him behind the shelter of the wall. Further shots thudded into the concrete floor a foot from where they hunkered down.

Alexa rose on one knee and returned fire through the opening. 'What was that?' she hissed over her shoulder.

Jackson's eyes dilated with anger. 'What was—hell, I was only trying to save your skinny ass!' he barked.

'I don't need your help,' she retorted furiously.

'Lady, there's a whole load of things I think you're in serious need of,' he said between gritted teeth. A shot flashed past his head. 'But now's not the time to get into that,' he added hastily.

Chips of concrete and plaster rained down around them as a barrage of bullets slammed into the walls of the arch. The sound of running footsteps reached Alexa's ears above the fading echoes of the gunshots. She straightened and dashed out onto the church terrace. Jackson followed on her heels.

The shadows on the rooftops melted in the darkness as their attackers bolted in the night. Alexa leapt on a low wall and climbed onto the nearest building.

'Oh, for the love of—' Jackson blurted behind her.

She chased the last two fleeing figures across the icy canted roof of the monks' living quarters to a spiral fire escape that backed onto a commercial complex overlooking the main avenue. The men slid down the bars of the metal frame enclosing the staircase and dropped along a series of narrow ledges to the church forecourt.

She landed after them seconds later and sprinted up the steps onto Istiklal Avenue, her breath pluming in small, white puffs in front of her face.

Armed officers stood on the road in front of the Russian Consulate to her left. They stared at her warily when she emerged from the shadows of the church stairs.

Alexa turned and scanned the road. Her gaze fell on two figures just as they merged into a noisy parade coming down the avenue some hundred feet to the right. One of the men glanced over his shoulder. Light from an overhead street lamp illuminated his face briefly before he disappeared in the crowd.

She froze.

'Hey!' someone called out behind her. Panting, Jackson appeared at her side. 'Wasn't that one of the men you shot back at the tavern?' His perplexed gaze shifted from the spot where the two figures had vanished. He stared at her.

'No,' said Alexa stiffly.

It was a blatant lie and Jackson was not falling for it. 'I don't forget a face easily,' he said. 'How the hell did he survive that injury? He took a bullet to the head!'

She refrained from replying. There was only one possible explanation to Jackson's question.

The man had to be an immortal. Which meant that they had gravely underestimated the enemy.

The magnitude of the situation did not escape her. There was more at stake here than her original mission ever encompassed. She had to talk to Reznak.

The blare of sirens rose in the distance. Windows and doors opened along the avenue as the residents of Istiklal came out on the street, their faces reflecting alarm and morbid curiosity. Several monks appeared on the stairs to the church.

Ignoring the suspicious stares from the sentries outside the Russian Consulate, Alexa turned and headed up the road.

'What the hell's going on?' said Jackson, storming after her. 'You're hiding something, aren't you? Talk to me goddamnit!'

The guard outside the Dutch Consulate caught sight of her through the gathering mob. He darted inside his cabin and grabbed the phone on the desk again.

She scowled and broke into a trot. The last thing she wanted was attention from the local authorities.

'Hey, wait up!' Jackson called out.

A glow in the sky caught her eyes. Above the clamor of the police cars, Alexa detected the distinct, high-pitched sirens of several fire engines. Suspicion bloomed in her mind. She started to run.

By the time she retraced her steps to the alley that backed onto the rear of the tavern, the entire building was ablaze. She stopped and stared at the flames that engulfed the beer hall.

Sleet and rain fell lightly from the sky, the icy drops hissing and steaming as they made contact with the fire.

There was no doubt in her mind that the building had been set alight deliberately.

Anger flashed through her as she thought of the documents and map in the back room; she should have secured them before chasing after the fleeing men.

Jackson's footfall sounded behind her. 'Shit,' he gasped when he reached her side. Out of the corner of her eye, she saw him bend over with his hands on his knees. 'Look, I don't think we should be here. The cops are gonna be crawling all over this place any minute now. Besides, I—'

Alexa turned to look at him. Movement beyond his shoulder captured her gaze.

A saffron-robed figure stood in the alley a hundred feet from them, in the opposite direction to Istiklal. The man's face was cast in the shadows of an overhanging porch. He turned and ran.

She bolted after him.

'For Pete's sake—' Jackson groaned behind her.

Alexa chased the monk out of the dark passage and onto a vertiginous road that looked down to the Golden Horn and Topkapi Palace in the distance across the water. He grinned at her over his shoulder. Although the Asian man was shorter and should have been encumbered by the outfit he wore, she found the distance between them growing wider by the second. She gritted her teeth and accelerated.

He darted into a side street and disappeared from view. By the time she entered the steep, terraced lane lined with busy cafes and restaurants, the monk had scaled the barred window of one of the buildings and was pulling himself up onto a first floor balcony. He looked around. She caught another flash of white teeth in the darkness.

Her gaze dropped to the packed street.

She ran down a couple of steps, jumped, and grabbed a vine-covered metal beam that spanned the width of the passage. Swinging herself up into the air, she spun and landed feet down in a wide stance on the horizontal bar. Gasps and cries of amazement rose from the crowd below. The monk nodded in approval before turning and moving nimbly up the face of the building.

Alexa leapt onto an adjacent balustrade and climbed along a parallel path. She reached the flat terrace at the top of the edifice seconds later.

The monk had already cleared the gap to the next apartment complex. She went after him.

The chase was silent but for the sound of their breathing and their rapid footsteps. They dropped and climbed across the ice-covered rooftop landscape of the city, crossing buildings, leaping over shadowy alleyways, and dancing along the edges of balconies. All the while, Alexa could not shake the strange feeling that the monk was toying with her. She smiled grimly and gathered speed.

The distance between them shrank.

She was a dozen feet behind him when he suddenly disappeared. Alexa rocked to a standstill on the edge of a fifty-foot drop and stared down. The monk had vanished. She looked up and scanned the shadows of the surrounding rooftops. Although her every instinct told her he was close by, the saffron-robed figure was nowhere to be seen.

She gazed thoughtfully at the lights along the Bosphorus while her heartbeat slowed down. Finally, she turned and made her way back to Istiklal.

JACKSON WAS SITTING ON THE HOOD OF THE TAURUS WHEN SHE reached the side street where she had parked the car. His body was rigid and his eyes were dark.

'Are we done here?' he asked.

Alexa got in the car wordlessly. He joined her and slammed the passenger door forcefully. They sat and stared at the avenue a hundred feet ahead.

The busy crowd from earlier had scattered. The majority of the pedestrians had shifted a safe distance from the scenes of the incidents; a morbidly curious few had moved closer to get a better view of the action. Sirens blared and lights flashed against the frontage of buildings as patrol cars and ambulances raced into the neighborhood.

'If Reznak and you want my help beyond this, we're gonna have to lay down some ground rules,' said Jackson in a low, flat voice. 'No more secrets—or I walk.'

Alexa remained silent. It was the first time she had heard genuine anger in Jackson's voice. This was hardly a surprise after what he had just experienced. Still, it troubled her.

She switched the engine on and pulled away from the curb. After heading down the hill and crossing the Galata Bridge, she turned left toward Seraglio Point. Moments later, she stopped the Taurus on the seafront next to a lighthouse beyond the defensive sea walls that once protected Istanbul and Topkapi Palace. Grabbing the satellite phone from her bag, she climbed out of the car and crossed the road to the promenade that looked out over the bay. At this late hour, the concrete walkway was practically deserted.

Jackson got out of the Taurus and leaned against the hood while she made the call.

'It's Alexa,' she said bluntly when Reznak answered.

'What's wrong?' said her godfather tensely at her tone.

She gave him a brief rundown of the events of the last twenty-four hours, starting with the attack in Port Said and ending with her chase of the monk. Now that the excitement of the recent fight had abated, the gravity of the situation impressed itself upon her once more.

'Do you have a name for this…sect?' Reznak asked after she finished her account.

'No. Jackson's friend didn't know either, nor do the Crovir techs,' said Alexa. 'The only thing we can be confident of is the *Rose Croix* connection.' A ferryboat drifted past slowly less than half a mile from where she stood, its thrusters churning the waters of the Sea of Marmara. A phosphorescent glow tipped the waves in its wake. It started to snow heavily.

'I've come across a few of these esoteric societies in my time,' said Reznak. 'Some of their members were not the most...balanced individuals I have ever met.'

'Did you ever encounter one with associations with the immortal societies?'

'No,' said Reznak firmly. 'That I can be certain of.'

She stared into the night and recalled cold gray eyes and an inscrutable face. 'The red-haired man I fought an hour ago knew I was an immortal.'

'He won't be the first or last human who is aware of the existence of our races,' said her godfather steadily.

'And the monk?'

Static travelled down the line. 'Do you think he meant you harm?' asked Reznak.

Alexa pondered the question for silent seconds. 'No,' she replied. 'I don't believe he's part of the group who raided the tombs either.'

'Hmm,' murmured Reznak. 'I wonder—' He lapsed into silence.

'Is there something you're not telling me?' she asked in clipped tones.

'I think I might know who the monk is,' said Reznak in an enigmatic voice. 'I'll have to look into it further.'

She glanced across the street to where Jackson was leaning against the hire car. She could feel the heat of his gaze on her face. 'We have a problem,' she said quietly into the mouthpiece. 'Jackson saw the immortal I killed rise again. He won't cooperate unless we tell him the truth.'

Reznak's breathing froze at the other end of the line. 'Damn it,' her godfather muttered, exhaling sharply. 'You're certain he won't buy—'

'He's too smart for that,' she interrupted brusquely.

'What do you want to do?' said Reznak after several seconds.

Alexa was startled by his words. 'You're happy to leave this decision to me?'

'Yes,' said Reznak. He sighed. 'Frankly, I wish we could do without the man, but I fear we're going to need his skills even more in the coming days.'

She stared blindly at the falling snow. 'I agree,' she said slowly. There was no denying that Jackson's presence was crucial to her mission. He was better than any database system she had ever had access to and was an expert hacker to boot.

'But bear this in mind,' said Reznak in a warning tone. 'If you do decide to tell him about us, he will have to keep it a secret for the rest of his life.' Her godfather paused. 'You more than anyone know the potential ramifications if he doesn't. The Crovirs do not forgive easily.'

Alexa mulled over his words silently. 'Will you talk to the

First Council?' she asked finally. 'This recent incident exceeds the remit of the Immortal Culture and History Section.'

'Yes,' said Reznak. Another sigh left his lips. 'I have no choice, though I sorely wish I did. We're about to appoint a permanent Head of the Order of Crovir Hunters. I guess now is as good a time as any to broach the subject.'

She frowned at this latest news. 'Is this likely to affect the mission?'

'No,' said Reznak adamantly. 'It's in our interest to secure those tombs.'

Her gaze shifted to the dark waters washing onto the rocky shore fifty feet away. 'Have you got anything on Dragov?'

'Yes,' said Reznak. 'A man matching the description you gave was spotted in Budapest and Rome in the last month. I have people on the ground making enquiries.'

Alexa digested this information thoughtfully. 'Budapest is closer,' she murmured absent-mindedly.

She felt the shift in Reznak's mood. 'Stay put,' her godfather said curtly. 'I'll have more information in the next few hours. In the meantime, you need to lie low.' He ended the call.

She lowered the phone and studied the white curtain of sleet for a moment before walking back to the car.

'Well?' said Jackson, raising his eyebrows. Snow had melted in his hair and soaked through his clothes.

She glanced at his injured arm. 'We need to see to that.'

CHAPTER TWELVE

Alexa drove to a small hotel in the Sultanahmet district of Istanbul and booked them into a suite. The receptionist overlooked their unkempt attire and smiled diplomatically while he took down the details of the fake passports.

Jackson whistled appreciatively when they entered the room. He crossed the polished parquet floor and dropped onto a beautiful, silk-upholstered, gilded chair. The duffel bag thudded dully to the ground next to his feet. A sigh left his lips and he closed his eyes.

Alexa locked the door and closed the curtains on the French doors and windows that overlooked the old city. She removed her medical kit from her bag and turned to Jackson. 'Strip,' she said.

His eyes snapped open. 'Huh?' His surprised gaze darted to the king-sized bed that dominated the room before focusing on her face.

'Your wound. I need to examine it,' she said steadily.

'Oh.' A faint look of what might have been disappointment

flitted across his features. He shrugged out of his jacket and unbuttoned his shirt. She pulled a bed end stool across to the chair.

The bullet had carved a gash in the flesh of his outer arm. He would not need any stitches. She set about cleaning the injury quickly and efficiently.

A faint hiss escaped Jackson's lips when she dabbed the wound with an antiseptic preparation. His breath washed over her cheek, making her skin tingle. She tensed slightly and tried to ignore the dusting of freckles across his shoulder.

'Thanks,' he murmured when she finished applying the dressing.

Alexa looked up. His face was inches from hers. The blue eyes had darkened to cobalt. His eyelids lowered as his gaze dropped to her mouth.

A hot, unfamiliar feeling uncoiled inside her chest. She stood and strode to the bed.

'You should be fine in a few days,' she said, her back to him while she put away her kit. She thought she heard him sigh.

'What did you and Reznak talk about?' he asked. 'I hope you told him I'm not gonna play ball until you guys come clean about whatever it is you're so determined to hide from me.' His tone hardened on his last words.

Alexa turned and watched him guardedly. She had played out this conversation several times in her head during the drive to the hotel.

A crucial aspect of all the assignments she had ever undertaken for the Crovir Councils had been to keep the existence of immortals a secret from the eyes of ordinary humans. Deliberately having to expose the reality of her race was a novel and disturbing experience for her.

Yet, as she was coming to realize, Jackson was no ordinary

human. He possessed one of the most brilliant minds she had ever encountered in her three centuries of existence to date.

He was also one of a handful of people who had ever managed to elicit an emotional response from her.

With that in mind, she walked to the French doors and moved one of the curtains aside slightly. Golden light from the Ottoman mosque on the other side of the road spilled across the darkness outside. 'What were you looking for when Reznak sacked you from his project in ancient Mesopotamia ten years ago?' she asked.

Jackson grunted. 'He told you about that, huh?'

'Yes.' She turned to stare at him.

He ran his fingers through his hair. 'I always felt there was something off about Reznak and the organization that financed that dig,' he said finally. 'I can't be more specific about what triggered my initial suspicions. Call it a gut instinct if you must,' he added with a shrug. 'I didn't find much at the time. Reznak's security people were pretty sharp. The only thing I came up with was that this organization had a major base somewhere in east Germany.'

Alexa kept her expression neutral. The Harvard professor had come unerringly close to the truth; the headquarters of the Crovir First Council was in Dresden. She replayed his words in her mind. 'You didn't find much *at the time*? Does that mean you've uncovered more since?'

Jackson did not reply immediately. Instead, he reached inside his duffel bag and took out a book. A black and white photograph fell out from between the pages and landed on the parquet floor. He picked it up and handed it to her.

She froze when she saw the picture.

The photograph had been taken on an archaeological site in ancient Numidia, or what was now modern Algeria, in North

Africa. Two Caucasian men stood talking animatedly in the foreground next to a large excavated pit; from their expressions, they had probably been unaware that they were being photographed. Several dark-skinned laborers were visible in the trench behind them. A carefully laid collection of pottery sat on the dusty ground next to their feet.

The two white men wore Norfolk jackets over breeches and sturdy boots. One of the bridges of the city of Constantine rose against a cloudless sky behind them. The figure on the left was Reznak.

'That dig took place in 1895,' said Jackson. 'I checked.'

Alexa's gaze shifted from the picture. 'Where did you get this?' she asked stonily. She was certain Reznak did not know of the existence of the photograph. Immortals were notoriously camera shy in the presence of humans.

Jackson leaned against the wall next to the French doors. 'I came across it five years ago, when I was going through some stuff one of my professors left to me in his will,' he said. 'Needless to say, I was stunned when I saw it. I tried to pass it off as a striking resemblance or one of life's little coincidences, but I got curious after a while. All my efforts to solve the mystery of that photograph were in vain. I hit so many obstacles and dead ends, it felt as if a higher authority was at play behind the scenes and was determined to stop me at every turn.' The corners of his mouth tilted in a wry smile. 'The Dean of the Faculty even walked into my office one day and asked me to stop whatever private research project I had going on the side, or else he'd show me the door.' His expression sobered. 'I don't think he was kidding. Strange thing was, I hadn't told anybody what I was doing at the time.'

Alexa remained quiet. What Jackson had just described

fitted the modus operandi of the Crovir operatives whose task it was to preserve the anonymity of the immortals.

'After a while, I stopped that line of questioning: I didn't want to lose my job. Instead, I decided to go and look in a place where no one could interfere with my research, because the facts would be indelibly carved in stone.' He gazed at her unwaveringly. 'I turned to the past.'

She felt her scalp prickle at his words.

'Did you know that I majored in history at Princeton?' he continued, unaware of the chilling effect his words had on her. 'Funny thing, history. Some take it as an art, others consider it a science. I view it as both. What dawned on me at the time I was doing my dissertation were certain...irregularities that cropped up at various points in the historical timeline of the world. At that stage in my career, I wasn't intrigued enough to pursue the matter further; anthropology was fast becoming my main interest. When I found that photograph, something told me to go take a closer look at the history books.'

Jackson's face became inscrutable. 'It took me a while to figure it out. When I did, I was so dumbstruck by my findings, I went and drank myself into a stupor for two days. You see,' he said, staring at her with such an intense look his eyes turned cobalt blue again, 'what I discovered were patterns. They were faint and carefully hidden within the plethora of records and archives, but nevertheless there. To put it simply, it seemed to me that at every major turning point in human history, events occurred that were never completely or satisfactorily explained. What really happened to the last king of the Assyrians? How did Alexander the Great die? How could the son of a Mongol chief become the ruler of one of the largest empires in the world? These inconsistencies were strangely repetitive and seemed to coincide with the rise and fall of great leaders. It was as if an external force was determined to shape the very course of human civilization.' He inhaled deeply and ran his fingers through his hair again. 'The conclusion I reached was this: I believe there is another race of intelligent beings that walks the Earth besides humans. I think they've been around for millennia.' A grimace crossed his face. 'And I suspect they are incredibly powerful.'

Alexa was not aware she had been holding her own breath until she released it in a soundless rush of air. She wondered whether Reznak had any idea how close Jackson had been to uncovering the existence of the immortals. The answer was quite likely that he did not; her godfather would never have approached the Harvard professor for this mission otherwise.

'You believe Reznak belongs to this…race of beings?' she asked, her tone calm despite her racing heart.

'Yes,' said Jackson.

'What about me? Do you think I'm one of them as well?'

His eyes widened slightly. He cocked his head to the side and studied her for a moment. Alexa could practically hear the wheels spinning in his mind and felt curiously exposed under his scrutiny.

He nodded. 'Yes. Possibly.'

She turned and looked at the brightly lit mosque across the street, her fingers clenching unconsciously at her sides. 'After what you've just told me, I should technically be putting a bullet through your brain,' she said. She felt Jackson go rigid at her side. Her gaze shifted to his wary face. 'However, Reznak gave me a choice in this matter. You are more useful to me alive than dead, so I will tell you what you want to know. But realize this now: you will have to keep what I'm about to say a secret for the rest of your life.' She looked at him steadily. 'It won't be an easy task. The few humans who know of our existence are kept under close surveillance by our operatives.'

Jackson was quiet for some time. 'Okay,' he eventually assented with a nod.

'You'd better sit down,' said Alexa.

She spent the next hour telling him about the two immortal races. She described the long and bloody war between the Crovirs and the Bastians and how the emergence of the Red Death, the plague that killed more than half of the immortals on Earth in the fourteenth century, finally compelled the two races to reach a truce that proved to be vital to their survival. She related each race's ability to survive up to sixteen deaths, how crows came for most of them at the end of their final life, and acknowledged their influence on the course of human history, cultures, and religions for over two millennia. She finally narrated Reznak's findings in the caves in Egypt and how the latter suspected that the artifacts they were after were quite likely the tombs of the original Crovir and Bastian.

She left out the part about the carving of the trishula in the second cave and the embalmed hearts.

A hush fell over the room when she stopped talking. Alexa watched Jackson carefully.

The Harvard professor stared blindly at the floor for what seemed like minutes before slowly raising his head and looking at her. Unease clouded his eyes. 'Have you died?' he asked quietly.

She kept her face blank. 'No.'

'And Reznak?' said Jackson.

'I believe he has perished ten times before.'

His gaze was unwavering. 'How does it feel?'

'From what I've been told, it's like going to sleep and waking up again.' She wondered if he had been hoping for a more spiritual experience. Belatedly, she recalled what Sadik had said about Jackson; he was also a professor of philosophy and religious studies.

'Huh. So, none of that "white light" stuff then?' he continued, confirming her suspicions.

'No.'

Jackson studied her quizzically. 'Is that why you're so strong? Because you're an immortal?'

She did not reply immediately. 'I am…unusual among the immortals,' she said finally.

'Oh.' He mulled over her words. 'What else can you people do? I mean, do you have other supernatural abilities?'

Alexa blinked rapidly to hide her confusion. She had assumed Jackson would be nervous and frightened after what she had told him. Although he had seemed troubled mere seconds ago, she could no longer perceive any apprehension in his eyes. Instead, the Harvard professor looked eager to learn more.

His reaction left her feeling strangely off balance.

'We're stronger and faster than humans,' she admitted reluctantly. 'And we heal more quickly.'

'How quickly? said Jackson doggedly.

She removed her jacket and showed him her arm. The scar from the bullet wound she had suffered in Port Said had almost disappeared.

'How long does it take to recover from a death?' he murmured, his gaze fixed on her skin.

Alexa shrugged. 'It depends on how powerful the immortal is. It may be minutes for some, an hour for others.'

He looked up. 'And your fighting skills?'

'We practice a lot,' she said. 'After all, we have hundreds of years in which to perfect them.' She did not see the need to tell him that she had mastered all the combat arts before she reached immortal adulthood.

Jackson digested this for a while longer. 'All right,' he said finally. A guilty grimace flittered across his face. 'I guess I should come clean as well.'

Suspicion blossomed at the back of her mind. 'What do you mean by that, exactly?' she said coldly.

He removed a grubby piece of paper from the inside pocket of his jacket. 'I grabbed this off the table in the back room of the beer hall.' A wry smile darted across his lips. 'I might have had time to get my hands on more if I hadn't needed to go after a certain somebody.'

Alexa's fingers twitched. She was starting to feel the urge to shoot him again.

She took the sheet from his hand and studied the clusters of paired numbers and equations that covered the first few lines. 'Are these Cartesian coordinates?'

'Yes,' said Jackson.

She glanced at him. 'What do they mean?'

He shrugged. 'My best guess? They're position vectors indicating distance and direction.' He sighed. 'Unfortunately, they mean nothing without a point of origin.'

'Could this be a map to the location of the tombs?' she asked sharply.

'Possibly,' he replied.

The satellite phone rang in the silence that followed. Alexa looked at the number and answered the call.

'Have you told him?' said Reznak without preamble.

Her gaze shifted to Jackson. 'I have.'

'You can guarantee his silence?' said Reznak after a pause.

'Yes.' She decided not to tell her godfather how close Jackson had been to the truth in the first place.

'Good,' said Reznak. He sounded relieved. 'There's someone in Rome who has intelligence on our secret sect. I'm sending Fawkes and Carrington to collect you.'

Alexa went still. 'Is Dragov in Italy?'

'Not that I'm aware,' said Reznak. 'He seems to have vanished off the face of the Earth.'

'And this other person?' she said.

'He's an old friend,' said Reznak. 'Be kind to him.'

Surprise flashed through her. Reznak's contact in Rome must be a very close acquaintance indeed. She wondered why she had never heard of him before.

'Fawkes will give you further details when you see him,' her godfather continued. 'Oh, and Alexa?'

'Yes?'

'The monk is on our side. Don't kill him.' Reznak ended the call.

Alexa stared at the phone.

'We're going to Italy?' asked Jackson, interrupting her thoughts.

'Yes,' she replied, still puzzling over her godfather's last statement. 'Reznak found somebody in Rome who has information on the sect.'

'What's wrong?'

She looked up and detected concern in his eyes. 'Nothing,' she stated in a firm voice. She glanced at the bed. 'I'll take the couch.'

Concern was replaced by incredulity. Jackson scowled. 'You're kidding, right?'

In the end, they shared the bed. Instead of the unsettled night she had anticipated, Alexa's eyes closed the minute her head hit the pillow. She was lulled into a deep and restful sleep by the sound of Jackson's breathing and the heat of his body close to hers.

CHAPTER THIRTEEN

THE GULFSTREAM JET STOOD PARKED OUTSIDE A PRIVATE HANGAR at Ataturk airport the next morning. Alexa stopped the Taurus close to the aircraft and walked toward the two men waiting by the steps.

Jackson studied the silent figures as he followed in her wake. 'Are they immortals as well?' he said quietly.

She glanced at him over her shoulder. 'Yes.' She greeted the two men briskly and climbed the stairs to the cabin.

'I see you're still in one piece,' said the man called Carrington. He grinned at Jackson wryly, the scar on his cheek pale in the sunlight. 'I didn't think you'd last a day with her.'

Jackson stopped at the foot of the steps. 'She does take some getting used to,' he admitted with a faint smile. He felt Alexa's gaze on his face and turned to find her frowning down at him.

'Let's go,' she said.

The flight to Rome took just under two hours. Jackson spent most of it furtively appraising the immortals while he pretended to study the photographs from the excavation of the caves in Egypt. He did not have to look at them again; the images were engraved in his mind.

Although he had lived with his suspicions about Reznak's origins ever since he came across the photograph of the archeological dig in Constantine, the truth had turned out to be more shocking than he had ever anticipated. The revelation that two races of powerful supernatural beings had walked the Earth with humans since before the dawn of civilization had turned his entire world and belief system upside down in a single night.

Jackson knew it would be some time before he fully came to terms with the disquieting disclosures Alexa had made; he had been careful to hide the full extent of his reaction from her. It was not every day that he came across the most incredible discovery in human history. Her warning echoed in his mind once more. He was now a marked man, so to speak.

He looked up from the computer display and found her observing him with an unfathomable expression.

It amazed him that she looked so human. Even more troubling was his growing attraction for her.

The fear that had gripped him when she went chasing after the men from the beer hall in Beyoglu had shocked and almost paralyzed him in its intensity. The bitter taste of it still lingered in his mouth. That was when he started to realize the escalating strength of his feelings.

Sharing a bed the night before had only intensified his physical desire for her. Stopping himself from reaching out and touching her had been sheer, unadulterated torture.

A self-deprecating smile crossed Jackson's lips at that thought. If she suspected even half the wanton things going through his mind, she would no doubt put him out of his misery with one of her guns. But probably not before she broke a few bones.

A voice behind him interrupted the dangerous turn his thoughts had taken. 'Those the pictures from the boss's trip to Egypt?' asked Carrington.

'Uh-huh,' said Jackson. He was similarly surprised by how normal Reznak's men appeared to be. Carrington came across as friendly and quick-witted. Fawkes was harder to read; although the pilot was polite and accommodating, his eyes were as old and as inscrutable as the Sphinx.

Carrington swung himself into the seat across the aisle. 'Do the scriptures mention anything about who might be behind this supposed secret sect?' he said.

Jackson saw Alexa tense behind the immortal. 'I don't have access to the full transcriptions, but from what I can gather from these images, they don't appear to mention any such group,' he replied casually.

Her brow furrowed. 'You've translated the cuneiform scripts?'

'Yes, some of them,' he admitted with an awkward shrug. 'What I've deciphered doesn't make any sense to me, though.'

She studied him for a moment. He could tell from her expression that his words did not please her in the least. 'It would be in your best interests not to examine them too closely,' she said finally, a trace of reservation modulating her voice.

Jackson felt a sudden thrill dart through him. Was she worried about him?

'If you find out any more of our secrets, I might be forced to kill you,' she continued, quashing any such hope.

Carrington froze. 'What secrets?' he said, his gaze swinging slowly between the two of them.

Alexa turned to the immortal. 'He knows.'

Carrington's eyebrows rose. 'You mean—'

'Yes,' she interrupted in the same cool tone.

The immortal looked dumbstruck. 'How?' he blurted out. He glanced at Jackson distractedly before scowling at Alexa. 'Is the boss aware of this?'

'I told him. And yes, Reznak knows.' The look on her face discouraged further questions.

Carrington looked at him uneasily before disappearing in the direction of the cockpit.

Jackson saw the immortal exchange heated words with the pilot. 'He doesn't look too happy.'

Alexa's gaze shifted to the window. 'The choice to tell you about the existence of immortals was mine to make,' she said calmly. 'I will handle the consequences.'

He wondered whether that statement included taking care of him if he ever broke his promise to her. He could think of worse ways to die.

A COLD WIND WAS BLOWING FROM THE NORTHEAST WHEN THEY touched down at Fiumicino Airport an hour later. The gray clouds marching across the sullen sky held the promise of an afternoon downpour.

The Gulfstream jet turned off the landing strip and taxied up to a private hangar at the far end of the grounds. Jackson exited the plane behind Alexa and paused at the top of the steps.

A stationary, black sedan stood some hundred feet from the

nose of the aircraft. The driver's door opened and a man in a dark suit stepped out.

Alexa headed toward him. Jackson followed slowly in her wake.

The stranger watched them cross the tarmac. He handed the sedan keys to Alexa wordlessly when she reached him.

'Thanks,' she said curtly. The man's blank expression did not change. He turned on his heels and walked to an SUV with tinted windows that had pulled up outside the hangar.

Jackson eyed the other vehicle curiously while they climbed in the sedan. 'Is that one of Reznak's men?'

She turned the key in the ignition. 'No.' She glanced at him impassively. 'He's a Hunter.'

He frowned at her words. The night before, Alexa had touched briefly upon the hierarchy of the councils that governed the two immortal societies. The way she described it, the Hunters were the police force and bodyguards of the nobles who ruled the immortal races. In Jackson's eyes, they sounded very much like the councils' private armies.

'He looked nervous,' he commented. Alexa remained silent and guided the sedan off the tarmac.

Carrington and Fawkes watched them leave from the steps of the jet. They were staying put on Reznak's instructions, in case the information supplied by his contact directed Alexa and Jackson to another port of call. Carrington had thawed slightly in the last half hour of the flight and even grumbled a stilted farewell when they left the aircraft. Fawkes remained resolutely poker-faced.

The pilot had provided them with a phone number for Reznak's associate in Rome. It directed them to an answering service where they were instructed to leave a message and their contact details. Jackson could only presume they would be notified of the specifics of their meeting when they reached Rome.

They took the motorway and headed east toward the capital. Hills and villages dotted the flat and mostly rural landscape around them. Winter had turned the normally green landscape stark and gray. Less than ten miles after they left the airport, they turned north onto the ring road that encircled Rome.

They had just entered the outskirts of the city when the satellite phone rang.

Alexa brought the handset to her ear. She listened for several seconds before ending the call abruptly. 'The coordinates for the point of contact are 41.902° North, 12.457° East,' she said in a clipped tone.

Jackson's eyebrows rose as she handed him the GPS. 'This is all rather cryptic, isn't it?' he said while he entered the data in the machine. 'I mean, who *is* this guy?'

Traffic thickened when they crossed into the Aurelio quarter of the town. The cream and terracotta apartment blocks crowding the skyline gave way to imposing mansions built in the Romanesque and Renaissance styles. The dark clouds scattered and sunlight streamed down from the lightening sky.

Jackson looked around. He had been to Rome several times in the last twenty years and knew the city fairly well. The neighborhood was starting to look eerily familiar. Minutes later, they crested a hill west of the river Tiber.

'Isn't that the Vatican City wall?' he said slowly, staring straight ahead.

Alexa looked unfazed as she gazed at the towering, fortified rampart rising beyond the junction they were headed for.

Jackson looked down at the device in his hands with a

sinking feeling. Reznak's contact was leading them straight into the sovereign territory of the Holy See.

They drove past the entrance to the Vatican Museum on Viale Vaticano, turned south by the Piazza del Risorgimento, and went under the Porto Angelica. Seconds later, Alexa parked the sedan along a side street on the left.

They got out of the vehicle and walked the rest of the way. The GPS beeped after eight hundred feet. They had reached their destination.

They stopped and looked up at the Obelisk in the center of St. Peter's Square.

'Well, this sure beats a crummy bar in the backstreets of Istanbul,' said Jackson dully.

Although the monument was supported by four bronze lions and flanked on either side by an impressive granite fountain, it was overshadowed by the magnificent Renaissance church behind it. At the head of the large elliptical piazza enclosed by a pair of massive, semicircular Tuscan colonnades, the travertine stone that made up the facade of St. Peter's Basilica glowed warmly under the midday sun; above it, Christ and the Apostles looked down benevolently upon the crowded square.

Alexa's eyes flickered over the sea of people while she dialed a number on the satellite phone. 'We're here,' she said curtly into the mouthpiece and disconnected.

It was several minutes before they saw a short, elderly figure in a black cassock approaching swiftly from the north of the piazza. Although the man was not wearing the purple sash of his office, the pectoral cross he wore and the ring on his finger indicated that he was an archbishop.

The stranger's gait visibly slowed when he saw them waiting in the shadow of the obelisk. A hesitant expression dawned on his lined face. He stopped several feet from where they stood. '*Signorina* King?'

'*Si*,' said Alexa with a brief nod.

'I am Monsignor Francesco Lorenzio,' said the archbishop in a rich, cultured accent. His wary gaze shifted to Jackson. 'And this would be?'

'Professor Zachary Jackson,' said Jackson pleasantly. He extended a hand.

Recognition dawned in the archbishop's blue eyes. His face brightened. He crossed the gap that separated them and shook Jackson's hand warmly. 'You are *the* Professor Jackson, of Harvard University?'

Jackson glanced at Alexa. 'Yes, I am,' he replied, bemused.

'I read your recent paper on the initial findings coming out of the Paracopan project in Honduras,' said the archbishop amiably. 'It was truly fascinating.'

Jackson's eyebrows rose at the older man's words. 'I didn't think a member of the Secretariat of State would be interested in one of our archaeological digs.'

It was Lorenzio's turn to look surprised. 'How did you know I was part of the Secretariat?'

Jackson shrugged. 'It's the only department of the governing body of the Roman Catholic Church that has offices in Vatican City.'

Lorenzio nodded approvingly. 'You're as sharp as your papers suggest. And you are indeed correct.' A smile spread across his face. 'Archaeology happens to be one of my pet interests, among other things.' The smile gradually faded and he glanced around nervously. 'I'm glad Dimitri has you working on this task. I can't think of a better mind to tackle this complex matter. Come, follow me,' he said in a low voice. He turned and retraced his steps across the square.

Jackson glanced at Alexa and saw his own unease reflected in her face. They headed after the archbishop.

Lorenzio led them to a pair of large bronze doors at the top of a flight of stairs. He nodded distractedly at the two Swiss Guards guarding the imposing entrance to Vatican Palace and murmured, 'They are with me.' He indicated Alexa and Jackson with a tilt of his head.

The sentinels watched them blankly as they swept past. Jackson saw Alexa's gaze skim across the handguns resting in their sword belts.

They followed the archbishop into the bowels of the palace until they reached a brightly lit office in a private corridor on the second floor. An open window at the end of the room overlooked a courtyard. The sun-drenched facade of St. Peter's Basilica was visible beyond it.

'Please excuse the secrecy,' said Lorenzio apologetically as he ushered them to a pair of chairs. He locked the door and took the seat behind the desk. 'I'm afraid the subject matter we need to discuss is too delicate for me to risk our words falling on the wrong ears.'

'Dimitri said you had information on a secret sect whose members bear a *Rose Croix* tattoo?' said Alexa.

The archbishop leaned forward on his elbows. 'Before I say anything, tell me what you know so far,' he said carefully.

Jackson spent several minutes narrating Ismael Sadik's experiences and impressions of the secret society that had infiltrated the corridors of power in Turkey and its neighboring states in the last fifty years. When he finished talking, Lorenzio sat back and drummed his fingers on the desk, a thoughtful frown on his brow.

'Your friend is an emeritus professor of philosophy and religious studies in Istanbul?' the archbishop asked finally.

'Yes,' said Jackson with a nod.

'I believe I met him at a seminar once.' Lorenzio's expression remained brooding as he slumped in his armchair. 'He has done well to have discerned so much during his time within the academic sphere in Turkey,' he said slowly. 'But I'm afraid his theory is only the tip of the proverbial iceberg.'

CHAPTER FOURTEEN

ALEXA STRAIGHTENED IN HER SEAT AT THE ARCHBISHOP'S WORDS. 'What do you mean?' she asked flatly.

Lorenzio did not reply immediately. Instead, he rose to his feet and crossed the room to the window, his footsteps silent on the polished parquet floor. 'Did Dimitri tell you how we met?' he murmured, his gaze focused on one of the Apostles crowning the facade of the Basilica.

'No.'

The archbishop turned and studied her with a shrewd expression. 'Being a close associate of Reznak, I take it that you are also...special?'

Alexa stared at him. 'You must know Dimitri very well.' She was annoyed at her godfather for not having revealed more about his relationship with this man. She wondered what else the archbishop knew about the immortals.

Lorenzio smiled faintly. 'And Professor Jackson?' he added with a raised eyebrow, glancing at the man beside her.

'He's not one of us,' said Alexa. 'But he knows.'

Jackson nodded in agreement.

Relief flashed in the older man's eyes. 'I didn't think you were,' he said to Jackson apologetically. 'But it's good that you're aware of the remarkable circumstances of this situation. It will make the rest of our discussion less awkward.' He returned to his seat, removed a key from an inside pocket of his cassock, and unlocked a drawer in his desk. He took out an old, worn folder and laid it carefully on the desktop.

'In 1849, six months after the assassination of the Papal government's Minister of Justice and Pope Pius IX's subsequent flight to the city fortress of Gaeta, Napoleon III sent troops to Rome to restore the Pope's seat and the temporal power of the Holy See,' said Lorenzio. 'This formidable show of power resulted in Pope Pius's eventual return to Rome in 1850. Alas, when the Franco-Prussian War began two decades later, Napoleon was forced to withdraw his soldiers from Rome.'

'If I remember correctly, there were also grave political tensions between France and Italy at the time,' said Jackson.

'Indeed.' Lorenzio nodded. 'Italy had remained neutral with regard to that particular war, but the French feared that the Italians might use the presence of Napoleon's garrison in Rome to join the Prussians. Napoleon did not take the decision lightly and was tortured by the fact that he had in effect removed his sovereign protection from Rome and abandoned the Pope. Although the Italians demanded their government retake the city under the ongoing unification process, the Italian King, Emmanuel the Second, did not make his move until Napoleon lost to the Prussians at the Battle of Sedan in September of that year. In his resolve not to hand over the political powers of the Roman Catholic Church to the Italian government, Pope Pius resisted all attempts at a peaceful takeover of the city by the Italian army. There followed a short, ten-day battle that was to be a symbolic stand, at best.'

'Ah,' said Jackson. 'The infamous Capture of Rome.'

'Yes,' said Lorenzio with a sad smile. 'Pope Pius's troops were easily defeated and Rome was officially annexed to Italy the following month.' He removed a thick, yellow parchment from the folder and lowered it carefully onto the desk in front of them. 'Does this look familiar?'

Faded and cracked, the paper curled slightly at the edges. Alexa stared at the sketch depicted on it in bold strokes. 'It's a drawing of the *Rose Croix*,' she said.

'It does look similar to the tattoos of the men we saw in Istanbul,' said Jackson reluctantly.

'That's because it is,' said Lorenzio.

She noticed the initials and date at the bottom of the page. 'FL, Rome, 1880?'

'Yes,' said Lorenzio. 'It was I who drew that picture.'

The muted roar of the crowd from St. Peter's Square was the only sound that broke the hush that followed.

Alexa gazed steadily at the archbishop's lined face. 'You are not an immortal,' she stated.

A brief smile touched Lorenzio's lips. 'You are correct. I am not an immortal.' He rested his arms on the table. 'I met Dimitri in 1850, when he accompanied Pope Pius IX on the pontiff's return to Rome from Gaeta. He was part of the entourage that negotiated the agreement between Napoleon III and the Pope to the effect that the French would not meddle in the affairs of the Church. At the time, I had only just become a member of the Papal Court. It would be another ten years before I entered the Roman Curia. Dimitri and I shared a few common interests, and we became friendly acquaintances. We did not see each other for another twenty years, when he returned at the head of a group of powerful nobles determined to protect the Pope's interests after the Italian army took the city.' A wry grimace flitted across his face. 'At that stage, it became obvious to both of us that the other party was not exactly…human.' His gaze became direct and strangely forceful as it settled on her face. 'You see,' he said quietly, 'I am the descendant of an immortal-human offspring.'

Jackson tensed. He glanced at her, his fingers suddenly gripping the armrests of his chair. 'Is that even possible?'

Alexa did not reply immediately. 'I am aware that immortals and humans have successfully mated in the past,' she said after a while, her eyes never leaving the archbishop's face. 'But the children of such couplings did not inherit the abilities of their immortal parent.'

'That is true,' said Lorenzio with a careful nod. 'For example, I do not boast the healing powers, strength, or speed of the immortals, and I would most certainly not survive a death. I do, however, possess one of your most important assets: longevity.'

'How?' asked Jackson in a strained voice, mirroring the question going through Alexa's mind.

'Because the immortal progenitor of my lineage was a pureblood,' said Lorenzio.

'A pureblood?' the Harvard professor repeated.

Alexa had related the genealogy of the immortals to him briefly the night before. Purebloods were immortals who could trace their ancestry all the way back to the original forefathers of their races. According to Reznak, there were none still alive today. The significance of the archbishop's words slowly sank in.

'I was born in Naples in 1800,' Lorenzio continued in a steady tone. 'It wasn't until I turned sixteen that my mother first relayed to me the strange reality of our origins.' A self-deprecating smile crossed his face then. 'I didn't believe her at the time. Once I reached my forties however, I could no longer deny the truth. While everyone around me was aging, I was not.' His expression sobered. 'After I met Dimitri for the second time, that fact became irrefutable.'

Jackson's expression turned wary. 'Are there many others like you?'

Lorenzio shook his head. 'I wasn't aware of the existence of beings with our unique bloodline outside my own family at the time.' His gaze shifted to the sketch on the weathered paper before him. 'It wasn't until the Italian army marched into Rome that I met another descendant of a pureblood immortal-human offspring.' He looked up, his troubled expression lost in the distant past. 'Among the soldiers who breached the Aurelian Walls at Porta Pia was a young brigadier general by the name of Alberto Cavaleti. It was several decades before I came to know of his similarly remarkable ancestry.' His eyes focused on them once more. 'That drawing is a depiction of the tattoo he bore on the back of his neck. He was not the only soldier I saw with such a mark in the days that followed the capture of Rome.'

'Did Dimitri know about this at the time?' said Alexa sharply.

The archbishop shook his head. 'No. I never saw the need to tell him. Twenty-five years after my first encounter with Cavaleti, I saw him again in Budapest, where I was attending a religious seminar. Like me, he had barely aged in the time that had passed. I approached him on that occasion.' Lorenzio hesitated. 'His reaction was quite different from Dimitri's. He wanted nothing to do with me and became aggressive. I did not take offense, as I understood his need for privacy. After all, my own family had lived in anonymity for most of their lives. Over the decades that followed, however, I started to note the appearance of more individuals bearing the *Rose Croix* tattoo. Like your friend's observations in Istanbul,' he glanced at Jackson, 'these sightings were not confined to one arena. It soon became apparent to me that what I was seeing was a slow and focused infiltration of the geopolitical and socioreligious spheres of a number of European states by a determined sect. The subtle physical changes I discerned among these beings over time led me to believe that they were not true immortals, but more likely half-breeds like myself.'

'Were they aware of your existence?' said Alexa.

Lorenzio shrugged. 'Cavaleti was, at least. I became curious about their intentions and started to follow their movements more closely. But it wasn't until twenty years ago that I began to gain an insight into their true motives.' The older man's eyes darkened and he looked at Jackson. 'I take it you've heard of Cardinal Eduardo Morettii?'

Jackson's brow furrowed slightly. He nodded. 'He was a former President of the Pontifical Commission for the Cultural Heritage of the Church.'

Alexa glanced at him. 'Is that another branch of the governing body of the Holy See?'

'Yes,' said Jackson. 'It's one of its many institutions.' He stared at the archbishop. 'Cardinal Morettii died in a car accident in Breggia in 1989. If I remember correctly, the vehicle he was in slipped down an embankment and crashed at the bottom of a gorge. The cause of the accident was presumed to be a landslide.'

The archbishop's eyes grew inscrutable. 'Eduardo visited

Breggia in August of that year,' he said. 'It was the driest month on record for the canton of Ticino in half a century.' He reached inside the folder before him. 'The police report did not comment on any significant geological disturbance in the area that would have accounted for the supposed ground movement. Furthermore, these pictures taken at the scene of the accident tell a different story.'

He removed three prints and handed them across the desk.

Alexa took the photographs and studied the images. They had all been taken from an elevated position and showed different views of a road that snaked along the side of a forested mountain. The land dropped away into a steep, green valley beyond the narrow shoulder that bordered the cracked asphalt.

'There are two sets of tracks at the edge of the road,' observed Jackson.

She stared at the dark rubber streaks that marked the blacktop. It would have required a considerable amount of pressure on the tires to produce the imprints. She looked up at the archbishop. 'Are you saying that the Cardinal's death was not an accident?'

'Yes,' Lorenzio replied quietly. 'I believe his car was deliberately pushed off that road. An analysis of the tire tracks by several private forensic experts hired by the Vatican support that theory. Another vehicle was present at the scene and was directly involved in the incident.' A muscle twitched in his jaw. 'The charred bodies of Eduardo and his assistant were eventually recovered from the burnt remains of the wreck a few days later. The boot of their car was riddled with bullet holes.' He stared at his hands. 'They were both close friends of mine.'

'Why was this never made public?' asked Jackson in a troubled voice.

A sigh left Lorenzio's lips. His lined face suddenly looked decades older. 'For very good reasons, Professor Jackson. You see, Eduardo went to Breggia to investigate a disturbing rumor. It concerned the possible discovery of a historical document that would have put the cultural heritage and ideology of the Catholic Church in great jeopardy should it become common knowledge.' He hesitated. 'I take it you've heard of the *Mutus Liber*?'

Jackson's eyebrows rose. '*The Wordless Book*? Yes. It was an alchemist text and manual consisting of a series of fifteen illustrations that allegedly outlined a process for manufacturing the Philosopher's Stone. There's a hand-colored, copper-engraved copy of the plates in the Library of Congress in Washington. The authenticity of the claim aside, experts in the field of alchemy, theology, and philosophy have long argued that the images do not accurately represent the first manuscript. In fact—' His eyes suddenly widened. 'Wait, you're not suggesting that Morettii was on the trail of the *original* text?'

'That is exactly what I'm proposing,' said Lorenzio calmly. 'Although the manual's author was said to have been a French apothecary in La Rochelle, the truth will probably turn out to be stranger than fiction,' he continued, ignoring Jackson's dumbfounded expression. 'Unfortunately, Eduardo was murdered before he could uncover the veracity of the rumor. By the time a second contingent from the Church, of which I was part, travelled to Breggia and reached the abbey where the document was said to have been hidden, the complex had been burnt to the ground. The subsequent police investigation came to the conclusion that it was an act of arson. The culprit was never found. There was, however, one witness.'

The archbishop took another photograph from the

document wallet and laid it on the desk. 'A monk who survived the fire spoke of a man he saw near the abbey grounds the night the blaze started. We managed to trace some of the tourists who visited the monastery on that fateful afternoon and took copies of the pictures they had taken. This,' he tapped the picture, 'is the man the monk glimpsed that night.'

Alexa's breath froze in her throat as she gazed at the image. Although the distant figure was slightly blurred, she recognized his face and posture. It was the man with the red hair and deep-set gray eyes.

'That's Alberto Cavaleti,' said Lorenzio.

Jackson glanced at her with a frown. 'It's our guy from Istanbul.'

'You've met him?' asked the archbishop sharply.

'I fought him last night,' Alexa admitted reluctantly. She related the rest of their tale from the previous twenty-four hours.

Lorenzio sat rigidly in his chair while he listened. 'This is news indeed,' he said after a short silence. He took a deep breath and released it slowly. 'Cavaleti has not been sighted in public for almost five years,' he explained at their puzzled expressions. 'Which brings me to the second reason why Eduardo's murder was never publicized. Shortly after the incidents in 1989, the Pope ordered the creation of an independent commission to investigate the sect behind these crimes. No one outside the Secretariat knows of the existence of this secret council. It answers directly to the Pontiff. I was placed in charge of that commission.'

'This is—' Jackson started to say in a dazed voice.

'Does the sect have a name?' Alexa interrupted.

Lorenzio shook his head, a contrite grimace flitting across his face. 'Not that we've managed to uncover in the twenty-odd years we have been investigating them. Even though we suspect them of having been behind dozens of political and religious assassinations in the last century, as well as the theft of important archaeological and theological artifacts, they have kept the identity of their group surprisingly well concealed. The only distinctive characteristic their members bear is the *Rose Croix* tattoo on their necks. That and the fact that the majority appear to be of a pureblood immortal-human lineage like myself.'

She studied the photograph on the desk, her mind whirling with the information they had just learned. 'There are also immortals amongst them.'

Lorenzio drew a breath in sharply. 'Are you certain?'

'Yes,' Alexa replied.

The archbishop's hands shook slightly as he placed them on the desk. 'Is Dimitri aware of this?'

'He is,' she said with a nod. The direction the conversation had taken troubled her as well. The connection between the secret sect behind the disappearance of Reznak's tombs and the Catholic Church was not good news.

Immortals had shaped the course of human religions since the very dawn of civilization, and none more so than the Catholic Church. To this day, both the Crovirs and the Bastians held positions of power within every single faith group in the world. The fact that Reznak's Immortal Culture and History Section was unaware of the existence of Lorenzio's commission indicated that immortals were not part of the group that had been assigned the task of investigating Cavaleti's sect.

Alexa wondered how the Crovir First Council would react when she relayed what the archbishop had told them. The ramifications, she sensed, could be explosive. 'Have you reached any conclusions as to their objectives?' she inquired curtly.

Lorenzio hesitated. 'Like Professor Sadik, I have been suspicious for some time that they are planning an…event of sorts.'

A chill ran down her spine at the archbishop's words. She exchanged a glance with Jackson and saw the same concern reflected in his gaze.

The older man's face had grown pale. 'Although the members of our commission disagree heavily on this matter, I for one have come to only one logical conclusion as to their possible motive,' he said finally in a low voice. 'I think they're planning the downfall of the Catholic Church.'

'What do you mean?' asked Jackson, stunned.

'It's exactly as it sounds,' said Lorenzio, his eyes dull with fear. 'I believe Cavaleti and his sect are planning the destruction of the single largest religion in the world today.'

'That's impossible,' the Harvard professor said hoarsely. 'You must be wrong. If that were to happen…'

'Yes. It would bring a magnitude of chaos the world has never seen before,' said Lorenzio, finishing Jackson's unspoken thought. 'Society as we know it would fall apart, and millions would die in the resulting wars that will scorch the Earth.' He clasped his hands tightly together. 'Sodom and Gomorrah would look like child's play in the face of the destruction that would transpire.'

An icy feeling raced across Alexa's mind as she stared at the archbishop. Although she personally held no strong feelings about religion, she could not deny its crucial role in the world. It was the glue that had held many a civilization together through times of woe, and it had united entire races in ways that surpassed the bonds of blood.

'But *why*?' said Jackson.

Lorenzio sighed and sat back in his chair. 'If we go by the

assumption that Cavaleti's sect abides by the principles of esoteric wisdom, then we can assume that its members believe, as do so many other disciples of esotericism, that they are special, mystical beings who belong to an inner circle of enlightened individuals destined to discover and preach the divine truths.' A humorless chuckle left his lips. 'It may sound farcical and utterly mad when it's voiced out loud, but I am convinced that this is their underlying ideology.' He glanced at the document wallet in front of him. 'I believe that the purpose of the sect's infiltration of the geopolitical and socioreligious spheres of the most powerful countries in the world is to allow them to wield greater influence on the human race once the Catholic Church falls. Some of the individuals we suspect of being part of Cavaleti's group are important members of society, from businessmen and cultural leaders, to religious figures and politicians.'

Jackson studied the archbishop for a moment. 'Could he be trying to establish his own religion?'

Lorenzio's eyes glimmered with strong emotion. 'That thought has crossed my mind. I think Cavaleti is insane enough to think that he is a god. But the connection with the *Mutus Liber* is one aspect of the sect's actions I have yet to comprehend.' His fingers drummed a short beat on the polished surface of the desk. 'The fact that Cavaleti has come out of hiding troubles me. I fear their plans are now accelerating and the Event may not be far away.'

Alexa looked at the photographs again. 'Isn't one of the reputed properties of the Philosopher's Stone its ability to transform common metals into gold and silver?' she queried.

'Yes,' said Lorenzio with a nod. 'It is also said to possess the ability to heal all ills.'

'And prolong the life of any person who consumes part of it,' said Jackson in a distracted voice. He was staring at the depiction of the *Rose Croix* on the yellow parchment on the desk.

Alexa went still. 'Prolong? To what extent?'

'The other name for the Philosopher's Stone is the Elixir of Life,' said Jackson. 'Nicholas Flamel was said to have discovered it in the fourteenth century and achieved immortality, along with his wife.'

His words made the hairs on the back of her neck rise.

'I would not concern myself too much with that possibility,' said Lorenzio dismissively at her expression. 'The search for the Philosopher's Stone is one of the most protracted and unsuccessful ventures of all alchemists, scientists, and philosophers since the dawn of their respective fields. I doubt Cavaleti's sect possesses the knowledge and ability to discover what is essentially thought to be a mythical entity.'

Jackson suddenly stiffened. He looked up from the *Rose Croix* illustration and gazed at Alexa blindly, his face ashen. 'The tombs,' he whispered.

She stared at him grimly. The exact same thought had flashed through her mind in the last minute. The link between the *Rose Croix* sect and the *Mutus Liber* could very well be Reznak's discovery in Egypt. The how and why still remained to be determined, if the connection did indeed exist.

'Tombs?' Lorenzio asked with a puzzled frown. 'What tombs?'

They had not told the archbishop about Reznak's findings in the Eastern Desert. Alexa hesitated; judging from Lorenzio's expression, neither had her godfather. 'About a month ago, Dimitri discovered a pair of caves in Egypt. He believes it was the resting place of the original immortals who gave birth to our two races,' she finally admitted reluctantly.

The older man's face cleared. 'You mean he finally found what he had been seeking for all those years?' he uttered slowly. A smile broke across his lips. 'He didn't mention it when we spoke last night. That's—'

Two shots shattered the clamor of the crowd in St. Peter's Square and drowned out the archbishop's next words.

CHAPTER FIFTEEN

LORENZIO JERKED TWICE. A TRAIL OF BLOOD TRICKLED OUT OF the corner of his mouth and a crimson bloom erupted above his right ear. He fell forward slowly, his open eyes gazing blindly at Alexa and Jackson.

Alexa was on the ground before the dead man's head thudded on the desk. She grabbed Jackson's sleeve and yanked him sharply out of his chair just as a salvo of rounds ripped through the open window and peppered the leather upholstery of the backrest he had occupied. He landed heavily next to her, air leaving his lips in a startled gasp. Fragments of feathers and foam rained down around them.

For a single breathless moment, shocked silence fell outside the Basilica. It was replaced by panicked screams.

Alexa rolled to one knee, pulled the Sigs out in one fluid movement, scanned the view framed by the open window, and fired at the figure standing in the shadow of the travertine statue of St. Matthias on the northern end of the Basilica's rooftop. Stone chips erupted from the pedestal beneath the

Apostle's feet, inches from the semi-automatic sniper rifle held by the assassin. The man moved back, folded the bipod of the gun, and disappeared from view. Anger surged through her veins.

The killer had been wearing the regular duty uniform of a Swiss Guard.

Keeping out of the line of sight of the neighboring roof terraces, she sprang to her feet and strode to the side of the window.

'Shit,' said Jackson dully. He sat up on the floor and stared at Lorenzio's still figure.

Alexa ignored him and studied the scene outside.

Chaos reigned inside the square as tourists fled down the steps of the Basilica and across the vast piazza toward the Via della Conciliazione. In the seconds it took her to inspect the grounds, she identified ten officers wearing the dark blue uniforms of the Vigilanza, the Vatican's police force, as well as eight Swiss Guards; the men surged resolutely in the opposite direction of the retreating crowd and spread out in an organized fashion toward the openings to the church and the Apostolic Palace. More would undoubtedly follow.

Running footsteps echoed in the corridor outside the archbishop's office. Alexa's gaze skimmed over the man slumped lifelessly over the desk as frantic pounding erupted at the door. The doorknob twisted and rattled loudly against the ornate escutcheon plate.

'Barricade it,' she instructed Jackson sharply. She turned to scrutinize the window for an escape route.

There was a sharp intake of breath behind her. 'Look, I'm sure if we explain what happened here—' Jackson started to say as he climbed to his feet.

Alexa scowled at him over her shoulder. 'We cannot account

for our presence here,' she said abruptly. *Not without losing precious time and getting the Crovir Councils involved,* she thought. She knew without a doubt that the two of them would be arrested as the prime suspects in the archbishop's murder. Whether the assassin had planned it that way remained to be seen.

A muscle clenched in Jackson's jaw and his eyes darkened.

She turned her back on him. There was a grunt and the dull, grating noise of a heavy object being pushed across the parquet floor. As she contemplated scaling the wall to the courtyard two floors below, several Swiss Guards appeared inside the enclosure. One of them looked up and pointed excitedly in her direction.

A thump sounded from the other side of the room. She looked around. Jackson was leaning against the walnut cabinet he had shoved in front of the door. The muscles in his arms and neck bulged, and another grunt left his lips as his feet shifted an inch across the floor.

'I don't know how much longer I can keep this up!' he managed to utter between gritted teeth.

Angry shouts erupted from the guards in the corridor outside. A narrow gap had appeared between the door and its jamb. Someone yelled out Lorenzio's name. As Alexa watched, the breach expanded by another half-inch.

Less than a minute had passed since the first shot that killed Lorenzio was fired.

Alexa's gaze shifted sideways. She grabbed the army knife from the pocket of her cargo pants, yanked on the bulky drapes that framed one side of the window until the rod tore from the wall, and swiftly cut the thick nylon cord from the tracks.

'Whatever you're gonna do, do it now!' Jackson shouted

from the doorway, his feet skidding another inch across the parquet.

She snatched the document wallet from the desk, shoved it inside her jacket, and tied one end of the makeshift rope around one of her sais. She lifted a leg over the windowsill. Cries of alarm rose from the guards in the courtyard as she balanced on the edge some sixty feet above the ground.

Alexa ignored the men below as she spun the cord in her hands in increasing circles, her eyes never leaving her target. Five seconds later, she let go of the end of the rope attached to the dagger.

The blade glinted in the sun as it sailed straight and true through the air. It dropped across the railing of the balustrade that topped the straight wing connecting the north colonnade of St. Peter's Square to the Basilica, and looped around the stonework once.

She tugged on the rope. The makeshift grappling hook held.

A crash resounded from the door. The cabinet moved. Jackson was pushed a foot across the floor. The head of an angry guard appeared in the narrow opening behind him.

Alexa raised her other leg over the windowsill until she stood on the narrow shelf outside the building. She extended a hand toward Jackson and barked 'Let's go!'

He inhaled sharply and sprinted across the room toward her.

She closed her fingers around his wrist as he scaled the window ledge, twisted the nylon cord around her left fist, and stepped off the edge of the facade.

A strangled gasp escaped Jackson's lips as they fell through empty space. The sai dagger ground against the stone of the balustrade and the rope frayed under their combined weight.

In the courtyard below, the guards froze in their tracks and watched aghast as they soared above their heads.

It took but seconds for them to travel the fifty feet to the colonnade. At the end of their arc, Alexa swung Jackson up. He reached out and his fingers made contact with the stone parapet. He grasped the railing firmly with one hand and pulled her toward him. She stepped up lightly against the outer edge of the balustrade and leapt onto the roof of the colonnade.

Snatching the sai free, she raced alongside him toward the Basilica. Angry cries rose from the guards and officers on the ground. Someone shouted 'Stop!' in Italian.

They skidded to a standstill next to the statue of St. Thomas Aquinus at the end of the colonnade. 'Now what?' exclaimed Jackson.

The crack of a bullet tore the air behind them and chipped the stonework by their feet. Alexa glanced over her shoulder toward the palace.

The guards had discovered Lorenzio's body. An officer stood at the window of the archbishop's office. A second figure joined him. Their guns glinted in the sunlight as they took aim.

She turned, vaulted over the balustrade, and jumped toward an arched balcony in the bell tower that formed the north vestibule of the Basilica's portico. A grunt left her lips as she struck the stone railing with her chest. She grabbed it with an iron grip and steadied herself on the narrow ledge beneath.

'You're kidding me,' said Jackson dully from the rooftop of the colonnade. He stared at the large drop that separated them. Shots pelted the ground around him. He swore and moved into the narrow shelter afforded by the statue.

'Jump!' Alexa ordered.

He hesitated for a heartbeat before climbing over the

balustrade. 'I can't believe I'm doing this,' he said, then leapt toward her.

She caught his outstretched arm and heard a whoosh of air escape his lungs. 'Ever been to the circus?' she said. She looked down at him, the buzz of the chase sending a flush of heat to her cheeks.

Jackson dangled from her grasp and gazed incredulously from her face to the Basilica's facade below his feet. 'You are one crazy chick, you know that?' he said, shaking his head.

Alexa smiled grimly and swung him effortlessly down the wall until his feet found purchase on the stone sill of an alcove. She dropped past him to the balustrade of the vaulted window below, grabbed his wrist as he jumped, and lowered him to the next ledge.

They reached the base of the bell tower moments later and landed in the square.

Confusion still reigned outside the Basilica. Hundreds of harried visitors were pouring out through the entrances to the church and spilling down the wide stairs toward the piazza's ellipse. Sirens rose in the distance beyond the borders of Vatican City.

They broke into a run and were rapidly engulfed in the sea of people. As they entered the shadow cast by the statue of St. Paul, five uniformed Vigilanza officers closed in on them. The men had their weapons drawn.

'Stop!' the lead officer shouted. He stopped a dozen feet away and pointed his gun in their direction, his outstretched arms locked in a shooter's stance.

Alexa skidded to a halt. Jackson stumbled to a standstill beside her.

'Hands behind your head! Get down on your knees!' the

officer continued harshly in Italian. He took a careful step toward them.

Alexa caught a flash of blue out of the corner of her eye. She turned her head and froze.

Twenty-five feet beyond the circle of officers that surrounded them, a figure in the duty uniform of the Swiss Guard was strolling down the steps of the Basilica. As he hefted the bag on his back, a dark mark that looked like the top of a *Rose Croix* tattoo peeked above the white collar at his nape. The man glanced at them over his shoulder before continuing in the direction of the piazza.

It was the sniper from the rooftop.

Her hands fisted at her side. Alexa headed resolutely toward Lorenzio's killer.

Four of the Vigilanza officers wavered and glanced at each other uneasily.

The lead policeman showed no such hesitation. He scowled and moved directly in her path. 'I said stop—'

She spun and side-kicked the gun out of his hand. The man staggered back, his eyes wide with shock and anger. This time, the other officers did not hesitate.

Alexa blocked a blow aimed at her head, jabbed a man in the solar plexus, hook-kicked a third officer in the stomach, and back-fisted the fourth man in the nose. A cross-punch sailed toward her head. She slipped out of the way, grabbed the policeman's head, and drove her knee into his face as she yanked him down. A shot flashed past her cheek. She looked over her shoulder.

Jackson held the lead Vigilanza officer in a chokehold and slowly forced the man's arm down. The policeman pulled the trigger of his gun once more. A second bullet left the barrel and struck the cobblestone by her feet. Jackson swore and thrust his knee in the Italian's lower back. The officer crumpled to the ground, face pale and mouth open in a silent scream of agony.

Alexa turned and swiftly scanned the crowd. The blue uniform of the assassin was barely visible in the crush of people fleeing past the Obelisk. She ignored the groaning men struggling to their knees around her and started to run. Jackson followed.

Lorenzio's killer looked around at the sound of their footfall. Alarm flashed on his face. He darted rapidly through the sea of bodies.

'Who is he?' gasped Jackson as they raced across the packed piazza.

'The man who killed Lorenzio,' she replied, her breathing slow and steady despite the anger thrumming through her. 'He has a *Rose Croix* tattoo on his neck.' She saw Jackson frown out of the corner of her eye.

The blare of the sirens grew louder. Several blue and white squad cars of the Italian State Police screeched down the Via della Conciliazione and braked to a stop just outside the piazza. The flashing lights of ambulances followed behind them.

Alexa glanced around the square. A dozen Vigilanza officers and as many Swiss Guards had materialized from the cover of the colonnades and were moving purposefully in their direction. A single warning shot boomed above their heads.

Fresh screams rose to the skies as terror gripped the crowd once more. They were jostled by the people fleeing past. Seconds later, a score of uniformed officers surrounded them.

She jumped into a reverse roundhouse kick without breaking her stride and took out three men. She hook-kicked another two officers in the chest, pivoted, and back-kicked a pair of Swiss Guards in the gut, her movements lightning fast.

Jackson jabbed at a Vigilanza officer, took a straight punch in the stomach from another man, delivered an elbow thrust to his attacker's face, and narrowly avoided a half-hook a Swiss Guard aimed at his head.

As she kicked, punched, kneed, and elbowed the officers and guards in their path, Alexa spotted a dozen Italian policemen approaching from the east end of the piazza. Her gaze shifted to where she had last seen the killer. The man in the blue uniform had disappeared.

She scowled, dropped in a low reverse sweep-kick that toppled four officers, and rose to deliver a flurry of side-kicks to another three. Two blows glanced off Jackson's head and he retreated a step toward her. Alexa straightened and positioned her back against his.

The Harvard professor's breaths came in shallow pants and rigid tension coursed through his body. Unease suddenly flickered through her. Although she could keep fighting for the rest of the day, she sensed Jackson would not last much longer. Her knuckles whitened as she faced the next wave of officers. She heard Jackson grit his teeth.

As they prepared to do battle once more, a yellow blur sailed past them and landed on the cobblestones a couple of feet ahead. The men encircling them stumbled back and gaped at the strange figure. Alexa's breath caught in her throat.

It was the short, saffron-robed monk with the bald head.

CHAPTER SIXTEEN

THE ASIAN MAN HELD A PLAIN, RED OAK JŌ STAFF EXPERTLY IN HIS hands. White teeth glinted in the sunlight when he flashed a grin at her over his shoulder. He took something from within the folds of his robe and threw it in her direction.

Alexa caught the jangling object in one hand. It was a three-sectional bō, a martial arts staff weapon slightly longer than the monk's own jō when in full extension.

'Who the hell is he?' hissed Jackson.

She hesitated. 'A friend.'

Alexa stared into the monk's limpid eyes, nodded a brief acknowledgement, and snapped the staff open. Her fingers closed firmly on the familiar weapon. She spun it through a full revolution before whipping it into position under her right arm.

The monk turned to face the line of dumbfounded Vigilanza officers, Swiss Guards, and Italian State policemen. 'My most sincere apologies,' he said brightly and gave them a quick formal bow. The men glanced at each other uneasily.

The smile slipped from the young man's face. He assumed a basic aikido fight stance, his face composed in solemn concentration.

The next seconds blurred in an explosion of movement as Alexa and the saffron-robed figure whirled around each other, their staffs gliding, spinning, and twisting in a flurry of strikes and thrusts that sent six men sprawling to the ground.

Jackson punched another two in the face. A grim smile crossed Alexa's lips. His uppercut had definitely improved.

Angry cries erupted from the officers at the rear when they saw their colleagues fall. Several men drew their weapons.

Alexa stepped up against a startled guard's chest, jumped into a forward flip over his head, touched off the ground, and sailed into a reverse roundhouse kick that took out three gunmen. She landed lightly on her feet before wheeling the bō smoothly in an expanding swirl of figure-eight strikes and stabs. Firearms clattered to the ground around her, and the remaining men staggered back, faces contorted in grimaces of pain.

Another four officers rushed forward.

Alexa slammed the staff in a gap between two cobblestones, leapt, and thrust her feet in a circle of flying side-kicks. She dropped to the ground and twisted the bō under her right arm while the men dropped around her.

A high-pitched squeal drew her gaze to the edge of the piazza, where a dark van had braked to a stop. Half a dozen men spilled out from the rear of the vehicle and raced toward them, weapons in hand.

She frowned as she recognized the uniforms and Socimi submachine guns of the NOCS, the tactical assault team of the Italian Police. A second van skidded to a halt inches behind the first one.

Alexa looked to where the monk and Jackson fought back to back against the growing tide of officers and guards. Though there was no doubt in her mind that she could defeat the men surrounding them, she knew it would cost many of them their lives. Despite her irritation at having lost the trail of Lorenzio's killer, she saw no point in the senseless shedding of innocent blood.

Her eyes scoured the square for an exit. She snapped the bō staff closed and shouted, 'Let's go!' at Jackson and the monk.

The staccato shots from several automatics raised sparks at her heels as she took off toward Bernini's fountain. Alexa pulled a Sig out and returned fire at the NOCS team.

Wide-eyed onlookers scattered when she stormed through the narrow breach in the crowd to the south of the piazza. As she entered the cool shadows of the colonnade, a pair of Vigilanza officers appeared on her left and stepped in her path. She blocked a hook-punch from the first man, palm-heeled him in the face, and snapped a front kick that sent the second officer sprawling against a Tuscan column. Jackson and the monk followed in her steps as she vaulted over a barrier and bolted down a road.

Three hundred feet later, they reached an intersection next to an old stone tower.

Alexa stepped out in the middle of the busy thoroughfare and raised the Sig at the cars coming toward her.

The first vehicle swerved out of the way and narrowly avoided crashing into a bus in the opposite lane. The bus driver honked his horn while the owner of the car desperately maneuvered his vehicle back on track.

The next car screeched to a halt scant inches from her knees.

The middle-aged man behind the wheel of the powder blue

Fiat 500 stared at her open-mouthed. Terror blanched the face of the woman beside him. Traffic slowed and juddered to a stop in a squeal of tires and brakes behind the little car. A van smashed into the back of a sedan. A cacophony of horns and colorful cursing followed.

Alexa strode to the driver's side of the Fiat and yanked the door open. 'Get out,' she snapped.

The man scrambled from his seat and landed heavily in the middle of the road. The woman exited through the passenger door and dashed for the safety of the sidewalk. Jackson took her place. Alexa turned and looked impatiently at the monk.

The saffron-robed figure had placed his palms together and was bowing to the dumbstruck man sitting on the asphalt. 'We are very sorry,' he said cheerfully.

The Fiat's driver nodded shakily.

The monk turned and grinned blithely at her dark expression before squeezing in the back seat of the car. She climbed behind the wheel and slammed the door shut. As she engaged the transmission, two Subaru squad cars appeared ahead and hurtled down the road toward them.

She slammed on the gas pedal, flicked the steering wheel to the left, and sent the Fiat careening through a controlled skid across the intersection. Jackson gripped the door and the dashboard, a tiny groan slipping past his lips when the car fishtailed. The tires screamed in protest and the Fiat clipped the side mirror of a sedan in the adjacent lane as it completed a one-eighty revolution. Alexa shifted gears, stepped on the accelerator, and charged down a dark underpass.

A giggle rose from the back seat. Jackson stared over his shoulder at the laughing monk. 'You're kidding me, right?' he said dully.

The monk chortled. 'Relax, Mr. Harvard. Lady is a fast driver!'

'That's what I'm afraid of,' muttered Jackson. He yanked his seatbelt across his chest and snapped it into place.

Alexa glanced in the rearview mirror. The blue and white squad cars were close on their tail. Another pair of patrol vehicles appeared from the direction of the Basilica.

Her gaze switched to the road ahead. She weaved expertly in and out of the dual lane traffic in the tunnel until they emerged into bright sunlight, and drove up to a bridge spanning the Tiber River. A chorus of angry klaxons and sirens rose around them as they crossed the dark green waters. Seconds later, they came to a bustling crossroad.

Alexa veered around a bus and shot onto the wide pavement to the right. Startled pedestrians scattered in their path. Jackson's knuckles whitened on the dashboard. She twitched the steering wheel. The Fiat hurtled back onto the two-lane road.

'This is fun!' the monk declared behind them.

Jackson rolled his eyes.

A blue and white Alfa Romeo squad car with flashing lights and blaring sirens appeared on the other side of the road. As it tore down the opposite lane, the policeman behind the steering wheel turned and stared open mouthed when they shot past him.

Alexa saw the vehicle spin around sharply in the side mirror of the Fiat.

'Watch out for the coach!' Jackson shouted in warning.

Her eyes shifted to the road ahead. They were two hundred feet behind and closing rapidly on a white tourist motor coach cruising in their lane.

'Big coach! Big coach!' the monk chanted from the back seat.

'Oh shit,' Jackson said quietly.

'Big bus! Big bus!' added the monk.

A shuttle bus was crawling in the lane next to the coach, effectively blocking their route.

Alexa twisted the steering wheel and sent the Fiat across double white lines into the oncoming traffic on the other side of the road. The Alfa Romeo followed close behind.

Vehicles veered out of their way as they tore through the contraflow at a crowded junction. Jackson swore. The monk laughed.

As she guided the little car back into the dual lanes to the right, movement in the mirrors caught her gaze.

The Alfa Romeo was right on their bumper. She saw the policeman gesticulate wildly a second before the squad car rear-ended the Fiat. Jackson's breath left his lips in a harsh gasp as he jerked against the seat belt.

Alexa scanned the avenue ahead, slammed her hand on the horn, and drove the car across another intersection. They shot into a contraflow lane and darted down a one-way road.

The Alfa Romeo stayed on their tail.

A shuttle bus materialized in front of them. The driver's eyes widened in horror behind the cabin windshield when he spotted the Fiat hurtling toward him.

Jackson blanched. He braced himself against the dashboard, murmured something that sounded like a prayer, and closed his eyes.

Alexa flicked the steering wheel. The little car mounted the sidewalk inches from the front grille of the braking bus and stormed along the wall next to it.

The monk giggled. Jackson opened his eyes slowly and stared over his shoulder.

The Alfa Romeo had come to an abrupt stop a foot from the

bus. It reversed sharply, turned, and climbed the pavement after them. Alexa glanced at the rearview mirror. The Italian policeman was reaching for his radio.

The Fiat hurtled through another junction, careened around a motorbike, and clipped a stone planter outside a police station on the left side of the road. The two uniformed officers standing guard at the entrance gaped at them. Moments later, a blue squad car pulled out from the precinct and joined the Alfa Romeo.

Alexa ignored the flashing lights and sirens behind her as she navigated the Fiat through the traffic clogging a busy piazza before charging up a large avenue beyond it. As they whizzed around a curve at the top of the shallow incline, a blue and white BMW Stradale police sports bike appeared out of a side road and drew level with the little car.

Jackson stared at the scowling, helmeted officer motioning frantically for them to stop. 'Hi! How are you?' he shouted with a manic, wide-eyed grin and a slow wave. 'Get us the hell out of here!' he grunted to Alexa out of the corner of his mouth.

They were coming up to a roundabout populated with a grassy island and trees. Alexa changed gears, twisted the steering wheel, and drove the Fiat into the oncoming traffic on the left. The sports bike followed. A grim smile flashed across her lips. She flicked the car toward the motorcycle.

The policeman's mouth opened on a shout. He veered to the right, rode onto a shallow sidewalk, struck some steps, and crashed into the green knoll in the middle of the junction.

'When I said get us the hell out of there, I didn't mean kill him!' said Jackson, staring over his shoulder.

Alexa glanced in the side mirror. 'He'll live,' she said. The policeman was sitting up on the grass and shaking his head dazedly. She took the next corner, dropped gears, and sped up a steep slope.

Jackson's breath froze on his lips as he stared ahead. 'Oh no,' he said grimly.

They were heading toward a square on a hill. A fountain stood in the middle, beneath an obelisk and four gigantic marble statues of a pair of Roman figures and their horses. Beyond it rose the palace and official residence of the President of the Italian Republic. A coach had pulled up on the side of the piazza, and tourists milled across the open square.

Three patrol cars appeared about a hundred and fifty feet in front of them and raced down the incline on an interception course.

Alexa turned the Fiat sharply to the left and sent it tearing through the piazza in a high-pitched shriek of tires, her hand on the horn. The crowd dispersed with a burst of shocked cries at the sound of the klaxon.

'Oh no! No! No! No!' Jackson shouted in a rising tone, his interjections punctuated by vigorous head shakes.

She shifted gears and grinned savagely.

The monk whooped in delight as the Fiat slipped between two concrete bollards past the entrance to the palace and sailed down the wide cordonata stone staircase beyond. They touched down on a landing with a violent jolt before juddering past another two flights of steps to the street below.

The squad cars screeched to a halt at the edge of the square above them. Alexa glanced in the side mirrors. One of the Subarus backed up and wheeled around sharply. The Alfa Romeo was nowhere in sight.

'You're going to get us killed!' yelled Jackson.

'Not time to die yet, Mr. Harvard,' chanted the monk with a smile.

As she pondered the Asian man's enigmatic words, Alexa was distracted by movement on the left. The Alfa Romeo stormed out of a side street and moved in to ram them. She stepped on the gas pedal and sent the Fiat careening across a small junction. There was a bang from behind when the squad car glanced off their tailgate.

She turned into a small lane on the left and drove up a shallow incline.

Towering walls rose inches from the doors of the car. 'Oh crap,' said Jackson, staring ahead.

The road narrowed at the top of the slope. Sparks erupted from the wing mirrors as Alexa guided the Fiat through the confined space. She accelerated down the wider road beyond, took a right, then a left. Sunlight glinted off something behind them. She looked up, saw the Alfa Romeo in the rearview mirror, and braced as the vehicle rear-ended them once more. Jackson swore.

The steering wheel spun between her fingers, and the Fiat glanced off a row of parked cars on the left before she brought it under control once more. She turned sharply to the right at a three-way junction and shot down a short street.

The patrons of a small cafe on the side stood up with panicked cries and flattened themselves against the wall when the Alpha Romeo followed in a squeal of tires.

They came to another junction. The road opened up on the left. Alexa twisted the wheel and darted down a wide avenue.

A patrol car appeared up ahead and accelerated toward them.

Jackson closed his eyes and groaned.

Alexa slammed on the brakes, slipped into second gear, and sent the Fiat flying around in a controlled skid. The acrid smell of burning rubber rose around them as the little car did another one-eighty spin. She gunned the engine and drove straight for the pursuing Alfa Romeo.

The Italian policeman's jaw dropped open behind the windshield. He twisted his steering wheel sharply seconds from impact.

The Alfa Romeo clipped the front bumper of the other patrol car and smashed into a line of mopeds on the sidewalk.

Jackson gazed wide-eyed over his shoulder while the Fiat darted up a no-entry. 'Un-freakin'-believable,' he said, turning to stare at her.

Alexa shrugged and took a left at the next junction. She guided the car through a series of tight twists and turns along the narrow streets of the city until the blare of sirens faded behind them. The sky darkened with storm clouds. It started to rain. Moments later, they were back on a main road and headed out of the center of Rome.

CHAPTER SEVENTEEN

'WHAT HAPPENED?' ASKED REZNAK STIFFLY. THE DRONE OF THE Gulfstream's engines could not mask the distress in the Crovir noble's voice as it came over the speakers.

Half an hour had passed since they lifted off from Fiumicino Airport. Alexa had called Fawkes from the stolen car and asked him to update Reznak about Lorenzio's death. They left the city moments after driving onto the airport tarmac.

She glanced from the screen of the onboard computer to the aircraft's phone. She had put it in speaker mode while she scrolled through the CCTV footage the Crovir techs had sent her in the last ten minutes. Images of the chaos inside St. Peter's Square and its surroundings streamed across the monitor.

Jackson sat opposite her and studied the contents of the dead archbishop's folder.

The monk was perched cross-legged in the leather seat across the aisle from them, his eyes closed and his expression serene. He had been particularly unforthcoming with information on the drive from Rome to the airport, and had since fallen into a meditative silence. Alexa sensed that he was biding his time.

Carrington stood behind Jackson, his arms crossed in a defensive posture while he stared at the saffron-robed figure.

Alexa gave her godfather a matter-of-fact account of the morning's incident. 'I'm uncertain whether Lorenzio's assassination was planned to coincide with our visit,' she said at the end. 'It was probably fortunate that it happened while we were there.'

'I'm sorry, but I fail to see anything fortunate about this situation at the moment,' snapped Reznak.

Alexa stared at the phone's speaker. She had rarely heard such unrestrained anger in her godfather's voice. 'I saw Lorenzio's killer,' she explained calmly. 'He was murdered by a member of the *Rose Croix* sect.'

Reznak drew a breath in sharply. 'Are you certain?'

'Yes.' She related the archbishop's revelations about Alberto Cavaleti. 'Lorenzio was in charge of a secret commission put together by the Pope to investigate the activities and motives of the *Rose Croix* sect,' she added. 'It followed the apparent murder of a close friend of his who had been on the trail of the original *Mutus Liber*.'

'The *Wordless Book*?' Reznak said in a low murmur.

'Yes.' Alexa looked across the table. 'Jackson and I believe there might be a connection between the tombs and the *Mutus Liber*, if such a document does exist.'

'I've also just realized something that's been bothering me for a while,' the Harvard professor said quietly, wrinkling his brow. 'The *Rose Croix* is an alchemical symbol for the Philosopher's Stone. The link exists, I'm certain of it now. But I don't know what it is yet.'

'Did Francesco say anything else?' asked Reznak.

Alexa could visualize her godfather's worried expression at the other end of the line.

'Cavaleti has apparently not been sighted in public for the last five years,' she replied. She told him of Lorenzio's suspicions about the sect's involvement in scores of assassinations and thefts in the last one hundred years. She also reported the archbishop's impression about their possible objective.

'Jackson's friend in Istanbul came to a similar conclusion about a future "event",' Reznak stated uneasily. 'If Lorenzio was correct in his assumptions, the *Rose Croix* sect's plans will cause anarchy for the human race,' he added in a frustrated voice. 'The immortals will not stand idly by and let that happen.'

Alexa stared at the phone. 'You never mentioned Lorenzio's immortal roots.' She could not mask the trace of accusation in her tone. Although she hated to admit it, the fact that Reznak kept secrets from her irritated her to no end. He was the only person in the world who she trusted unconditionally.

'To be frank, I didn't think it was my right to reveal something so personal,' said Reznak bluntly. 'Stranger things have happened in the history of our race, Alexa,' her godfather continued in a softer tone. 'I've never felt the need to tell you about them because I didn't think you would be interested.'

Alexa knew what he said was true. Still, it did nothing to diminish her ire.

The monk's lips twitched in a smile. He opened his eyes. 'It is amazing what one can see when one truly opens one's inner eyes,' he declared.

'From that cryptic statement, I gather that was the monk talking,' muttered Reznak over the speakerphone.

'Hello, Mr. Crovir,' he chirped.

'Reznak will do, thank you, Yonten,' said Alexa's godfather

in a stilted voice. The monk's smile broadened at hearing his own name. 'I spoke to Abbot Kelsang at length this morning. An old Bastian friend pointed me in his direction.'

The monk's expression did not change. 'And how is Master Kelsang?'

'He is well,' replied Reznak. 'He is, however, concerned that your actions have become somewhat…reckless since you set out on your assignment. He wishes me to remind you that, although you are one of his best field agents, you are neither the most subtle nor the most accommodating of his acolytes.' He sighed. 'I can sympathize with him on that subject.'

Alexa saw a flicker of amusement cross Jackson's face as he stared at the papers in his lap. Carrington chuckled behind him; the immortal stopped abruptly when he saw her expression and cleared his throat.

'What's this assignment you mentioned?' she said coolly, glancing at the smiling monk.

'Yonten was sent by the Abbot to observe and report the *Rose Croix* sect's activities,' said Reznak. 'He was only to intervene directly in matters after strict discussion with the Abbot, but that doesn't appear to have happened in this instance—a fact that vexes Yonten's master considerably.'

The aircraft's engines hummed steadily in the silence that followed.

'Abbot Kelsang is the current head of a twelve-hundred-year-old Buddhist order,' said Reznak. 'Its sole purpose is to preserve the secret of our existence and maintain peace between humans and immortals. The order is said to have been created by Guru Rinpoche.'

Jackson drew a breath in sharply. 'The lotus-born Second Buddha?'

Alexa stared at him questioningly.

'Rinpoche was an Indian sage who famously brought the doctrines of esoteric Buddhism to Tibet,' the Harvard professor explained slowly. He glanced at the grinning monk. 'He was also one of the founders of the Nyingma, the oldest school of Tibetan Buddhism.'

'You're correct as always, Jackson,' said Reznak. 'From what I learned this morning, Rinpoche apparently crossed paths with an immortal during the second half of the eighth century, while on his way to attend the court of King Detsen, the first Emperor of Tibet. He met many more immortals over the decades that followed and came to know the secrets of our races.' He cleared his throat. 'Rinpoche believed immortals stemmed from original divine beings and, as such, their existence needed to be concealed from humans until such a time when mankind as a whole would be able to deal with this reality in a tolerant and wise manner.'

Jackson's eyebrows rose at Reznak's words.

'Rinpoche predicted that this was unlikely to happen for several millennia,' her godfather continued. 'It was for that reason that he founded the order.' He hesitated. 'Yonten, show them your tattoo.'

The monk slowly turned his right hand up and opened his fist. Etched into the skin in the middle of his palm was a black trishula mark.

The hair on the back of Alexa's neck rose and an uncanny presentiment flashed across her mind.

Carrington stared at the design. 'It's your birthmark!' he blurted, glancing at her.

Jackson's puzzled gaze switched between Alexa and Carrington. 'What birthmark?'

She hesitated briefly before twisting in the chair and pulling down the collar of her jacket.

A gasp left the Harvard professor's lips. 'It's Rinpoche's trident!'

Alexa turned and frowned at the monk. Yonten's smile had turned inscrutable.

'The trishula is not just a symbol of Buddhism,' said Reznak.

'Of course,' said Jackson. 'It's a weapon that has been wielded by many powerful deities in Asia.' His eyes flickered to her face, his expression troubled. 'The three spears of the trishula are said to represent the trinities of nature, namely creation, preservation, and—'

'Destruction,' said Reznak. A somber hush fell inside the cabin. 'According to Abbot Kelsang, one of the oldest Nyingma scriptures ever discovered indicates that Rinpoche chose the trishula as the symbol of his order based on a tale related to him by the first immortal he met.'

Her godfather's voice grew strained as he continued talking. 'Though many of his followers considered the story to be a fanciful myth, Rinpoche was confident that the legend was based in fact. The tale was about an incredible female warrior of ancient times who defeated the original immortals. This warrior was thought to have been of Crovir's bloodline and fought with the very first trident weapon ever seen. The immortal who recounted this story told Rinpoche that the descendants of the warrior still walked the Earth and would do so until the end of days—and that there may come a time when the warrior's soul will be reborn within the immortal bloodlines. Rinpoche promised that if such an age ever came, his order would lay down their lives for this immortal.'

Yonten's expression turned solemn and he gazed at Alexa with eyes that seemed to penetrate her very core. She slowly released the breath she had been holding and met his stare unflinchingly.

'That's—' said Jackson.

'Do you really believe this?' Alexa interrupted in a hard tone, her eyes not shifting from the monk's face.

It was several seconds before Reznak replied. 'I only found out about the Abbot's order last night, and I spoke to him for the first time today. But I will vouch for Victor Dvorsky, the Bastian who told me about Abbot Kelsang, with my own life.' He sighed. 'There's also the matter of the engraving we discovered in the floor of the second cave.'

Jackson raised his eyebrows. 'What engraving?'

Alexa was still digesting her godfather's words as she turned to the computer and opened a file. She had heard of Victor Dvorsky, the former Head of the Bastian Counter Terrorism Section and current leader of the Bastian race, but had never met the immortal noble in person. That Reznak trusted him to such an extent was yet another remarkable truth she had learned about him in the last week. She wondered how many more secrets he had kept from her.

She shifted the screen and brought up the images of the trishula marking in the floor of the smaller cave in Egypt.

Jackson paled as he stared at the marking. His stunned gaze moved to her face briefly before returning to the display.

'Members of Abbot Kelsang's order have been aware of the *Rose Croix* sect for some time, ever since an important artifact was stolen from their monastery three hundred years ago,' said Reznak. 'The Abbot is also of the impression that the sect's activities have increased in the last century and escalated exponentially over the past five decades. However, I do believe he was unaware that the sect members were of a pureblood immortal-human lineage.'

'Mr. Crovir is right,' said Yonten with a gracious nod.

Reznak sighed again. 'Jackson, have you found anything new in the files you took from Lorenzio's office?'

'Not yet,' replied Jackson.

'Keep working on it,' said Reznak curtly. 'I'll speak to the First Council. We have to decide what to do about the *Rose Croix* sect's potential plans. We also have to clear things with the Vatican. Your faces have already made it into Interpol's criminal database.'

A buzz rose from the speakers after he disconnected.

Having operated below the radar of the human authorities for almost three centuries, Alexa was not pleased to have achieved this level of notoriety in so short a time. But she was hardly surprised after their actions at the Vatican; they had not exactly been subtle. Nonetheless, the fact remained that this latest development could lead to unnecessary complications. She did not want to have to hurt the human agents who might get in her path. Her irritation with the *Rose Croix* sect rose another notch.

She looked at the monk. 'What was taken from your monastery?'

'A relic bestowed on us by an immortal,' said Yonten calmly. He closed his eyes and assumed a meditative pose once more.

Alexa suspected that was all he was going to say for some time. She turned her attention to the CCTV footage. Though she did her best to try and ignore the most recent revelations imparted by Reznak, the image of the trishula mark on the monk's palm kept flashing through her mind.

Was it a coincidence that she had chosen to carry a pair of sai daggers even before she became an agent for the Crovir First Council?

Alexa could recall with crystal clarity the first time she had ever laid eyes on the weapons as a child. They had seemed strangely familiar even then, like they belonged in her hands. And there was no doubt that she fought with them like they were extensions of her very being.

She frowned and concentrated on the recordings.

It was another hour before she found something useful in the films. Her fingers stilled on the keyboard.

A frozen screenshot showed Lorenzio's killer getting into a van on the Via della Conciliazione moments after he had fled St. Peter's Square. She zoomed in on the grainy picture. Half of the vehicle's registration number was visible. The image had also caught the reflection of a face in the side mirror of the van.

A thrill ran through Alexa when she recognized the coarse features of Boyko Dragov. She picked up the phone and called the Crovir techs.

'There's no vehicle matching that description and partial number plate?' she said into the handset a couple of minutes later. Somehow, this fact did not surprise her. 'I want you to run that combination through every number plate recognition software we have. Call me if you get any hits.' She disconnected and turned to look at Jackson. 'Have you got anywhere with those yet?' she asked, indicating the documents on his lap.

'I'm not sure,' he replied with a frown. 'The folder contains reports of the sect's suspected deeds, as well as the minutes of the meetings Lorenzio's commission had with the Pope. There's also another drawing by him.' He removed a thick, yellow sheet from the pile and placed it on the table between them.

Alexa stared at the watercolor painting on the faded parchment.

'I know I've seen it somewhere before,' said Jackson, frustration evident in his tone.

The sketch was of a pretty, small flower with five petals.

Lorenzio had shaded the corolla a pale blue and the center golden.

Yonten opened his eyes and glanced at the illustration. '*Myosotis scorpioides*,' he murmured and closed his eyes once more.

There was a noise behind them. Carrington strolled down the aisle from the direction of the cockpit. 'We cleared Italian airspace a while back. Fawkes wants to know where we're headed.'

Alexa ignored the immortal and gazed unblinkingly at Jackson.

The Harvard professor was staring at the monk with a glazed expression. 'What did you say?' he whispered.

'*Myosotis scorpioides*,' repeated Yonten calmly. 'The—'

'Forget-me-not flower!' Jackson interjected feverishly. His ice-blue gaze glinted as it moved to her face. 'The Freemasons.'

She watched while he rifled frantically through the contents of the document wallet. Seconds later, his fingers stilled on a file.

'In December 1995, there was a major incident at the Freemasons' Grand Lodge of Scotland,' said Jackson. He glanced at her while he spoke. 'It resulted in several deaths and was thought to have been a botched robbery by the local police. Lorenzio's commission concluded that it was probably a failed attempt by the *Rose Croix* sect to steal something of value from one of the private Freemason collections held at the Lodge.'

Alexa drummed the fingers of her right hand on the table. 'Have there been any other incidents involving the Freemasons since then?'

'No,' he replied. He stiffened suddenly, his gaze locked on a distant memory. 'But I know where security has recently been heightened in the Freemasons' world; the United Grand Lodge of England in London. Just last month, a friend told me he had great difficulty gaining access to their old records.'

'What are you saying?' she asked carefully.

'There's a good chance the Freemasons would have moved whatever object the *Rose Croix* sect was looking for in Scotland around their numerous Lodges across the globe. But none is more sacred or well guarded than the Freemasons' Hall, the headquarters of the United Grand Lodge of England. Even if the item the *Rose Croix* sect was after is no longer there, their archives may hold more information on the group.'

Alexa looked at Carrington. 'Ask Fawkes to set a course for London.'

CHAPTER EIGHTEEN

Rain was falling in gray ribbons across the darkening sky when they landed at Heathrow Airport an hour later. Carrington opened the Gulfstream's cabin door and was doused with a shower of drops carried by the cold wind coursing across the tarmac.

Lights flashed in the gloom ahead. A black Mercedes SUV splashed through puddles and rolled to a stop a few feet from the aircraft. A familiar, suited figure climbed out from behind the steering wheel.

Alexa grew still as she studied the man by the vehicle. 'What's he doing here?'

Carrington shrugged. 'He was in London on Crovir business and asked Reznak whether he could tag along. The boss thought it might be a good idea.'

Frank Schmidt, the Crovir Hunter she had delivered Abraham McIntyre to six days ago in Las Vegas, watched with an unreadable expression while they strolled down the steps toward him. 'Alexa,' he said with a brief nod. His eyes shifted beyond her shoulder. 'And these would be?'

Jackson straightened. 'Zachary Jackson,' he said carefully. Schmidt was a couple of inches taller and heavier in the shoulders than the Harvard professor.

Alexa watched the two men exchange wary stares.

'And the monk?' said the Crovir Hunter, his gaze moving to the robed Asian man.

'My name is Yonten, oh great warrior,' said the monk. He bowed formally.

'Is he kidding?' Schmidt said dully.

'Just be grateful he greeted you,' said Carrington. 'All Reznak got was "Mr. Crovir".'

'Does that mean they—' Schmidt started.

'Know about the existence of immortals?' Jackson interrupted. 'Yes. We do.'

Schmidt stared at him stonily for a moment before climbing behind the wheel of the SUV. The whine of the Gulfstream's engines rose behind them as they followed him inside the vehicle; Fawkes was leaving on another assignment for Reznak.

Her godfather had insisted Carrington accompany them this time around. Alexa suspected he had agreed to Schmidt's request for similar reasons. Reznak was being overly cautious.

'Is something wrong?' asked Schmidt as he headed toward the M4 motorway. He glanced at her guardedly. 'You look like you're gonna kill someone.'

She unclenched her teeth and forced her facial muscles to relax. 'It's nothing,' she said.

Despite the heavy traffic clogging the arteries of the city, they made it to the outskirts of London in record time. Only Yonten's giggles and the occasional sharp intake of breath from Jackson punctuated Schmidt's wilder driving antics.

Night was descending on the capital when they drove past Hyde Park. A flurry of snow fell from the sky and melted almost instantly under the feet of the crowds swarming Trafalgar Square. Minutes later, they took a left off Kingsway and drove down a one-way road.

The Crovir Hunter continued past the art deco façade of the Freemasons' Hall and parked the SUV on a side street around the corner. He turned the engine off. 'So, what're we doing here?' he asked.

Alexa reached into the bag by her feet and removed the slim hardback case that held her field computer. She brought up the floor plans sent by the Crovir techs during the flight to London.

'These are the blueprints of the Hall,' she said briskly. 'Besides the main doors, there are several side entrances to the building. They're all reasonably well guarded, and there are CCTV cameras covering pretty much every square foot of the complex.'

Schmidt went still. 'We're breaking into the place?'

'Yes,' she replied.

'Those cameras can easily be disabled,' said Carrington from the rear seat.

'Yes, they can,' said Alexa. A faint frown marred her brow. 'We could storm this place with a squad of Hunters if we wanted to, but not without causing a major scene.' She scrolled through the plans and images on the screen. 'Underground access is possible but would take hours, require heavy drilling equipment, and be too noisy. Our best bet is the roof. We can get to it from here.' She tapped a shot of a building at the rear of the Freemasons' Hall.

'What are we looking for when we get inside?' said Schmidt.

'We want access to their private archives and collections,'

said Jackson. 'We suspected they might be in the Library, but then—'

'We found this,' interrupted Alexa. She brought up a three-dimensional, infrared image of the Hall and zoomed in on a section of the frame.

Twenty-three thousand miles above the Earth, a network of private satellites owned by the Crovirs orbited the planet and contributed vast amounts of information to the databases held by the immortal race. They had been updated with the latest in ground-penetrating radar technology several years ago and had provided clear, in-depth pictures of the Freemasons' building.

Thirty feet below the Lodge and directly underneath their Grand Temple was a small circular chamber that did not feature anywhere on the original blueprints. The array of heat signals around the enclosed space indicated the presence of an elaborate security system. The walls were three feet thick and made of concrete. It was almost certainly a vault.

'Our techs can override the cameras in the Hall as well as any alarms they may have on our signal,' said Alexa. 'That should buy us time to make it to that room.'

'Can they disable the security network in the chamber?' queried Jackson, indicating the frozen image on the computer screen.

'No,' she replied. 'The alarm system for the vault is on a separate internal framework. It'll be up to us to figure out how to get inside when we reach it.'

'And the guards we might come across?' said Schmidt carefully as he studied the multiple heat signals that dotted the interior of the building. Each one corresponded to a living body.

As Jackson had anticipated, there were a lot of sentries patrolling the Hall.

Alexa gazed steadily at the Crovir Hunter. 'This is a strict no-kill assignment.' Her eyes narrowed slightly at the expression that flashed in his gaze.

'Yeah,' said Jackson in a hard tone. 'We don't want the slaughter of innocent humans.'

Yonten shook his head solemnly.

Carrington sighed. 'Seriously, Reznak and you take all the fun out of our missions.'

Alexa left the hardback case on the floor of the SUV, grabbed her backpack, and followed the men out of the vehicle. They stuck to the shadows as they headed toward the Freemasons' Hall. A narrow alley off a side road brought them to the goods entrance of the building that abutted the rear of the headquarters of the Grand Lodge.

She slid the blade of a sai inside the gap where the two doors met and jimmied the lock. The metal panel opened with a loud groan. They slipped into the darkness inside just as a couple of women strolled down the passageway toward them, voices raised in conversation.

Schmidt took a pen torch out of his suit jacket and flicked the bright beam across an empty, tiled corridor. The place was as silent as a tomb. They moved quietly into the gloom and went in search of the service stairs. Moments after they entered the building, they walked out onto a rooftop terrace.

After the stillness of the last minute, the sounds of the city hit them like a wall. An icy wind ruffled Alexa's hair and brought a small burst of snowflakes that melted rapidly on her face. She strolled to the west end of the terrace and studied the drop before her. She removed a small grappling hook attached to a sturdy, nylon rope from her backpack, secured the iron claws to the low parapet, grasped the rope, and stepped off the edge of the building.

Seconds later, her feet touched down on the roof of the Freemasons' Hall. The four men followed swiftly.

Soft light shone through skylights and stained glass ceilings, casting their shadows briefly on the rooftop as they ran over the canted surface toward the outline of the Grand Temple. An access door soon appeared in the gloom. They stopped outside it.

Carrington took his cell out and made a call. 'We're good to go,' he said once the Crovir techs acknowledged his caller ID. He listened briefly before disconnecting. 'Their security system will be offline in five seconds.'

Schmidt picked the lock on the door. Alexa glimpsed Yonten's small, enigmatic smile while she watched the Hunter work.

'I'm starting to get a bad feeling about this,' murmured Jackson when Schmidt pulled the door open moments later.

'Everything will be all right, Mr. Harvard,' said Yonten brightly. The monk stepped past them and followed the Crovir Hunter through the opening.

Carrington stared at Yonten's back. 'How the hell can he know that?' he muttered.

A flight of narrow steps lay on the other side of the door. They proceeded down it in single file. A dim glow appeared around a corner after fifteen feet, and soon they came to a brightly lit landing.

Alexa took the lead and turned left down a marble passage. Glossy cherry wood paneling glistened softly in the light cast by ornate chandeliers and wall lamps. They reached the balustrade of a majestic double staircase.

The overcast night sky was visible through a beautiful mosaic glass ceiling some twenty feet above their heads.

Beneath a series of tall arches, paintings of Freemasons past sat in elaborate frames lining pale walls on either side of the two stairs. The polished wood of the brown railing and cream balusters glittered under the muted lighting that bathed the stately space.

'Pretty,' commented Carrington.

Hushed conversation and the sound of quiet footsteps suddenly rose from their left. They took the stairs to the landing below and flattened themselves against the walls underneath. The footfall paused briefly above them before continuing along the corridor. The voices of the two sentries faded in the distance.

A soundless sigh of relief escaped Jackson's lips and prickled the skin on the back of Alexa's neck. She ignored the disquieting sensation and headed down the next flight of steps toward the ground floor. She stopped at the bottom of the stairs and looked around.

Chandeliers cast a soft glow on the beautifully adorned ceiling, marble walls, and gleaming tiled flooring of a wide hallway that branched off on either side.

'We must be at the back of the Grand Temple,' whispered Jackson.

Alexa turned right and headed soundlessly toward a recessed portal a dozen feet away. She glanced dismissively at the surveillance camera above it, twisted the heavy handle of the door, and stepped across the threshold. A curtained vestibule lay beyond. She crossed it briskly and stopped just inside the cavernous chamber of the Grand Temple.

An immense and elaborate mosaic coving framed a dark blue ceiling some sixty feet above her head. The bright sun disc at its center was surrounded by a speckling of stars and moons that shone brightly on the inky background. Masonic figures and symbols spanned the molded cornices, with the four cardinal virtues of Prudence, Justice, Fortitude, and Temperance dominating the corners.

A pedestal on the left held a tall, gold-colored ceremonial chair and pulpit mounted on an ornate frame with four pillars. It was flanked by another pair of smaller chairs and ringed on either side by rows of seats that rose in tiers toward an organ loft at the back of the chamber, where an altar-like table sat between a pair of gilded columns.

A second pedestal holding another ceremonial chair stood at the opposite end of the temple. Beyond it was a pair of twelve-foot tall, heavy-looking, sculpted bronze doors. A third ornamental chair occupied the edge of a checkerboard floor that ran down the middle of the chamber. Banks of seats lined the enormous spaces on the sides, with galleries supporting further tiers above the ground floor.

The coat of arms of the United Grand Lodge, with its border of lions and the Latin motto *'Avdi Vide Tace'* emblazoned in gold on a blue background, punctuated the vast assembly room of the Freemasons.

'"Hear, See, Be Silent",' translated Carrington as he studied the closest blazon. He looked around the Grand Temple. 'Nice digs they've got here.'

Jackson rolled his eyes.

Alexa's gaze shifted to the head of the room. She strode to the gilded mount holding the chair and pulpit, and scrutinized the structure. According to the satellite images, it concealed the access to the underground chamber.

They carefully examined the protrusions and crevices of the ornate design for several minutes. The monk finally stood back and studied the frame with an absorbed expression. Moments later, he lifted the jō staff and gently touched a knot below a small cherub at the corner of the support.

A low, grinding noise rose from the gilded mount. They took several steps back as the ceremonial chair and pulpit moved forward four feet and revealed a square opening in the floor. A flight of steps dropped down into darkness.

'Well done,' said Schmidt quietly. 'How did you figure it out?'

Yonten smiled and pointed at the statue of the angel.

'"Hear, See, Be Silent",' said Jackson slowly. The cherub's eyes were wide open and its hands covered its mouth. Admiration glinted in his eyes as he turned to look at the monk.

A soft click broke the silence of the room. Alexa's finger moved off the decocking lever of the Sig she was aiming at Schmidt's left temple. The Crovir Hunter went still, his fingers frozen on the Beretta Storm pistol that had appeared in his hand.

'Hey—' said Carrington with a frown. He took a step forward.

'Who are you working for?' Alexa interrupted harshly, her gaze not shifting from the Hunter's grim face. Schmidt glared at her defiantly out of the corner of his eye and remained resolutely tight-lipped.

'What's going on?' demanded Jackson, glancing between the two of them.

The monk watched silently, the enigmatic smile still hovering around his lips.

'You shouldn't be here,' the Crovir Hunter finally said in a hard voice.

Alexa suspected she knew the reason why Schmidt was

acting the way he was, but she had to be certain. From Yonten's expression, he had also guessed the truth.

'Do you answer to Cavaleti?' she asked coldly.

Schmidt turned to look at her. 'Who the hell is Cavaleti?'

She couldn't detect any trace of deception in his voice. Relief flashed through her. 'Then, there's only one reason you would do something so foolish as to draw your gun on us.' She lowered the Sig and stepped back. 'You're a Freemason.'

Carrington's jaw sagged open. 'What, you mean like…secret handshakes, passwords, and that dancing naked in the moonlight stuff?'

Alexa and Schmidt looked at him icily.

'We do not dance naked in the moonlight,' said the Hunter between gritted teeth.

Carrington's face fell slightly. 'You sure? 'Cause I heard rumors.'

Schmidt holstered the Beretta. 'I'm afraid I can't let you go farther than this,' he said. 'I was curious to see what you were up to when I heard you were coming here. The Freemasons' secrets must remain just that—secrets.'

'A man called Alberto Cavaleti wants to use those secrets to destroy the Catholic Church,' said Alexa.

Schmidt went still.

'You can imagine what would happen if that came to pass,' she continued in an even tone. 'His sect will stop at nothing to get their hands on what may lie in the vault below this temple—and that includes destroying the Freemasons.'

'Cavaleti's sect was behind the incident at the Lodge in Scotland in 1995,' said Jackson quietly. 'We think they'll try to break in here as well. The recent escalation in the security measures is bound to have alerted them to the fact that the

English Freemasons are currently in possession of a very important object.'

Schmidt's lips twisted in a cynical grimace.

Alexa ignored the wave of impatience coursing through her limbs. 'This is where you decide where your loyalties lie, Frank. You're either with us or against us on this.'

The Crovir Hunter's head snapped around at the use of his first name. She had not uttered it in a long time. Alexa saw Jackson glance uneasily between the two of them once more.

Schmidt looked at her for a long moment. He finally closed his eyes briefly and snorted in disgust. 'I can't believe I'm doing this,' he muttered. 'I'll be kicked out of the fraternity for sure.'

Carrington grinned and slapped him on the back. 'You can always go back to just being a plain old immortal.'

Schmidt scowled at the Crovir before leading the way down the stairs, pen torch in hand. The opening closed ponderously behind them.

The steps spiraled through two full revolutions before ending in a circular vestibule thirty feet below ground. Dim light spilled over the sconces in the rock walls that framed the foyer and washed across the wide marble corridor beyond it. A pair of steel doors stood at the end of the passage.

Their footsteps echoed on the polished floor as they strolled toward the vault.

'I've never been down here before,' said Schmidt as he shone his light on the metal doors. A trace of unease underlaid his words. 'My Lodge is in the States.' He hesitated. 'Although I've visited this Hall on several occasions, I didn't know this place existed until you showed me those satellite images.'

Jackson raised his eyebrows. 'I'm surprised an immortal would fraternize with an organization such as the Freemasons.'

Schmidt grunted. 'I'm not the only immortal in their ranks.

And I happen to like the way they do things,' he said. 'Besides, hanging out with immortals gets grinding after a while.'

Alexa looked at him steadily for silent seconds. 'You can always walk out of here,' she said. 'Pretend this never happened. I won't tell Reznak about your alliance with the Freemasons.'

The Crovir Hunter frowned. 'No,' he said. 'If what you're saying is true, then what's at stake here goes far beyond the Freemasons.' He turned to stare at the doors. 'So, anyone spot some kind of access panel yet?'

They studied the polished surfaces.

The doors met each other almost seamlessly. Alexa stepped up to the closest one and skimmed her fingers along the corners and sides. There was nothing to see. She suspected they were as thick as the concrete walls that enclosed the chamber. They would not be able to break into the place by sheer brute force.

Her gaze shifted to the steel itself. She took a few steps back and stared at the gray, burnished metal at an angle. Seconds later, she went still.

She could just about discern the suggestion of a faint line on it.

'You see it too?' murmured Jackson. He was standing three feet from her and gazing intently at the doors, his head tilted to one side.

'Yes,' Alexa replied in a low voice.

'We need the lights off,' said Jackson suddenly.

They turned and inspected the walls. Alexa saw Carrington reach for his gun out of the corner of her eye. Before she could shout out a warning, the Crovir took out three of the lights. The suppressor at the end of the weapon muffled his shots to dull thuds.

'Switch is here, Mr. Crovir,' said Yonten cheerfully. The monk pointed at a small silver knob near the vestibule.

'Oh,' said Carrington. 'Look, it was an honest mistake,' he added with a sickly grin as he beheld her dark stare.

Yonten pressed the switch. The corridor was plunged in darkness.

'Holy crap,' whispered Carrington a heartbeat later, all embarrassment forgotten.

CHAPTER NINETEEN

HUNDREDS OF BRIGHT, GLOWING SYMBOLS COVERED THE METAL doors ahead of them. Among the Masonic figures and emblems in the complex arrangement, Alexa recognized the coat of arms of the United Grand Lodge.

'It's a code,' said Jackson finally, in a voice filled with wonder.

She glanced at his dim shadow to her left.

'What do you mean, a "code"?' asked Schmidt irritably.

'There's no key. No access panel to break into to open those doors. The only way to get inside that room is to figure out the Freemasons' code,' said Jackson animatedly. 'And I bet we only have one guess.'

Alexa could tell he was impressed by the intricate puzzle before them. She shifted impatiently; they did not have time for riddles. 'Can you decipher it?' she asked.

'I think so,' said Jackson with a nod.

'Schmidt?' She turned to the Crovir Hunter.

Schmidt shrugged. 'I can give it a go, but I don't think I'll be of much use. I suspect only the Grand Master of the Lodge knows the code.'

'Get on with it,' she ordered.

Ten minutes later, Jackson's breath left his lips in a harsh exhale. He was sitting cross-legged in the middle of the marble floor and staring at the symbols, his elbows on his thighs and his chin propped on his fisted hands. Schmidt stood close to him.

Neither man had made any progress in solving the code.

Alexa leaned against the rock wall next to the Harvard professor. Her eyes had adjusted to the weak luminescence emanating from the polished steel surfaces, and she could make out the scowl darkening his features.

Carrington had retreated to the vestibule, while the monk sat perched in a meditative pose on the bottom step of the stairs.

'If I knew I was going to have to decipher a bloody cryptogram, I would have brushed up on my Freemasonry before we came here,' Jackson muttered. Schmidt glanced at him with a disgruntled expression.

Alexa looked down at the luminous dials on her watch. She was confident that if anyone could break the code, it would be Jackson. Her only concern lay in the timeframe it might take for him to achieve this; they had been inside the building for almost forty minutes.

Though the Crovir techs would remain in control of the Hall's security system for however long she wanted them to, she could not help but think of the sentries inside the Freemasons' headquarters. She had no doubt there was a security room somewhere in the complex where they were monitoring the camera feeds. It would only take one very astute guard to detect that the footage had been tampered with for the alarm to be raised.

She was about to suggest they try another method to get inside the vault—one she suspected would involve heavy explosives after all—when Jackson suddenly straightened.

'Yonten,' he said in a low voice, his eyes not shifting from the mass of symbols that crowded the doors, 'how many steps do those stairs have?'

'Sixty, Mr. Harvard,' said Yonten.

'And the number of lights in the vestibule and this corridor?' said Jackson, his tone rising with barely concealed excitement.

'Nine,' said Schmidt curiously.

'Three on each wall and three inside the vestibule?' said Jackson sharply.

'Yeah,' said Carrington, joining Schmidt. 'Where are you going with this?'

'There are three degrees of Freemasonry. And Schmidt is right—only Grand Masters would be able to access this chamber,' Jackson explained. 'Nine lights on the walls. Sixty steps. They are all multiples of three.'

Alexa stared at the doors. 'But there are no numbers among those symbols.'

'There doesn't need to be,' said Jackson with a shake of his head. 'The code is all about heraldry.' He leapt to his feet and took a step toward the vault's entrance. 'The current coat of arms of the United Grand Lodge of England is actually a combination of two arms, namely those of the "Modern" and the "Ancient" Grand Lodges,' he continued, pointing at various figures and emblems on the steel panels. 'The "Modern" Grand Lodge was the original Grand Lodge of England, formed in 1717 when four London Lodges met up for the first time. The "Modern" Grand Lodge chose to adopt the three castles and

Masonic compasses as their coat of arms. Another Grand Lodge, the "Ancient", or "Antient" Grand Lodge as it was also called, was formed in 1751 as a challenge to the first Grand Lodge. *Its* coat of arms featured the man in the crimson robe, the golden lion, the black ox, and the golden eagle. The two Lodges were eventually united in 1813, and the coats of arms were joined, with the addition of the ark crest and the supporting cherubs. The border of golden lions was added more than a century later by the College of Arms and King George V.'

'Okay,' said Schmidt with a skeptical nod after a short silence. 'History lesson aside, what's the code, Sherlock?'

'There are three distinct symbols in the coats of arms on these doors that we need to press in a predefined order to get inside the vault,' said Jackson, bright eyes scanning the burnished surfaces. 'Help me find them.'

Carrington stared at the convoluted network of motifs before them. 'There are at least a hundred replicas of these coats of arms on here!' he blurted out.

'There are ninety-nine to be exact,' said the Harvard professor. 'Trust me,' he added in a self-assured tone, 'three of them will be different.'

Yonten found the first symbol. On a shield near the far upper corner of the right door, the robed man was without his robe. Alexa spotted an extra golden lion on the border of another shield on the top outer edge of the left door.

They searched in vain for the third symbol.

An irritated growl escaped Jackson's throat. He twisted on his heels, strode toward the stairs, and turned back to face the doors.

'Two Lodges,' he muttered to himself, glaring at the steel panels as he walked to and fro. 'The Square and the Compasses.

Four sides to the Square and the Compasses. Two…four…three —' He suddenly stopped pacing.

Alexa felt a strange shiver run through her at the expression on his face. He had the code.

The Harvard professor's eyes shifted to where she and Yonten stood in front of the shields they had each identified. His gaze dropped to the bottom of the doors. 'It's a chevron,' he whispered hoarsely. 'A V-shaped code.'

She looked at the monk with a faint frown. Yonten shrugged.

'The castle,' said Schmidt suddenly, his eyes focusing on where Jackson was staring.

The Crovir Hunter moved to touch a coat of arms near the foot of the right door. The compass on it was ever so slightly skewed and seemed to be pointing at one of three castles.

'Wait!' shouted Jackson, rushing forward. 'There's a fourth symbol!'

Schmidt's fingers froze millimeters from the polished steel. 'You said there were three,' he said accusingly.

'I was wrong.' Jackson pointed at the missing joint on the pair of compasses in a blazon at the top of the left door.

'What makes you think you're right this time?' argued the Crovir Hunter.

'I'm never wrong twice,' Jackson retorted confidently. 'Besides, the pattern needs to be symmetrical.'

Alexa felt a headache throb at her temples. She could feel the underlying current of machismo running between the two men. She resisted the urge to reach for one of her Sigs.

'So what order do we touch them in, genius?' said Schmidt challengingly.

'Give me a minute,' said Jackson in a distracted voice.

'You've already had several of those,' muttered the Crovir

Hunter. 'What?' he added defensively when Alexa shot him a cold stare.

Features locked in concentration, Jackson paid no heed to his words. A tiny gasp suddenly passed his lips, and a grin flashed across his face. 'Okay, I'm first,' he said excitedly. 'Schmidt, you're second. Alexa and Yonten, you're last.' He looked at the monk and her intently. 'The two of you have to touch the symbols at the exact same moment.'

Alexa glanced at Yonten. The monk smiled beatifically.

'You sure about this?' asked Schmidt with a scowl.

'Yes,' said Jackson. 'Now, on the count of three. One.' He pressed the missing hinge of the compasses. 'Two.'

Schmidt pushed his fingers against the castle.

'And three,' breathed Jackson.

Alexa and Yonten depressed the last two symbols.

For a second, nothing happened. Then, the four symbols flashed to green and retracted almost half a foot inside the doors. They stood back as a series of bolts audibly engaged inside the steel panels. The vault doors finally slid aside with a low, pneumatic hiss.

Spotlights sprang into life beyond the three-foot-thick threshold and bathed the interior of the chamber beyond in white brilliance. They stepped forward cautiously and stopped just inside the entrance.

The room was a perfect oval and measured roughly twenty by twenty-five feet. Dozens of manuscripts, faded scrolls, and parchments lay in display cabinets arranged in a circle around the periphery of a marble floor. Bookcases punctuated the gaps between them, while the walls themselves were occupied with glittering artifacts in secured glass frames and stands.

The air inside was cool and dry. Alexa suspected the environment had been artificially engineered to preserve the priceless contents within. She could see no passive infrared sensors on the walls; the Freemasons obviously felt the coded steel doors would be enough to deter any intruders who ever managed to make it this far.

She felt Jackson suddenly stiffen at her side. She glanced at him and saw his blue eyes widen and his face blanch. A spasm of alarm darted through her and she tensed as she followed his unmoving gaze.

On the back wall of the chamber, diametrically opposite the steel access doors, stood a tall plinth hewn out of bare rock. The thick marble had been cleverly cut around the base to preserve the original foundation of the stand. Sitting atop it was a glass case. A thick tablet made of sparkling green stone was propped on metal supports inside. Carved into its surface were complex words that glittered in the light.

'My God! The *Tabula Smaragdina*,' whispered Jackson. He crossed the floor slowly and stopped before the stand, his eyes gleaming in the reflection of the light cast off the glass case and the shimmering artifact within.

'The—what now?' asked Carrington.

'The Emerald Tablet,' the Harvard professor translated hoarsely.

Somewhere in the back of her mind, Alexa recognized his words. She raised her eyebrows slightly. 'Isn't that one of the artifacts said to be behind the *Magnus Opus*?'

Schmidt startled at her words. He stared at the tablet. 'The Philosopher's Stone,' he said in a low voice.

Carrington raised a hand. 'Sorry but, what's the *Magnus Opus*?'

'It's the alchemical terminology for the four-stage process used to create the Philosopher's Stone,' said Jackson. He glanced at Schmidt briefly before focusing on the tablet under the glass.

'This must be what the *Rose Croix* sect was after. It would explain the *Mutus Liber* connection. Both those documents were said to have been used for the *Magnus Opus*.'

'The Philosopher's Stone?' repeated Carrington.

'Yes,' said Jackson. 'The Elixir of Life.'

'That's just a myth, isn't it?' asked Carrington. No one seemed to want to answer his question.

Alexa joined Jackson. 'Can you translate it?' she said.

The Harvard professor hesitated. 'Given time and access to a specialist lab, yes, possibly,' he finally replied.

She studied the shimmering words on the green stone. The text was compact and the writing strongly resembled the Sumerian-derived scripts from the walls of scrolls in the cave in Egypt. 'We have to take it with us,' she stated firmly.

Jackson drew a breath in sharply. 'You want to *steal* the Emerald Tablet?'

Alexa shrugged. 'Do you have a better suggestion?'

'Even though I shouldn't be saying this, I would rather the tablet end up in the possession of the Crovirs than this *Rose Croix* sect,' said Schmidt. 'Immortals have a better chance of guarding it than the Freemasons.'

Jackson looked between Schmidt and her. Alexa knew she had won the battle even before he sighed and muttered, 'All right. Just be goddamned careful with it.'

Her fingers got to within an inch of the glass case before Carrington called out a warning. 'I wouldn't do that if I were you,' said the Crovir.

Alexa turned and looked at him with a frown.

'Although there are no infrared motion detectors in the room, that display case has its own security system,' said Carrington as he approached the plinth. 'The tablet is mounted on a pressure and vibration sensitive plate.' This statement earned him a battery of stares. 'I used to be a thief in a former life. Before I started working for Reznak, obviously,' he added hastily at her expression. 'I've kinda kept up with the new technology.'

She glanced at the artifact. 'How can you be certain of this?'

Carrington shrugged. 'It's the most valuable item in the place. The Freemasons are not fools.'

She shifted impatiently. 'What do you suggest we do?'

'First, we need to lift the case off,' said Carrington.

He grabbed the edges of the glass box on one side and looked at Jackson. The Harvard professor joined him and placed his hands on the opposite end. Together, they slowly lifted the case off the plinth.

No alarms broke the silence inside the chamber. They released a collective sigh of relief.

Carrington placed the box on the marble floor and studied the tablet. 'Now we need to find something of the same weight and size to stabilize the plate.'

Alexa glanced around the vault. Her gaze fell on a cabinet on the wall to the right. She strode toward it, broke the glass with her elbow, and removed the heavy clock inside. 'Will this do?' she asked, staring down their shocked expressions.

Yonten smiled from where he stood looking at the contents of a bookcase.

A sigh left Jackson's lips. 'That display case could have been alarmed, you know.'

'It wasn't,' she said dismissively.

Carrington muttered something under his breath and took the clock from her. He weighed it thoughtfully in his hands while he stared at the tablet. 'This will do,' he finally said gruffly. He turned to Jackson. 'Our timing needs to be perfect on this.'

The Harvard professor nodded and wiped his sweaty hands on his jeans. His fingers shook slightly as he reached for the tablet. He flexed them once, took a deep breath, and started again. His grip was steady when he finally touched the green stone.

'On three,' said Carrington. A bead of sweat rolled down the Crovir's face as he held the clock a millimeter from the edge of the plate.

Jackson nodded, his gaze not moving from the artifact in his hands. Alexa tensed.

'One…two…three!' said Carrington. Jackson slid the tablet off the base at the same time that Carrington shifted the clock onto it.

Everyone's breathing resumed in the stillness that followed. The Harvard professor stared wide-eyed at the precious artifact in his grasp. Alexa could see the passionate emotion it engendered reflected in his cobalt gaze. Something twisted inside her chest, startling her.

'Well, that seemed to do the trick,' said Carrington with a relieved expression. He wiped sweat from his brow. 'Now, let's get the hell out of—'

The boom of an explosion somewhere above rocked the foundations of the building. The clock shifted on the pressure plate. Carrington's eyes widened in horror.

Before he could reach out to stop it, the clock tilted forward and smashed onto the marble floor. A piercing alarm tore through the underground vault as small springs and coils cartwheeled around them.

'Oh shit,' said the Crovir.

CHAPTER TWENTY

THE STEEL DOORS RUMBLED INTO LIFE ON THE OTHER SIDE OF THE chamber. They raced for the closing exit.

Jackson stumbled several feet from the opening, the tablet held firmly in his arms. A snarl of irritation left Alexa's lips. She grabbed the artifact from his grasp and pushed him toward the doorway. He darted through with a couple of feet to spare on either side and skidded around to watch her in wide-eyed horror. She gritted her teeth.

She was not going to make it.

From the other side of the doors, Yonten threw his jō staff into the closing gap.

Alexa clasped the tablet to her chest, dropped on her side, and slid under the weapon as it bowed and shattered above her, slowing the steel panels by a mere fraction of a second. She felt the whisper of air from the closing portal on the back of her head as she slipped through the exit.

She glided to a stop in front of Jackson, sprang to her feet, and dropped the stone tablet in his hands.

'Don't let go of it,' she instructed curtly before handing him her bag.

He nodded, his expression hardening. He placed the artifact inside the backpack and slung it on his shoulders.

Red emergency lights guided their path to the stairs that led to the Grand Temple. Further explosions sounded in the distance above them. The slab of stone hiding the secret opening retracted with a ponderous groan seconds before they reached it. Schmidt went through first, Beretta in hand. Alexa drew the Sigs and followed a heartbeat behind him.

A cloud of smoke and plaster dust accompanied three Freemason sentries as they staggered through a door on the left. Tears streamed down their faces and they coughed and gasped hoarsely. More guards poured into the galleries above. Some of the men had bleeding wounds on their heads and hands. Their angry shouts punctuated the shrill alarm blasting through the building.

The Freemasons' attention remained focused on the double doors that guarded the entrance to their Grand Temple.

Alexa stared at the thick bronze panels; they had buckled under the force of a significant impact. Chunks of plaster and brick littered the polished floor inside the chamber. A second later, the doors swung open in a gray billow of smoke. A squad of twenty black-clad men fitted with gas masks, machine guns, and pistols stormed inside the room.

'Looks like you were right about that sect,' said Schmidt grimly, glancing at Alexa.

Carrington looked pointedly at Yonten. 'I thought you said everything would be all right,' he said accusingly. The monk shrugged, the cryptic smile back on his lips.

One of the guards finally noticed their presence near the ceremonial chair. He shouted a warning to his comrades.

Confusion dawned on the faces of the sentries as they stared from the small group by the gilded frame to the armed strangers marching across the floor of the temple.

The black-clad men slowed just beyond the end of the checkerboard floor and spread out around the dais. The two figures in the lead lifted their masks from their faces.

A muscle twitched in Alexa's cheek.

It was the fair-skinned man with the pale blue eyes she had killed in Istanbul. The other immortal she had shot in the head stood beside him. Jackson inhaled sharply next to her.

'Don't kill the Freemasons,' Alexa ordered, her muscles tightening in anticipation of the upcoming battle. She holstered her right Sig and slipped a sai out of its sheath.

Carrington grunted. 'That might prove to be a tad difficult,' he said, looking at the guards approaching cautiously from the periphery of the chamber.

'Try hard,' she snapped.

About a dozen armed sentries now stood inside the temple. More slipped through the bronze doors behind the sect members and the openings on either side of the organ loft.

Although the Freemasons seemed unsure as to whom their enemy was, Alexa sensed they would not hesitate to engage them for much longer. She knew they would be willing to fight to the death to protect the relics held within their sacred grounds. She would have to be careful not to inflict any fatal blows.

'The authorities have already been alerted!' shouted a bulky Freemason with red hair. His gaze shifted from the silent sect members to Alexa and the four men. 'Put your weapons on the floor and get down on your knees!' The barrel of his gun swung between the two groups.

'No can do,' said Schmidt with an unhappy shake of his

head. Remorse clouded his face as he stared at his fellow Freemasons.

Alexa moved at the same time that Yonten opened his lips to shout out a warning. She raised the Sig and fired at the blue-eyed immortal just as he turned to shoot the red haired guard. His bullet thudded into the Freemason's arm. The wounded man swore and clutched at his limb, the gun clattering out of his hand.

The immortal staggered back a step before staring at the hole over his heart. He looked up slowly, his eyes gleaming with savage zeal. His lips curled back in a grin.

'Flak jackets?' muttered Schmidt.

'Looks like it,' said Carrington grimly. 'Inconsiderate bastards.'

Gunfire erupted inside the temple as the Freemasons started to shoot at the *Rose Croix* sect. Half of the black-clad men returned fire; the others charged up the steps toward the ceremonial chair.

Alexa ducked below the fist aimed at her head, punched the snarling blue-eyed immortal in the flank, and twisted to deliver a back-kick to his companion. She felt a rib snap under the heel of her boot and smiled ferociously.

She blocked a strike to her side, trapped the barrel of the blue-eyed immortal's gun with the prongs of the sai, and pushed the weapon down. He pulled the trigger reflexively. The bullet whistled past her hip and struck the second immortal in the thigh.

A growl of rage left the blue-eyed man's throat. It turned into a gurgle when she raised the Sig and shot him in the neck. He brought his hands to his throat, panic flashing in his eyes as blood spurted past his fingers. Alexa kicked him in the chest and sent him stumbling into a pair of sect members.

Heat streaked across her left shoulder as a bullet scorched a gash in her flesh. Scowling, she dropped to avoid a second shot from the other immortal and brought him down with a scissor kick. Her elbow slammed into his groin and she back-fisted him in the face. Satisfaction coursed through her when his nose broke under her blow.

A Freemason appeared on her right. She jumped to her feet, slipped out of the way of his punch, and head-butted him in the chin. He crumpled to the ground, unconscious. She deflected blows from three more sect members and looked around.

Schmidt and Carrington were fighting their way toward the exit on the left. About twenty feet to her right and a shorter distance still from another door, Jackson weaved and bobbed to avoid strikes to his head and body. Encumbered by the bag on his back and the precious tablet he was trying to protect, he could not avoid all the blows; blood already smeared his lips and left eyebrow, where his skin had split. His counter-punches landed on the Freemason guards around him with deadly accuracy.

Yonten stood close to Jackson and glided through a combination of martial art moves while he tackled four sect members, evading their fists, kicks, and shots with practiced ease.

Alarm flashed through Alexa when she saw a fresh wave of Freemasons charge toward the two men from the main chamber floor.

She leaned out of the way of the barrel of a submachine gun and took out the sect members in her path with a reverse roundhouse kick, before grabbing the three-sectional bō staff from inside her jacket. Shouting the monk's name, she threw the weapon toward him.

Yonten kicked up against a guard's chest, jumped, and

caught the staff smoothly in midair. He had it open and delivered two swift strikes before his feet touched the ground.

Alexa looked to the left. Schmidt and Carrington had made it through the exit. She flicked the sai in her grip and darted across the floor, the blade moving in a series of fluid blocks and thrusts that rapidly incapacitated the guards in her way. The Sig sang in her other hand as she fired at the *Rose Croix* sect.

She reached Jackson and the monk in seconds and shouted 'Let's go!' sharply as she raced past them toward the other door.

They darted through a curtained vestibule and entered a smoke-wreathed hallway outside the Grand Temple. Yonten and Jackson turned and closed the doors on the guards behind them. Alexa broke the leg of a nearby console table with a kick, grabbed the makeshift bolt, and jammed it inside the handles. Angry shouts erupted from inside the temple as the Freemasons surged against the blocked exit. The bar held.

A metallic noise suddenly reached her ears. Alexa whipped her head around. A line of armed Freemasons appeared through the clearing smoke on the right. She frowned when she saw the automatic weapons in their hands. One of men had just clicked the safety catch off his submachine gun.

Footsteps rose from the opposite end of the hallway. A group of men in assault vests rushed down the passage and stopped abruptly about twenty feet away.

Alexa recognized the uniforms of the London Metropolitan Police specialist firearms unit. Above the alarm that still clamored through the Freemasons' Hall, she discerned the sirens of squad cars outside the building.

The first line of Met officers dropped to their knees and raised the MP5 submachine guns in their hands. Their team leader barked 'Stop!' before leveling his Glock 17 at Alexa and the two men.

Shadows suddenly shifted at the end of the hallway on the right. A second squad of *Rose Croix* sect members had materialized behind the Freemasons. The Met officer shouted a warning. The Freemason sentries looked over their shoulders.

Alexa sheathed the sai and slipped the second Sig from her body holster.

'Stay back,' she ordered, glancing at Jackson and the monk over her shoulder. Yonten bowed, grabbed a startled Jackson by the bag on his back, and yanked him inside the shelter of a shallow alcove next to the doors.

Adrenaline buzzed through her as she raised the Sigs toward each end of the hallway. The excitement of the fight brought a savage, fearless smile to her lips. She saw the Met officer's eyes widen. Still grinning, Alexa squeezed the triggers of both guns and ran at the wall in front of her.

Bullets whined through the air as both groups of men fired.

She pushed up against a marble pillar, used the momentum of her leap to climb toward the ceiling, kicked off the edge of a sculptured coving, and spun head down in the air toward the middle of the hall, the Sigs still singing in her grip.

Her shots riddled the fixtures of two chandeliers. She flipped backwards and landed smoothly on her feet just as the towers of sparkling prisms crashed onto the marble floor, causing the Met officers and the Freemasons to jump back to avoid the deadly debris.

'This way!' she shouted. She reloaded the guns and darted straight for the scattered line of Freemasons, Jackson and Yonten on her heels.

Yells erupted behind them as the Met officers started to give chase. Several of the Freemasons raised their weapons.

Alexa jumped into a flying roundhouse kick as they charged through the fractured group. Four sentries fell to the ground.

Yonten dropped in a low sweep that took out another three. He whirled the bō staff in a circle of strikes as he rose. Machine guns clattered to the floor around them.

They were past the Freemasons a heartbeat later.

Alexa raised both Sigs and fired at the *Rose Croix* sect a second before they pulled the triggers on their automatic guns. She was careful to aim anywhere but at their chests.

A blur flashed by her as Yonten twirled the bō in figure-of-eight spins, the staff connecting with flesh and metal with his every strike and block.

One of the black-clad men suddenly snatched at the bag on Jackson's back. The Harvard professor wheeled around, swung an uppercut at his jaw, kneed him in the stomach, and carried on running.

Shots pelted the tiles at Alexa's heels as they raced down the rubble-strewn passage toward the rear of the building. A bullet slashed a tear in the fabric over her right hip. She twisted, dropped to one knee, and skidded backward across the floor while she fired a barrage of warning shots at the pursuing Met officers. She rose and sprinted after Jackson and the monk.

They reached a junction and turned left. A door at the end opened into a large room. Alexa caught a glimpse of bookcases and display cabinets as they charged across a polished parquet floor.

'Oh shit, not the Museum!' cried Jackson, his eyes widening in alarm. He raised his arms and covered his head when the glass cases next to him shattered under a storm of bullets. Lethal fragments of glassware and porcelain streaked through the air. A stray shard slashed across the back of Alexa's hand.

She reloaded the Sigs, jumped on a low cabinet, dropped on her back into a spinning slide across the smooth surface, and fired at the Freemasons in the galleries above them. She leapt off the edge of the glass table and raced for the exit through which Jackson and the monk had just disappeared.

They came to a bolted door. The two men stood back while Alexa shot at the padlock. She yanked the shattered metal aside and kicked open the exit. They emerged onto a road at the side of the building.

Snow fell thick and fast from the overcast sky. The lights from a cluster of squad cars and tactical intervention vehicles flashed across the street thirty feet or so from their position. A shout erupted from one of the policemen gathered in front of the Freemasons' Hall. Alexa saw him lower the radio in his hand and point in their direction.

A bullet zinged through the doorway behind them and punched a hole in the bag on Jackson's back.

'Let's go!' snapped Alexa. She turned and took off down the street, the two men close on her heels.

Clusters of curious bystanders from neighboring bars and restaurants dotted the pavements around the Freemason building. A scream rose above the blast of the alarm still rending through the Hall and the blaring sirens of the police vehicles. Someone had spotted the guns in her hands. The crowd scattered.

The roar of an engine firing up rose behind them. Alexa glanced over her shoulder and saw the tires on one of the squad cars spin on the icy asphalt as it started to give chase. Yonten skidded to a stop in the middle of the road and turned to face the oncoming vehicle.

'You go. I'll stay,' he said over his shoulder. His teeth gleamed in the night as he flashed a smile at her.

Jackson stumbled to a halt. 'No!' he said vehemently. 'We're not leaving you!'

Alexa stared into the monk's limpid eyes with the faintest of misgivings. She nodded once, grabbed Jackson's arm, and forcibly pulled him after her.

'Wait!' he yelled, struggling in her grip.

'He'll be fine,' she said firmly.

Jackson's jaw clenched. He stopped fighting her, swallowed another protest, and followed in her footsteps as she started to run.

Alexa looked back when they approached the corner of the street. She saw the monk face down the approaching police car, an impish grin on his lips. He looked like he was having fun.

The snow and sleet sweeping across the city helped them disappear in the crowd. It was several minutes before Alexa felt confident that they had lost all traces of their pursuers.

An hour after their escape from the Freemasons' Hall, they stopped in front of an exclusive apartment block overlooking the Thames. Though the winter storm had abated slightly, an icy wind still blew off the waters and caused their breath to mist in the night air.

'Where are we?' asked Jackson. He looked around curiously while she typed a code in the security keypad outside the glass doors; his lips had taken on a slightly purplish hue, and shivers racked his body.

It was the first time he had spoken to her since they left Yonten. Alexa sensed he was still upset at having abandoned the monk. 'It's a Crovir safe house,' she said quietly.

The doors slid open and they entered the building. Jackson followed her across a wide lobby to a bank of elevators. A blast of warm air washed over them when they entered the lift. He shuddered, a low groan escaping his throat. She entered a second code into the interior control panel and pressed her hand against a biometric sensor.

'How many of these safe houses do you guys have?' He stared at the changing numbers in the electronic display next to her.

'Six in London,' she replied.

The lift stopped at the penthouse level of the building. The doors opened soundlessly to reveal a cavernous, dark space. The lights of the city cast a dim glow through the glass wall on the other side of an expansive floor.

Alexa stepped out onto the heated marble tiles and said, 'Lights on' in a loud, clear voice.

Jackson blinked when brightness flared into life around them. He walked out of the elevator and came to an abrupt halt. The metal doors closed behind him with a soft ping.

Given the external appearance of the building, she suspected he had been expecting a sleek and modern décor. Alexa could tell he was pleasantly shocked by the rich colors and elegant lines of the priceless antique furnishings that adorned the luxurious suite.

Jackson crossed the foyer and stepped down into the sitting room. He ignored the exquisite set of period French furniture and the magnificent pianoforte that stood on its own dais as he strolled toward the glass wall that made up the southern aspect of the penthouse. He stopped and gazed at the stunning view of London for timeless seconds before turning to inspect the open-plan apartment with a measured stare. 'You people really don't spare any expenses, do you?' he commented drily.

Alexa allowed a small smile to cross her lips.

The upscale apartment building was owned by a Crovir noble with close ties to the First Council. The penthouse itself was exclusively reserved for use by the Council members and their guests. She had a certain fondness for the place. It reminded her of her own apartment in Manhattan.

She headed into the state-of-the-art kitchen on the left and opened the door of the larder fridge. It was stocked daily by a concierge and contained fresh food and drinks. She reached past a bottle of champagne, took out a can of beer, and threw it to Jackson as he walked toward her. He caught the drink with a grateful expression, snapped the metal ring open, tilted his head back, and drank straight from the can.

A slow heat spread through Alexa's body as she watched the muscles in his throat work. Jackson caught her stare.

'What? Have I got some on my chin?' he asked, wiping his jaw with the back of his hand.

She shook her head and twisted on her heels, a faint frown marring her brow. She would have to analyze the unwelcome sensation coiling inside her chest later. She took a pizza out of the fridge, popped it in the microwave, and took a pair of plates out of the cupboard.

They ate standing at the counter while they inspected the precious artifact they had stolen from the Freemasons' Hall.

'We should take this to a lab with the appropriate facilities,' said Jackson. 'I can't examine it here—some of the text is too small for me to make out.' He had been reluctant to handle the tablet and had insisted they keep it carefully wrapped. The bullet had penetrated the backpack an inch from the edge of the stone.

Alexa looked up and studied the lines on his face. It had been a busy few days. She doubted the Harvard professor had ever been in as many life-and-death chases and combat situations as he had experienced in the last forty-eight hours. She was surprised he wasn't more shell-shocked.

'Reznak has a facility in Europe,' she said. 'I'll talk to him again in the morning.'

She had called her godfather on the way to the penthouse. Schmidt and Carrington had made it out of the Freemasons' Hall unscathed. Though the police radio messages the Crovirs had intercepted reported injuries sustained by the Freemasons at the site, there were no fatalities among the wounded. There had, however, been several casualties among a group of unidentified men wearing body armor. No arrests had been made, which indicated that the remaining members of the *Rose Croix* sect had gotten away.

There had been no word from the monk.

Jackson looked at her hesitantly. 'We're staying the night?' he asked, glancing around the silent apartment.

'You need some rest,' she said bluntly.

The penthouse had six bedrooms, each with its own bathroom and walk-in closet. Alexa showed Jackson to one of the suites and took the one opposite his.

She shrugged her jacket off and dropped it on the beautifully carved Baroque bed that dominated the room. She cleaned and dressed the wound on her shoulder before strolling across the marble floor to the glass wall that formed the south aspect of the suite. French doors looked out onto the wooden deck that wrapped around the penthouse.

She stood motionless and stared at the dazzling lights of the capital while she tried to dissect the unwarranted emotions that had plagued her in the last week.

The only other time she had ever worked as part of a team was the brief period she had spent in the Order of the Hunters with Frank Schmidt many years ago. Even then, she had never felt anxiety over her fellow Hunters' wellbeing like she had with Jackson in the few days that she had known him. From his fight with Boyko Dragov in Port Said to their more recent encounter with the *Rose Croix* sect members on the rooftop of the church in Istanbul, she had found her breath catching in her throat whenever he was exposed to danger. Even more irritating was the growing intensity of her reactions to the man. What was it about him that triggered such extreme responses from her? Even Reznak, who had been part of her life for centuries, had never engendered so many forceful feelings in her in such a short period of time.

She was still looking out over the city minutes later when a knock came at the door. She watched it open in the reflection cast by the mirror-like glass.

Jackson entered the room and stopped by the console table next to the door. 'I thought you might want this back,' he said, holding her bag in one hand.

Realization suddenly hit her with the force of an earthquake. She stopped breathing.

Jackson stiffened. 'Alexa?'

Her heart thudded rapidly inside her chest as awareness bloomed across her consciousness. She wanted this man. She wanted him like she had never wanted another being, immortal or human, in the three hundred and ten years of her known existence. The long-denied hunger that had been building up inside her for the last week flooded her senses and washed away the last fragments of her irritation.

Jackson took a step toward her. 'Hey, are you okay?' he asked in a low voice that danced down her back.

Alexa turned around slowly and stared at him. This time, she made no attempt to mask the expression on her face. He froze.

She carefully undid her body holster and let it fall to the floor. His gaze never left hers as the guns and sai daggers clattered noisily on the marble tiles. Heat flashed through his darkening eyes, and a faint flush tainted his cheekbones. His breathing accelerated slightly and his pupils dilated.

Alexa walked toward him, her steps slow and steady. She took her bag from his unresisting hand and dropped it on the console table. Her eyes shifted to his mouth. His lower lip was still swollen from the blows he had suffered during their earlier fight. She raised her hand and touched the wound lightly.

A soft groan left his throat and warmed her fingertips. Her skin tingled and desire pooled inside her. His gaze dropped to her mouth.

The hunger thrumming inside her rose to fever pitch. Her hand snaked to the back of his head and she tugged his face to hers. She stopped when their lips were an inch apart, savoring the feeling of his breath mingling with hers. He grasped her shoulders and closed the distance between them with another groan.

His mouth, when it made contact, was shockingly gentle.

Alexa stared into his eyes as he brushed his lips across hers, slowly learning their contours. His cobalt-blue gaze shifted to dark indigo a heartbeat before his kiss turned hot and fervent. His tongue invaded her mouth with a passion that sent a sudden shiver down her spine. Her eyelids fluttered closed.

For the first time in her immortal life, she felt her legs go weak. The alien sensation was like a cold slap that brought her back to her senses. Her eyes snapped open and she broke free from his embrace, her chest heaving with the effort to control her ragged breathing.

Confusion clouded Jackson's eyes. 'Alexa?'

The sound of her name on his lips made her blood sing with yearning. It was all it took to break the iron control she was attempting to regain over her unruly emotions. She felt the impenetrable barriers that guarded her inner core come crashing down under a deluge of torrid lust.

She slammed the door shut and pushed him down on the bed. Jackson gasped when he landed heavily on the mattress. She kicked off her boots, shrugged her shirt over her head, and slipped out of her cargo pants. He rose on his elbows, his heated gaze skimming her nearly naked body.

Alexa climbed on the bed, straddled him, and started to unbutton his shirt. Halfway down, she snarled in impatience and ripped the material from his chest.

A throaty chuckle escaped Jackson's lips. 'Are we about to indulge in some kinda kinky immortal sex?'

The laughter rumbling through his chest caused his body to vibrate between her thighs and sent a quiver of anticipation racing across her skin. Alexa leaned down and kissed him hard. His fingers skimmed down the sides of her breasts and waist before gripping her hips with an urgency that betrayed his desire. He pulled her down until their bodies melded together.

They came up for air timeless seconds later. 'Oh boy,' breathed Jackson, his eyes glazed. He suddenly flipped her on her back.

A gasp left her lips when the weight of his body pressed her into the mattress. She fought down her instinct to push him off and allowed herself to savor the heavy heat of his limbs entwined with hers. His knee slipped between her legs and his fingers closed around her hip. She shivered beneath his touch. Her hand glided across the hard muscles of his abdomen before pausing on the zipper of his jeans. She felt the shudder that coursed through his body as she slowly pulled the metal down.

'Have mercy,' said Jackson with a slow, sinful smile.

❄

PART III
KILL

CHAPTER TWENTY-ONE

CONSCIOUSNESS RETURNED LANGUIDLY. ALEXA BECAME AWARE OF bright sunlight penetrating through the thin skin of her eyelids and warming the skin on her back. She stretched her pleasantly sated body and sighed.

Her eyes snapped open a second later. She twisted, clutched the cotton sheet to her naked chest, grabbed one of her Sigs from the floor next to the bed, and whipped the weapon around smoothly as she sat up.

Reznak stared impassively into the barrel of the gun from where he sat in the armchair across the room.

Alexa clenched her jaw and scanned the suite. Schmidt was leaning against the French doors that led to the terrace and gazing at the views of the city across the river. Yonten sat in a meditative pose on the deck outside the glass wall. The monk opened his eyes and winked at her. Schmidt looked over his shoulder stiffly.

There was a noise from the direction of the bathroom. Jackson strolled through, a towel perched precariously on his hips while he briskly rubbed his wet hair with another one. It took him a couple of seconds to note the presence of the other men in the room. He froze.

Schmidt's expression darkened.

A knock sounded on the door. Fawkes walked in with a tray of fresh coffee and Jackson's duffel bag. He placed the drinks on the console table, handed the bag to Jackson, smiled warmly at Alexa, and left.

Jackson sighed. 'Seriously, I wish you guys would call or something.'

Her stare focused on him. She noted his swollen lips and the marks her teeth and nails had left on his body. Heat ignited in her gut. She'd thought her desire for the man would abate after sleeping with him. She was wrong.

Jackson's eyes shifted to the color of a storm-swept sea as he stared back. It reminded her of the way he looked above her last night—all feverish and hot and wanting. They had barely slept, their need for each other too strong to deny.

Reznak sighed at the overt sexual tension coursing through the air. 'We need to talk,' said her godfather bluntly.

Alexa scowled. 'I want everyone out. Now,' she ordered icily, holding the sheet to her breasts.

Jackson straightened when her gaze fell on him. 'What, you mean me too?' he said incredulously. 'Don't tell me you're feeling shy, not after everything we did last night?' he added.

Reznak rose from the chair and headed stiffly for the door. Schmidt turned and followed her godfather, his stance rigid.

'I mean, there was some stuff I can honestly say I've never done before,' Jackson continued drily.

Schmidt grimaced and slammed the door behind him.

Alexa could not help but feel that Jackson had deliberately been taunting the immortal.

'It was the best night of my life,' continued the Harvard professor. 'My hips are still sore—'

A sai thudded into the wall next to him. The smile never left Jackson's face. He strolled toward the door at a leisurely pace and opened it. He walked out, stopped, and peeked his head around the corner. 'By the way, would it be terribly wrong to say that you look very sexy this morning and that I want to crawl into that bed with you again?'

His laughter sent a quiver along her spine. The second sai hit the wood inches from his face. He grinned and left the room, his bag in hand.

Alexa glanced at the deck. The monk had disappeared. Despite her best attempts to suppress it, she could not stop the smile that crossed her lips. She dropped the sheet, climbed off the bed, and strode into the bathroom. As the hot water pelted her skin, she summoned all her willpower to suppress the sensual images of the hour she and Jackson had spent in the luxurious shower the night before.

Fifteen minutes later, she stepped out into the open-plan living area, her guns and blades securely ensconced in the custom-made holster under her jacket. She looked around.

Reznak was sitting in one of the French chairs and staring at the priceless artifact on the coffee table before him. Carrington stood leaning against the backrest behind him. Yonten perched cross-legged on the pianoforte, while Schmidt lounged against a marble pillar to the right. Reznak's bodyguards stood silently on either side of the lift.

' 'morning,' said Carrington, a knowing grin dawning on his face and stretching the silver scar on his cheek. Alexa shot him a warning look. 'Here. It was still in the SUV outside the Hall.' He put the hardback case that held her field computer on the table.

'Thanks,' she murmured grudgingly.

Dressed in a fresh pair of jeans and a clean shirt, Jackson stood downing a cup of coffee at the kitchen counter. His eyes glided appreciatively down her body for a second.

Alexa felt heat flare across her skin where his gaze had landed. She turned to Schmidt. 'When did he turn up?' She indicated Yonten with a head tilt.

'He was on the terrace outside when we got here,' replied Schmidt coolly.

She ignored the Crovir Hunter's hostile tone and raised her eyebrows at the monk. Yonten smiled beatifically. 'Karmic signal,' he said in a sedate voice.

'The *Emerald Tablet*,' Reznak murmured. 'In all the centuries since I first heard of it, I honestly thought it was just a myth.'

'So did I,' said Jackson. He crossed the marble floor and took the seat opposite Reznak. 'I have to admit, it wasn't exactly what I was expecting to find when we broke into the Freemasons' Hall.' He grimaced. 'I'm just annoyed that we never got round to examining their archives. They might have held more information on the *Rose Croix* sect.'

A grin flashed across Yonten's face. He reached inside his robe, took out a slim tome, and lobed it across the room to Jackson. The Harvard professor caught it deftly. 'What is it?' he asked curiously, skimming through the faded pages. His fingers froze on the book. His chin came up sharply and he stared at the monk. 'Is this from the Freemasons' vault?'

Yonten nodded. 'Parts of the book are encoded. You must decipher it,' said the monk.

Jackson looked down at the tome in wide-eyed wonderment.

'I have other news,' said Reznak, his expression darkening. 'From the initial investigation by the Corps of Gendarmerie of

Vatican City, it appears that there was a hidden microphone and tracking device in Francesco's ring. The *Rose Croix* sect must have heard our conversation two nights ago. They obviously didn't want him to talk. This can only lead me to conclude that Cavaleti has spies in the Holy See.'

Alexa silently digested this information. Lorenzio's assassination had to have been a last-minute decision on the part of the sect. The measures the archbishop had taken to arrange their meeting had evidently given him enough time to divulge most of the information he had wanted to disclose.

'I spoke to Abbot Kelsang again this morning and asked him to send me a sketch of the artifact that was stolen from their monastery three hundred years ago,' said Reznak.

Carrington brought out a slim laptop from behind the chair and flipped it open on the coffee table. Reznak turned the computer around so she and Jackson could see the screen. 'What do you think?' he asked, gazing steadily at the Harvard professor.

An image occupied the display. It showed a beautiful, thick, intricately designed, gold sun cross pendant.

Jackson leaned forward and examined the picture closely. 'Interesting,' he murmured. 'But I'm afraid it would be impossible to come to any definitive conclusions about this object from a simple drawing.'

A shrewd light appeared in Reznak's eyes.

Alexa watched her godfather guardedly.

'Would it be helpful if you could see an identical item in person?' he said.

Jackson's eyebrows rose. 'Yes.'

'Good. I know someone who possesses a pendant almost indistinguishable from the one in that sketch,' said Reznak. 'We're meeting her in Paris in a few hours.'

THEY LEFT THE PENTHOUSE AND WERE IN THE AIR WITHIN NINETY minutes. Shortly before midday, the Gulfstream jet landed on an abandoned airstrip several miles outside the French capital. The sky was a crisp, clear blue, and the air had an icy chill that promised frost for the night.

Alexa glanced curiously at Reznak while they waited by the steps of the aircraft. Her godfather had remained resolutely tight-lipped since they left London. Apart from admitting that the woman they would be meeting was an immortal, he had not said another word on the matter.

Although she sensed his disapproval of her relationship with Jackson, Alexa felt there was more to his silence than petty punishment for her actions.

It was another hour before they heard the distant roar of a vehicle approaching from the east. Seconds later, a black Jaguar XK120 roadster appeared from under a line of trees and raced toward them.

The vehicle rolled to a smoothly controlled stop thirty feet from the jet. As Alexa admired the lines of the immaculate vintage car, the doors opened, and a couple stepped out.

The woman wore a thick coat with the collar turned up against the blustery wind blowing across the airfield. Knee-high boots covered her legs and ended just beneath the hem of a woolen dress that hung perfectly on her slender frame. Her chestnut colored hair tumbled in soft curls around her face and past her shoulders. As she walked toward them, her alluring, olive-green eyes studied them neutrally from beneath thick eyelashes.

A genuine smile parted her lips when she spotted Reznak.

That simple act transformed her face from beautiful to stunning.

Alexa's gaze switched to the man who strolled at her side. She stiffened. Although the woman was unknown to her, she recognized her companion. Schmidt, Carrington, and Reznak's bodyguards tensed behind her godfather. The Crovirs undoubtedly knew the identity of the male figure heading their way.

He was as tall as Jackson and had short, black hair that curled slightly at the collar of his bomber jacket. Black jeans encased his long legs, the ends tucked inside a pair of practical boots. His blue eyes were a shade darker than Jackson's. His body was lean and his face as striking as the woman beside him.

'Lucas Soul,' murmured Schmidt warily.

Reznak frowned at the Crovir Hunter. 'He's a friend.'

The woman with the green eyes ignored the exchange as she stopped in front of Reznak. 'Dimitri. It's good to see you again,' she said in a soft voice underscored by a thin veneer of steel. She rose on her toes and kissed him on the cheek.

'Anna,' Reznak acknowledged with a warm smile. He nodded cordially at the man. 'Lucas.'

Lucas Soul, once the most hunted man in the history of the two immortal societies, inclined his head briefly and murmured, 'Dimitri' in a steady voice.

'I'm sorry to trouble you,' said Reznak, a contrite grimace flashing across his face. 'And in the days before your wedding as well.'

Alexa glanced at the simple yet exquisitely detailed engagement ring on the woman's left hand.

'Will you be able to make it?' asked the woman called Anna. 'It was a pretty impromptu decision,' she admitted with a sheepish smile. 'Pierre and Solange only arrived two days ago. It'll be a small ceremony.'

'I would love to be there, but I'm afraid the matter at hand requires all my attention,' said Reznak. His eyes brightened slightly. 'Will Victor be in attendance?'

'He's walking me down the aisle,' said Anna, golden speckles dancing in her eyes.

Sadness flooded Reznak's face, much to Alexa's surprise. 'I'm glad. Tomas would have wanted it so,' said her godfather quietly.

Anna smiled and nodded, her green eyes glittering with a sudden, wet sheen.

'I take it Reid's going to be best man?' asked Reznak, turning an enquiring stare at the quiet, blue-eyed man.

A wry grin flashed across Lucas Soul's face and softened his features. 'He threatened to shoot me if I didn't ask him,' he said.

Reznak laughed out loud.

Alexa was startled at how relaxed he seemed in the presence of the two immortals. Her godfather was only ever this carefree in the company of people he trusted unconditionally. There was a hidden history between the three that she did not know of.

'I really wish I could come, truly,' said Reznak. His expression grew sober. 'Unfortunately, there are schemes afoot that may have far-reaching implications for the immortal societies.'

He introduced the couple to the group. Alexa noted how he carefully abstained from revealing her identity as his goddaughter. A frown dawned on her face when he started updating the two immortals with the unsettling events of the last week.

Soul's eyes grew still and Anna listened intently while

Reznak spoke. From what Alexa gleaned of their discussion, the pair already knew of the caves in Egypt and the extraordinary contents Reznak had discovered within.

Jackson watched silently, his curious stare shifting from Schmidt's increasingly strained face and Carrington's cautious countenance to the couple's contrastingly composed demeanors. Though the Harvard professor seemed aware of the tension coursing through the two Crovirs, he remained quiet.

Yonten stood frozen at Alexa's side. The strangest expression unfolded across his features as he stared at the two immortals. It took her a couple of seconds to grasp the emotions on the monk's face: it displayed deep-seated reverence mixed with awe.

Schmidt finally spoke, interrupting Reznak. 'Should you really be telling them all of this?' he asked harshly. 'Some of this information is privy only to the highest members of our Councils.'

Reznak turned and looked at the Crovir Hunter with cold eyes. 'Anna Godard is the granddaughter of Tomas Godard, the previous Head of the Bastian Hunters and the leader of the Bastian race. She is one of the highest-born immortal nobles in existence today,' he said. He glanced at Soul. 'Though they have yet to accept the offer, both Anna and Lucas have been invited to be members of the Crovir and Bastian Councils. As far as I'm concerned, they have the same security clearance as any individual in our First Council.'

Schmidt looked dumbfounded at Reznak's words. He stared at the immortal couple with newfound, albeit begrudged respect in his eyes.

Alexa was similarly surprised at her godfather's revelations. She could not suppress the scowl that flashed across her face; the number of secrets Reznak had kept from her seemed to be escalating with the passage of each new day. She sensed a steady stare on her face.

Lucas Soul was appraising her with a carefully blank expression. Although he stood completely motionless with his arms relaxed by his sides, the quiet, understated power in his gaze ruffled her raw nerves.

In all the centuries that she had served as an agent of the Crovir First Council, Alexa had never been ordered to hunt and kill Soul. She had always suspected Reznak of having had a hand in bringing about that strange state of affairs, quite likely because of the fearsome reputation of the man who stood watching her silently.

Soul was the only immortal in the extensive history of the two races who could truly kill another immortal, with a single strike at that. It mattered not if it was their first or fifteenth death. If the weapon that he wielded had a direct physical connection between his body and their heart, he would shatter their entire existence in one fell swoop.

Anna Godard glanced at Soul before looking at Alexa. Although the same understated power emanated from her green eyes, they also contained a wealth of compassion and empathy that overshadowed her undeniable strength.

Alexa blinked. The woman had just given her a gentle, knowing smile.

'Be still, warrior,' said a quiet voice at her side. Alexa looked at Yonten. The monk's eyes did not shift from the couple. 'They are not your enemies.'

Though his words dampened the hunter's thrill humming through her veins, Alexa could not help but discern another meaning behind them. Was the monk suggesting that she would not be the winner in a battle with *either* of the two immortals?

Her gaze flickered back to the blue-eyed man. For the first

time since he'd stepped out of the car, she detected an emotion she had not picked up on before in his expression.

Lucas Soul was at peace with himself and the world around him.

The stab of envy that flashed through her consciousness shocked her to the core. Her jaw clenched instinctively and her body reflexively tightened for battle.

Jackson took a step toward her, anxiety evident in his eyes. Reznak looked at her stiffly.

Alexa ground her teeth together and inhaled shallowly. A heartbeat later, she answered the unspoken question in her godfather's stare with a brief nod. She had her emotions under control once more.

Relief replaced the concern in Reznak's eyes. He took the laptop from Carrington and typed briefly on the keyboard. A moment later, the image of the sun cross pendant appeared on the monitor.

Anna Godard grew pale as she stared at the display. Her hand fluttered to her neck. Something glittered under her fingertips in the harsh sunlight. She pulled the collar of her coat aside and brought out a thick, intricately designed sun cross pendant suspended on a fine chain. It was the mirror image of the one on the screen.

Jackson gasped and strode forward. 'May I?' he breathed, stopping in front of Anna. His eyes never left the gold pendant at the base of her throat.

She hesitated for a brief moment before unclasping the necklace and dropping it in his hand.

They all watched silently while the Harvard professor examined the sparkling relic in his palm. Alexa heard his breath catch in his throat.

'Do you know how old this is?' he asked, his eyes focused on the complex motif engraved in the gold.

Alexa was probably the only one who detected the slight tremor in his voice. She stared at the pendant, a flash of intuition darting through her mind.

Anna shook her head, her dark locks swinging around her face. 'I'm not certain, but I suspect probably fifteen centuries or so,' she said hesitantly. 'It belonged to my father. I believe it has been passed down through the generations in his family.'

Reznak gazed at Jackson with a guarded expression. 'What is it?'

The Harvard professor looked at him blindly. 'This pendant is at least 4,000 years old,' he said hoarsely.

The shock that coursed through the group was almost palpable.

'Are you sure?' gasped Anna.

Jackson nodded. 'There are symbols on here that stem from the original Sumerian language,' he said in a stronger, more confident voice. 'Although it would be impossible to prove without physically seeing it, I suspect the pendant stolen from Yonten's monastery is also from that period of history. But I don't think the two artifacts are identical,' he added, cocking his head at the image on the computer monitor. 'There are subtle differences, even from examining the picture.' He stared thoughtfully at the relic in his hand. 'I would have to analyze this in an archaeological lab to be certain.'

Reznak's gaze shifted briefly to Anna Godard. 'I don't think that would be possible—' he started to say.

'Wait, Dimitri,' said Anna quietly. She turned and looked questioningly at Soul.

The immortal feared by so many others stepped forward

and entwined his fingers with hers. 'I'm happy with whatever you decide,' he murmured.

'It's as much your legacy as it is mine,' said Anna softly.

Soul smiled at the woman in front of him, making Alexa realize once more how staggeringly attractive he was. 'Will the pendant help you find and stop this sect?' he asked bluntly, his gaze switching to the Harvard professor.

'Yes, I believe so,' Jackson replied with a firm nod.

'Then I agree with Anna's decision,' said Soul. 'We will leave the pendant in your care.'

'Are you sure?' said Reznak incredulously, staring at the two immortals. 'That pendant is a priceless family heirloom.'

Soul shrugged. 'Whatever is going on here sounds pretty serious. All we ask is that you keep it safe.' His eyes met Alexa's for a fraction of a second, and she knew beyond a doubt that his request had been directed at her.

The couple dismissed Reznak's profusely expressed gratitude with quiet smiles and bade their goodbyes. Soul paused by the door of the vintage car. 'Dimitri?' he called out.

'Yes?' said Reznak.

'Give us a call if you need a hand,' said Soul. He dipped his head at Alexa and Jackson, and flashed a brief grin at Yonten. 'Say hello to the Abbot for me.'

The monk bowed solemnly as the immortal climbed inside the roadster. A second later, the Jaguar spun round and bolted down the tarmac.

'He's as crazy behind the wheel as you are,' said Jackson.

Alexa stared until the vehicle disappeared in the shadows beneath the trees. It was dawning on her that she had more in common with Lucas Soul than she would care to admit.

❄

CHAPTER TWENTY-TWO

THEY WERE AIRBORNE MINUTES LATER, HEADED EAST INTO Europe. Schmidt stayed back in Paris at the request of the Order of the Hunters; he had been assigned another mission by the First Council.

Carrington kept Fawkes company in the cockpit for most of the flight. Reznak and Jackson sat at one of the tables and engaged in an animated discussion about the pendant and the Emerald Tablet.

Alexa stared at the sea of clouds drifting outside the aircraft through the porthole next to her seat. Her fingers absentmindedly drummed a beat on the arm support as she puzzled over the flash of jealousy that had shot through her in Soul's presence.

She had always thought herself reasonably content with her existence over the last three hundred years. Her missions for the First Council fulfilled some of her hunger for the excitement that came with a hunt, and she engaged in enough adrenaline-filled outdoor and competitive combat sports on the side to temper her craving for danger. She was also wealthy enough to live in luxury for another ten mortal lifetimes and never lacked for willing partners to satisfy her physical needs.

Yet she had never realized there was something missing from her life until she saw the expression in Soul's eyes.

Alexa had not detected any bitterness or animosity in his gaze, feelings that should righteously be his after the centuries of torment he had suffered at the hands of the two immortal societies. She was only dimly aware of his history, but ever since she started to walk the halls of the Councils, she had heard of his deaths at the hands of the Hunters. The savage excitement that coursed through the higher echelons of Crovir society at having bested the dangerous immortal was evident for days after the deed.

She knew of the concept of immortal soulmates. Very much like human soulmates, they were individuals who were destined by fate to spend their many lives together. It took some several lifetimes to find their other halves, and not every immortal was successful in the task.

She had not been curious about the notion or even considered it with regard to her own self until she saw the two immortals today.

There was no doubt in her mind that they completed each other perfectly, not just physically and emotionally, but on a higher, supernatural level. The combined strength afforded by their union was subtly evident in the way they stood, moved, and even spoke. Although Alexa sensed that they were individually very powerful, together they seemed invincible.

Her gaze shifted to Jackson. Desire coiled inside her almost instantly. The fact that they were physically compatible was undeniable, yet she sensed there was more to her passion for the man than mere lust.

Yonten opened his eyes and gazed at her silently from the other side of the cabin. Alexa frowned faintly at his expression. She had the uncanny suspicion the monk could read her mind.

Less than two hours after it left Paris, the jet landed in the middle of a blizzard at a former military airport outside the city of Ceske Budejovice, in the South Bohemia region of the Czech Republic. Two black Mercedes four-by-fours sat waiting on the edge of the tarmac where the jet rolled to a stop. The vehicles' roofs were already buried under a three-inch-thick blanket of snow. A pair of hard-faced, silent drivers bundled in thick winter coats stood impassively next to the cars.

Jackson winced at the icy rain and sleet that pelted his face when he stepped off the plane. Yonten skipped down the steps past him, bare arms exposed to the harsh winter conditions. Jackson stared at the monk.

A smile dawned on Reznak's face at the Harvard professor's expression. 'It can get pretty cold in northern Tibet,' said the Crovir noble.

'I know that,' said Jackson darkly. 'Still, I get the feeling the yak milk may have gotten to his brain.'

Alexa climbed into the welcoming warmth of the first vehicle behind Jackson, Yonten, and Reznak. Fawkes joined Carrington and the two bodyguards in the second vehicle, and the convoy rapidly got under way.

'Where are we going?' asked Jackson. He stared curiously out of the window.

'To my estate,' replied Reznak.

'I thought we were heading for your lab,' said Jackson, raising his eyebrows.

'It's on the grounds of the property.'

❄

ALEXA GAZED SILENTLY AT THE SNOW-COVERED FIELDS THAT stretched out to the low hills undulating across the horizon. The occasional bare tree punctuated the barren landscape, dark branches rising starkly against the white backdrop.

Frozen streams and abandoned logging mills dotted the sparsely populated countryside as the four-by-fours headed toward the mountainous ridge soaring to the west. The gradient grew steeper, and ice-covered snow patches appeared on the freeway. The vehicles' snow tires gripped the frosty asphalt securely as they negotiated the tortuous roads that wound through the foothills of the looming peaks. Spruce and pine trees loomed out of the gray vista, their boughs heavy with the fresh snowfall. They drove through tunnels of towering trunks, the rays of the sun filtered to an eerie twilight by the branches above them.

A solid line of trees soon appeared in the distance, a dark smudge that lay across the entire skyline. An hour after leaving the airport, they entered the Bohemian Forest and headed deep into the Sumava National Park.

Situated in the same named mountain range, the park was part of the largest preserved forested area in Central Europe, extending west across the border into the Bavarian Forest in Germany, and south into Austria. It was the last remaining wild heart of Europe and encompassed almost three hundred square miles of forests, glacial lakes, peat bogs, wetlands, and flower meadows. It was also home to some of the last remaining populations of lynxes, grouse, European elks, and Ural owls on the continent, which made it a fiercely contested topic for debate between the conservationists, who wanted to preserve the natural habitat of the forest, and the logging industry, who wanted to fell its trees.

Much had changed in the three hundred and ten years since

she first laid eyes on the forest. Memories of the years she had spent exploring the wilderness around Reznak's estate flooded Alexa's mind as she studied the hauntingly beautiful landscape outside the window.

She recalled rustling leaves in hundred-year-old fir trees, wild otters fishing for salmon in rivers, raindrops falling silently on still water, and the shelter afforded by the abandoned gold and silver mines that dotted the mountains on the occasions when she got caught out in bad weather. She had hunted game with the lynxes, killed her first deer at the age of twelve, and run with the last wild wolves that had inhabited the forest. Though she would most likely never recall the first eight or so years of her life, Alexa was grateful to Reznak for having provided her with an unparalleled second childhood.

The rutted forest track finally ended in front of a set of imposing, black, wrought iron gates. The driver of their four-by-four glanced at the security cameras atop the eighteen-foot stone pillars framing the impenetrable gateway. Seconds later, the doors swung open on arm-thick hinges. He guided the vehicle onto the wide, graveled, stone-lined driveway beyond. The gates closed ponderously once the second four-by-four was through.

The trees thinned out on either side of the drive and the shadows under the canopy grew lighter. Jackson leaned eagerly forward in his seat. The outlook suddenly opened out after a thousand feet. Alexa heard him draw in a sharp breath.

Reznak's estate was set in twelve thousand acres of Bohemian Forest. Although an impressive three-mile wall extended along parts of its eastern and southern borders, the rest of the property was opened to the wild. Only discrete signs posted at regular intervals indicated that the land was privately owned. Strategically positioned surveillance cameras around the perimeter ensured a degree of privacy from intruders and helped the team of park rangers and guards employed by her godfather oversee the protection of the extensive natural habitat and the lab within the grounds.

He had been in possession of the land since before the forest acquired its current name of Sumava.

The driveway carved through a thirty-hectare park and exquisitely maintained, formal, French-style gardens to an imposing, three-winged, baroque chateau at the opposite end. The gray clouds and approaching storm dulled the normally warm colors of the cream limestone walls and red, chimney-studded, mansard roofs. Soft lights glittered behind the leaded glass windows that lined the elegant facade.

They passed several ornamental ponds and fountains before pulling to a stop in a large courtyard framed by the secondary wings of the castle.

'*This* is your home?' uttered Jackson incredulously.

'It used to be,' said Alexa with a shrug. 'I haven't lived here for some time.'

They exited the vehicles and climbed the split-level terrace to a wide portico. The taciturn drivers drove the four-by-fours toward the extensive garages at the side of the property, Reznak's bodyguards in tow.

A pair of thick oak doors embellished with a simple pattern of wrought iron guarded the entrance to the castle. One of them opened to reveal a thin, middle-aged woman with a shock of silver-blonde hair. Fawkes leaned down to kiss her cheek.

'Marie,' he said gently, affection warming his voice.

She smiled and kissed him back before greeting Reznak and Carrington. Her blue eyes lit up when she saw Alexa. 'It's good to see you again, child,' she said huskily, engulfing her in a warm embrace.

Alexa wrapped her arms around the frail, older woman and inhaled the familiar aroma of baking spices drifting from her hair and clothes. 'It's good to see you too, Marie,' she murmured, her smile hidden in the soft blonde curls.

Marie Fawkes was the closest thing to a mother she had ever had. When Fawkes retired from the Order of Hunters and came to work for Reznak, she joined her husband and took over the role of housekeeper for the estate. Both Marie and her husband were survivors of the deadly plague that decimated the immortal races in the fourteenth century and left the majority of survivors infertile. As a result, the couple had no children. The disease had also left Marie in poor health for a long time, and she remained somewhat delicate to this day. When Reznak brought Alexa to his home after the Battle of Narva, the pair doted on her as if she were their own flesh and blood.

Although Marie studied Yonten and Jackson with a quizzical expression, the older woman greeted them just as warmly as she would any other guests.

The Harvard professor stopped inside the entrance of the castle and looked around the marble foyer. A majestic staircase rose in the middle of the hall and split into symmetric branches on a common landing, rising to a gallery on the floor above. 'How long have you had this place?' he asked.

Reznak shrugged his coat off. Fawkes took the garment from him and headed for a closet on the left. 'The estate and the castle are four hundred years old,' said her godfather. 'I've owned the land longer.'

'Impressive,' said Jackson. His eyes assimilated the fine art and skilled craftsmanship on display for several seconds before displaying a sudden gleam of impatience. 'So, where's the lab?'

Reznak smiled faintly. 'Let's wait for the storm to abate. It'll be easier to get there.'

Alexa suppressed a grin and caught Marie's shrewd glance.

Her godfather was correct in one respect. On the other hand, he had just told Jackson a barefaced lie. Few people knew of the existence of the underground tunnel that connected one of the extensive cellars of the castle to Reznak's research facility three miles away. When he had the original lab built in the early 1900s, he had ordered the construction of the secret passage as a secondary escape route. Only the site managers were aware of the location of the tunnel's entrance inside the facility. Weather permitting, Reznak normally walked the distance to the lab above ground.

It was a few hours before the blizzard began to ease. Reznak gave Jackson an extensive tour of the castle before returning to the vast study that looked out over the rear gardens. Alexa glanced over her shoulder when they walked in the room.

'Is it stopping yet?' said Jackson, coming to stand at her side by the windows.

'No,' she replied. She could hardly make out the shapes of the trees beyond the boundaries of the park. The skies had darkened in the last hour, the storm hastening the arrival of twilight.

They stood quietly for a while. Jackson finally looked to where Reznak stood stoking the fire in the hearth and talking on his cellphone. 'By the way, did Schmidt and you have a...thing going at some stage?' asked the Harvard professor.

Alexa stiffened slightly and gave him a hard look. 'Why do you ask?'

Jackson shrugged. 'Well, the guy was acting as if he'd like to put a bullet through me this morning.'

She recalled Schmidt's expression at the London penthouse. 'Yes,' she eventually murmured. 'It was a while ago.' What she did not tell Jackson was that the Crovir Hunter had made it clear for some time that he wished to resume their old relationship.

'You know, although I'm thrilled to be here, I'm kinda wishing we were still in London,' Jackson said in a low voice.

She turned her head and met his cobalt-blue gaze. Desire licked a treacherous path through her body, and she felt her heartbeat start to rise. A flicker of light outside drew her eyes. 'The snowfall is lightening,' she said in a steady voice that masked her emotions. She thought she heard a sigh leave his lips.

The door opened behind them and Carrington strolled in. 'I've brought the Jeep around,' he said. 'I don't think the weather is going to get better than this.'

Yonten met them in the foyer. He had disappeared in the direction of the kitchen shortly after being shown to his room; to Alexa's surprise, the monk had proven to have a sweet tooth and had kept Marie company most of the afternoon while she baked. He finished the slice of honey cake in his hand and flashed a large grin. 'The cake is good,' he stated emphatically, patting his skinny belly and wiping the icing sugar from around his lips.

A mud-covered Jeep stood in the courtyard beyond the portico. Carrington took the wheel while they climbed in. Moments later, he guided the vehicle into the forest north of the park.

Jackson's eyebrows rose slightly as he gazed at the untamed wilderness on either side of the established dirt track. 'Your lab's in the woods?'

'Sort of,' said Reznak with a shrug.

Alexa glanced at her backpack on Jackson's lap. It held the Emerald Tablet and the sun cross pendant. It had not left the Harvard professor's sight since they left Paris.

The track widened and they came to a large clearing. An abandoned sawmill stood in the middle of the desolate scenery, the rusting remains of old machinery dotting the forlorn space around it. A second, wider track was visible at the eastern edge of the clearing.

Carrington steered the Jeep toward a stone barn next to the sawmill.

'It's inside the barn?' Jackson said skeptically.

'Not quite,' murmured Reznak.

Carrington slowed the vehicle to a crawl and took a small biometric remote control from his pocket. He pressed one of the keys.

The derelict wooden doors slid open smoothly on invisible rollers to reveal a yawning space. The crunch of tires across fresh snow changed into the slick glide of wet rubber on concrete. The Jeep's beams cut through the oily gloom ahead.

The darkness intensified when the doors closed behind them.

Floodlights came on above and illuminated the vast interior of the barn. Except for piles of old circular saws and conveyor belts, the place was deserted. Jackson stared out the window at the multiple snow and mud tracks on the floor.

Carrington braked in the center of the barn. He grinned at the Harvard professor in the rearview mirror and pressed a second key on the remote. A rumble rose outside. A forty-by-sixty-foot rectangular section of the concrete floor on which they were parked started to sink vertically into the ground.

CHAPTER TWENTY-THREE

JACKSON GAZED WIDE-EYED AT THE WALLS RISING AROUND THEM. 'What the—'

'This is the primary elevator shaft to the first level of the lab,' said Reznak. 'The roof over the facility, including this lift, is made of steel-reinforced concrete interlaced with silica-based ceramic and clay to reduce detection by ground-penetrating satellite technology.'

The light slowly faded above them, and they were engulfed by shadows. The beams from the Jeep's headlights bounced off the soaring wall in front and were soon the only light source in the vertical tunnel.

Jackson glanced at Alexa, his eyes gleaming in the reflection from ahead. 'How far down does this go?'

'It's a hundred and fifty feet to the first level,' said Alexa steadily. 'There are eight more beneath it.'

The last time she had been to the facility was over three years ago. With the acceleration in new technologies, Reznak had had to make considerable changes to the site over time. The biggest redesign had been the installation of the extra materials to ensure the structure was invisible to human satellites. To date, her godfather had spent close to sixty million dollars on the entire venture.

Dazzling radiance suddenly shot up from the edges of the dropping floor. The concrete elevator ground to a stop moments later.

'Wow,' Jackson murmured in a stunned voice.

The momentousness of the occasion was spoiled by a loud crunch. Yonten had pulled a biscuit out of his robe and was biting into it enthusiastically while he looked around in earnest interest. The Harvard professor scowled at the monk.

The lift was situated at the south end of an immense, vertical, T-shaped deck. The highest level of the complex was occupied by parking bays that could accommodate over a hundred cars, several loading areas with assigned service lifts, banks of regular-sized elevators, and a complex of offices and rooms. All looked out onto the middle of the platform, where a two-hundred-foot-long, oval-shaped opening descended into the earth. A metal railing enclosed the edges of the drop, with a promenade running around its periphery. Vivid green topiary shrubs and hedges grew in planters along it.

Jackson looked around wordlessly when they exited the vehicle, seemingly oblivious to the silent armed guards staffing the security cubicles on either side of the concrete lift. He walked toward the center of the vast underground deck, the bag holding the artifacts slung over his shoulder, and stopped at the railing overlooking the chasm. Reznak and Alexa joined him.

The hollow core of the complex was three hundred feet deep. Another five levels were visible below, all running circumferentially around the gigantic borehole. Large, floor-to-ceiling glass walls looked out onto the epicenter of the facility;

busy figures in white coats were visible in the brightly lit labs behind them.

A carpet of moss and ferns covered the floor at the bottom of the vertical tunnel.

Jackson turned and examined the shrub next to him. He ran his fingers over the richly colored leaves before staring at the high ceiling above them. 'Light wells?' he asked inquisitively, glancing at Reznak.

Reznak nodded, a faint smile on his lips. 'There are periscope-like light and ventilation shafts in the forest above us. You can't really see the full effect at the moment, but on a clear summer day, it gets fairly bright down here.'

Carrington wandered off to talk to the security guards. Yonten strolled toward them.

Jackson looked at Alexa. 'You said there were nine levels. I only see six, including this one.'

'The basement contains the utilities for the facility, as well as the backup generators and computer servers,' she said.

'The other two levels are for our most…private of enterprises,' said Reznak with a carefully neutral expression.

There was a faint crunch next to him. Yonten had magicked another biscuit out of his robe and was eating it with unrestrained relish.

Reznak glanced at the monk distractedly. 'The complex is essentially self-sustaining,' he said, a hint of pride evident in his voice. 'There's an underground river supplying water and hydroelectric power, and the waste from the site is recycled.' He looked around the airy promenade with its bright, living plants. 'I wanted to make the place as pleasant as possible for the staff who work here,' he added quietly. 'I spend hours within these confines myself.'

'Where do the scientists live?' asked Jackson, gazing at the white-coated figures behind the glass walls on the floors below.

'Most of them reside within an hour's drive of the estate,' said Reznak. 'At any one time, we have several visiting professors from universities around the world. They're normally my guests at the castle, unless they wish otherwise.'

A wry smile dawned on Jackson's face. 'Let me guess—they've all signed one of those complicated confidentiality agreements you like so much?'

Alexa felt her lips twitch.

Reznak shrugged. 'You can surely see the logic of it, now that you're aware of the existence of immortals. It would look exceedingly strange if we never aged during the span of a human's career. More than half of the scientists here are immortals anyway.' He turned and headed toward one of the lifts in the west wall.

Excitement replaced surprise on Jackson's face. 'So, what kind of labs have you got?' he asked as they followed the Crovir noble.

'Being that I'm the Head of our Immortal Culture and History Section, we pretty much have every discipline you can imagine under one roof, from geoarchaeology through to paleoanthropology and anthropological genetics,' said Reznak when they entered the elevator. 'The artifact analysis room is our largest lab, followed by our archival research facility.'

They descended one level and stepped off the lift into a bright corridor decorated in pastel colors. Security doors with biometric LCD displays guarded the entrances to the vast spaces behind the glass walls that lined the east aspect of the passageway.

'The complex has a canteen, rest rooms for the staff, a gym

with a swimming pool, and an entertainment center,' said Reznak. 'This is the molecular and nano archaeology lab.' He entered a code in one of the doors, pressed his fingers in the dual finger sensors, and stared into the face recognition camera.

A musical tone sounded, and a soft, computerized female voice said, 'Welcome back, Dimitri. It has been three days, seven hours, and two minutes since your last visit. I see you have new visitors. Please enter their biometric details before I grant you access.'

Jackson's eyebrows rose.

'The facility is run by an artificial intelligence system,' said Reznak, grinning at the Harvard professor's expression. 'She controls everything from security to the temperature of the swimming pool. If the two of you could please oblige.' He looked at Jackson and Yonten, and indicated the security screen.

The two men took turns staring into the camera and pressing their fingers against the sensors. The monk eyed the computer warily while Reznak approved their IDs.

'She recognizes changes in voice modulation and fingerprint sweat pattern that may indicate stress or fear,' said Reznak. 'Even if anyone managed to get through all the security to this level, they would not be able to force one of the staff to open the doors.'

A beep sounded and the lab door slid open a second after the AI scanned Alexa and informed her that her last visit was over three years ago.

'Does she have a name?' asked Jackson distractedly, his attention immediately captured by the state-of-the-art lab they had entered. A few of the scientists working at the counters dotted across the floor raised their heads and called out a greeting to Reznak.

He nodded in response before looking at Jackson quizzically.

'The AI?' clarified Jackson.

'Oh,' said Reznak. Alexa was the only one present who knew the Crovir noble well enough to detect the infinitesimal flicker of sadness that flashed in his eyes. 'Yes. Her name is…Eva.'

Despite Alexa's persistent questioning over the years, Reznak had never once explained the origin of the AI's handle to her. A sorrowful look almost invariably dawned on his face when the subject was brought up, and although Fawkes and Marie appeared to know the truth of the matter, they remained as resolutely tight-lipped as Reznak. Alexa had always suspected the name belonged to someone from his past.

Jackson strolled around the room, his ice-blue eyes keenly observing every aspect of the research lab. He stopped next to a complex workstation. 'If I'm not mistaken, this is a prototype of the next generation of ultra-high resolution, electron microscope that's been getting so much attention in the research community in the last few months,' he said, looking at Reznak steadily.

'It is,' he agreed with a small nod. 'The Crovir R&D Section was involved in its development. We're testing it out for the company.'

Reznak introduced Jackson to the other scientists. Most seemed to know him on sight and greeted him warmly. As her godfather took Jackson on a tour of the other labs, it became obvious to Alexa that the Harvard professor was not only highly regarded in his own field, but across the broader scientific community.

She listened to their conversations with mounting unease. It was dawning on her that there was still a lot she did not know about the man who had become her lover.

Alexa detected rising impatience in Jackson's eyes as he hefted the bag containing the artifacts on his shoulder. She suspected Reznak was stalling for a reason, possibly to impress upon the Harvard professor the extent of the expertise available for the undoubtedly daunting task that lay ahead.

They finally headed down a passage to one of the service elevators. Jackson studied the biometric display on the wall next to it curiously; it was different from the others in the facility in that it had an additional integrated digital keypad. The AI acknowledged Reznak's identity after he entered a long code into it. A beep sounded and the doors opened.

'Now, this is what I call an elevator,' said Jackson dully. The interior of the lift was immense and could easily have accommodated a medium-sized truck. 'Why do you need something this size?'

'You'll see soon enough,' Reznak replied.

They stepped inside. The doors closed behind them, only to open again seconds later on the seventh floor. They exited the metal cage.

Alexa had rarely visited this part of the facility, her work having never required much involvement with the Immortal Culture and History Section. Her eyes narrowed at the same time that Jackson's breath caught in his throat.

A fifteen-by-twenty-foot foyer stretched out before the lift. It was empty save for the heavily armed guard seated at a desk in front of a trio of security monitors. Thick, bullet-resistant glass formed a floor-to-ceiling wall behind him and extended to the two sides of the lobby. Beyond it was the secret core of Reznak's research facility.

This lab occupied the length and breadth of the complex. A pair of security doors in the sidewalls opened onto an oval-shaped mezzanine that ran all the way around the periphery of the massive space. It was occupied by an extensive library, with ceiling-high bookcases lining the walls. Secured display tables protecting fragile, ancient manuscripts dotted the gaps between islands of desks and chairs.

Several flights of stairs led to the lower deck of the lab fifteen feet below.

The outer edges of the vast concrete floor were occupied by workstations that formed a half circle to the right and left, the lines of the tables mirroring the curves of the mezzanine above. A group of twenty scientists busied themselves at the plethora of complex equipment and banks of computer monitors that occupied the desks.

Jackson's gaze never wavered from the center of the lab floor.

There, in the middle of the two-hundred-foot-wide space, lit by half a dozen floodlights, stood the carefully reconstructed second cave that Reznak's team had discovered in Egypt.

The Harvard professor took several cautious steps forward until he reached the glass wall. 'That's—' He shook his head dazedly, his eyes glazed with wonderment. 'How?' he murmured, staring over his shoulder at Reznak.

'We excavated the whole thing and transported it here,' said Reznak.

Yonten's expression grew solemn. 'Warrior's mark,' he said quietly, gazing at the trishula in the floor of the cave.

Alexa glanced at the monk before turning to look at the carving laid bare under the harsh artificial light. The pictures had not done the image justice. Her birthmark tingled on the back of her neck.

The guard manning the security desk nodded at Reznak before buzzing them through the door on the left. Jackson's steps quickened as he crossed the mezzanine and headed for the nearest stairwell. He descended the steps swiftly and started toward the center of the room.

'Oh. Professor Jackson! What a pleasure to see you here!' someone called out in a distinctly British accent. An elderly gentleman with frizzy gray hair and glasses approached them, a white lab coat flapping behind him and a tablet computer in one hand.

Jackson froze. 'Professor Ingram?' he said incredulously.

The scientist reached their side and vigorously shook hands with the Harvard professor. 'I read that last paper of yours in the American Journal of Archaeology. Fascinating stuff,' said the man, his head bobbing while he spoke. He turned and smiled at Reznak. 'Is Professor Jackson joining our team?'

'He'll be assisting me on some other matters,' said the Crovir noble smoothly. 'I wanted him to see the cave.'

'Oh,' said the silver-haired professor blankly. Someone shouted his name from the other side of the room. 'Excuse me,' he said distractedly. He nodded at the rest of the group and started to walk off. 'It's good to see you again, Jackson.'

The Harvard professor stared at the departing figure. He scanned the room slowly before looking at Reznak. 'How the hell did you get the world's leading Assyriologist to come work for you? Never mind the other big names in here right now.'

Her godfather smiled. 'The same way I persuaded you to accept this mission: money.'

Jackson muttered something indistinct under his breath. He suddenly went pale. 'Wait—*please* don't tell me he's an immortal!' he said in a stunned voice.

Reznak's grin widened. 'He isn't.'

'Thank God for that,' said Jackson. 'The man has been one of my heroes since I was twelve.' He glanced around again before focusing on the gigantic artifact in the middle of the lab.

From what Alexa recalled of her first conversation with Reznak, it had taken days of meticulous and cautious drilling to remove the cave from its original location within the Egyptian desert mountains. His team had subsequently reassembled the different sections exactly as depicted on the hundred or so photographs pinned to a large board to the left, down to the position and width of the doorway.

A clothes rack held hooded plastic suits with boots and gloves to the left. They donned the unflattering garments before approaching the looming granite walls.

Jackson hesitated on the threshold of the doorway, his blue eyes brimming with emotion. Alexa looked away from his expression and tried to ignore the strange twisting sensation inside her chest.

'Go ahead,' said Reznak gently.

CHAPTER TWENTY-FOUR

JACKSON TOOK A DEEP BREATH AND STEPPED INSIDE THE chamber. Yonten followed hesitantly, his normally limpid eyes looking unusually nervous. Alexa was the last one to enter the cave.

They spent a long time simply gazing at the complex pictographs covering the walls and the trishula carved into the floor.

Alexa kept her face expressionless while she studied the stone imprint of her birthmark, laid bare for all to see under the bright lights. The back of her neck felt as if someone had scorched it. She noted Yonten's anxious glance and wondered whether the monk could see the eerie flames dancing across her skin.

'Have they completed the translations?' asked Jackson.

'Not quite,' replied Reznak.

'And these alcoves were really empty?' The Harvard professor walked toward one of the twin pillars and inspected the hollow compartment inside.

Reznak glanced at Alexa. 'I haven't told him,' she said quietly.

Jackson turned. Before he could phrase the protest that was bubbling up his throat, her godfather sighed and raised a hand.

'I shall tell you what the alcoves contained—but not here,' said Reznak quietly. 'Let's go.' He turned and headed for the doorway.

'Go?' repeated Jackson in a puzzled tone. 'Go where?'

Reznak looked over his shoulder. 'To the eighth floor.'

Instead of heading for the mezzanine level and the lift, he strode across the floor toward a narrow, dimly lit passage in the north wall of the lab. A door guarded by another biometric LCD display stood unobtrusively at the end.

'There is elevator access to the eighth floor but I prefer to go this way,' said Reznak in a low voice as he operated the panel. A flight of stairs stood on the other side of the door. 'Only a handful of people have security clearance to this level of the facility.'

They followed him down the steps and through another security door at the bottom of the concrete staircase. Beyond it lay the north end of a long, curved corridor that spanned the length of the complex.

Halfway down the passage, light spilled out through a twenty-foot-wide glass section in the east wall. Reznak accessed the security display embedded in one of a pair of large, transparent doors in the middle. Eva's modulated voice sounded through invisible speakers seconds later.

Jackson seemed oblivious to it as he stared at the massive chamber beyond.

'Welcome to the heart of the facility,' said Reznak when the doors slid open. The Harvard professor strolled in after him, his gaze spanning the interior of the cool, shadowy space.

Sleek, three-foot-tall flatscreen monitors ran in a semicircle around a large hub in the center of the room. There were three chairs at the workstation. A man sat typing on a keyboard in the middle one.

Different images flashed across the screens. A monitor showed live feeds from the security cameras around Reznak's estate and inside the research complex; Alexa could see herself and the others in one of them. Another monitor appeared to be working through a complex image-processing program for an archaeological artifact. A third showed a game of chess in progress, with a live Nintendo Mario chase happening in a separate window.

'I see you're still trying to beat Eva at chess,' said Reznak wryly, strolling toward the workstation.

The man in the chair wheeled around. 'Oh. Hi, Dimitri.' He looked about twenty-five years old and sported a shock of dark hair and sharp, brown eyes. An exasperated sigh left his lips. 'I haven't managed to win a single game against the damn woman yet.' He blinked in the glow from the monitors as he stared at the figures behind Reznak. A smile lit his face. 'Alexa, long time no see! Hey, you fancy a game of Gran Turismo? I'm testing the latest software for the company.'

'I'm afraid not,' she replied curtly. Her neck still prickled warmly and she curbed the impulse to touch the skin over her birthmark as she gazed at the young man.

Jordan Montague Banks was the immortal genius who had constructed Eva. A graduate of several world-class universities and the holder of a dozen degrees in computer, electrical, and mechanical engineering as well as AI technology, he now oversaw the networks for Reznak's estate and research facility. His abilities were matched only by the large team of Crovir techs who manned the central security and intelligence systems for the councils. Reznak had recruited the immortal from the Crovir headquarters more than two decades ago, when Banks was a mere ninety years old.

Reznak introduced Jackson and Yonten briefly before glancing at a steel door to the south of the computer lab. 'Is it all set up?'

Banks nodded. 'We moved the last of the equipment in there this morning. It's got everything you wanted, from luminescence dating to isotope analysis.' He wheeled himself to one of the displays and typed on a keyboard. 'I've freed up this monitor for any digital analysis Professor Jackson may need. Image processing, 3D visualization, mathematical modeling—you name it, he'll have it. Eva's also just informed me that she will graciously put aside five percent of her memory and function for the professor's personal use.'

'Oh,' said Jackson. 'Er, thanks Eva.' He looked around hesitantly.

'You're welcome,' the AI replied. 'I have been reading your papers from your first publication twenty-three years ago. I am very much enjoying them. You are one of the brightest minds of the last century.'

Bemusement washed across Jackson's face. 'That's...very kind of you,' he murmured. He glanced at Reznak. 'Did you tell her to do that?'

Reznak shook his head. 'Eva didn't know you were coming,' he said in an amused tone. 'She's been checking your credentials ever since you inputed your biometrics outside the molecular and nano archaeology lab. She's quite curious that way.'

Jackson looked at the monitors disconcertedly.

Banks was frowning. 'Oh really, Eva? What about me?' he said, staring up into the air. 'I don't see you harping on about my genius.'

'You are, of course, a very clever man, Jordan,' said Eva. 'After all, you invented me. As for the genius part, I will only acknowledge that after you beat me at chess.'

While Banks grumbled under his breath about AIs who were too smart for their own good, Eva spoke again. 'By the way, Dimitri, I am afraid to report that I have still not found any information on the young Asian man accompanying you. He appears not to exist on any biometric or other demographic database in the world.'

Yonten beamed at this piece of news.

'I wouldn't worry about it,' said Reznak with a sigh. 'He belongs to a very…secret organization. Eva, can you open the primary vault?'

'Yes,' said the AI.

Alexa watched Reznak cross the floor to a second steel door to the north of the computer lab. It hissed ajar moments before he reached it. She left Banks at the central hub and followed Jackson and Yonten as they headed after her godfather.

The chamber beyond was similar to the strongroom they had broken into under the Freemasons' Grand Temple in London. A number of relics lay within glass display cabinets around the walls and under glass boxes scattered across the floor of the vault.

A steel safe took up a quarter of the east wall. Reznak walked up to it and worked the security display swiftly. A soft beep sounded and the heavy metal door swung open.

The safe was divided into sections, one of which was a large liquid nitrogen freezer. Reznak put on a pair of gloves and carefully extracted a metal case from the frigid compartment.

He laid it out on a nearby table, unlatched the clasps, and lifted the lid.

The stench of the embalming chemicals had all but faded. Alexa stared at the hearts on display and felt the invisible flames blaze across her nape once more. At the same time, her pulse accelerated. The minuscule hole where Reznak's scientists had taken a biopsy to study the genetic composition of the organs was barely visible.

Yonten murmured a short prayer and bowed respectfully.

Jackson gave the monk a puzzled look before turning to Reznak. 'What are we looking at, exactly?' he asked.

'You are aware that the tombs stolen by the *Rose Croix* sect quite likely contain the remains of Crovir and Bastian, the original immortals?' said Reznak, gazing steadily at the Harvard professor.

'Yes, so you say,' replied Jackson.

'These,' said Reznak, indicating the contents of the metal case, 'are their hearts. They were inside individual clay pots in the alcoves of the pillars in the second cave, which were positioned exactly beneath what I believe were their respective tombs in the larger cave above.'

Jackson's breath left his lips in a faint gasp. He glanced at Alexa as if to ascertain the veracity of Reznak's words. 'That's impossible,' he finally stated. 'Besides, I thought you people turned to ash after your final deaths, and that crows came for you.'

'What you have to remember is that, as the forefathers of our races, Crovir and Bastian were incredibly unique beings,' said Reznak calmly. 'Genetic analysis has started to show how special they truly were. The clay pots we found the hearts in date back to more than four millennia ago.'

Jackson's skeptical expression faded only partially while

Reznak closed the metal case and placed it back in the safe. The Crovir noble disposed of the gloves and headed out of the chamber. Alexa was the last to leave, the metal panel closing behind her with a soft, pneumatic hiss. Her birthmark almost immediately stopped burning, and she unclenched her jaw.

Her godfather crossed the floor to the second steel door south of the computer room. A newly assembled lab lay beyond it. Glittering metals and shiny plastics covered the half dozen workstations arranged in a rough semicircle around a central table.

The room had been kitted out with every possible piece of gear Jackson would need to analyze the unique artifacts in his possession.

The Harvard professor's eyes glittered with rising excitement. 'I'm officially impressed,' he murmured.

'There's a resting lounge down the corridor outside the computer lab,' said Reznak. 'Let me know if you need any extra equipment.'

'I don't think I will, but thanks,' said Jackson distractedly. He walked to the middle of the floor and carefully placed Alexa's bag on the table. A faraway expression dawned in his eyes, his gaze lost on an invisible horizon that only he could see. 'I'll start now.'

Reznak's eyebrows rose. 'Won't you have dinner first? Marie is preparing one of her special feasts.'

'Oh.' Jackson flushed slightly. He glanced longingly at the bag before nodding. 'Can I come back afterwards?'

Reznak smiled. 'Yes. I'll bring you to the lab myself.'

The evening meal was a warm affair, Reznak assuming his role as host with his usual aplomb. They retired to the study briefly for coffee. Soon, the Crovir noble headed out of the back door with Jackson in tow. Carrington offered to drive them. Reznak refused and shooed the immortal away.

'If I don't get behind the wheel once in a while, I'll get rusty,' her godfather grumbled.

Jackson halted in the doorway and turned to look at Alexa. Since there was no need for her presence at the lab, she was staying back to keep Marie and Fawkes company. 'See you later,' he said.

Alexa could tell that it was more of a question than a statement. She gave a quick nod, aware of Marie's watchful gaze.

The antique grandfather clock in the entrance hall was chiming midnight when she climbed the steps to her old room in one of the castle towers a few hours later. Although Alexa rarely visited the estate these days, Marie had kept her chambers exactly as she had left them. She looked over the familiar books lining the shelves on the walls, the beautiful antique bed, and the matching wardrobe and chests of drawers. There was even a dressing table, which she had barely used in all the time that she had lived there.

Alexa crossed the wood floor to a pair of French doors. A balcony lay on the other side. She walked out into the night and leaned against a cream, stone baluster.

The air was cold and crisp. The snowfall had finally abated. Stars dotted the inky sky, brilliant diamonds around a full moon that shed its ethereal light over the white, sparkling landscape. Her breaths plumed the air in front of her lips as she stared silently across the park to the Bohemian Forest.

Her birthmark still throbbed faintly on the back of her neck.

She was still standing there at two o'clock in the morning when she heard the door to her room open. Footsteps sounded softly on the floorboards. She saw the edges of the gauzy French curtains billow past her as someone stepped onto the balcony.

'Hey,' said Jackson quietly behind her.

Alexa turned, put her arms around his neck, and kissed him.

CHAPTER TWENTY-FIVE

He was gone when she woke the next morning. Alexa lay in her bed and stared at the ceiling while she tried to analyze the complex emotions churning through her mind.

Her passion for Jackson showed no sign of abating. They had made love with a raw intensity that matched their first night together, only succumbing to sleep after dawn had broken across the land.

She sighed, threw the covers back, and strode naked into the bathroom.

'What will you do today?' Marie asked her pleasantly when she joined the older woman in the kitchen for a late breakfast.

Alexa was not fooled by her benign expression. Marie was bound to have noticed that Jackson had not slept in his bed.

'I'm going to the lab.' There were still plenty of things she could do while Jackson worked on deciphering the mysteries of the artifacts.

Marie smiled. 'Good,' she said with a faint nod.

Alexa took one of the spare Jeeps and headed to the research facility shortly before midday. She found Yonten in the computer lab on the eighth floor. The monk was playing a video game with Banks. The young Crovir immortal was scowling at him.

'Are you sure you haven't played this before?' said Banks suspiciously. Alexa got the impression that this was not the first time he had asked the question.

Yonten shook his head and beamed.

'He is telling the truth,' said Eva smoothly. 'Analysis of his heart rate, pupillary reactions, and facial expressions confirm this. Face it, Jordan. You are a poor loser,' the AI added smugly.

'Are they in there?' asked Alexa, indicating the door leading to the private lab.

'Uh-huh,' said Banks distractedly. 'Okay! Let's go for another round,' he told the monk. Yonten nodded amiably and took a biscuit out of his robe.

She found Jackson seated behind one of the workstations in the lab. Reznak was leaning against the back of the Harvard professor's chair. Oblivious to her presence, the two men talked excitedly about the crisp, enhanced images on the large monitor before them.

The Emerald Tablet and Anna Godard's sun cross pendant stood propped under a pair of sleek, high-resolution, digital magnifiers on the table in the middle of the room.

'See the markings here and here?' Jackson was saying as he pointed to two lines of small, wedge-shaped characters in the middle of the tablet. 'Although the rest of the text appears to be Assyrian, these are undoubtedly Akkadian scripts, which would put the origin of the stone to at least the third millennium BC. The carbon fourteen data from the mass spectrometer also gives that period as the approximate era for its source.'

Alexa cleared her throat.

'Oh. Hi,' said Jackson. He turned to her with a preoccupied smile.

Reznak observed the silent look she exchanged with Jackson with a carefully neutral expression.

'Any progress yet?' she asked in a steady voice.

Jackson nodded. 'Yes. We've successfully dated the tablet, which will help with the translation. And I was correct about the pendant—the filigree and granulation design on the sun cross and the presence of Sumerian scripts puts its origin at the end of the fourth millennium BC.' He looked at the two artifacts on the table. 'I believe the pendant is older than the Emerald Tablet.'

Alexa's gaze fell on the bag she had given to Jackson. She crossed the room and picked up the slim tome resting atop it. It was the book that Yonten had stolen from the Freemasons' vault. 'Have you examined this yet?' she said, turning to look at Jackson.

A guilty grimace crossed the Harvard professor's face. 'No. I'm afraid I've been concentrating on the tablet and the pendant.'

She leafed through the pages of the book. 'Mind if I take a look?' she asked as she studied the tiny, calligraphic lettering that covered the thick sheets.

'Er, no,' said Jackson. 'Knock yourself out.'

Lorenzio's folder peeked out from beneath the bag. Alexa left the room with the book and document wallet in hand, took the last chair at the central hub in the computer lab, and put her feet up on the worktop. Banks looked away from the screen and gave her boots a frown. She raised her eyebrows coolly. He sighed and returned to his virtual Mario race against the monk.

She picked up the phone and called the main Crovir intelligence network. 'Hi,' she said after they acknowledged her

ID. 'I'm at Reznak's place in Sumava. Can you send Eva the image of the van from Rome? Thanks.'

She disconnected and turned to the tome. Although the text had been written in Medieval Latin, she found a date in the margin of the second page. It read 1695.

Eva interrupted her a second later. 'Hi, Alexa. I've received the picture you requested. Would you like me to process it?'

Alexa looked up. The shot of Lorenzio's killer and the van outside St. Peter's Square was in the top left corner of the monitor in front of her. 'Yes. We're trying to find a match for the vehicle. A current location would be ideal. Can you help?'

'Of course,' said Eva smoothly. 'I will use my access to our satellites and recognition softwares straightaway.'

'Thank you,' said Alexa. She ignored Banks's little yelp of frustration at losing another match to Yonten and settled down in the chair.

An hour later, she asked Banks for a scanner and uploaded the entire volume to the screen in front of her.

The first half of the Freemason's book had been a candid observation on the esoteric societies that had started to emerge across Europe shortly after the inception of Freemasonry around the fourteenth century. The second half was encoded.

Alexa had Eva bring up the decryption softwares from the central Crovir security network and had the pages deciphered within the next ninety minutes. Her eyes narrowed as she continued reading on the screen. Things were starting to get interesting.

The author of the book appeared to have fixated on a single esoteric society for the remainder of his work. The activities of this particular group had evidently perturbed him enough for him to encrypt the words he had put down on paper.

Alexa knew without a doubt that he was talking about the *Rose Croix* sect.

Her fingers flicked across a track pad as she highlighted specific sections and cross-referenced the associated historical events against Eva's vast database. The words 'Rosa Crucis' and a drawing of a *Rose Croix* finally appeared in the margin of a page. By then, she had taken over a second display.

She occasionally rubbed the back of her neck as she studied the complex data on the monitors; her birthmark had started to feel hot again the moment she had come within a thirty-foot radius of the Egyptian cave and the pair of immortal hearts. She was certain Yonten and Reznak would find a cryptic significance behind the phenomenon if she mentioned it to them. Since there was nothing to be gained from alluding to it, she chose to remain silent on the subject.

Banks left the computer lab to go work elsewhere in the facility. Yonten started to play chess with Eva. At five in the afternoon, Alexa felt coldness start to trickle through her mind at the information displayed on the two monitors.

A pattern was starting to emerge.

She recalled what Jackson had said in Istanbul about his research into human history and how he had detected anomalies in the timelines, which aroused his suspicions about the existence of another race. As she turned to Lorenzio's folder and opened it, something small and white fluttered out. She leaned down and picked it from the floor.

It was the piece of paper with the Cartesian coordinates that Jackson had stolen from the tavern in Istanbul. Alexa stared at it for a moment before tucking it inside her jacket.

She started to methodically examine the evidence gathered by the Pope's secret commission over the last twenty years. At the back of the folder, she found several private documents by the dead archbishop recording his observations of the *Rose Croix* sect over a period spanning a hundred years.

Except for a couple of centuries, most of the data was there.

'Eva,' Alexa said quietly, 'can you bring up the geographical and historical locations of the events I've underscored? I'm going to scan some more documents for you to upload.'

Yonten paused the game and turned to look at her. His solemn gaze shifted to the monitors.

Fifteen minutes later, the information was on the system. Eva spread the data across three screens. Alexa rose from the console, took a few steps back, and stood with her arms crossed while she studied the displays. Finally, she turned, crossed the floor to the private lab, and opened the steel door.

Reznak and Jackson were examining the sun cross pendant on the table.

'You need to see this,' she said.

They did not question her tone of voice. Banks walked through the doors of the computer lab just as she led the two men into the main chamber.

'Whoa!' said the young Crovir immortal. 'What'd you do to my screens?'

He did not get an answer.

'What are we looking at?' asked Reznak, glancing curiously from her face to the monitors.

'The *Rose Croix* sect goes by the name of Kronos,' said Alexa, tilting her head at a highlighted paragraph decoded from the second half of the Freemason's book. 'Aside from a period of time spanning nearly two hundred years, this is as thorough an account as we're likely to get about their activities over the last six centuries.'

Her godfather inhaled sharply. 'Kronos? You're certain?' The color drained from his face.

Alexa tensed. 'Yes, I am. What's wrong?'

Reznak was silent for several seconds. 'The scriptures in the cave walls above us give a partial account of Crovir's life. He had six children,' he finally said in a low voice. Muscles twitched in his jaw. 'The name of his third son was Kronos.'

The cold feeling that had invaded Alexa's mind intensified. She thought of Lorenzio's account of pureblood immortals who had mated with humans and the resulting halfbreed offsprings. 'Does this mean that Cavaleti could be a descendant of Kronos?'

'It's within the realm of the possible,' Reznak admitted reluctantly, his expression darkening.

Alexa watched him for a moment before turning back to the screens. 'Lorenzio's speculation as to the motives of the sect appears to be validated by the pattern emerging from combining the data from the Freemasons' book, the Pope's secret commission, and the archbishop's own observations in the century before that.' She pointed at half a dozen sections on the screens. 'All the major religious wars and disputes that have ever threatened to topple the Catholic Church have apparently been influenced by the actions of the sect.'

'Holy crap,' uttered Banks. 'What's this about toppling the Catholic Church?' He stared at their solemn faces.

Alexa glanced at Jackson. 'The *Mutus Liber* and the Emerald Tablet are also mentioned in the Freemasons' book,' she said.

Jackson's gaze focused on the highlighted paragraphs she indicated.

'It seems that Cavaleti's sect has been searching for both items for centuries,' she continued. 'The Emerald Tablet was entrusted to the Freemasons in the fifteenth century by someone who sounds very much like an immortal. By the end of the seventeenth century, when the book's timeline ends, the location of the *Mutus Liber* still remained a mystery.'

'Hey, are you guys talking about the Philosopher's Stone?' asked Banks.

'Yes,' Alexa replied curtly.

'Wow,' whispered the young immortal.

'Eva, split the screens,' said Alexa quietly. The monitors changed, the data separating into two distinct streams. 'I asked Eva to perform an extrapolation from the information available to help guide us as to Kronos's next move.' She pointed at the first monitor. 'I think the reason their activities have accelerated of late, and that Cavaleti made such a rare public appearance after half a decade under the radar, is because they are close to their goal. If we put what we know about Kronos's actions to date and their primary objective of bringing about the downfall of the Catholic Church, it's safe to assume the immortals' tombs are a big part of the picture.' She watched understanding begin to dawn in her godfather's eyes. 'What would be an absolute and irrevocable way of denying the fundamental importance of the Catholic Church?'

Horror washed across Jackson's face. Yonten frowned faintly.

'By proving that its foundations are possibly based in lies,' said Reznak, his expression hardening. 'By revealing the existence of immortals.'

'If we assume that the timeline of the history of Christianity is correct, then the Son of God could theoretically be a descendant of the original immortals,' Jackson continued in a dull voice.

Alexa looked at the monitors. 'Lorenzio suspected that Cavaleti wished to establish his own brand of religion. He thought the man wanted to be a living god. If Cavaleti believes he is from the lineage of Kronos, then he has every justification to indulge in that sick fantasy.'

'But, even if this Cavaleti character were to succeed, he'd have to face the real immortals,' interrupted Banks with a frown. 'The Crovirs and the Bastians would never let him get away with this. Not after all the blood, sweat, and tears they've invested in the human race.'

A grim smile crossed Alexa's lips. 'Well said,' she murmured, nodding curtly at the computer genius. 'That's where the second equation comes in.' The stream of data on the other screen faded. Only three sets of words remained. 'Lorenzio could not see the connection between the sect's plans and the *Mutus Liber*. Add in the Emerald Tablet and the original immortals' tombs, and it starts to make sense.' She glanced at Jackson and could see rising awareness reflected in his cobalt eyes. 'Cavaleti knows that the Crovirs and the Bastians are the only ones who can stop him. That's why he's obsessed with finding the Philosopher's Stone.'

'He wants to achieve true immortality,' Reznak stated coldly in the taut silence that ensued.

'If deciphered correctly, the Emerald Tablet and the *Mutus Liber* apparently describe the process of making the Elixir of Life,' said Alexa. 'As to the tombs—'

'He must think that they somehow contain the ingredients to making the Philosopher's Stone!' Jackson concluded in a breathless rush of words. Admiration glowed in his fevered gaze as he looked at her.

'But, surely he wouldn't be able to challenge the combined forces of our two immortal races,' said Banks dubiously. 'The Crovirs and the Bastians are embattled veterans who have been fighting wars for millennia!'

'That might have been true seven hundred years ago,' Alexa said quietly, 'but the Red Death decimated us almost to the point of extinction. Our races are nowhere close to the numbers they were at before the plague.' She ran a hand through her hair. 'Ismael Sadik said this sect was ancient. I believe him. I think Kronos has been around in one form or another for a long time. I would not underestimate the size of their faction. From what is written in those,' she indicated the documents on the screens with a head tilt, 'Cavaleti has been assembling a veritable army. Boyko Dragov is his right hand and principal disciple. There are immortals among their ranks, too. If he succeeds, we could be looking at the birth of a third, more powerful race of immortals.'

'Damn,' muttered Banks with a trace of admiration.

The soft, modulated voice of the AI interrupted them. 'Alexa, I have a hit on the van's registration plate,' said Eva. 'It was spotted in Budapest an hour ago. I've managed to trace its current location.'

A satellite image sprang up on one of the monitors. It showed a twilight view of a conglomeration of dark buildings in the middle of an empty countryside.

Alexa grew still as she studied the faint illumination outlining the distinct patterns of lines in the large field next to it. 'Is that a military airbase?'

'Yes,' said Eva. 'My data banks show that it was last occupied by the Soviet Armed Forces during the Cold War. It is currently classified as disused.'

Alexa turned to Reznak. 'Dragov and Cavaleti could be there right now,' she stated in a steady voice that managed to mask the anticipation building up inside her.

Her godfather was not fooled by her expression. 'Take however many men you need,' he said tersely. 'I'll talk to our First Council and the Bastians.'

She looked at Yonten. The monk smiled and bit down on a biscuit.

WARRIOR

CHAPTER TWENTY-SIX

ALEXA LEFT THE ESTATE WITH THE MONK AND CARRINGTON IN tow. They lifted off from the airport outside Ceske Budejovice shortly before nine and were in Budapest within the hour. Snow was falling steadily from the dark skies when they stepped onto the tarmac where two black SUVs and a van stood waiting. A group of twelve Hunters were joining them from the local Crovir base in Hungary.

As the convoy headed swiftly toward the abandoned airfield thirty miles outside Budapest, her thoughts turned to Jackson. He had not been pleased at being left behind in Sumava and had voiced his protests quite eloquently. It was Reznak who finally convinced him that his best chance to assist with their mission lay in solving the mystery of the two relics in their possession.

Though they had parted without exchanging words, Alexa recalled the expression in his eyes with a small shiver. He had looked like he wanted to brand her with his mark.

Half a mile from the boundary of the airfield, she ordered

the vehicles to a halt under a copse along a deserted country lane. They regrouped in the back of the van.

'I want your guys here, here, and here,' she said briskly to the Crovir Hunters' team leader. She pointed at three positions on the live picture of the old military base on the screen of her laptop. Satellite thermal imaging showed eighteen heat signals in the abandoned structures. 'No one is to fire a single shot until I say so, unless your life is under direct threat. Even then, I'd rather you take a bullet than break our cover.' The Hunters glanced at each other warily. Alexa could tell her reputation had preceded her once more. 'I want to find out what they're up to in there. Look out for a pair of tombs. They may be in one of those buildings.'

Moments later, they proceeded to their designated positions.

Carrington and Yonten followed her as she ran across an open field to a metal fence that spanned the perimeter of the facility. She stopped before it and studied the chain links thoughtfully. The enclosure was relatively new.

Carrington snipped across the bottom of the barrier with a metal cutter and pulled up a narrow section. They crawled through the gap, raced low along the cracked asphalt, and halted in the shadow of a large, dilapidated, two-storey structure.

Alexa slipped the Sigs from her body holster and stared at a window to her left. Dim light escaped around the edges of the metal blind on the other side.

From what they had seen of the recon images, the largest number of heat signals on the abandoned base was in the building she stood against. She leaned across and peered through a narrow gap in the metal slats. A shadow moved across the window. She pulled back and raised four fingers at

Carrington and Yonten. They nodded, the monk's teeth flashing in the darkness.

Alexa murmured, 'Go!' softly in the wireless transmitter pinned to her collar, strode to the fire exit further along the wall, and opened the door. A dim, deserted corridor lay beyond. She entered it, the Sigs covering her line of sight. The door to the room with the window she had spied through was on the left.

She stood still for several seconds.

The low hum of a powerful generator came from somewhere below and caused the floor to vibrate faintly beneath her boots. The mutter of voices rose from further inside the building.

Alexa walked to the door, opened it, strode inside, and shot the man sitting at a table on the other side of the room. The figure next to him fell a fraction of a second later. The suppressors muffled the thuds of the bullets.

Carrington shot the sect member next to the window while Yonten delivered a powerful chopping blow to a vital point in the neck of the man behind the door.

She stepped over the dead bodies and picked up the two-way portable radio transceiver the man at the table had been holding. Seconds later, a low voice came through it. She noted the channel frequency before tossing the transceiver across to Carrington. The Crovir caught it deftly, depressed the transmitter switch, and murmured a response in passable Bulgarian. The voice at the other end acknowledged the security check and disconnected.

Alexa took the satellite smartphone out of her jacket and texted the Crovir Hunters' team leader to change the band of the microphone devices they were using. She waited five seconds before talking softly in the transmitter. 'They have a security team guarding the perimeter of the airfield. Stay watchful.'

'We know. We almost walked into one of them,' the Hunter responded. 'The bastards are wearing camouflage gear.'

Her gaze shifted to the old computer on the table. Before they left Reznak's estate, Eva had attempted to connect to the network at the old airfield. All of the AI's efforts had been in vain.

Alexa removed a slim device from a pocket in her cargo pants. Banks had given it to her before she left the lab; it was a tap that would allow Eva to remotely access the data flowing across Kronos's system. She connected it to an ethernet port at the back of the terminal.

A second later, the AI buzzed quietly in her earpiece, confirming that a successful connection had been made.

Alexa walked out of the room and headed inside the building, Carrington and the monk on her heels. A shadowy stairwell appeared to their right after twenty feet. She looked up and saw faint light spill over the banister one storey above.

They continued down the corridor and explored the rest of the ground floor. The other rooms were deserted. The tombs were not in this building.

They returned to the stairwell and headed toward the basement.

A steel door stood at the bottom of the steps. Alexa opened it and stepped carefully across the threshold. The noise of the generator grew louder.

She stared at the banks of old computer mainframes ahead, caught movement out of the corner of her eye, and saw a startled man disappear around the corner of the L-shaped room. She went after him and shot him twice in the back. He fell across a table, the phone in his hand clattering to the metal surface.

She picked up the handset, listened to the dial tone, and placed it back on its base.

A voice came over the microphone receiver in her ear above the dull drone of the large generator to the right. 'I don't want to alarm you, but a Tornado fighter plane just came out of a hangar at the end of the runway,' said the Crovir team leader. 'What the hell are these guys up to?'

Alexa's gaze shifted to the generator. Before she could utter a word in response, the phone on the table started to ring. She stared at it. It stopped after ten seconds.

'Get ready,' she said curtly into the transmitter. 'They know we're here.' She crossed the floor and flicked off the generator switch.

The basement was instantly plunged into darkness. The lights came back on seconds later.

'Shit!' exclaimed Carrington. 'They must have backup generators elsewhere.'

The faint but unmistakable sound of gunfire rang out in the distance.

Alexa turned and strode out of the room. Bullets pelted down around her when she entered the stairwell. She looked up. Figures leaned over the railing two floors above, the muzzles of their Shipka submachine guns flashing in the gloom.

She returned fire, Carrington at her side. Three of the shadowy shapes jerked and slumped over the banister, their weapons dropping from their limp grasps. Carrington grabbed one as it fell past him.

They were on the ground floor within seconds.

The exit door through which they had entered the building slammed open to their left.

Alexa emptied the Sigs in the four camouflaged figures who came over the threshold, reloaded, and started up the stairs. A voice shouted a harsh command above them. She recognized the gravelly tone.

It was Boyko Dragov.

A bloodthirsty smile flashed across her lips as she discharged her guns at the silhouettes on the first floor. Carrington fired the Shipka next to her.

The enemies' shots suddenly stopped when Alexa and the two men reached the next landing. The sect members were falling back.

The Crovir team leader suddenly swore in her ear. 'Shit, I think they're gonna bomb someone!' he panted. It sounded like he was running. Gunfire erupted across the comms line. 'There's a mother of a missile strapped to the belly of this jet!'

Alexa glanced at Carrington. His expression mirrored her sudden unease. Throwing caution to the wind, she raced up the final steps. The immortal and the monk followed behind her.

A bullet grazed her right thigh when she stormed into the passage at the top of the stairs. She ignored the wound and took out the two men at the end of a long corridor to her right. They fell in front of a heavy-looking metal door.

Boyko Dragov stood in the room beyond. His eyes darkened when he saw her. The door slammed closed and she heard bolts slide across on the other side.

The rising whine of powerful twin engines suddenly shattered the air outside the building. As she strode down the passage toward the metal door, Alexa saw the Tornado jet thunder past through the windows of one of the empty rooms that lined the corridor. Glass rattled in metal frames. A muscle twitched in her jaw when she spotted the large bomb beneath the aircraft.

Eva's voice came over the microphone receiver. 'Alexa, I'm getting some strange readings from Kronos's network. They appear to be getting ready for a massive airstrike.'

'I know,' she replied with a frown. 'A fighter jet just lifted off from this airfield. Keep an eye on it.' She studied the metal door at the end of the passage, walked back a few steps, and entered one of the vacant rooms. She crossed the floor to a broken window and leaned out. The roof of the building was a few feet above them.

'Yonten, take the roof,' Alexa said quietly. He grinned and nodded.

She returned to the corridor with Carrington while the monk climbed out of the window. Eerie silence shrouded the building.

'I don't like this,' murmured the Crovir. He glanced over his shoulder toward the empty stairwell.

'Alexa,' said Eva in her ear. 'We appear to have a perimeter breach around the estate. Dimitri wanted me to warn you.'

Alexa's heart lurched inside her chest at the AI's words. Carrington was right; something was very wrong.

She raised the Sigs at the lock on the metal door and fired both guns rapidly. Sparks flew around them. She snarled, raised a booted leg, and kicked the panel. It dented beneath her blow.

Gunfire exploded on the other side of the door. Faint shouts punctuated the shots.

Alexa holstered the Sigs, grabbed the Shipka off Carrington, and emptied the submachine gun at the hinges. She dropped the weapon at her feet seconds later and kicked the door again. Another dent appeared beneath her foot.

Ignoring Carrington's shout of warning, she took several steps back, ran, and rammed her shoulder into the metal panel. Air left her lungs in a harsh grunt. The frame shuddered under the impact. She scowled and stepped back once more.

The door came off its hinges after the third blow and crashed into the room beyond. She was through the opening in a heartbeat, Carrington on her heels.

Six men lay incapacitated around the floor of a large, makeshift command center. A bank of monitors occupied the workstations ahead.

A choked noise rose from the right.

Alexa turned and saw Yonten struggling in Dragov's grasp. The giant had his arms wrapped around the skinny young man and was squeezing the air out of his lungs. His face an unhealthy shade of red, the monk continued to strike steadily at his adversary, his movements measured and accurate.

Her gaze shifted briefly to the bright computer screens. Her stomach dropped when she saw the satellite image on the middle display. 'Shut them down!' Alexa barked at Carrington. Sliding the sais out of their sheaths, she spoke swiftly into the transmitter on her collar. 'Eva, get everyone out of the lab, now! That jet is heading your way with a bomb. You don't have much time!'

She bolted across the room, jumped, and front-kicked Dragov in the small of his back.

The giant staggered forward a step. He dropped the monk and lumbered around to face her. His lips twisted in an ugly grimace. He raised his arms and brought his open hands toward her head in a power slap intended to crush her skull. Alexa spun the sais and blocked the blows, the blades pressed flat against her forearms.

Dragov grunted. Veins throbbed on his forehead.

She gritted her teeth as his palms slowly forced her arms closer together by an inch.

Someone kicked him in the thigh. His leg buckled slightly. Dragov turned and punched Yonten in the stomach. A whoosh of air left the monk's lips as he sailed across the room and struck the wall with his back. Alexa heard bone snap. Yonten pushed himself up and sagged, a sliver of blood staining his lips. A shadow of pain darted across his pale face. He took a determined step forward.

'Stand down!' snapped Alexa as she slipped out of the way of the giant's arcing fist. The monk froze at her command, his expression unreadable.

She raised each leg alternately in a rapid succession of savate kicks to Dragov's legs. Using the knuckle ends of the sais, she followed through with a series of powerful jab and hook punches to his trunk. The giant stumbled a couple of steps.

Alexa stepped behind him, hooked the top of her foot against the back of his ankle, swung an uppercut at his chin, and swept his leg out from under him when he leaned out of the way. Dragov fell heavily on his back.

She raised a heel and dropped it in an axe-kick toward his groin. He rolled, his quick movement catching her unawares once more. Alexa jumped up when his hand snaked out to grab her foot, twisted sideways in the air, and landed elbow down on his chest with the full weight of her body behind the strike.

She felt the breath leave his lungs in a low, guttural wheeze and saw a short spray of blood stain his teeth. She rolled free as he staggered to his feet.

Dragov swung at her again.

She ducked beneath his fist, grabbed his arm as it sailed above her head, lifted off the floor, and threw a hooking knee strike at his groin. This time, she made contact. The giant's eyes crossed and he doubled over. She dropped down lightly on the balls of her feet.

Shots rang out from the direction of the command center. Alexa looked over her shoulder.

Carrington was firing at the computer terminals. 'I've tried everything!' he shouted, glancing at her. 'I've even unplugged them. The damn things are running on battery power!'

A crash ahead brought her head back around. She saw Dragov disappear through a broken window.

Alexa ran to the sill and saw him rise from the ground fifteen feet below. Dragov looked up at her, a smug grin dawning on his lips. Tires squealed in the distance; a van was headed swiftly across the tarmac toward him. He leapt through the open side door as it slowed down. The vehicle performed a screeching U-turn and vanished into the night.

Something twisted painfully inside her chest. She turned and strode across the floor.

Less than ten minutes had passed since the fighter jet lifted off the airfield.

Alexa reached the monitors in time to see the explosion bloom brightly across the center screen. Acid burned the back of her throat. A shout of horror left Carrington's lips.

She raised a leaden hand to the microphone in her ear. 'Eva?' she said numbly. 'Eva!'

There was nothing but static in return.

CHAPTER TWENTY-SEVEN

THEY WATCHED THE ASSAULT ON REZNAK'S RESEARCH FACILITY ON the ride back to the airport. Carrington drove with one hand on the steering wheel of the SUV, the other alternating between the horn and the gearstick. The four-by-four lurched precariously around the vehicles on the motorway, its speed never dropping below a hundred and ten kilometers per hour. The Crovir immortal's eyes kept straying back to the laptop on Alexa's lap.

In the backseat, Yonten finished strapping his broken ribs and leaned across her shoulder. She could see his frown out of the corner of her eye. Her gaze remained fixed on the carnage on the screen.

Designed to penetrate hardened targets, specifically bunkers buried deep beneath the ground, the HOPE bomb had blasted through the reinforced concrete and the compact earth protecting the lab like a flamethrower through marshmallow. In the disastrous aftermath of the explosion, which had uprooted trees in a half-mile radius around its epicenter,

Kronos had swarmed in for the attack. Multiple points of gunfire still flared through the gray clouds of smoke and the blizzard that shrouded the site. The rain and sleet had put out most of the forest fires before they raged out of control.

Alexa's nails dug into her palms so hard she drew blood.

The Crovir team leader finished updating the central Crovir network from the backseat of the SUV. 'I'm sorry,' he said quietly. 'I hope you find the bastards who did this. Reznak is held in high regard in the Order.'

The Gulfstream jet's engines were already running when they drove onto the tarmac at Budapest Airport moments later. Fawkes stood in the doorway of the cabin, his expression flinty.

'Have you been able to reach Marie?' asked Alexa tensely as she climbed the steps toward him.

'No,' he replied, his tone frigid.

They were airborne within ten minutes.

Halfway to Ceske Budejovice, her satellite phone rang. Alexa grabbed it from the seat next to her. It was Reznak. She put it on speakerphone as she joined Fawkes and Carrington in the cockpit. Yonten followed behind her.

'Are you okay?' snapped Alexa into the mouthpiece.

The sound of coughing came over the line. 'Yes, I'm fine,' Reznak finally rasped. Other voices sounded in the noisy background. 'Tom? Marie's here with me. She's all right.'

Relief flashed across the pilot's face and his shoulders visibly sagged. 'Thank you,' Fawkes murmured in the direction of the phone.

'Did you suffer many casualties?' said Alexa. She stared blindly through the cockpit windscreen before asking the question she had been dreading to put forward. 'How's Jackson?'

'Apart from spitting nails and vowing eternal, bloody

vengeance on Cavaleti and Kronos, he's fine,' said Reznak wryly. 'He's helping Marie look after the wounded. We lost four humans.' His tone sobered with those words. 'About the only silver lining to this attack is that it took place so late at night. Most of the lab staff had already left for the day. There were eight deaths among the immortals, none of them final. Your warning gave us the time we needed to get to the emergency tunnel.'

Alexa digested this information slowly and felt a weight drop off her shoulders.

'The bomb reached the second level,' Reznak continued. 'Most of the labs on that floor were destroyed.'

She went still at the bitter note in her godfather's voice. She sensed he was holding back on news she was not going to like.

'Kronos got their hands on the Emerald Tablet and Anna's pendant,' said Reznak. 'We tried to recover the items, but we were heavily outnumbered. They threw tear gas and flash bombs into the crater after the explosion. Eva calculated the trajectory of the missile before she moved her data banks to her backup servers in the Crovir central facility in Dresden. She believes it was tracking something inside the lab. She suspects Kronos may have tagged one of you with a GPS device in your last encounter at the Freemasons' Hall.'

Alexa's hand stilled on the phone as a memory flashed through her mind. 'The bag I gave Jackson to put the tablet in,' she said grimly. 'One of the sect members tried to get it off his back.'

'That would explain their movements,' said her godfather after a short silence. 'They seemed to know exactly where it was inside the facility. The pendant will come as an added bonus for Cavaleti.'

She could almost hear him grit his teeth across the line. 'Did Jackson get somewhere with his translations?' she asked.

A stilted pause followed. 'Yes,' Reznak finally replied. 'Jackson believes that Anna's pendant, and by default the one that was stolen from Yonten's monastery three centuries ago, are seals for the tombs. Without them, Cavaleti cannot access the immortals' remains.' He sighed. 'Which means he is now in possession of everything he needs to make the Philosopher's Stone. '

Coldness flooded Alexa's veins.

'How far out are you?' said Reznak, interrupting her thoughts.

She glanced at Fawkes, her mind still resonating from the ramifications of Kronos's latest move.

'We'll be landing in fifteen minutes,' said Fawkes.

'Good,' said Reznak. 'There's a lot we need to do. Eva is tracking the vehicles that left the estate after the attack. They're heading north across the country. I'll start assembling a team to intercept them.'

One of Reznak's bodyguards was waiting for them when they reached the airport in the Czech Republic. Alexa strode up to the immortal and put a hand out. He stared at her moodily before dropping the keys of the SUV in her hand. She took the wheel as he climbed in the backseat with Fawkes and the monk.

Despite the blizzard, they made the return trip to Sumava in record time.

A faint red glow appeared above the tree line as they approached the boundaries of the estate. Carrington cursed beside her. Alexa's breath unconsciously caught in her throat when the iron gates swung open. She drove onto the icy driveway, her eyes straining as she peered into the darkness. The castle appeared through the trees, lights blazing through the tall glass windows. It stood untouched behind a thick veil of snow. She started to breathe again.

She braked in the courtyard and gazed darkly at the two ambulances parked with their lights off. A figure stood framed in the bright, open doorway under the portico. Marie met Fawkes halfway down the steps and was engulfed in his embrace. A smile of relief dawned on her lined face when she spotted Alexa.

Reznak was pacing the foyer when they entered the castle, his cellphone in hand. Icy anger prickled Alexa's skin as her eyes moved over the cuts on his face and hands, and the blood on one of his trouser legs. He was walking with a noticeable limp. 'I'll call you back, Victor,' he said abruptly into the mouthpiece when he saw them. He disconnected and headed toward her.

A figure overtook him.

Alexa caught a glimpse of Jackson's bloodied features before his arms closed around her in a vise-like grip. Surprise made her stiffen in his hold. He did not appear to notice.

'God,' he whispered in her hair. 'I thought I'd never see you again.' He leaned back and scrutinized her face, his expression fierce.

She scowled at the fresh bruises and cuts beneath the thin layer of grime covering his skin. The anger thrumming through her veins focused into icy determination.

She would make Alberto Cavaleti pay for this transgression.

Her fresh resolve came to a grinding halt when Jackson's mouth landed on hers. She tasted plaster dust and blood on his lips. He deepened the kiss, his tongue invading her mouth. Heat flooded her body and she raised her fingers to the back of his head.

'Would you mind very much if I say hello to my own goddaughter now?' said Reznak behind him.

Jackson's eyes snapped open and he stared at her blankly. 'Oh.' He let go of her and stepped back, an awkward grimace flashing across his face.

Reznak closed the gap between them and held her tightly to his chest for a long moment. Senses still reeling from Jackson's kiss, Alexa could only raise her eyebrows. This was another first in her relationship with Reznak.

Her godfather looked past her shoulder at Yonten. 'Abbot Kelsang is sending reinforcements,' he said quietly.

The monk nodded and winced. Marie took his hand and led him toward the kitchen.

'We were lucky. Several of the immortal scientists who work at the lab are qualified surgeons,' said Reznak in a low voice as he watched them leave. 'They were able to obtain medical supplies from the closest hospital.'

'The ambulances?' said Alexa.

Reznak nodded. 'They kind of...borrowed them.' He ran a hand through his hair. 'I've managed to stop the local authorities from swarming over the estate for the time being. I'm not sure how much longer they'll buy the lie that this was a gas leak. It should hopefully give us enough time to mask the fact that we were bombed. The weather being what it is, hopefully none of the locals noticed the fighter jet or the missile before it struck.'

Banks stepped out of the corridor on the right. His left eye was purple and almost swollen shut. Blood oozed from a split in his lower lip. 'Hey, Alexa,' he said weakly.

'You look like hell,' said Carrington bluntly.

'Yeah, well, I'm not used to being an action man,' muttered

the young immortal. 'The last time I punched someone was in 1960.'

'Are you all set?' asked Reznak briskly.

'Yes,' Banks replied with a careful nod that made him grimace in pain nonetheless.

They gathered at the temporary command center he had installed in the study.

'They're on Route 4, just outside Pribram,' said Banks. An infrared satellite image flashed up on a monitor on the desk before him. It tracked a convoy of army vehicles traveling up a northbound carriageway. 'Although I'm unsure as to their final destination, I asked Eva to check the closest airports and train terminals for any unusual activity, just in case. Eva?'

'There has been an unscheduled flight plan logged with the control tower at Prague's Ruzyne Airport in the last ten minutes,' came the AI's steady, computerized voice over the speakers. 'It's an Ilyushin Il-476 military plane bound for Perm, Russia. There is no information available on the owners of the aircraft.'

Banks stared at the display. 'If they're heading to Prague, they'll be there in under an hour.'

Carrington glanced at Reznak. 'There are Crovir Hunters based near the city. They could try to hold them off until our team gets—'

'No,' interrupted Reznak. His expression was strangely thoughtful as he studied the vehicles on the screen. 'I want to see where they're going.'

'Isn't that risky?' said Carrington with a frown. 'They've already got the tablet and the pendants.'

Reznak glanced at Alexa. 'What do you think?'

Now that her anger had started to abate, a hunter's thrill

buzzed through her veins once more. 'I agree with Dimitri,' Alexa said curtly. 'They'll lead us to the tombs.'

'Making the Elixir of Life is a process that could take days,' Reznak explained at Carrington's expression. 'We've only managed to decipher one fifth of the Emerald Tablet.' His gaze switched briefly to Jackson. 'I doubt they'll have anyone in their ranks who can match Zachary's skills.'

'Eva, did you manage to get anything else out of their systems before you moved to the Crovir data servers?' said Alexa.

'No,' replied the AI. 'If they're holding information somewhere, it must be in a physical format. They shut their network down after the attack.'

Reznak spoke to Abbot Kelsang again before spending the next forty minutes coordinating the Crovir response team that would join them in Russia. It took him nearly half an hour to convince the First Council of the urgency of the matter; by the end of the conversation, his voice had dropped to icy depths Alexa had rarely heard before. With the details of their mission confirmed and the Council finally agreeing to spare a group of fifty Hunters, she turned to leave the study.

Her godfather was calling Victor Dvorsky as she exited the room. Alexa pursed her lips as she made her way to the armory in the basement of the west wing of the castle.

Although she had been born well after the great war that had threatened to consume the two immortal races, she felt strangely ambivalent about working together with the people who had once been their sworn enemies.

She finally reached a narrow corridor and headed down the winding staircase at the end. A thick, iron-plated oak door appeared at the bottom of the steps. She opened it and walked across the threshold.

As well as holding one of the larger arsenals on Reznak's estate, the basement had also served as one of her training grounds during the years she had lived in the castle. She headed past the ring where she had won her first boxing match at the age of eleven, the faded punching bags that had had to be replaced on many an occasion, and the polished fencing floor where she had learned to use the sais. A large storeroom occupied the northern aspect of the cellar. Its walls were lined with dozens of ammunition crates and weapon cabinets. She opened one of the chests and started to load magazines in a compact tactical waist and thigh belt.

Footsteps sounded behind her and paused in the doorway. 'I'm coming with you,' said Jackson in a steadfast tone.

Alexa turned and studied the stubborn light blazing in his icy blue eyes. Her hands fisted at her sides.

She was still controlled by an all-consuming and somewhat irrational urge to keep Jackson as physically close as possible—especially since she had witnessed the blast that had devastated Reznak's research facility. But she was also level-headed enough to see that the Harvard professor would be unable to contribute much to their current predicament.

'Why?' she finally asked.

He inhaled sharply. 'Why? What the—'

'You can't fight as well as immortals,' Alexa interrupted bluntly. 'You'll only get in our way if we have to protect you.'

Jackson looked like he was about to explode. He took a deep breath and stared at the floor. 'Okay, I'll admit that I'm not as strong or as fast or as deadly as you guys,' he said bitterly. 'But I'm *way* smarter than any of you. And you're gonna need smarts in your dealings with Cavaleti's sect.'

Alexa could not deny the truth of his words. Still, something inside was screaming at her to not let him get anywhere near the battlefield. 'We have Eva,' she said steadily.

Jackson's expression darkened. He stormed inside the room and backed her against one of the cabinets. 'Eva is a goddamned robot!' he said between gritted teeth. 'Granted, she's clever, but you need human eyes on the ground and a brain that can analyze the enemy's actions instantly!'

Alexa scowled. She grabbed his arms, spun him round, and slammed him against the wall. 'I don't want you there!' she snarled.

His words of protest suddenly died on his lips. The anger in his eyes cleared. His irises turned cobalt blue. 'Are you worried about me?' he whispered.

She turned away.

He reached out and seized her arm in an iron grip. 'That's it, isn't it?' he said, his tone growing more confident.

Alexa closed her eyes briefly against the storm of emotions raging through her heart, whirled around, and kissed him savagely.

'Don't go,' she finally murmured against his lips, her breathing ragged and her heart pounding against her ribs as she tasted his blood on her tongue.

She tried hard not to make her words sound like a plea.

The expression on his face made her shiver and sent a sharp ache stabbing through her.

'I won't leave you,' said Jackson quietly.

CHAPTER TWENTY-EIGHT

THEY LEFT THE ESTATE SHORTLY BEFORE TWO IN THE MORNING. As their vehicles ate away the miles to the airport outside Ceske Budejovice, Eva confirmed that the convoy of SUVs and vans that had attacked Reznak's research facility had reached Prague.

Alexa was aware of Jackson's eyes on her throughout most of the drive.

Reznak's refueled Gulfstream jet lifted off the tarmac forty-five minutes after the Ilyushin Il-476 departed Ruzyne Airport.

'Tom, do you think you can beat them to Perm?' asked her godfather as he leaned in the doorway to the cockpit.

Fawkes studied the flight display before him with a cold expression. 'Yes.'

'Good,' said Reznak. He walked back into the main cabin and stopped by Yonten's seat. 'How're you holding up?'

The monk smiled and nodded once. The color had returned to his cheeks. Alexa suspected this had more to do with the biscuits Marie had given him than the painkillers the older woman had forced down his throat before they left the chateau.

Reznak turned to her. 'Get some rest,' he ordered curtly.

Despite her godfather's advice, sleep eluded Alexa as the jet soared through the dark skies. Out of the corner of her eye, she could see Jackson staring blindly through the porthole on the other side of the aisle.

THE SUN ROSE ON THE HORIZON SHORTLY AFTER THEY PASSED Moscow. They flew over the frozen landscape of the Eastern European Plain and the Kama River before landing at the deserted Bolshoye Savino International Airport nine miles outside the city of Perm just before midday. Storm clouds raced across the gray skies from the foothills of the Central Ural Mountains and brought a flurry of sleet over their heads as they made their way to the four-by-fours waiting on the edge of the tarmac.

'Where are the rest of your men?' asked Reznak stiffly of the Crovir Hunter who appeared to be in charge of the team of ten immortals.

The Hunter shifted awkwardly. 'I'm afraid the new Head of the Order delayed their deployment by two hours,' he replied in a low voice. 'Something came up in Germany.'

Reznak swore. 'I should have brought men from my own bloody Section!'

'Yeah, but they're not exactly warriors, boss,' said Carrington with a grimace.

Reznak scowled. 'They didn't do too badly against Agatha Vellacrus's army a month ago.'

They climbed in the vehicles and made their way east along a motorway. Soon, they exited a main road and pulled up under a copse on the edge of a military airbase southwest of the city.

The lights of the Il-476 blazed brightly as it taxied at the end of a runway a thousand feet from their location. It turned onto a side ramp before slowly rolling to a stop. The cargo hold opened moments later.

Alexa raised a pair of powerful binoculars to her eyes and stared at the fleet of SUVs that drove out of the aircraft. A muscle twitched in her jaw when she glimpsed the immortals who had attacked them at the Freemasons' Hall.

'I don't see Cavaleti or Dragov,' she said after a few tense seconds. She shared a troubled glance with Reznak.

They got back in the four-by-fours and caught up with the convoy of vehicles on the road heading into Perm. They followed cautiously from a distance.

The SUVs finally turned onto a dirt track after several miles, crossed an empty industrial estate, and parked next to an abandoned warehouse. Carrington switched off the headlights of their vehicle and brought it to a stop in the shadow of a building about four hundred feet away.

Reznak stared through the windscreen from the rear seat. 'What the hell are they up to?' he murmured.

The snowfall had almost doubled in the last ten minutes and an eerie twilight had fallen across the city. Icy rain pelted the roof of the four-by-four, the noise of the drops mimicking the ricochet of gunfire.

They were at one of the train stations that served the city of Perm and the Trans-Siberian Railway. Up ahead, the shadowy figures of Kronos started to unload crates from the rear of the stationary SUVs. Light flared across the frozen ground next to them when the doors of the warehouse opened. A pair of forklift trucks rolled out of the building. A second group of men followed behind.

'Looks like they're going somewhere,' said Jackson.

'Eva's viewpoint above us is not going to be of any use,' said Reznak, frowning at the gray screen of the computer on his lap. 'Even infrared imaging will prove futile in this weather.'

Alexa looked at the rail tracks on the right. She opened the passenger door and stepped out of the vehicle. An icy wind whipped sleet across her face and the hood of the white parka she wore over her jacket. Her gaze shifted to the dim shapes in the distance. 'I'll do some recon.'

Reznak looked at her steadily from the rear seat. 'Take Yonten with you,' he ordered. He turned to Carrington. 'Go around the opposite way with a couple of the Hunters.'

The Crovir grinned and slipped out of the driver's seat.

Alexa looked at Yonten. Although he had been unhappy about it, the monk had been persuaded to change into a snow camouflage suit before they left the jet. He had, however, insisted on wearing the saffron robes beneath it.

They used the cover of the worsening blizzard to cross the two hundred feet of open ground that separated them from the rows of goods wagons to the right. Alexa halted in the shelter of the first boxcars and moved slowly forward across the icy ground. Light stabbed through the gloom in front of them. Muffled thuds rose above the whistling of the wind.

Moments later, they dropped and crawled under one of the wagons. Alexa shuffled forward and suddenly froze in the shadows beneath the carriage.

Boyko Dragov stood fifty feet ahead and to her left. He was talking to the immortal with the pale blue eyes. Behind them, the forklift trucks loaded the crates from the SUVs onto a train. Smoke curled from the roof of the diesel locomotive at the head of the linked goods wagons. The muted roar of the engine shook the metal tracks and sleepers she and the monk lay against.

She studied the busy scene for several seconds before rolling carefully out from under the boxcar. She signaled to Yonten. The monk nodded and followed her as she crept back along the line for some twenty feet. They moved behind the next column of cars before edging forward again.

'Dimitri, they're getting ready to leave on a freight train,' Alexa said into the wireless transmitter pinned to the hood of her parka. 'The tablet and the pendant must be in one of the carriages.'

Reznak's voice came through the receiver in her ear. 'Carrington can't get to the other end of the tracks. He's in the line of sight of two of their vehicles.'

Alexa finally stopped and scrutinized the train thirty feet to their left through a gap between two cars. The first three carriages behind the locomotive were passenger coaches; shadows moved behind the steamed-up windows above the tracks.

Unease darted through her. They had to move *now*.

'I'm going in,' she said in low voice.

There was a long pause. Alexa heard the words of caution her godfather did not express in the tone of his voice. 'Okay,' said Reznak reluctantly.

She looked at Yonten over her shoulder. The monk grinned at her.

They slipped under the coupling of the two cars, ran across the gap to the freight train, and halted in the shadow of a wagon. Yonten looked up and quickly scaled the side of the boxcar. Alexa followed him to the top.

The icy wind whipped at their clothes and stung their faces when they slithered onto the roof of the train. Their snowsuits protected them from the worst of the cold as they lay exposed to the harsh elements.

Doors slammed somewhere below. The metal carriage shuddered under Alexa's hands. She shifted carefully to the edge of the snow-covered surface and looked down. Dragov had disappeared from the edge of the tracks.

She peered ahead to where the last sect members were climbing into the passenger carriages. A burst of smoke accompanied the rising rumble of the diesel locomotive as the train slowly pulled away and started to move east.

Ten seconds later, Yonten tapped her on the shoulder. Alexa looked back to where he pointed. A shadowy figure in a snow camouflage suit was climbing onto the roof of the last boxcar some hundred and sixty feet behind them.

It was Jackson.

Alexa stifled a curse, turned, and moved swiftly toward the Harvard professor. Yonten stayed put, an anxious smile hovering on his lips as he watched her leave.

The train started to gather speed after it exited the station. The frozen waters of the Kama River materialized to the left of the tracks. She had just cleared the second of the three wagons separating her from Jackson when he suddenly disappeared from view.

Her heart thudded painfully inside her chest. Alexa rose and ran across the shaking rooftop.

The train lurched beneath her when she landed on the final boxcar. She staggered to the edge of the wagon as it swerved north onto a bridge that spanned the river and caught a glimpse of the distant ice-covered waters below. She steadied herself a second before she lost her balance.

Frost coated her eyelashes and a glacial rain numbed her face as she peered into the deepening gloom. Relief flashed through her. There was a faint, square-shaped brightness ahead. She crouched and inched carefully to the edge of the skylight. As she peered over the metal lip of the opening, the birthmark on the back of her neck started to throb.

A feeble glow illuminated the interior of the carriage below. It was an old livestock wagon with louvered windows making up its east wall and a pair of stalls at the north end.

It was empty—except for two large stone tombs strapped heavily to the middle of the floor.

Alexa stared at the sarcophagi, the trishula burning fiercely at her nape. A heartbeat later, she spotted the figure creeping from the shadows beneath her toward the tombs. She choked back another curse and dropped through the opening.

Jackson turned around at the soft sound of her landing. His ice-blue eyes were bright with barely concealed excitement and frustratingly devoid of all apprehension. 'It's the tombs,' he whispered shakily, his hand inches from the dark stone.

'What the hell do you think you're doing?' she hissed, storming toward him.

A guilty grimace dawned on his face. 'I was coming to join you. I just happened to spot these through the skylight,' he said defensively, indicating the sarcophagi.

Alexa glanced at the bulkhead behind him. A door stood in the middle of the wall. The boxcar had a second compartment. She looked around. There was an exit in the north wall of the carriage, between the two stalls.

'We need to get out of here,' she said briskly.

'But—' started Jackson.

The bulkhead door opened and the immortal she had shot in the head in Istanbul stepped over the threshold. He backed into their compartment as he talked to someone in the adjacent room. A second later, he turned and stared into the twin barrels of the Sigs.

Alexa smiled grimly and pulled the triggers. The immortal

jerked as the bullets slammed into his chest. Wide-eyed incomprehension flared in his eyes before he slumped to the floor. Shadowy figures shifted in the dimly lit chamber behind him.

Still firing, Alexa stepped swiftly backward toward the opposite end of the wagon. She glanced over her shoulder.

Jackson was already at the exit door. He grabbed the handle and pulled; the door slid open half an inch before jamming in its tracks. He swore. It was locked.

Gunfire erupted from across the compartment. Alexa grabbed Jackson's arm and ran into the shelter of the stall to the left. Bullets pummeled the boards in front of them as they landed heavily on the floor. Wood chips and splinters rained down on their heads and slashed across exposed skin.

She checked the magazines in the guns, rose on one knee, and shot at the three men framed in the doorway next to the tombs. A lightbulb exploded in a shower of shards in the other room. One of the figures cried out and fell under her bullets. The other two retreated in the gloom behind him. She dropped behind the shelter of the stall wall.

Jackson's rapid breaths warmed the skin on the back of her neck in the deadly hush that followed. Alexa glanced at the skylight in the roof of the boxcar and formulated an escape plan.

A faint, metallic noise suddenly reached her ears. She looked over the top of the stall and saw the immortal with the pale blue eyes standing with a grenade launcher on the end of an AK-74 rifle. Instinct took over. She turned and pushed Jackson toward the second stall on the other side of the carriage.

A second later, the world went white around her.

❄

CHAPTER TWENTY-NINE

Awareness slammed into her with the force of an earthquake. Alexa gasped and sucked freezing air into her starving lungs. Deep, shuddering breaths wheezed past her numb lips as oxygen flooded her blood. She lay still for timeless moments as she concentrated on simply inhaling and exhaling.

Inch by slow inch, she became conscious of the cold shroud that encased her body. Her eyes fluttered open, dislodging a thin crust of frost from her lashes.

Snow fell thickly from a dark, overcast sky framed by a ring of trees. The flakes landed silently on her chilled skin and melted into icy trails. She turned her head slowly.

She was lying on her back in a shallow, frozen stream fifty feet from the edge of an embankment that ran alongside the railway line. The faint gurgle of flowing water reached her ears from beneath the inch-thick ice.

Pain suddenly washed over her in a blinding wave. She choked on her breath as dark spots danced across her vision. Wetness stung her eyes.

Alexa panted unevenly for several seconds. She gritted her teeth before slowly rolling onto her side. She froze and stared at the crimson stain spreading in an irregular circle across the whiteness around her. Beyond it, charred chunks of the wagon dotted the landscape in a semicircular blast radius. She looked down.

The fragments from the grenade had ripped through the snowsuit and slashed her body from her chest to her thighs. She was bleeding from dozens of cuts and jagged tears. She could make out a particularly large wound on her upper abdomen.

Alexa sat up unsteadily and bit her lip when fiery trails of agony stabbed through her once more. She had dislocated her left shoulder and broken a couple of ribs when she landed on the ground.

She took another deep breath, bent her left arm at the elbow, and rotated it out sharply. A hiss escaped her throat when the bone slipped back into the socket. Blood dripped from a slash on her forehead. She wiped the red drops from her eyes and scanned her surroundings.

She was in the middle of a forest that flanked the tracks. Metal glinted in a snowdrift about twenty feet ahead of her. She pushed herself onto her knees and slowly lurched to her feet.

The darkness swirled around her in hazy circles. Blood gushed from the wound in her abdomen.

Alexa stood still while she fought down a wave of nausea. It took all her willpower to raise one foot and put it forward in front of the other. By the seventh step, her gait was steadier.

Her Sigs had fallen some thirty feet from the rail lines. She picked them up and looked around. A frozen vista of trees stretched out before her for what seemed like miles. Although she suspected Perm lay somewhere to the southwest of her position, she could see no semblance of life through the blizzard and the solid barrier of pines and conifers.

She walked to a tree on the embankment and sat down against the trunk. Her breaths clouding the air with white puffs, she stared at the sky through the branches above her head before closing her eyes. Jackson's face swam across her dark vision.

This time, the ache that shot through her had little to do with her injuries. The fact that she could not see his body next to the tracks meant he was still on the train—and probably still alive.

A slow, burning anger seeped into her heart and started to flow through her veins. Alexa allowed the rage to build up until it drowned out her physical discomfort. She looked down at the gaping gash in her abdomen, grabbed a handful of snow, and started to pack it methodically against the wound.

Something white fluttered out of her torn jacket and fell against her hand. Dark drops dripped past her eyes and landed on the fragment of paper. She picked it up slowly. Scarlet trails smudged the Cartesian coordinates scribbled across the dirty sheet.

She was still staring at it sometime later when someone shouted her name. Lights flashed through the heavy curtain of white. Seconds later, the beams of a four-by-four washed over the tracks and zeroed in on her. The vehicle crunched over the snow and came to a stop several feet away.

Alexa rose slowly from the ground.

The passenger door opened and Reznak stepped out. He ran to where she stood propped against the tree, his boots sinking awkwardly in the foot-deep drifts. His eyes grew wide with horror as he took in her injuries.

'It looks worse than it—' she started to say.

Reznak grabbed her shoulders and hugged her fiercely to his chest. Alexa winced and stifled a groan.

He stood back, a remorseful grimace flashing across his face. He suddenly went pale. 'Did you die?'

'No,' Alexa said firmly. She wasn't sure how she knew. She just did.

Carrington appeared behind Reznak. 'Holy shit,' the immortal said hoarsely. He turned to the Hunters spilling out of the other vehicles pulling up behind the first four-by-four. 'Get the medical kit!'

'How did you find me?' asked Alexa.

As Reznak wrapped one arm around her shoulders and walked her to the open tailgate of the closest vehicle, she reached inside the snowsuit and took out her satellite phone. It had been smashed during the explosion and her subsequent landing. She looked at him with a frown.

A strangely defensive light dawned in her godfather's eyes. 'There's a GPS tracking device in your Timex,' he finally admitted. 'I'm sorry we couldn't get here any sooner. We had to take a detour across the river.'

Alexa stared at him for a moment before looking at the expensive and miraculously intact watch on her wrist. It had been a gift from him ten years ago, on the tricentennial anniversary of the day he had found her on the battlefield outside Narva. Her gaze shifted to his unrepentant face.

'I'm not apologizing for it,' Reznak said bluntly.

She mulled over his words and the unexpected feelings they engendered while he helped her remove the damaged snowsuit. A fortnight ago, the mere fact that Reznak had effectively tagged her would have enraged her beyond belief. Now, she felt differently.

Her short time with Zachary Jackson had changed her in ways that she could never have imagined in a hundred years.

A muscle clenched in her godfather's jaw when he uncovered the dozens of gashes and tears that dotted her flesh.

Carrington studied her wounds with a low whistle. 'God, Alexa, I don't think I've ever seen you this banged up.' He grabbed a steel hip flask from the trunk of the vehicle and tossed it at her. 'Here, drink up.'

She opened the cap of the container, got a whiff of strong spirits, and downed a mouthful of the liquid. Heat flooded her throat and spread flaming trails through her body. She took another mouthful as Carrington started to clean the worse of her injuries.

'What happened?' asked Reznak.

Alexa glanced at the suture kit that one of the Hunters had just opened. 'Jackson found the tombs,' she said steadily. 'They were in one of the goods wagons on the train. Kronos surprised us when we were trying to get out of the carriage.' She barely felt the needle when it pierced her cold skin. 'He's still on the train. As is Yonten.'

The only thing keeping her from losing her composure was the knowledge that the monk would protect Jackson. Of course, neither of them was bulletproof, but she had yet to see a single shot get close to striking the Asian man in the battles they had fought together thus far.

Reznak muttered an expletive in Czech. 'The rest of our team are more than an hour out,' he said at her quizzical expression. 'And we have no idea where the train's gone. Eva was unable to analyze the satellite images over this part of the plains.'

Alexa handed him the piece of paper with the Cartesian

coordinates. 'Jackson found this in Istanbul. The point of origin must be Perm,' she said curtly.

Five minutes later, they were staring at a dot on a map on Reznak's laptop. 'That's 180 miles northeast of here,' he said thoughtfully. He studied the craggy terrain around the target. 'It's in the Ural Mountains.'

Strength was steadily flowing back into Alexa's limbs. The pain that stabbed through her body had turned into a dull ache; her wounds were already healing. 'They needed the diesel locomotive to reach their final destination,' she said as she stepped into a spare snowsuit. 'They must be using sections of non-electrified tracks to get there.'

Reznak turned to one of the Hunters. 'Give the guys who're joining us the new coordinates. We'll meet them there.' His gaze shifted to the snow-covered railway line next to the vehicles. 'Let's go.'

They drove alongside the tracks for eighty miles before turning to follow a branch line that veered north by northeast into the wooded wilderness. Although the freezing winds that howled across the plains eased slightly, there was no respite from the steady snowfall.

Boreal forests draped in heavy white blankets rose around them as they headed through the foothills toward the soaring peaks of the Urals. Apart from the empty tracks and the occasional power cable, they saw no signs of civilization.

The snowstorm finally abated around five thirty. At six in the evening, a signpost appeared in the beams of their headlights. They rolled to a stop next to it and studied the Russian wording under the coating of ice and snow.

'"Danger. Mining area ahead. Trespassers will be prosecuted",' translated Carrington. He glanced at the computer screen on her lap.

They were four miles from their target.

'We go on foot from here,' said Alexa coldly.

The excitement of the impending hunt sent a burst of adrenaline through her veins. Injuries long forgotten, her muscles tightened in readiness for battle.

In her long, immortal life, she had never wanted a fight as much as she wanted this one.

Reznak spoke to the team leader of the forty Crovir Hunters waiting for his instructions ten miles northwest of their position. With the blizzard finally easing, Eva had managed to beam some useful satellite pictures their way.

'Your target is in the mountain ahead. To reach it, you will have to go through a narrow valley,' said the AI smoothly over the laptop speakers.

Alexa studied the infrared images on the display. 'Can you see any structures that look like buildings?'

'No. There are no visible signs of human habitation above the tree line,' said Eva. 'The rail tracks follow the banks of a river to the south face of the mountain at the head of the valley. Apart from some evidence of animal life, the area appears deserted.'

'What's below the mountain?' asked Alexa.

Static came across the speakers while the AI communicated with the Crovir satellite network. 'Interestingly enough, the ground-penetrating radar is showing impressions of a vast network of underground caves and tunnels,' said Eva moments later. 'The first two levels seem to be supported by reinforced concrete. The underlying rock appears to be limestone. I cannot tell you how deep the complex is.'

'Are the caves man-made structures?' said Reznak.

'It is difficult to ascertain this with absolute certainty,' said

Eva. 'Some look like natural formations. Others have a more traditional, symmetric design.'

'Can you access any computer network in the area?' said Alexa.

'No,' said Eva. 'But I am detecting underground power cables running into the mountain.'

Moments later, they finished gearing up, parked the vehicles under the cover of the trees, and headed into the forest on foot.

Apart from the occasional thud of snow falling from the laden branches and the faint crunch of their steps in the white drifts that covered the rising land, the silence around them was complete. The wind soon died down.

Alexa stared through the overhead canopy. Stars appeared in the clearing skies above, diamond-bright in the darkness.

She would have preferred the cover of the blizzard for their assault.

The sound of rushing water finally broke the stillness of the night. A mile after they started out, they came to the confluence of two rivers hedged by the conifer forests. A low bridge carried the rail tracks over the shallow rapids.

They crossed the waterway a hundred feet down from the overpass.

The gradient increased steeply when they reached the mouth of the valley. Shadowy slopes rose on either side of the thinning river, great blocks of rock that blotted out the stars. The rail line followed the curve of the canyon toward the north.

Fifteen minutes later, Alexa stopped abruptly and put a hand up to signal the others to halt.

An owl hooted in the unearthly hush that shrouded the forested inclines.

She studied the pile of snow next to a tree, crouched down,

and gently cleared the base with a gloved hand. A small, black, metallic device strapped to the trunk was exposed.

They stared at the sensor through their night vision goggles.

'Tell the rest of the team that there's a wireless, infrared, perimeter intrusion system within one and a half miles of the target,' said Alexa to one of the Crovir Hunters, her gaze shifting to the gloom ahead. The immortal nodded and spoke quietly into the microphone transmitter on the hood of his snowsuit.

They covered the remaining ground carefully, their progress hampered by their search for more hidden sensors. They had travelled another two thousand feet when Carrington picked out the flare of a cigarette in the darkness. They froze behind the trees and studied the camouflaged watchtower on the slope to their left.

A pair of figures stood at the top of the wood and metal structure. The low mutter of conversation floated down toward them. Ten seconds passed before one of the Crovir Hunters spotted the second tower to the right.

'Should we eliminate them?' the immortal murmured.

'No,' replied Alexa. She stared at the armed guards atop the structure. 'They might sound an alarm. We should use the element of surprise to our advantage as long as we possibly can.'

The land grew more barren the deeper they ventured into the valley. The grassy slopes and trees were soon replaced by loose rocks and towering boulders. The river became a stream. Eighty minutes after leaving the four-by-fours, they finally arrived at the head of the gorge.

The tree line ended abruptly some three hundred feet from the base of a giant cliff. Water gleamed against the dark surface as it rushed down from the peaks above to form a shallow creek.

They stopped in the shadows under a copse and studied the terrain. Irregular protrusions rose from the snow-covered ground in front of the elevation. Alexa stared at the tree stumps. Whatever vegetation had survived the harsh conditions of the mountains had been deliberately felled to expose the ground.

She stared at the south face of the mountain. To the untrained eye, the rail tracks appeared to run straight into the rock. It took but a few seconds for her to make out the outline of a cleverly disguised tunnel in the cliff face. The giant, gray metal doors under the camouflage netting looked large enough to admit a freight train.

Another pair of watchtowers stood under the bluff at the extremities of the canyon.

'They'll have security cameras covering this area,' said Alexa in a low voice.

'How can you be so sure?' asked the team leader of the Hunters. He glanced at her with a frown. 'I can't see anything through the IR goggles.'

'Because I would have them,' she replied curtly.

'I agree,' muttered Reznak.

'Eva, can you see anything that resembles manhole covers or ventilation shafts close to our position?' said Alexa into the microphone transmitter.

'There is a small segment of ground close to the cliff wall on your left that has a slightly enhanced heat signal from the rest of the land,' the AI replied after several seconds. 'I can detect three more similar areas within a four-hundred-foot radius of the mountain face.'

'Good. Let the other Crovir Hunters know their locations,' said Alexa.

'I will,' said Eva. As they turned to head toward the sector the AI had indicated, she came back on the line. 'Alexa, I am detecting movement behind you.'

They dropped to the ground behind the cover of the trees, weapons in hand.

'I've just received a communication from Banks,' said Eva in her ear. 'It's Frank Schmidt. He said he was bringing some friends.'

Alexa slowly rose to her feet. Shapes shifted in the shadows under the branches. She took the night vision goggles off and stared at the tall figure climbing the incline toward her.

The man stopped a few feet away and pulled down the ski mask covering his lower face.

'Hi, Alexa,' said Schmidt. He acknowledged the Hunters next to her with a nod.

They looked as surprised at his presence as she felt.

Carrington stared at the group of ten men behind the immortal. 'Hey, what the hell is this, a freaking picnic?' he muttered to Schmidt.

'What are you doing here?' asked Reznak coolly. 'Did the Council send you with the other Hunters?'

'No,' said Alexa before Schmidt could reply. She studied the silent figures behind the immortal. Her gaze shifted to the Crovir Hunter's face. 'You brought the Freemasons with you.'

Schmidt nodded as shocked gasps rose around them. 'I helped them negotiate an agreement with our First Council. In exchange for not causing a stink about the incident in London, they have been allowed in on this mission.' He shrugged. 'Since one of their most prized possessions is currently in the hands of this sect, they wanted in on the action.'

'Are you here in your capacity as a Crovir Hunter or a Freemason?' Reznak asked, his tone still guarded.

Schmidt smiled wryly. 'Since this directive doesn't cause any conflict between my two roles, I've come as both.' He peered closely at Alexa. 'What happened to you?'

'It's a long story,' she said.

They spent a minute coordinating their next move with the rest of the Crovir Hunters and the second team of Freemasons heading up the valley, before proceeding toward the area that Eva had pointed out.

Alexa used the butt of a Sig to tap the snow-covered ground gently. A dull metallic ring erupted from under the gun seconds later.

They dug at the frozen soil and loose gravel with their gloved hands until they uncovered a square metal plate.

She glanced at Carrington. He nodded. Reznak, Schmidt, and the other men raised their guns to cover them as they carefully lifted the hatch.

An unlit well appeared below. Metal rungs descended into the gloom.

Alexa took the lead and headed down into the darkness.

CHAPTER THIRTY

TWENTY-FIVE FEET BELOW GROUND, SHE STEPPED CAREFULLY onto the floor of a narrow tunnel. She aimed the Sigs at the empty ends of the passage while the men joined her.

A low ceiling rose above them. Dim wall lights shed a muted glow on bare concrete. Alexa studied the thin accumulation of dead plant debris and water on the ground at her feet thoughtfully.

'Is this a storm drain?' asked Carrington in a low voice.

'No,' said Alexa. 'It's an emergency exit.' She turned and headed north along the tunnel.

A junction appeared after a hundred and fifty feet. The tunnel split into two branches, the first continuing north, the other veering east. She took Schmidt and a group of Hunters and Freemasons along the second channel. Reznak continued down the first one with Carrington and the rest of the men.

A minute later, the passage began to rise. Alexa moved cautiously up the shallow incline. A low din gradually grew in the distance. Occasional shouts punctuated the solid rumble of background noise. The shadows ahead faded as another source of light entered the tunnel. The slope leveled out.

Alexa stopped abruptly and pulled back into the shadows. The men flattened themselves against the wall behind her. Schmidt peered over her head.

An opening lay ten feet in front of her. Beyond it was a wide platform that looked down on a set of rail tracks; the freight train that had departed Perm several hours ago stood on them.

A pair of dark-clad figures armed with guns moved hurriedly past the mouth of the passage. A forklift trundled slowly behind them, lights flashing above its cabin and an audible alarm sounding from a speaker box; two of the crates Kronos had loaded onto the train sat on its forks.

Alexa stripped out of her snow gear, checked the suppressors on the ends of the Sigs, and adjusted the body holster holding her sais and the ammunition belts around her waist and thighs. Schmidt stared at the bandages across her abdomen with a grimace before removing his own snowsuit.

She wrapped the end of her discarded parka around her fist and quietly smashed one of the lights on the wall. The tunnel grew darker, almost doubling their cover.

Alexa inched to the edge of the opening and looked out. She froze when she got her first full view of the space around the platform.

The tunnel that carried the tracks through the cliff lay on her right. A hundred feet after passing the metal doors that concealed its entrance from the outside world, it entered a cavernous space inside the mountain. The chamber was about the width of a football field and twice the length. Floodlights dotted a vaulted, rock ceiling thirty feet above the ground. A second platform rose on the other side of the tracks and joined with the first one at the north end of the cavern, where the walls opened up to accommodate a large staging area packed high with pallets of crates and containers. A second tunnel lined with concrete walls opened at the north face of the cave, its distant end curving around and down a shallow slope.

Alexa could see other openings in the walls of the cavern. Guards armed with submachine guns dotted the platforms.

'What's with all those boxes?' muttered Schmidt in her ear, his gaze fixed on the extensive stockpile on the staging area. 'What the hell are they planning?'

'The end of the world,' she said in a low voice.

Alexa's gaze returned to the livestock wagon that had held the tombs. She scanned the platform quickly, darted to the tracks, and dropped into the narrow gap underneath the train. She started to move toward the damaged carriage.

Schmidt landed behind her a second later, followed by half of the Hunters and Freemasons. 'What are you doing?' he hissed.

'I need to check something,' she replied.

She reached the wagon, moved under the metal coupling, and peered over the edge of a jagged piece of singed timber. Half of the carriage's east wall was missing; the bomb had completely destroyed the stall she had been in. She stared at the opposite wall and breathed a small sigh of relief. The second stall stood relatively intact.

The chains that had secured the tombs inside the wagon lay coiled on the empty floor.

'What happened here?' whispered Schmidt. His eyes widened and he glanced at the bandages at her midriff. 'Is *that* how you got hurt?'

Alexa did not reply. She was staring at the mouth of a tunnel on the east wall of the cavern, directly opposite the damaged carriage. A familiar shape had just flashed past in the passage beyond.

Two guards approached from the north end of the cave. She sank into the shadows beneath the train. The pair walked past, oblivious to their presence a few feet away.

Alexa climbed onto the platform and raced low over the ground to the opening across the way. Schmidt and the others followed in her footsteps.

An intersection appeared some twenty feet inside the concrete tunnel. Seconds before she reached it, a dark figure came into view around the corner from the left.

Alexa shot the man before he could shout out a warning. The bullet struck him between the eyes with a muffled thud. As he slumped against the wall, a second figure appeared behind him. She shifted her arm to fire again. Her finger froze on the trigger when he suddenly collapsed.

She stared at the apparition who had administered the blow to the now unconscious man. 'Yonten,' she said in acknowledgement.

The monk grinned. He had changed out of the snowsuit and held the bō staff in his hands.

'Where's Jackson?' she asked, her tone hardening.

He turned and beckoned them to follow him just as the rest of the Hunters and Freemasons rushed inside the passage behind them.

'Please don't do that again,' said the team leader of the Crovirs with a heavy frown. He stared at the monk. 'And who is this?'

'A friend,' said Alexa.

They had barely travelled thirty feet along the next tunnel when an alarm suddenly tore through the underground complex. Gunfire sounded in the distance.

'Dimitri!' she said sharply in the microphone transmitter on her collar, breaking the strict radio silence they had kept since entering the facility.

Reznak's voice came over the receiver. 'We're okay,' he said in a low voice. 'One of the other teams must have triggered a security sensor. Looks like the game's up.'

'Yonten's taking us to Jackson,' said Alexa as she headed briskly after the running monk. 'The tombs have been moved from the train.'

Footsteps sounded ahead of them. Four armed sect members appeared from a side passage eighteen feet from their position. The man in the lead shouted a warning to his companions before raising the Shipka submachine gun in his hands.

Alexa, Schmidt, and four of the Hunters returned fire as bullets pelted past them. The other Crovirs and the Freemasons turned to face the second group of guards who had materialized at the opposite end of the corridor.

'This way!' said Yonten. He opened a metal hatch in the floor and disappeared from view.

Alexa followed him and dropped down the rails of a vertical ladder into a tunnel below. Her boots and cross training gloves squeaked against the metal poles as she suddenly broke her fall. She came to an abrupt halt a foot from the monk's head.

Yonten had stopped on a rung three feet above the ground. The staff spun in his right hand as he kicked and jabbed at the two armed guards below him.

Alexa jumped down on the shoulders of the man on the right, brought him to the floor, and punched him in the face. He went limp beneath her. She rose smoothly, turned, and fired at the armed figures racing toward them from the south end of the corridor.

The edge of Yonten's foot collided with the neck of the remaining guard. The man crumpled to the ground.

Schmidt landed beside them with the rest of their team; of the ten men who had been with them, only seven remained. A hail of shots followed their passage down the ladder.

They maintained steady gunfire cover at their backs as they followed the monk down the passage. Moments later, they emerged from the sidewall of a huge tunnel that spiraled gently down into the earth to their right.

It was the concrete borehole that opened up at the north end of the massive cavern directly beneath the mountain. Alexa registered this in the same second that her gaze fell on the fifteen sect members occupying the tunnel floor.

The Sigs sang in her hands as she discharged them with deadly accuracy into the bodies of the armed men. Schmidt fired the Beretta pistol next to her. A Hunter and a Freemason fell under the enemy's bullets.

Yonten darted across the angled floor, the bō staff blurring around his body while his feet moved in a flawless dance. His strikes and kicks incapacitated four guards in as many seconds.

'This way!' he shouted. He turned and raced down the slope. They headed after him just as another wave of guards appeared at the top of the incline.

Bullets slammed into the wall next to Alexa, raising chips of concrete. She twisted and fired one of the Sigs behind her while she sprinted after the monk. The gunfire eased off when they turned the corner of the borehole. Fifty feet later, the ground leveled out and the ceiling dropped. Concrete was replaced by solid rock.

The artificial glare of floodlights faded behind them and was superseded by the glow of flames from torches sitting in iron brackets on the walls. Fat, stone pillars surfaced from the gloom, rising out of the limestone bed to support the roof of the tunnel. Archways materialized on either side of them.

In the wavering, yellow light, Alexa caught glimpses of other corridors and rooms.

More sect members appeared in their path and succumbed swiftly under their bullets. Two more Freemasons and another Hunter fell at their sides. All the while, the alarm echoed shrilly through the rock around them.

Yonten suddenly swerved into a passage to the left and disappeared down a steep, winding staircase. Alexa went after him, Schmidt and the remaining men hot on her heels.

They were soon inside a honeycomb of tunnels and caves deep beneath the ground. She recalled what Eva had said about the complex. The structure looked very old. It reminded her of the ancient, underground cities in Turkey, built before the Byzantine era.

Giant, stone roller doors leaned against the walls next to the main entrance of every floor, ready to be moved to close off the access to that level of the complex. They passed ventilation shafts dropping hundreds of feet into the earth and narrow wells that carried the rush of a distant, subterranean river.

The monk finally staggered to a halt at the junction of a pair of tunnels two hundred feet below the ground. Shadows shifted at the end of the passage on the right. Alexa raised the Sigs, her fingers on the triggers. She froze, before slowly lowering the guns.

Reznak and Carrington stormed into the intersection with a large company of men; they had met up with the Freemasons. Although Reznak's team had fared better than her own party in terms of numbers, they had still incurred significant injuries. Alexa could see blood trailing from bullet wounds on the legs and chests of several of the men.

'Any sign of the rest of the Hunters?' she asked briskly.

Reznak shook his head, a scowl darkening his face. 'They're two and a half miles down the valley.' He glanced at the men behind him. 'This is it for the time being.' His gaze shifted to the monk. 'It's good to see you again.'

Yonten nodded distractedly and pointed at the staircase at the end of the opposite tunnel. 'Hurry,' he said, breaking into a run.

They went after him.

'We're close to the tombs,' said Alexa seconds later as they pounded down the wide stone steps.

'How do you know?' said Reznak beside her.

'Because my birthmark is burning.'

Alexa felt her godfather's stare on the back of her neck. They reached the bottom of the staircase.

A pair of thick, oak doors with wrought iron hinges stood at the opposite end of a shallow vestibule. An empty alcove was visible on the left. A small corridor disappeared into the gloom to the right.

'Is Jackson in there?' said Alexa stiffly, indicating the closed doors with a sharp head tilt.

Yonten nodded, his expression sober. 'There are a lot of sect members on the other side,' he said. He motioned her toward the recess to the left of the doors.

Bullets thudded into the ground behind them as a group of guards poured down the stairs. The Hunters and the Freemasons returned fire.

Alexa and Reznak followed Yonten into the alcove. The monk pointed to the wall ahead. A dim light washed across a slit-like opening at waist level. They crouched down and peered through the narrow aperture.

An enormous circular chamber with a barrel-vaulted ceiling

lay at the bottom of the short flight of steps that dropped down from the thick, oak doors to the right. Dotted in the thick limestone walls was a network of niches holding a collection of relics and ancient weapons; the gap Alexa and Reznak were spying through was at the back of one of these recesses.

A battalion of heavily armed sect members occupied the expansive floor space beyond the stairs. Half of the men stood guarding the entrance to the chamber. The rest were moving crates up a ramp and into a giant, arched opening on the opposite side of the room.

Alexa caught a glimpse of the tombs as they disappeared on a pair of electric, flatbed goods trolleys into the gloom of the tunnel beyond. Her gaze finally alighted on an altar in a wide alcove to the left of the chamber.

The Emerald Tablet and Anna Godard's gold pendant glimmered on the top of the solid limestone block that rose out of the ground. A document that might have been the *Mutus Liber* and a second sun cross pendent rested beside them.

She froze.

CHAPTER THIRTY-ONE

JACKSON STOOD SHACKLED TO THE WALL NEXT TO THE ALTAR, HIS wrists locked in iron fetters above his head. Blood coated his face and the exposed skin of his arms and chest where he had been beaten and cut. The knuckles of his fists were red and raw. His left eye and cheek were swollen and badly bruised.

Cavaleti stood close to him and pointed imperiously at the artifacts on the limestone block. Fresh crimson trails stained the polished edges of the Schiavona broadsword in the older man's hand as he shouted indiscernible commands at the Harvard professor.

A wry smile crept across Jackson's face. He murmured something through his bleeding lips. Cavaleti's eyes darkened. He nodded briskly at someone hidden behind the curve of the wall. Boyko Dragov stepped into view and punched Jackson in the stomach.

The Harvard professor gasped and choked as he struggled to catch his breath. Scarlet drops dripped down his chin and onto the floor.

Icy rage flooded Alexa's mind. The trishula blazed at the back of her neck. She rose to her feet and stormed out of the alcove.

Bodies crowded the staircase leading to the vestibule. The Hunters and the Freemasons were using the cover of the dead sect members to shoot at the men coming down the steps.

'Do you know where this leads to?' she asked the monk, jerking her head at the passage opposite the alcove.

Yonten glanced at the oak doors. 'Somewhere on the other side?' he hazarded.

Alexa turned to Carrington. 'Give me the C4,' she ordered curtly.

The Crovir immortal looked at the doors blankly before slowly sliding his backpack from his shoulders. He handed her two blocks of explosives, a handful of blasting caps, and a remote control detonator.

She finally looked at Reznak. 'Take half the men and go.' She indicated the narrow corridor on the other side of the vestibule.

Sporadic gunfire sounded in the distance. Her godfather gazed at her inscrutably for timeless seconds. Schmidt frowned at them from his position near the staircase.

'Okay,' Reznak murmured, his fingers whitening on the gun in his hand. This time, he spoke the words he had refrained from uttering earlier that day. 'Be careful.'

Alexa nodded and watched him leave with Carrington and a mixed band of Hunters and Freemasons. Six men stayed back to cover the stairs. She turned to the doors and packed the C4 around the hinges before joining the rest of the group in the alcove.

'Get Jackson and the artifacts,' she instructed in a hard voice, looking steadily at Schmidt and Yonten. The two men glanced at each other and nodded. The Crovir Hunter yelled at the men guarding the steps. They turned and rushed inside the alcove.

Alexa flexed her gloved fingers, took a deep breath, and depressed the switch on the detonator. The force of the explosion shook the ground beneath their feet.

She was up and running through the billows of dust and flying splinters of wood before the final reverberations died down. She flashed past the wreckage of the damaged doors, stepped off the top of the stairs beyond, and leapt into the air, the Sigs singing in her hands as she swung her arms out and wide.

The guards reacted too slowly. By the time her feet neared the ground, she had disposed of the first five men. Adrenaline streamed through her veins, sharpening her senses and focusing her hunter's skills. A grim smile dawned on her lips.

She had never felt more alive than she did in that moment.

She reloaded the guns a heartbeat after she landed and raced for the line of advancing men, the weapons unwavering in her grip. Her shots did not miss a single target.

Cavaleti yelled an order from the other side of the room. Alexa glimpsed an orange streak out of the corner of her eye and heard gunfire behind her. Yonten was heading for the altar with Schmidt.

She looked around and saw Cavaleti running toward the dark tunnel at the rear of the chamber. Dragov stood his ground and turned to face the monk and the Crovir immortal.

A second later, she was inside a ring of sect members. She holstered the Sigs, pulled the sais out of their sheaths, and jumped into a powerful roundhouse kick that floored three men.

A stranger dressed in saffron robes and wielding a jō staff dashed past her right as she spun a sai against her forearm to block a blow to her head. A second, similarly dressed figure armed with a lacquered bō appeared on her left just before she delivered an elbow slash to a guard's throat and back-fisted another one in the face.

Alexa looked over her shoulder at the dozens of men in orange robes pouring through the doorway behind her. The monks from Abbot Kelsang's order had arrived.

She slipped out of the way of an uppercut aimed at her temple, flicked the second sai against her forearm, and struck the man in the chest and head with the handles of the blades. She shifted, front snap-kicked another guard in the groin, and brought her leg around in a curving knee strike into the abdomen of a third sect member.

The three men folded to the ground. Four more surrounded her.

Grinning savagely, Alexa jumped in a high reverse round-kick that knocked out the first two men, flowed into a spinning hook-kick to bring down the third, and dropped into a floor-sweep that tripped the last sect member to the ground. She elbowed him in the face, rolled out of the way of a stamping boot, and rose smoothly to her feet.

A flurry of fists darted toward her. She ducked, blocked a low kick to her midriff, flipped the sais in her grip, and jabbed her two attackers in the neck and face. A blow glanced past her left hip. She stepped to the side, dropped her leg in a stomp-kick that broke her assailant's foot, twisted to avoid strikes from another pair of guards, palm-heeled one of them in the nose, and hammer-fisted the second one in the throat.

Across the way, Yonten engaged Dragov while Schmidt shot open the manacles that bound Jackson to the wall. The Harvard professor collapsed in the Hunter's arms and raised his head weakly. Bloodshot, puffy blue eyes blinked slowly. He froze when he saw her. Shock and relief flashed on his face.

A deep wrenching ache tore through Alexa's very being and made her breath catch in her throat. Flames licked the birthmark across her nape. Before she knew it, she was moving through the horde of men separating her from the altar in a deadly dance of kicks, punches, and strikes, the sais blurring in her hands as she snapped them through rapid grip changes.

A bullet whizzed past her head a second after she leapt into a butterfly kick. Another one grazed her right thigh when she landed on the ground, the three sect members she had struck in the head falling around her. She looked toward the mouth of the tunnel and saw the immortal with the pale blue eyes aim his gun at her again.

Alexa shifted to the side as a third bullet flashed past her hip, hurled a sai above her head, pulled a Sig out, and returned fire. Her shots slammed into the immortal's left shoulder and flank. He stumbled and collapsed against the wall of the tunnel. She holstered the Sig, grasped the dagger as it fell toward her, and looked toward the altar. Her breath froze in her lungs.

Schmidt was on his knees by the limestone block. He shook his head dazedly, blood dripping from his mouth and nose. Dragov's foot swung up like a sledgehammer and slammed into his gut. The Crovir Hunter's body rose three feet into the air before crumpling to the ground. Jackson struggled from the floor and staggered toward the giant.

As Alexa sprinted toward them, her body gliding automatically into a frenzied flow of strikes and blocks, Yonten stepped up against the altar and jumped into a powerful reverse roundhouse kick. His foot collided with Dragov's jaw with an audible snap.

The giant reared back. He reached out with lightning speed,

grabbed the monk by the arm, and swung him up against the stone wall with a sadistic smile. Yonten struck the rock face with a thud. Crimson jets streaked across the limestone.

Air left Alexa's lips in a hiss of anger. She sheathed the sais, whipped the Sigs from her body holster, and fired ruthlessly at the men in her path.

Dragov released the injured monk, scooped the four artifacts on the stone altar into a small wooden chest, and headed briskly toward the tunnel at the back of the room.

Movement drew Alexa's gaze to the right. Ice filled her veins. The blue-eyed immortal was back on his feet. He raised his gun once more and squeezed the trigger.

Her head whipped around. Time slowed.

Her mouth opened on a cry as the bullet hurtled through the air toward Jackson. She saw a figure rise out of the corner of her eye.

Yonten pushed Jackson out of the path of the bullet. The shot slammed into the monk's chest with a solid thunk.

'No!' screamed Alexa.

Jackson caught Yonten as the monk staggered backward into him. The two men stumbled to the ground. The Harvard professor sat up slowly, his eyes widening in horror when he saw blood bloom across the saffron robes.

She pointed the Sigs toward the tunnel and pulled the triggers until the magazines clicked empty. Dragov and the blue-eyed immortal retreated further inside the passage. A second later, she reached the fallen men near the altar. Schmidt stirred on the floor and coughed.

Alexa gripped Yonten's hand tightly, her heart sinking as she watched the crimson stain expand across his chest. Jackson pressed down firmly on the wound. Blood continued to pour past his fingers.

The monk looked up at her with a frail smile. Sweat beaded his pale brow. 'Time to die,' he gasped softly.

Alexa clenched her jaw and gazed into his limpid eyes, her fingers shaking tremulously around his.

Jackson stared at Yonten. 'Why did you—' he whispered, anguish flaring across his battered, ashen face.

The monk turned his head slightly. 'You still have a purpose to fulfill.' He raised bloodstained fingers and touched Jackson's face gently.

A figure landed beside them and dropped to its knees. It was one of the other monks. The jō staff in the young man's hands clattered to the stone floor. 'Yonten,' he said brokenly, dark eyes gleaming wetly.

Yonten's gaze shifted. 'Brother,' he acknowledged in a weakening voice. 'Now is not the time for tears.' His breathing grew ragged. 'I have...a request.'

'Anything,' said the other monk hoarsely.

'You must tell the Abbot that Guru Rinpoche was right.' Another gasp shuddered past Yonten's lips as he turned to Alexa. 'The immortal warrior truly lives on.' His eyelids fluttered closed and his hand went limp in her grasp.

Alexa's knuckles whitened as she squeezed his fingers.

A heartbeat later, Yonten opened his eyes one last time and stared at her. 'Death is but a door,' he murmured with a bright smile. 'See you in the next life, warrior.'

Alexa could dimly make out the sounds of the nearby battle as she watched the light fade in the monk's black pupils. She crouched motionless for long seconds before folding his fingers over the bloodied trishula mark on his palm and placing his hand gently on his chest. She closed his eyes with a steady hand and brought her lips to his forehead.

'I will avenge you,' she breathed in a hardening voice. The birthmark on her neck flamed at her words.

She rose to her feet and pulled Jackson up from the floor. He looked at her with a grim expression, his cobalt eyes blazing. 'Let's finish this,' he said coldly. She picked a gun from the floor, handed it to him, and reloaded her Sigs.

Schmidt joined them as they headed into the tunnel on the other side of the chamber. Moments later, the muted roar of a second battle rose ahead of them. They reached the top of a flight of crescent-shaped steps and looked down upon a scene of chaos.

Flame torches dotted an enormous cave before them, the yellow glow barely penetrating its dark fringes and inky ceiling. Alcoves and doorways punctuated distant walls. At the back of the cavern, a fast flowing, underground river poured through a deep channel, its roar echoing against the rock face; the stolen tombs stood on a stone jetty next to a barge moored in the rushing waters.

Backed by a battalion of Hunters and Freemasons, Reznak and Carrington clashed brutally with Kronos on the floor below. Gunfire and cries shattered the air. More Hunters and saffron-robed monks poured through a narrow opening in the wall to the right.

Alexa's gaze sought and found Dragov. The giant was storming across the floor of the cave toward Cavaleti, one large hand lazily swatting the men in his path as if they were flies, while the other clasped the wooden box holding the stolen artifacts.

The leader of Kronos stood next to the tombs and sneered at the battleground from behind a circle of armed guards. A group of men were tying iron chains around the sarcophagi and linking them to a mechanical hoist.

Her eyes shifted to the immortal on Dragov's heels. Alexa started down the stairs and reached the bottom in the blink of an eye.

Bodies fell in a wave around her as she entered the legion of fighting men. The Sigs roared in her hands, her aim steady and unerring. She bolted over the fallen and the wounded, her pace never slowing in her single-minded determination to reach her target. When the bullets ran dry, she holstered the guns, unsheathed her blades, and maintained her deadly charge. Crimson smears stained her hands and the metal of the sais as her blows broke skin and bone.

A brutal grimace distorted her lips when she finally spotted Yonten's killer. She covered the distance that separated them in a flash.

The immortal turned at the sound of her footsteps. Shock flared in the pale blue eyes as her foot arced toward his face and smashed into his jaw in a powerful, crescent kick. His head snapped back. Alexa grabbed his shoulders, raised her leg in a straight knee strike to his chest as she yanked him down, slammed the edges of her palms against his ears, and hammer-fisted him in the face.

Blood spurted from his fractured nose and burst eardrums.

She drove her shoulder into his abdomen, grabbed his legs behind his knees, and flipped him onto his back.

'Alexa!' shouted Jackson.

She turned. The Harvard professor pitched his gun at her. Her fingers opened on her left sai and closed around the weapon while the dagger fell toward the floor. She swung her arm down and shot the stunned immortal between the eyes before the sai hit the ground. The man blinked once and went still.

A harsh grunt suddenly sounded on her left. Alexa looked around.

Terror froze her limbs to the ground. Her mind went blank.

She tasted fear for the first time in her immortal life.

Ten feet from her, dark pupils dilated in a sea of ice blue. Jackson's shocked stare dropped from her face to the tip of the blade that had impaled his back and penetrated through his abdomen. A red blotch appeared around the metal and spread scarlet trails down his skin.

CHAPTER THIRTY-TWO

Cold triumph gleamed in the slate gray eyes behind Jackson. Cavaleti slowly withdrew the broadsword from the Harvard professor's back and watched him fall to his knees. An insane smile spread across the older man's face. He looked directly at Alexa, raised the blade, and dropped it toward Jackson's neck.

The hunter inside her took over. Her movements dream-like, Alexa moved and blocked the sword with her sai inches before it kissed the fallen man's skin. Cavaleti grunted and flicked his wrist. The blade sparked against the dagger. He grunted, stepped back, and lifted his sword once more.

Alexa felt herself slip out of the way of the blade. The broadsword whispered close to her skin once. It streaked past a second time, then a third.

As Cavaleti swung the sword down for the fourth time, she slid past his guard and brought the right sai up, a guttural snarl finally leaving her lips. The tip of the dagger arced through the air and punctured the floor of the sect leader's mouth. The momentum of her strike carried the sai through the base of his skull and into his brain.

A gurgle left Cavaleti's throat. Crimson drops sprayed past his thin lips and onto his beard. He stared at her in disbelief as he choked on his own blood. The crazed fury in the gray eyes dimmed and his features went slack. He sagged against her.

An animal bellow erupted from across the floor.

Dragov swept Schmidt aside with a powerful back-slap and barreled toward her, his face contorted in a mask of rage.

Alexa released her grip on the sai, stepped back toward the stone jetty, and ducked beneath Dragov's fists. The giant swung his arms around like a demon, his hands dropping toward her with furious speed. She moved out of his way and countered with a flurry of strikes, the skin over her knuckles splitting under the force of the impact as her punches landed with deadly accuracy.

The veins on Dragov's forehead bulged. Bloodstained spittle dribbled past his torn lips and onto his chin. He roared once more.

Alexa had just drawn her arm back to block his fist when a bullet slammed into the side of her right knee. Her leg buckled beneath her.

Dragov's first blow landed on her cheek with the force of a hammer. Her head snapped back and black spots danced across her vision.

His second blow slammed into her solar plexus. She doubled over and felt something tear inside her body. As the third blow curved through the air toward her, she became dimly aware of voices screaming her name in the distance.

Dragov's fist smashed into her sternum. Bones cracked inside her chest. The force of the impact lifted her off her feet. As she soared backward, Alexa caught a glimpse of her godfather's horrified face. Half a second later, she struck the closest tomb.

Pain knifed through her, searing and ice cold. Numbness bloomed in a wave from the middle of her back to the tips of her toes. She slumped against the sarcophagus and slid to the ground.

Someone dropped to the floor at her side. Alexa looked up weakly as Reznak lifted her in his arms and shouted her name. His voice came from far away, his words overlaid by the faint buzzing in her ears. Her head lolled forward and her hair fell across her eyes. Indistinct figures appeared beyond her godfather's shoulder. She blinked and vaguely recognized Carrington and Schmidt as they engaged Dragov.

Her gaze shifted to Reznak's face once more as her vision started to dim. A veil of darkness fell across the world and eclipsed his tortured features. The abyss beckoned, cold, infinite, and murky.

Someone whispered, 'Alexandria' from the shadows.

Alexa closed her eyes and fell into the void.

The trishula scorched the skin on her neck.

TIME PASSED. HOW MUCH SHE DID NOT KNOW. IT DID NOT REALLY matter in this place of twilight. Nothing mattered there.

Sound finally rose on the limitless horizon. It raced toward her for what seemed like an eternity before slamming into her ethereal form in thunderous waves of cacophony. Distorted images flashed across the inky landscape. A legion of flickering memories, thoughts, and feelings overwhelmed her senses.

A voice rose from the clamor, a faint susurration that spoke of a long-forgotten promise. At once strange yet achingly familiar, the words resonated with the core of her being and the essence of who she truly was.

In that timeless and enduring moment of remembrance, Alexa heard. She saw. She understood.

Her eyes snapped open, the roar of an ancient, hundred-day war still ringing in her ears. Her gaze zeroed in on the giant man fifteen feet away. She saw him strike Reznak. A saffron-robed monk stepped in front of her godfather as he fell and attacked Dragov with a staff weapon, the wooden stick blurring with the speed of his blocks and strikes. The giant knocked him away with the back of one hand.

Alexa's gaze sought and found the man who lay still on the ground to her left. She saw Jackson's back rise and fall with shallow breaths. Blood pooled beneath his body in a crimson puddle. His eyes were closed and his face deathly pale.

She rose to her feet, stepped down from the jetty, and started to run.

Schmidt and Carrington turned at the sound of her footsteps. Their eyes widened in dull incomprehension.

Heat erupted from her birthmark and flowed through her veins as she raced for the giant man. Alexa heard the whisper of the ancient immortal warrior in her ears and felt the incredible power flood her limbs.

She jumped, stepped off Dragov's back, somersaulted over his head, and landed thigh-down on his shoulders. Her palms slammed onto the sides of his jaws as he staggered backward.

Dragov raised his arms and gripped her thighs in an iron vise. He grunted as he tried to throw her off.

A pair of ghostly hands closed over Alexa's fingers. She threw her head back and opened her lips. A faint echo underscored the primitive cry that left her throat as she twisted the giant's head sharply.

Dragov's neck broke with an audible snap.

Alexa leapt off the falling man and landed lightly on her feet, her gaze unblinking. Dragov hit the ground with a dull thud.

A wave of shocked silence spread out across the cave. The remaining members of Kronos stared wide-eyed at their fallen leaders. Although they resumed the fight in the next breath, it was evident that the spirit of the battle had drained out of them.

'Dimitri!' someone shouted.

Alexa turned and watched a lean man with silver-speckled hair and a trim beard storm down the steps of the cave, a Beretta semiautomatic in one hand and a sword in the other. Scores of dark figures followed at his back and joined in the action.

Reznak's stunned gaze shifted from her to the man striding toward them. 'Victor,' he breathed. 'Thanks for coming.'

The leader of the Bastians looked at her briefly with intelligent, dark eyes. 'I'm sorry we couldn't get here faster,' said Victor Dvorsky, his tone contrite as he studied Reznak's bloodied face and the bodies around them. 'The storm delayed us.'

'I'm just glad you're here, old friend,' said Reznak with a weak smile.

Schmidt looked uneasily at the crowd of Bastian Hunters helping the Crovirs and Freemasons subdue the remaining members of Kronos. His wary stare moved to Alexa. Before he could say a word, she walked past him to the man lying unconscious several feet away.

Alexa dropped to one knee by Jackson's side and gently rolled him onto his back. The flow of blood from the stab wound had slowed to an ooze. She placed her hands over it and stared at his ashen features, an icy chill settling over her heart.

'No one has ever returned from a death that fast before,' she heard Schmidt murmur to Reznak. 'Especially not their first one.'

Alexa felt her godfather's eyes on the back of her head.

The monk who had been with Yonten at his death appeared on the other side of Jackson. He took the bleeding man's hand in one of his own and looked at her steadily. Their gaze shifted to the tombs on the stone jetty.

'The crows never came for them,' said Alexa in a low voice. The heat from her birthmark had started to fade. The whisper of a sigh reached her on the edge of hearing.

The monk's expression remained solemn.

Kronos was soon overpowered. Of the thirty Freemasons who had volunteered for the mission, sixteen had perished during the battle. Eight of the Crovir Hunters had suffered their final deaths. Yonten was the only monk who lost his life.

An hour after the battle ended, Alexa and a small group of men arrived at the mouth of the valley. Between them they carried the unconscious body of the Harvard professor. An Ansat air ambulance stood waiting on a flat outcrop of rock near the base of the mountain. The paramedic crew rushed out of the helicopter and swiftly transferred Jackson to a stretcher.

Reznak and Carrington climbed inside the aircraft after her and took the seat opposite to where she sat. Alexa's eyes never left the unconscious man's face while the crew worked desperately on his broken body.

Jackson's heart stopped beating moments before they landed in the grounds of the regional hospital in Perm. The paramedics got him back after eight minutes of resuscitation. He arrested again when they wheeled him into theatre thirty minutes later, and once more during the emergency surgery that followed.

Alexa stood in the waiting room outside the theatre wing, her nails digging into her palms while she stared silently at the steady snowfall outside the window. She had dismissed all attempts by the hospital staff to treat her injuries. The wounds had almost healed.

After repeatedly failing to engage her in conversation, Reznak and Carrington lingered silently by her side. Although she sensed her godfather's distress, Alexa could not bring herself to open her mouth for fear of the scream that might escape her lips.

She looked around once when the surgeon walked out to inform them that Jackson had survived the operation and was being transferred to the ICU. The silver-haired doctor rubbed the back of his neck tiredly and spoke in a guarded tone. He told them to prepare for the worst.

As evening fell, another blizzard swept across the city. Its ferocity matched the storm of emotions that raged endlessly through Alexa's heart into the darkest hours of the night. When dawn finally broke hours later, Jackson was still alive.

By the time night fell once more, he was deemed stable enough to be transferred.

Twenty-four hours after he was stabbed by Alberto Cavaleti, Jackson landed in Boston in a private medical plane leased by Reznak. He arrived at the Massachusetts General Hospital at ten in the evening, sedated and still ventilated. He was back in theatre at midnight.

Alexa remained at the hospital the entire time. She did not speak a single word to another soul. A day later, the Harvard professor had still not regained consciousness. It was another twenty-four hours before the doctors came to speak to her and Reznak.

Alexa listened numbly, her gaze frozen on the face of the unmoving figure attached to the life support machines.

CT imaging of Jackson's head had revealed brain damage from his repeated cardiac arrests. Though he would likely breathe if they took him off the ventilator, his chances of recovery were slim. They asked whether he had any next of kin.

Reznak looked at her at this point. Alexa gazed back at him dully, the first eye contact she had made with another being in three days. He reached for his cell phone and made a call.

Banks phoned him back ten minutes later. Apart from a distant cousin in Montana who was too ill to travel, Jackson had no other family.

An end-of-life care specialist came to speak to them in the hours that followed the grim news. Minutes into her introduction, the woman mumbled an apology and retreated from the room under Alexa's leaden stare.

Marie arrived with Fawkes on the fourth day. The older woman finally managed to force some food down Alexa's throat. She ate the meal at Jackson's bedside. It tasted like ash in her mouth.

In an attempt to distract her, Reznak started to relate the findings of the research team he had dispatched to the Ural Mountains in the days following Kronos's defeat. After recovering the tombs and the other precious artifacts stolen by the sect, the Crovir scientists had unearthed ancient Sumerian scriptures carved in the walls of the giant complex of caves beneath the mountain. The underground river where Cavaleti had attempted to escape with the tombs had led to a large subterranean lake and a second underground city further in the Urals. The scientists had also discovered dozens of relics that testified to the origins and history of the people who once lived there.

It seemed the underground cities had been the ancestral grounds of the immortal-human offsprings whose bloodline could be traced all the way back to Kronos, the third son of Crovir. They had also been the birthplace of the sect that would come to be named after him. From the early translations of the cuneiform scripts in the cave where Cavaleti had met his death, it appeared that they had been searching for the Philosopher's Stone for a very long time.

Six days after they arrived in Boston, Reznak came to her once more. It was late in the day. Marie and Fawkes had gone to get a drink in the hospital canteen. Alexa and an ICU nurse were the only ones by Jackson's bedside.

Her godfather waited until the nurse left the room before turning to look at her with a troubled expression. 'We found a stone box in the underground city a few days ago,' he said. 'It was the third artifact that Kronos had stolen in Egypt besides the tombs.' His stare touched briefly on where her fingers lay on the unconscious man's hand. 'From what we discovered in the first cave more than a month ago, we believe it stood between the two sarcophagi. It held more information about the origins of the immortals. More specifically, the scripts within it mentioned your birthmark.'

Her eyes remained steady on Jackson's face.

'If the initial translations are correct, then Guru Rinpoche was right,' Reznak continued in a quiet voice. 'You are the pureblood descendant of an immortal named Mila. She was one of Crovir's daughters. Her intended mate was Kronos.'

Alexa finally lifted her head and looked at her godfather.

'Though we have yet to complete our examination of the texts, the provisional reports indicate that the first war between the immortals started roughly four millennia ago. As I had suspected from the genetic analysis of their hearts, Crovir and Bastian were indeed brothers. They had three sons and three daughters each. Those siblings gave rise to our two immortal races.' Reznak took a deep breath. 'Only four people in the world know what I'm about to tell you next.' His gaze was unwavering as it met hers. 'Crovir and Bastian's father was a man called Romerus. The texts in the stone box appear to confirm what was suggested by the Sumerian scriptures in the smaller cave we excavated in Egypt—Romerus was a direct descendant of Adam and Eve.'

The beeps from the life support machines attached to the man on the bed punctuated the hush that followed.

'Unlike his sons, Romerus was not an immortal. But he lived for a very long time. Before his death, Crovir and Bastian established their dominion over a kingdom that extended for more than a thousand miles across Europe, Asia, and North Africa,' said Reznak. 'Their empire was larger than the Roman one that would follow a few millennia later, and they ruled their lands with their children for hundreds of years. During that time, both immortals and the human slaves who lived among them prospered. But they also suffered, especially at Crovir's hands. Several of their children eventually rebelled. Although Bastian initially joined their ranks, it seems he changed his mind in the days leading to the final battle and chose to stay by his brother's side.' Her godfather exhaled sharply. 'It was Mila who dealt the final blows that killed Crovir and Bastian. Of all their children, she was the greatest warrior.'

Alexa blinked. Her eyes shifted to the white sheets that covered Jackson's still body.

What she did not tell her godfather then was that she already knew. In that infinitesimal sliver of time between her first death and her resurrection, she had seen and felt it all.

The unease of an immortal soldier that had slowly grown into disbelief and despair. The rising anger at the injustices and cruel acts she had borne witness to over decades of increasing tyranny by a mad man. The desperate and irrevocable decision taken the night her father committed the final, unforgivable sin. The first trishulas being forged in the white-hot flames of a furnace. And finally, the warrior herself during the last days of the conflict. Lithe. Fast. Deadly. Icy rage filling her belly and fire overflowing her heart as her siblings and cousins fell around her.

Alexa had lived it through Mila's eyes and ears. In that moment, their souls and minds had been as one.

Although she had not felt the warrior's presence inside her consciousness since the battle in the Ural mountains, she sensed that Mila still existed somewhere inside her. And although Alexa now recognized that the idea of reincarnation put forward by Guru Rinpoche and Yonten himself was probably true, she also knew that she was her own being, with her own memories and experiences. Mila was only a part of her.

An alarm tore through the room and scattered her thoughts. Her head snapped up. The fear that had been her constant companion for the last seven days threatened to drown her as she stared at the flashing monitor above Jackson's bed.

Two nurses rushed inside the room. A doctor followed in their footsteps.

Half an hour later, the medical team spoke to them again. Jackson's organs had started to fail.

CHAPTER THIRTY-THREE

Dimitri Reznak stood at the window of an expensive hotel room overlooking the Boston Harbor waterfront. The suite was located on the twelfth floor of the building, which was owned by a Crovir. The room was reserved for the use of immortal nobles who visited Boston.

He stared blindly at the festive lights that glimmered gaily along the snow-covered promenades lining the wharf. The hotel was about a mile from the hospital where Jackson lay dying.

Footsteps rose behind him. Reznak turned and saw Marie.

'Are you coming to the hospital?' she asked softly. Her eyes were puffy and red from crying. Fawkes stood silently next to her. He placed a hand on her shoulder and squeezed it gently.

'I'll be there soon,' said Reznak quietly. 'Go ahead without me.'

The door shut after them moments later.

It had been three days since the doctors had given them the

news about Jackson's deterioration. In that time, Alexa hadn't left the Harvard professor's side once.

Today was the day they would turn off his life support.

A ragged sigh left Reznak's lips and his shoulders sagged. He would never forget the look on his goddaughter's face when the doctors told them their decision—not until his very final death.

Ten minutes later, a knock sounded at the door of the suite.

Reznak crossed the floor and opened it. Four familiar faces stared at him over the threshold. 'Thank you for coming,' he said hoarsely. He ushered them inside the room and closed the door.

They spoke for an hour before leaving for the hospital.

The ICU was quiet when they entered it just before midday. It was the week leading up to Christmas. The nurse in charge glanced at the group of visitors behind Reznak before frowning at him over the top of her glasses.

'Can we borrow your family room?' he said with a tired smile.

The woman's eyes softened. She nodded once.

Reznak went to get Alexa from Jackson's bedside. At first, she refused to leave him. 'This is important,' he finally said, his voice hardening.

She stared at him for a moment. His heart twisted at the deadened expression in her silver eyes. She glanced to where Marie and Fawkes sat by Jackson's side.

'Go,' whispered Marie tremulously.

Alexa rose and came around the bed.

Seconds later, she froze on the threshold of the room where Victor Dvorsky waited with Lucas and Anna Soul. A third man leaned against the wall to the right. He was as tall and as powerfully built as Frank Schmidt; sharp brown eyes watched them carefully from an impassive face.

'What's going on?' asked Alexa coldly. She looked at Reznak over her shoulder, faint misgiving evident on her face.

It was the first genuine emotion he had seen her express in over a week.

'Sit,' Reznak ordered curtly. He closed the door behind him.

Alexa hesitated before folding herself in a chair.

He almost smiled at her then. Despite the grief that was visibly crushing his goddaughter, she had chosen the best position in the room from which she could guard herself from a physical attack. The expression that flashed across the faces of the other three men in the room suggested that this hadn't escaped their attention.

'Before we begin, let me introduce you properly,' said Reznak. He took the seat next to hers. 'You saw Victor briefly in Russia.'

'We finally get to meet,' said Dvorsky. He glanced at Reznak. 'You are the most closely guarded secret this old fox has ever kept from me. And I've known him for a long time.' His lips twisted in a wry grimace.

Alexa watched the leader of the Bastians warily before tilting her head in brief acknowledgement.

'Anna and Lucas you've already met,' Reznak continued, indicating the immortal couple.

Anna's lips curved in a small, sad smile. Lucas Soul gazed at Alexa inscrutably.

'This is Reid Hasley,' Reznak added, indicating the man by the wall. 'He is Soul's business partner—and a human.'

Alexa stiffened. She turned to him again, her expression vigilant.

'I never told you how Eva got her name,' said Reznak.

His goddaughter's eyes widened. She had obviously not expected him to talk of such things.

Reznak glanced at the other people in the room and met Victor's stare briefly. 'Victor has known for centuries. In view of what I'm asking of Lucas, Anna, and Reid, they also deserve to hear this.' He took a deep breath as old memories flooded his mind. 'The original Eva was a cousin of Ivan the Third, a Grand Prince of Moscow and the founder of what would become the Russian state. She was, and always will be, the love of my life. She was also a human.'

He heard Alexa's breath catch in her throat. 'You know of the concept of immortal soulmates?' he asked.

She nodded once, her gaze unblinking.

'Very much like humans profess to have "soulmates" in their lifetimes, immortals also share similar bonds with each other,' said Reznak. 'But not every immortal will necessarily find a mate, despite their many lives. This situation has been made doubly worse since the advent of the Red Death. Many of us lost our soulmates during the plague.' He sighed. 'For an immortal to find their other half these days is in the realm of the truly miraculous.' His gaze shifted fleetingly to the immortal couple seated several feet away. 'But a few immortals will have a human soulmate.' He felt the surge of a familiar, centuries-old ache in his chest, and swallowed hard. 'I was one of them.'

Reznak saw Victor shift in his chair and glanced at his friend's sorrowful expression. He stared down at his own hands. 'I had sixty wonderful years with Eva. The day she died, I took my own life.' A humorless chuckle escaped his lips. 'Victor stopped me from doing it again. It was the only time he ever knocked me senseless.'

A hush descended on the room.

Reznak finally looked up into his goddaughter's tortured features. 'I could not bear to see you go through what I experienced,' he said hoarsely. He reached out and gripped her hand.

Alexa sat frozen for a moment before turning her palm over and clasping his fingers tightly. Her beautiful gray eyes glimmered.

'That's why I called Victor and Lucas,' said Reznak.

Confusion dawned on his goddaughter's face. She glanced at the two men.

'During the aborted immortal war that took place six weeks ago, Lucas suffered his seventeenth death,' Reznak continued. 'He survived it.'

Shock flared in Alexa's eyes. She turned to look at Soul. The immortal nodded at her briefly to confirm this fact.

'The reason why Lucas will continue surviving every death from now on, and the explanation for his other ability, lies in his bloodline,' said Reznak. 'Though he is a half-breed, his parents were pureblood descendants of the first immortals. In essence, Lucas carries the combined genes of Crovir and Bastian.' He hesitated. 'As does Anna.'

Alexa looked into Anna Soul's unwavering green eyes. Her gaze shifted briefly to the telltale bump under the immortal's dress.

'Reid was also badly injured in the course of that battle. In her attempt to save his life, Anna gave him her blood,' said Reznak. 'Reid survived. In fact, he did more than survive.' He glanced at Hasley's neutral expression. 'Since he received Anna's blood, his healing abilities have increased ten fold. They are now nearly as good as an immortal's regenerative powers. And not only are his new injuries recovering faster, his old ones are also disappearing with the passage of time.'

Alexa's breathing froze. Her pulse jumped where his fingers clasped her wrist.

'Twenty-four hours ago, I asked Lucas and Anna whether they could help Jackson. When I told them about the events that had taken place in the Urals, they came straight away,' continued Reznak quietly. 'Since you are aware of their origins, it was only fair of me to tell them about yours. They know of the reason behind Guru Rinpoche's sect, and about Mila, Crovir's daughter.' He looked between the silent immortals. 'For all intents and purposes, the three of you are cousins.'

Anna Soul spoke for the first time in the frozen silence that ensued. 'I cannot promise you that this will work,' she told Alexa softly. 'But Lucas and I decided it was worth a shot.' She looked at her husband and took his hand in her own. 'For us to find someone else to call family is something we never thought would happen again.' Her voice shook slightly.

'The decision is yours to make,' said Reznak.

His goddaughter was motionless for timeless seconds. Finally, she closed her eyes and nodded tremulously.

EPILOGUE

Alexa opened the door of Jackson's apartment and paused on the threshold of the narrow, familiar vestibule. She lifted the pile of unopened mail from the doormat and tossed it on the hallway table. She stood still and listened.

The place was as silent as a tomb.

She turned the central heating on full blast before walking slowly through the deserted rooms. Marie had been in the previous week and given them a thorough cleaning. Even the study looked pristine.

She headed past the bedroom and strolled into the sitting room, her boots squeaking slightly on the hardwood floor. She looked at the pictures and boxing trophies on the walls before turning to the bay windows.

The frozen waters of the Charles River Basin glimmered brightly at the end of the road. Down on the streets below, the Christmas lights were being taken down.

It was the tenth day of the new year.

A lot had happened since that afternoon when she met her

immortal cousins several weeks ago. Shortly after Alexa had agreed to Reznak's desperate plan, Anna Soul had taken over Jackson's care. Although the hospital initially protested, Anna's first-rate qualifications as a physician and surgeon quickly quieted their objections. The combined persuasive powers of her godfather and Victor Dvorsky—and a hefty private donation to the hospital—also helped.

It was Lucas who gave his blood to Jackson in the end. Anna supervised the entire process and stayed by the Harvard professor's side in the days that followed.

Twenty-four hours after the transfusion, Jackson's multi organ failure started to rescind. A day later, the electrical activity of his brain was back to normal. Several hours after Alexa left for New York, he finally opened his eyes.

Although her decision to leave initially shocked everyone, Reznak and Anna were the first ones who grasped the reason for her sudden departure. Anna kept her updated with Jackson's progress over the phone.

Alexa's days in New York passed swiftly enough. She spent most of them at her penthouse in Manhattan. One morning, she woke to find a saffron-robed figure on the terrace outside the apartment. Her heart lurched in her chest for a breathless moment before she recognized the monk who had been at Yonten's side when he died.

'My brother would have wanted you to have this,' he said when she walked out to meet him. He placed the bō staff in her hands. For the first time, Alexa detected nuances of Yonten's features in the younger man's face and eyes. She looked down at the staff weapon in her fingers. When she looked up, the monk had disappeared.

Reznak and Marie came to stay for a while. Though she was not used to having people in her personal space, Alexa was glad for their presence. They kept her from falling apart completely.

The truth of the matter was that she was scared. Alexa King, perfect immortal warrior, was utterly and completely terrified of her feelings for the man she had left in that hospital bed in Boston. The irony of the situation did not escape her. Physically, she was quite likely as invincible as Lucas Soul. Emotionally, she was about as strong as the stem of a crystal vase.

She understood why Reznak had taken his own life after losing his human soulmate. In the days that she had sat at Jackson's bedside and watched him slowly die before her eyes, she had resolved to do the same, and had thought of at least a dozen ways to accomplish her goal.

Now that Jackson was alive, she did not think she could survive the process of losing him all over again.

A key turned in the front door of the apartment. Alexa froze.

The door opened, then closed quietly.

Footsteps sounded in the hallway. They halted briefly before growing closer. Someone entered the sitting room and came to a standstill.

'Hi,' said Jackson behind her.

Alexa stared rigidly at the dim figure reflected in the glare of the windows. She saw him drop the unopened mail on the coffee table and shrug out of a winter coat. Still, she did not turn around. He stopped several steps behind her.

'This is all still quite strange,' he said finally. A rueful sigh left his lips. 'I remember what happened in the cave with Cavaleti. After that, everything went blank for a while. Next thing I know, I'm waking up in Boston, a medical miracle in the making.' His tone turned dry with his last words.

Despite the whirlwind of emotions threatening to engulf her, Alexa's lips twitched slightly.

'I had a very long and interesting talk with a guy called Reid Hasley, as well as the two immortals we met in Paris,' said Jackson thoughtfully. 'I believe they are related to you in a...strange and distant fashion.'

Alexa remained mute.

'After I listened to what they said, I told them to pull the other one,' Jackson continued with a chuckle, ignoring her silence. 'When I realized they weren't kidding, I was dumbfounded to say the least. Then, Reznak visited and imparted some more…how shall I say…critical knowledge about what he had found in the caves in the Urals.'

Alexa saw him rub his chin in a pensive gesture.

'The way I understand it, Hasley told me I'm now officially a superhuman,' Jackson mused. 'I asked him whether this included the ability to jump off tall buildings. He told me to stop being an ass. He also said that if I ever decided to try it, to save him and Lucas front row seats.'

Alexa bit her lip to stop from smiling. She had gotten to know Reid Hasley a little in the few days before she left Boston. The former US Marine and Boston PD detective was not a man in the habit of mincing his words. She could see why Lucas had chosen him as his best friend and business partner.

'I don't know whether you've spoken to Reznak recently, but I also had some crucial information to convey when we were in that cave in Russia. Unfortunately, Cavaleti kinda ruined my plans,' said Jackson. He took a step toward her. 'After I was captured by Kronos, they forced me to translate the artifacts they had in their possessions—at gunpoint I might add.' He paused and she glimpsed the dry grin that flashed across his lips. 'It was at that time that I experienced what can only be described as an epiphany. Call it that moment of clarity that comes when some bastard is threatening to shoot you in the kneecap. Anyway, I finally grasped the message behind the Emerald Tablet and the *Mutus Liber*. Of course, I spouted a lot of nonsense to Cavaleti. Not long before you barged into that room where he had me shackled to the wall, I finally told him the truth.'

Jackson took another step. Alexa felt the warmth of his body inches behind hers.

'The key ingredient to making the Elixir of Life was not the shells of the original immortals.' His breath stirred her hair as he spoke. 'It was their hearts. That was the secret to making the Philosopher's Stone. Despite the fact that the vault where they were stored was not damaged during the attack on Reznak's lab, Kronos completely overlooked them. The sect never knew of their existence. Needless to say, Cavaleti was pissed.'

Alexa did not dare to breathe.

'The tablet and the Wordless Book divulged another secret,' said Jackson, his tone sobering. 'You see, the power of the immortal races is this. The seventeen pieces of an immortal's soul physically reside inside their heart. I believe this in turn explains Lucas's ability to be able to shatter them in a single strike.'

Air left her lips in a soundless rush.

'Oh, by the way, Anna wanted me to tell you—she's expecting twins.'

This time, Alexa did not suppress the smile that came to her lips. Her vision blurred.

'So, is this gonna be the kind of relationship where I do most of the talking?' said Jackson after a while. 'Not that I mind or anything, but you might soon get—' He stopped abruptly.

She had turned to face him.

As she stared at him through a glimmering haze, Alexa realized something momentous.

He was here. He was whole. And he was hers for however many decades they would have together.

His ice-blue eyes once again turned to cobalt. Jackson took her in his arms.

'Don't cry,' he whispered softly in her hair.

THE END

The Immortals' adventures continue in Empire.

ACKNOWLEDGMENTS

To all my friends who helped make this possible. You know who you are.

To you, my readers. Thank you for reading Warrior. If you enjoyed my book, please consider leaving a review on Goodreads or on the store where you purchased it. Reviews help readers like you find my books and I truly appreciate your honest opinions about my stories.

Make sure to sign up to my store newsletter for special deals on my books and new release alerts. Or you can sign up to my author newsletter to get upcoming release notifications, sneak peeks, and giveaways.

FACTS AND FICTIONS

Now, for one of my favorite parts of writing my books. Here are the facts and fictions behind the story.

Battle of Narva

The Battle of Narva is factual. There have been several Battles of Narva. The one featured in the prologue of *Warrior* is the November 1700 skirmish, which saw Charles XII, the young Swedish King, defend his lands against the Russian Tsar, Peter the Great. The city was eventually captured by the Russians during the second siege in 1704.

Egypt Tombs

The tombs that Dimitri Reznak uncovered in the Eastern Desert mountains in Egypt are said to be the precursors upon which subsequent Egyptian dynasties would base the sarcophagus. This is obviously fictional. In 2002, archaeologists discovered the world's oldest sarcophagus on the Giza plateau in Egypt. It is thought to be 4,500 years old. The final resting places of Crovir and Bastian and the wall of scrolls in the second cave are inspired by the burial chamber of Tuthmosis III, an Egyptian king of the 18th dynasty, whose tomb was discovered in the Valley of the Kings, opposite Thebes (modern Luxor), in 1898.

Sai Daggers

Alexa King's trishula birthmark and sai daggers are inspired by the three-pronged spear used by the Hindu deities Shiva and Durga, as well as two gods of Greco-Roman mythology, Poseidon and Neptune.

Mutus Liber

The *Mutus Liber*, or Wordless Book, and the Emerald Tablet are two of several alchemical texts claiming to outline the process of making the fabled Philosopher's Stone. The latter is thought to be either a substance that could turn base metals into gold or a potion that could grant immortality; hence, it is also known as the Elixir of Life. A copy of the fifteen color illustrations of the *Mutus Liber* can be found in the Library of Congress in Washington DC. Alchemy and Rosicrucianism both exemplify the concept and principles of Esotericism. Notable historical figures thought to have been Rosicrucians include Leonardo Da Vinci, Napoleon Bonaparte, Rene Descartes, Benjamin Franklin, and Thomas Jefferson. The Rosy Cross or Rose Croix symbol of Rosicrucianism can also be found in Freemasonry, for example in the Knight of the Rose Croix, the 18th degree of the Scottish Masonic rite.

Guru Rinpoche

According to ancient scriptures discovered in the 14th century, Guru Rinpoche, the lotus-born Second Buddha, was invited to Tibet by King Trisong Detsen during the 8th century AD and was thought to have been responsible for introducing the doctrines of esoteric Buddhism to what was then the Tibetan empire.

Ural Mountains Underground Cities

The underground cities of Kronos in the Ural Mountains are fictional and are inspired by Derinyuku, a vast underground city in Cappadocia, a historical region in ancient Central Anatolia, Turkey. Derinyuku is thought to have been built between the 5th and 10th century BC and is one of several large underground cities that has been discovered in Turkey.

And that's it for the science and technology lesson folks. Visit my website at www.adstarrling.com to check out more Extras!

BOOKS BY A.D. STARRLING

Seventeen Novels

Hunted

Warrior

Empire

Legacy

Origins

Destiny

Seventeen Short Stories

First Death

Dancing Blades

The Meeting

The Warrior Monk

The Hunger

The Bank Job

The Seventeen Series Ultimate Short Story Collection (#1-6)

Legion

Blood and Bones

Fire and Earth

Awakening

Forsaken

Hallowed Ground

Heir

Legion

Witch Queen

The Darkest Night

Rites of Passage

Of Flames and Crows

Midnight Witch

A Fury of Shadows

Witch Queen

Division Eight

Mission:Black

Mission: Armor

Mission:Anaconda

Miscellaneous

Void - A Sci-fi Horror Short Story

The Other Side of the Wall - A Horror Short Story

ABOUT A.D. STARRLING

Visit Shop AD Starrling and buy all of AD's ebooks, paperbacks, hardbacks, audiobooks, and exclusive special edition print books direct.

Want to know about AD Starrling's upcoming releases? Sign up to her author newsletter for new release alerts, sneak peeks, giveaways, and more.

Follow AD Starrling on Amazon.

Join AD's reader group on Facebook
The Seventeen Club.

Check out this link to find out more about A.D. Starrling
Linktr.ee/AD_Starrling.

www.ingramcontent.com/pod-product-compliance
Lightning Source LLC
Chambersburg PA
CBHW020604310726
48979CB00008B/1345/J

* 9 7 8 0 9 9 5 5 0 1 3 6 2 *